HARBINGER
OF DARKNESS

RICHARD C. WHITE

I0662857

NWG™
NIGHTWOLF
GRAPHICS

StarWarp Concepts

www.starwarpconcepts.com
New York, NY

Harbinger of Darkness copyright © 2017 Richard C. White

A Nightwolf Graphics Production

StarWarp Concepts
P.O. Box 4667
Sunnyside, NY 11104

Visit our website: **www.StarwarpConcepts.com**

Visit Richard C. White on the Web at:
www.richardcwhite.com

Library of Congress Control Number: 2017953833

ISBN: 978-0-9982361-2-4 (trade paperback)
ISBN: 978-0-9982361-3-1 (e-book)

First Print Edition: September 2017
10 9 8 7 6 5 4 3 2 1

Cover painting by John Stone
http://john-stone-art.deviantart.com

Edited by Steven Roman
Designed by Raechel Henderson

Printed in the USA

To Mike Shields, Bill Bryan, Oscar Richie IV, and Chris Hackett — Roll Initiative.

PRAISE FOR THE WORK OF AUTHOR RICHARD C. WHITE

"Entertaining, old-school sword and sorcery, in the tradition of Fafhrd and the Gray Mouser." —**Jim C. Hines**, author of the Magic ex Libris, Jig the Goblin, and The Princesses series, on *For a Few Gold Pieces More*

"What a fantastic ride! If you like sarcasm and snark reminiscent of Harry Dresden, good doses of magic, treachery, and myth, this is the book for you." —**Goodreads**, on *For a Few Gold Pieces More*

"White's *Terra Incognito* is a solid introduction to the subject of world building. It succeeds in helping the apiring writer in creating a skeletal framework on which to hang the moving parts required of a believable fictional setting." —**The Gaming Gang**, on *Terra Incognito: A Guide to Building the Worlds of Your Imagination*

"A very good spin on the tried and true 'good-guys-for-hire' formula. All in all, an enjoyable read that I would recommend to anyone." —**Word of the Nerd**, on *Troubleshooters, Incorporated: Night Stalkings*

"An accurately dialogued epic set in a place and time of fantasy. If you like pirates or elves or fantasy adventure or pure swashbuckling, then pick it up." —**Comic Genesis**, on *The Chronicles of the Sea Dragon Special*

ACKNOWLEDGMENTS

This book could not have ever come together without the support and friendship of a host of people too numerous to name, but if you'll indulge me, I'll mention a few:

My Masters of English instructors at Bowie State University — thanks for inspiring me and stretching my limits by introducing me to literature I might never have found on my own.

Gary Huggins — thanks for years of mentoring and friendship. It's a lonelier place without you here to guide me anymore.

Errol Flynn, Douglas Fairbanks, Jr., Basil Rathbone, and Tyrone Powers — Thanks for making all those swashbuckling movies which were a great inspiration for me whenever I felt my writing momentum start to flag.

Steve Roman (editor), Raechel Henderson (designer), and John Stone (artist) — Thanks for taking this lump of clay and helping me make a cool piece of art out of it.

And of course, my wife, Joni, and my daughter, Katie — thanks for having the patience for putting up with me while I worked on this and other projects over the years. There's no doing this without you.

Chapter One

The stentorian clang of the cathedral bell tolled out one hour past midnight. It caught the attention of the young man who stumbled out of the noisy tavern and grabbed the nearest column holding up the awning over the tavern's door. He let out a loud belch and blinked several times, letting his eyes adjust to the darkness. A dumbfounded expression settled on his face as he looked out onto the dimly lit streets. Glancing to his left and then his right, it began to dawn on him that his companions weren't there.

Cursing under his breath, he drew himself up with the indignity of one too drunk to realize he was drunk. *Now, how do you like that? Gone off and left me to find another tavern. Couldn't wait for me to finish visiting with the barmaid here? Well, if they're too good to wait for me, then they can continue being boors without me to protect them. It's obvious they're upset because the ladies are paying more attention to me than them anyway. Jealousy is such an ugly emotion.*

He jingled the sack of coins on his belt and smiled. *At least the ladies here understand the simplest of facts. He who has the coin has first dibs on the ladies. If their fathers are stingy with the coin, is it my fault? After all, I paid their bar tab here.* Shaking his head to clear some of the tavern's fog from his brain, he made his way down the rickety steps of the tavern to the cobblestoned street. He felt a strange tugging on his throat and his hands flew up to thwart the assassin, only to find his cape had come askew again, the cord threatening to choke him. He straightened out the short cape with exaggerated care and noted a stain near the edge that resisted coming out with a liberal application of spittle. *Ah, the trials one goes through to keep up with the latest fashions. Still, the ladies seem to approve and that's all I need to tell me it's worth it.*

He looked up at the moon and noted it was beginning to descend. He debated whether he had time to visit one more tavern before heading back up the hill to the Royal Quarter. If he didn't head home now, though, it was likely to be completely dark before he reached the wall. The thieves of the city were brazen these days, and several of his friends had been waylaid during their visits to the Barrens.

Of course, the risk was part of the allure of this region. It was so delightfully low. So different from the staid and, yes, boring taverns that dotted the Royal Quarter. Places his father would be perfectly comfortable in. Places where he wouldn't be caught dead.

"Excuse me, milord."

The young man jumped, one hand dropping to the finely crafted rapier on his hip, startled by the voice that seemed to explode out of the darkness near him. He wheeled around, rapier half-drawn, when he saw a young woman cringing back, frightened by his sudden movements. "By the gods, woman, what were you thinking?"

"A thousand pardons, sir. I didn't mean to scare you."

"I'm not so easily frightened, my dear, just a bit caught off guard. You really should be more careful. If I didn't have the finely trained muscles of a fencing master, I might have struck you down where you stand. Never just come up on someone out of the darkness like that. It's not safe."

"Oh, dear. I hadn't even thought of that. You see, I saw you there and you seemed like a good man, someone I could trust, and I just wanted to speak to you before I lost my courage. I am in a spot of trouble, milord, and I was hoping you could aid me?"

He slid the rapier back into its scabbard and turned to face her. She was standing a few feet away, her dark hair hanging down as she kept her eyes downward, as if afraid to face him. He had no such qualms as she was a pleasant-looking woman. She didn't appear to be a peasant, but her clothes were certainly a few years out of fashion. Perhaps a daughter of a wealthy merchant or a minor lord. She shuffled her feet as if embarrassed to be in this situation.

He tried to keep his voice light, but some of the evening's earlier frustration crept into his voice. "Come now, my dear, out with it or I'm afraid I will have to leave you here to dither until morning."

"Oh, milord, please don't do that. You see, I was visiting with a sick friend and I have let the hour grow late. I am afraid to walk these streets by myself in the dark. It's simply not safe. I was hoping you might be persuaded to escort me to my house?"

The young man felt the heat rising in his face as she looked up at him, her dark eyes gazing at him in supplication. He swallowed hard, took a deep breath, and held himself a touch straighter as he felt her admiring gaze on him. He glanced past her and let his vision take in the empty streets. "I don't believe you have anything to fear. It appears everyone besides the noisy patrons of that tavern I just exited have called it a night. Still, you are right. A young and delicate thing such as yourself should not be walking these streets unescorted." He leaned closer to her and lowered his voice into his "seductive" range. "In fact, one as lovely as you shouldn't be unescorted even when it's broad daylight. Who knows what kind of scoundrel might try to snatch you up for himself."

She blushed and giggled at the comment before rushing forward and grabbing his left arm with her two delicate hands. "I do appreciate this and I hope I'll be able to properly reward you for your gallantry." She pressed her body against his side and even his ale-besotted mind had an idea about what she was implying. He felt his face burning.

"Don't worry about a thing, my dear. Just tell me which way to go and I'll be delighted to ensure you arrive safe and sound."

"Oh, if only every man were as brave and gallant as you."

"True. Oh, so true."

She gave his arm a soft tug and began leading him down the street. He found out her name was Penelope and her father was a minor government official who worked with the Royal Army in the Red Quarter. He gave her a polite smile and pretended to believe her story. He gave her a false name and mentioned he worked in the Royal Exchequer.

His story did have a thread of truth in it. While he hadn't worked a day in his life, his father was the counselor for the minister of the exchequer, and to hear him talk, he was the one who got all the work done while the minister dithered over how little of his master's money should be spent on the various projects the kingdom required. In fact, his father wondered if the old boy would even know to go to the privies if he wasn't there to remind him.

They made small talk as they walked down the broad thoroughfare. After a while, she slowed and pointed to a narrower street. The young man noted the streetlights were spaced farther apart here—those that the lamplighters had bothered to light this evening, that is. She pulled him toward her and spoke in a soft, husky voice. "It's the second house from the end on the right. The one with the light in front of it." She leaned closer against him. "You see why I am afraid to go home alone. It's too scary to face by myself."

She looked up at him expectantly and he knew she was waiting for him to make the first move. He bowed to her, extending his free arm toward the narrow street. "Never fear, I'll be happy to ensure nothing happens to you."

She gave his arm another squeeze. "I knew you were special the moment I laid eyes on you."

He felt his cheeks grow warm again. He took her arm in his and turned toward the darkened street, loosening his rapier in its scabbard—just in case—before they left the thoroughfare. He examined the house she'd pointed out and it did appear to be the kind of house a minor government official could afford. Still, he had no doubts someone else, perhaps calling himself her father, was making the payments on it. It was a secluded spot and off the beaten track, perfect for meeting one's mistress.

They walked on, her chatting like they were old friends, when another voice broke in. "Now, isn't this cozy. Just three old friends out for a stroll."

The young man shoved her behind him as he turned to face the dark figure walking out from between two of the houses. The girl's hand rose to her mouth to stifle a small scream when the faint light showed the man's lower face covered by a cloth and a rapier aimed at the young man's heart only a few feet away. The young man's hand fell onto the hilt of his own weapon, but the masked man shook his head with deliberation. "No, I think that would be a very bad idea. I'm pretty sure I can run you through before your blade would ever clear your scabbard. Even if I don't, I wouldn't want anything to happen to that lovely lady behind you. I mean, things happen in a fight no one intends. Why, if a sword were to be parried with the least bit of error, her pretty face could be scarred for life. And such a face it is. I mean, can you take a chance on something like that?"

A small shriek escaped from behind the fist clenched over her mouth. "Oh, you couldn't. You wouldn't."

"I hope it will not come to that. You do have a most pleasant face. Perhaps you could dissuade me from considering such an act?"

"You knave. How dare you speak to her like that?"

"Ah, the young pup does have teeth. So, boy, are you going to stop me?"

The young man tensed up and then realized he was playing right into the masked man's hands. He relaxed his body and took his hand away from his sword. "We both know you're not looking to kill anyone because you certainly could have struck me down before I saw you. What will it take to encourage you to go away and leave us in peace?"

The masked man's sword dropped a few inches and his

stance took on a less-threatening tone. He looked them over with a practiced air before continuing. "It is a pleasure to deal with someone who actually uses his head for something other than a place to grow hair and shove food. Very well, for your safe passage to wherever you're going, I think the necklace the young woman is wearing and the sack of coins on your hip. Oh, and that signet ring you're wearing."

The young man snatched the sack off his belt and tossed it to the ground near the masked man's feet. "Take this and be damned with you. This ring is a family heirloom and will be staying with me."

The masked man's sword rose into position. "Ah, perhaps this will not be so pleasant after all. Very well, I shall just have to cut it off your dead hand."

She rushed forward, moving between the two men, nearly impaling herself on the sword in her rush. "Please, please no. Here, take it." She tore the necklace from around her neck and thrust it at him. "Just take it."

He lifted the point of the sword toward her and she placed the necklace on the blade. He tilted it toward her delicate throat and the young man watched as the band of gems made its way down the length of the sword to rest against the hand guard. He turned the point slightly to the left until it was on line with the young man's heart. "And now you, sir?"

Growling a curse, the young man tugged the ring off his hand and threaded it onto the threatening sword's blade. He watched as the ring slid down the blade to join the necklace. "I do thank you for your kind and generous donations. Now if the two of you will be so kind as to take a few steps back, we'll get on with our separate lives." They complied with his request and watched as he knelt down and snatched up the sack lying on the ground. He slipped the necklace and the ring into the sack and gave them a mock bow before disappearing into the darkness between the houses behind him.

The young man snatched his rapier out of his scabbard and began running after the thief. Before he reached the end of the small alley between the houses, his common sense finally kicked in, wading through the alcohol sloshing around in his brain. He noted how dark the alley was and the fact was he had no idea where the thief had gone. If he kept moving forward, he might just as easily impale himself on a sword he never saw or else trip over something and break his fool neck. He muttered some dire threats into the darkness and made his way back to the street. He spotted movement coming toward him and had only a second to brace himself before Penelope nearly knocked him over rushing into his arms.

He could hear her sobbing as she pressed up against him. "Oh, I was so afraid when you rushed off like that. What were you thinking? There could have been more of them in the alley and then what would have happened? Don't do anything like that again."

"Not to worry, my dear. I doubt that ruffian will return anytime soon. I would have taught him a lesson he'd not soon forget, but when he threatened you, I confess, I felt weak in the knees. I decided discretion was better than taking a chance on you getting hurt."

She favored him with a warm smile. "Perhaps I can arrange a reward for you when we get to my house, my gallant knight."

He tried to keep the expectant look off his face as they continued down the dark street toward her home. She leaned closer, glancing around nervously; as if afraid the thief would appear out of the darkness again. They reached the front of the house and she moved toward the door, but halted as her fingers grazed the door pull.

"You're welcome to come in for a bit. I'm certain I have something that'll help settle your nerves before you continue your journey."

"A kind offer indeed, my dear."

She held up one hand and motioned him closer. He leaned forward, but instead of a kiss, she whispered in his ear. "However, do keep your voice down when we get inside. My husband is a light sleeper and he tends to be out of sorts when he gets woken unexpectedly."

"Your husband?"

"You'll have to forgive him; he spent so much time in the king's army that he just doesn't feel right without his crossbow by the bed. But I wouldn't worry too much; he's not a very good shot when he first wakes up. He just tends to shoot at the first noise he hears." She sighed before continuing. "I've lost more cats that way."

The young man swallowed hard. What little common sense he had was banging on everything it could to drown the lust he'd been feeling a second ago. She was good looking, but she wasn't worth catching a crossbow bolt. "I …ah …well, perhaps we shouldn't disturb him. Maybe we could get together another night and reminisce over our exciting evening. I think I probably should be getting home now."

She gave a small squeal and jumped into his arms. His eyes widened as he glanced up at the windows, waiting for a shadowy figure to appear armed to the teeth. "Oh, you are such a gentleman. I knew you were special the second I laid eyes on you. Of course, we will have to get together. I'll wait for you at that tavern you were in."

"Yes, you do that. Ah, my dear, I am counting down the moments until then." He waved to her and started down the dim street back toward the main road. He glanced over his shoulder a few times just to be sure. Reaching the thoroughfare, he turned toward the Hill and broke into a run. *If these are the kinds of people who live in the Barrens, then Ashanti take them all. I think I'll do my drinking in the Red Quarter for a while.*

* * *

A low chuckle came from the shadows next to the house after the young man disappeared from view. "Oh, if you could only have seen his face when you mentioned your husband. It's like someone kicked him right in the balls."

The young woman turned toward the shadows, a predatory grin spreading across her face. "Well, he's lucky. If he had tried to fondle me one more time, I think I would have kicked him out of spite. What Ginny ever saw in him, I'll never know."

"Speaking of her, how's she doing?"

"Bertok says she'll be fine in a few days. I should have taken her to a real healer, but I didn't have the crowns to get one that is halfway competent. I just wish we could have left him the same way he left her."

"Hey, she didn't want us to hurt him. Crap, it took us this long just to track him down." The masked man stepped into the light, carrying a sack. "Might I say you're looking most fetching, my lady Penelope?"

"You might, if you don't mind picking your teeth up, my daring highwayman. Now, give me the sack and let me get out of this ridiculous outfit, Jerek." He tossed it to her and she stepped into the shadows behind the house to change. She wasted no time pulling the dress over her head, revealing a linen blouse and leather pants beneath. She reached into the pack and pulled out a leather jerkin lined with steel plates and slipped it over her blouse before pulling a brace of weapons out of it as well as a thin leather backpack.

That feels a lot more comfortable. One last thing, though, before we're done. She reached into her blouse and pulled a small silver medallion out and held it between her hands. Speaking words only a few people in the city-state knew, she felt a familiar feeling settling on her. When she rejoined Jerek, her hair was shorter and her features more angular.

"Damn, that's a good trick, Raven. I don't know what you're using to disguise yourself, but there's a fortune to be made if you ever decide to let others in on your secret."

"Maybe when I retire, Jerek. But for now, my secrets are my secrets."

He pulled the cloth covering his face away, revealing a handsome man with dark eyes and curly, dark hair. Without his mask, there was little question he was a member of the Corconti, the nomads who respected no country's boundaries and their laws even less. He flipped his tunic inside out, revealing a green and black Corconti pattern on it.

She walked over and tousled his hair. "So, how did we make out tonight?"

"You know, for all our plans, we could have probably gotten more money by selling him to the local slavers. That signet ring? It's silver, all right, but it's low quality. Probably something he gives to his latest conquests. Only worth a few shillings at best."

"Well, the signet ring led us to him. Ginny had one in her possession when we found her."

"And that might be the whole sum of the treasure. The sack he gave me? Filled with copper pennies and a few silver shillings to make it look good. We already knew that necklace of yours was paste. I think we should have gutted him, Ginny or not."

"That's your problem, Jerek. You're a guy ... too single-minded. You're here to avenge a friend. Nothing more, nothing less."

"Oh? And what did you see that my single-mindedness didn't, O avatar of Kerthani?"

She gave him a dirty look. She wasn't a follower of the goddess of thieves and darkness, and the last thing she needed was to draw her attention. "Well, my simple friend, you don't think I gave him all those hugs because I was enamored by him? Gods, he probably hasn't bathed in a week." She lifted up the bottom of her blouse and withdrew two velvet pouches. "He had his real money stashed inside hidden pockets in his cape." She loosened the string on the first one and produced a small pile of gold crowns and double crowns. "The other one jingles like there are gems in there. I imagine this will go a long way to paying for Ginny's healing as well as getting her out of Sagras before he notices these are missing. Of course, that means we have to go see old Tobias before we can do anything with them."

"Tobias? Tobias the shark?"

"The same. You know the saying, 'you want to fence something in Sagras, Tobias is going to get his bite in first.' I just hope we can get a good deal considering what happened the last time we sold him something."

"Hey, it's not our fault the ring had a curse on it. I consider it part of the reason he gets such a good cut for being a fence."

"You tell him that. Last time I saw him, he sent two of his leg breakers after me.Took me all night to get rid of them. 'Course, I heard it took six weeks for his hand to quit glowing pink. I can imagine the guild didn't exactly let him live that down."

They snickered at the shared memory before turning serious again. Raven passed the two pouches to him. "Here, you take care of this. Explain to Tobias what it's for, he may give you a better break than usual. He's got a soft spot for Ginny. I've got some other stuff to take care of tonight."

"Slipping out early again? Where *do* you go every night, Raven? You come and go like a shadow and no one knows anything about you."

"Uh-uh, Jerek." She gave her head a playful shake, but there was a no-nonsense look on her face. "We agreed when we teamed up there would be no questions. I like working with you, Jerek. You're the best partner I've ever had. Don't blow it now by letting your curiosity get the better of you."

"Ah, but you know the Corconti. We love a good story and we love a good mystery … especially when it involves a beautiful woman."

"Don't even go there. I think Lady Penelope is more your type than I am."

Jerek looked up at the moon and saw it was dipping toward the horizon. "As you wish, Raven. Tomorrow night?"

"If I can. Look for me at the Green Gryphon after sundown." She blew him a kiss and turned away before he could ask any more questions. She hurried between two houses and crossed the thoroughfare, pausing in an alley long enough to watch Jerek emerge and turn toward the Merchants' Quarter. She watched to ensure he wasn't trying to follow her trail and after he disappeared from sight, she continued down the alley into the maze that made up the slum known as the Barrens.

Jerek, I do like you a lot, but I'm not ready to share some things with you yet. Not quite yet.

Moving down the alley, she paused at the smoldering remains of a house. She'd been there a few weeks ago visiting the family that lived here. She'd heard the family had come down with one of the rampant diseases the slum was notorious for spawning. *I guess the neighbors burned it down to prevent the disease from spreading. I just hope they weren't inside.* When people panicked, they often acted stupidly. The Barrens tended to do that to people—if you lived here, that meant there was nowhere else to go.

She pushed on, determined to check up on the family later. A few blocks away, she found a ramshackle building behind what might have been an inn long ago. She checked to make sure some squatters hadn't move in and then continued to an interior room filled with rubble. She reached beneath one particular pile and lifted up on the rope that was hidden beneath it. The lid to the trapdoor swung up, the wood and debris nailed to it to hide it from the casual observer. She eased into the darkness it revealed, feeling the cold rungs of an iron ladder beneath her feet and began climbing down, drawing the trapdoor down over her.

Even surrounded by total darkness, she climbed down with confidence. Twelve rungs later, she reached out and felt the stone walkway beneath her and heard the soft rush of water behind her. She reached into a pouch and pulled out a small stone that she cupped in her hand. Speaking a couple of soft words, the gem began to glow with a soft light and she spread her fingers just far apart for a sliver of light to fall on the path in front of her. She turned and began walking downstream, the cool damp stone to her right and the dark water on her left. Every so often, she could hear the soft running of feet as the sewer's normal inhabitants got out of her way. She paused to let them make their escape before continuing on.

She counted in her head the steps since she'd left the ladder. Reaching a curve in the sewer, she stopped and pressed on the third brick from the ceiling. A small crack appeared in the wall and she pulled the hidden door toward her, its well-oiled hinges making only the slightest whisper of sound. Hurrying inside, she pulled the door shut before spreading her hand open to let the gem light up the room. She climbed up the ladder in here and entered a storeroom filled with boxes and debris. She glanced to her left and noted the bricks that blocked the window. She knew, from the outside, it appeared they were just boarded up, but it would take a determined opponent a long time to break through that. She checked at the only door but nothing alarmed her as she listened, so she pulled the door open and went into the next room.

Lighting the lamp on the nearest wall, she noted the difference between the junk-filled storeroom and where she was in now: clean and immaculate, the wooden floor covered in expensive rugs and long tapestries hanging on the walls. A large padded armchair dominated the center of the room, with a sturdy cherrywood table next to it. On the table, a brandy snifter and a bottle waited for Raven's arrival. The walls were lined with rows of shelves where valuable knickknacks and porcelain figurines gave the room an opulent feeling. Raven's eyes were drawn to the far wall where a large mahogany armoire and full-length mirror stood. The glass in the mirror was nearly flawless.

An indulgence, perhaps, but what's the point in acquiring money if you don't spend a little on yourself once in a while?

Home.

This was Raven's lair. Her home away from everyone else. She sat in the chair and poured herself a drink while she reviewed the events of the evening. She was supposed to see Bertok tomorrow evening. With any luck, Ginny might be able to get out of bed and hopefully Jerek would be able to fence those gems soon. She had a feeling Ginny's paramour was likely to miss those gems sooner rather than later and, knowing his temper, he'd try to take it out on her if he could find her.

Some brave warrior. I don't think the king will be too impressed if your only conquests are beating women who don't know enough to put a knife in your kidney at the first opportunity. You'd better hope your father finds you a damn safe job somewhere.

Raven leaned back in the chair and rested her head against the cushioned back, soaking up the quiet and solitude. Still, she knew she had one more mission tonight. Standing up, she felt the weight of the evening on her shoulders.

She shrugged out of the leather jerkin and carried the sword belt and jerkin over to the armoire. Hanging the jerkin on its stand, she turned her attention to the belt. Removing the pouches that hung from it, she placed them in their individual drawers and then hung her weapons on their racks beside them. Then, she stripped off her clothes and boots and hung them next to her jerkin. She pulled the long green dress out of the armoire and slipped it over her head before putting on the comfortable slippers she'd worn earlier in the evening.

She examined herself in the mirror to ensure everything was in place. She reached down and withdrew the strange silver medallion. Again, words long thought extinct were spoken and she felt the metal grow cold beneath her fingers. As she looked in the mirror, her features wavered, the glamour fading away.

Turning back to the full-length mirror, she gazed at herself again. Ice-blue eyes gazed back at her, almost mocking the more common brown that had looked back seconds before. A self-satisfied smile ran across her full red lips. She ran a brush through her bright red hair and tucked it underneath a shawl. Pulling a cloak about her, she held the edges of the shawl up around her face. She bid adieu to the sanctuary and headed for the trapdoor to let herself out.

Every time she went through the transformation, she was amazed at how perfect the glamour was. The nights belonged to Raven, but dawn was fast approaching and it was time for Perrin to make her appearance once again.

Chapter Two

The smell of food cooking wafted up to Perrin as she made her way down the stairs. It wasn't like her not to notice when her father, Rory, woke up, much less to sleep in this late. She hesitated for a second before hurrying down the stairs from the living area above his store. She hoped Father wouldn't have a lot of awkward questions for her because she had slept so late.

She hurried down the stairs, trying not to make a sound in her padded shoes, and had almost made it to the store before her father's voice boomed out of the kitchen. "So glad to see you could join us, Perrin. Now that you're awake, sleepyhead, you might notice we received a shipment of books after you went out last night. When you get done with the cleaning, be sure to get those out and on the shelves. I have a couple of people coming by today to look at them."

"Yes, Father." She slipped past the landing that led to the kitchen and stepped into the bookstore. Its familiar shelves and piles of books greeted her like old friends as she grabbed the broom and duster from the small closet behind one of the counters to begin the morning cleaning.

Her eyes glanced around the store as she pushed the accumulation of dirt and dust around on the floor. As she pushed the dirt toward the front door, she felt a presence at her shoulder. Turning her head, she saw her father standing in the doorway, his light brown eyes gazing into the store with almost the same amount of pride he showed for her.

"You know, one of these days, this will all be yours. Or, yours and your husband's," he continued, dodging backward out of reach as she threatened him with the broom.

"Let's not get *that* started again." She knew he was scandalized that she was not only unmarried, but had no visible prospects. He'd even started bringing other merchants' sons home to meet her.

He started to say something else, but the threatening look she gave him brought him up short. A good businessman knows how to read a customer so he backed off and his shoulders slumped in mock defeat. Perrin wasn't fooled, though. This was a strategic retreat. The war wasn't over yet.

"I heard you received a letter from Janos yesterday. How's your grandfather doing?"

"Grandfather is fine. Says he's picking up a big shipment to haul to Wolf River and hopes he can stop for a visit on the return trip. He'll send word one way or the other." Her grandfather and Uncle Viktor ran a drayage business, hauling goods from the seaport town of Kolus to other cities in the realm.

"The capital? I wonder if he could pick up that lot of new books I ordered?" His voice brightened as moved around the kitchen. "That would save me the cost of shipping. Remind me to send a letter to the inn he stays in at Wolf River. They should be able to get it to him in time."

"Now, Father ..."

Rory waved his hands to shush her. "Of course I'm going to pay him. But he does give me the family discount. If he's coming this way, it'd be foolish not to take advantage of it." She shook her head, amazed once again at his single-minded devotion to this store.

Imagining her grandfather's trip, she recalled the map of the Empire. Her father had made her memorize it since a merchant should know where his or her goods were made. Sagras might be a city-state, but even King Marcus answered to a superior. Stephan Ironhand ruled a loose confederation of city-states and petty kingdoms besides his own Kingdom of Malios. He was a benevolent emperor, seldom interfering in the squabbles of his vassals as long as the taxes were paid on time and his vassals provided troops whenever he had to call up the imperial levy.

She looked over the large room with a sense of pride. *There aren't many merchants who have accomplished what my father has. We have books from all over the Empire as well as foreign countries. Each book's leather binding tells me where it's from and who created it.*

Her eyes moved from book to book as she dusted the shelves. They had a wide range of books, from some written for young children to great works of history and philosophy. The most expensive books in the store were the ones bound in white calfskin on the back wall. Published by a group of scholars in the imperial capital, they were only released once a year. Rory required anyone handling them to wear a special set of gloves, and they were kept well out of reach of any child.

The glass case at the back of the store held her father's most prized possessions: three books, each bound in unidentified rough golden leather and sealed with a small golden latch and leather strap. These ancient tomes were written in an obscure language. When she was younger, Perrin had tried to read them, but she could never figure out the words. According to Rory, they contained powerful spells and the leather was from a golden dragon. *I must have been gullible as a child. They're probably nothing more than props to get people to visit the store. None of the wizards up the hill have shown a single bit of interest in them.*

Her personal favorites were a set of leather-bound travelogues written by the explorer Tadzic Cerny. He had spent years sailing through the southern islands and his stories and pictures were dazzling. She dreamed of traveling about the Empire or sailing away on a fast ship, seeking adventure over the far horizon.

Instead, I come downstairs every day and clean and work in the shop, visiting with the same people about the same news. Nothing in Sagras ever seems to change. She paused and thought back to the night before. *Even the games that Raven plays on people are starting to fall into a rut. The only thing that seems to change is the faces of people I give money to, but for everyone I help, another family seems to get themselves into trouble. It's like they take turns with disasters.*

She finished straightening a shelf of books and snorted to herself. When it came to routine, her father could write the book on it. Every day was the same. Rory cooked breakfast while she prepared the store for the new day. In the evening, she cooked dinner while he did the books and closed the store. He bought lunch at the same inns and in the evening, he retired to his room to read before going to bed. They'd been doing the same things ever since her mother had passed.

She paused and realized it was ten years ago this month that her mother had died from the black fever. Perrin had only been eight at the time. She remembered they wouldn't let her go into her mother's room to be with her, afraid she'd catch the fever, too. She could still remember that final night. Everyone thought she was asleep and they didn't notice her on the steps while the healers talked to her father in the kitchen, discussing how lucky it was she'd gone quickly instead of wasting away like so many of the other victims.

It had been so long, it was hard to remember what her mother looked like. Still, there was the portrait that her father kept in his room. It hadn't hung on the wall in years, but she still slipped in from time to time to look at it. Grandfather had commissioned one of the best painters in the Empire and she still admired how lifelike the painting was. Her father had objected over the cost, but she knew secretly he treasured it over anything else in the house. Everyone always told Perrin how much she looked like her mother, and she admitted she had her mother's red hair and blue eyes, but her mother was beautiful and she … well, she was just Perrin.

"I'm not hearing much cleaning going on in there."

The gruff voice from the kitchen woke her from her reverie. She grabbed the duster and made sure she made enough noise to keep her father satisfied. Once she was sure everything was ready, she cut through the kitchen, dodged around her father, and grabbed a bucket next to the back door. Hurrying down the alley, she reached the closest well to draw some fresh water to wash the front windows. Her father had paid an exorbitant sum to have glass panes installed in their store, but he felt it was easier to sell books if people could see them as they walked past. However, it was a never-ending battle to keep them clean against the forces of dust and the fingerprints of curious children.

Lowering the pail into the well, she could see the harbor below. A merchantman was pulling into the dock and she couldn't quite make out the flag that flew from its quarterdeck. Some days, the desire to just walk onto one of those ships and sail off was overwhelming. Oh, to be somewhere, anywhere but Sagras.

I wish Father could take even a day off from the store so we could travel. The business did well, but Rory always put off talk of travel by claiming he couldn't afford to hire any extra help—and wouldn't trust them with his books even if he did. Perrin's grandfather had once offered to take her on one of his caravan trips while her cousin, Cyril, filled in for her at the store, but Rory turned him down. *I think he still sees me as that quiet little girl I was when Mother died and treats me like a porcelain doll. No, if I'm ever going to leave Sagras, it's going to have to be on my terms with my own money.*

That's one of the reasons Raven exists.

Looking away from the beckoning sea, she began drawing the heavy pail up out of the well. She was pouring the water into her bucket when she heard footsteps coming her way. Before she could look up, a familiar voice reached her. "Good morning, Perrin. Time to wash the windows?"

"Good morning, Angelina. Of course, if I could get kids like you to quit pressing your noses on the glass, it'd be a lot easier."

The younger girl frowned at her before responding. "I'm not a kid anymore, Perrin. I turned fourteen a couple of months ago."

Perrin stopped and looked at her friend. "Fourteen already? It doesn't seem that long ago I was staying with you in the evenings when your mother and father had to work nights."

Angelina's blond curls bounced as she skipped along while Perrin carried the bucket back to the store. "Yeah. Now Daddy has two men who work at night getting the jewelry ready for him to finish. Did you know we just got back from Wolf River? The capital is a huge city, Perrin. You could probably put six Sagrases in it with room left over."

Perrin tried to keep the jealousy out of her voice. "Really?"

Her friend continued on with her tale, oblivious to the tone in Perrin's voice. 'It was so wonderful. The palace is huge and made of gray and rose-colored marble with granite walkways so smooth you could almost skate on them. I thought I was going to fall over a dozen times. See, Daddy bought me these new shoes that are in fashion up there and they're so tall. I was afraid I would do something and look stupid, but I finally got used to them. Oh, and we got to meet some of the Emperor's personal jewelers. We even brought back a few pieces to sell here."

Perrin waited for Angelina to take a breath so she could speak. "It sounds like you had a great time. I'd love to see those pieces before he sells them."

"Sure, anytime. Just let me know when you're not busy and I'll have Daddy get them out for you. I better go now. See you later."

Perrin waved as Angelina went on down the alley before ducking into the last building on the block. Angelina's father, Bryan, ran the Crystal Lion, one of the nicest jewelry stores not on the Hill. Perrin knew if she went to the corner and looked to her right, she'd be able to see the wall that separated the Royal Quarter from the rest of Sagras. Her father's store was only two streets down from the wall, which was a tribute to his business skills. Like many things in Sagras, the higher on the Hill you were located, the more successful you were.

Still, the Old Wall was there and it was a barrier in more ways than one—not just physical, but social as well. No matter how successful you were as a merchant or scholar, if you didn't live in the Royal Quarter, you really hadn't made it. Perrin and her father had talked about trying to get a shop there once. It would have been a tremendous expense to find both a shop and a place to live, but it would have been offset by access to a wealthier and more influential clientele. However, many of the people who relied on Rory would no longer be able to reach him and that was enough to keep Rory on this side of the wall.

She carried the bucket of water through the store, unlocked the front door, and stepped out onto the high porch that overlooked Swan Street. Armed with her cleaning rags, she turned to attack the daily buildup of dirt and grime when she saw someone walking up the street. An older man in shabby clothes paused at the bottom of the steps, holding a rolled-up piece of parchment.

Perrin favored him with a smile. "I'm sorry, we won't be open before the top of the hour."

The man's smile faded a bit at her response. "I'm not here to buy nothing, miss. I hear your father reads stuff for people who don't know how to, and well, I …" He paused, obviously embarrassed to have to ask for help.

"Wait right there. I'll let Father know you're here."

She ducked inside and told Rory what the old man needed. Rory bounded through the store and caught the man who had turned to leave. "Hold on there. I believe you wanted to see me?"

"Well, I don't mean to cause no trouble, sir. I just got this document and I really need to answer it proper."

"Come right on in. You had breakfast yet?"

The old man looked at Rory with a confused expression. "Breakfast? Well, I had some bread and coffee couple of hours ago."

"That's not a breakfast. Come on in. You can have a bite while I go over these for you. Perrin, go set another place at

21

the table."

Perrin locked the front door behind them and then went to the cupboard while her father visited with the older man. She grabbed a pewter plate and cup as well as a knife and fork for their guest. She smiled to herself while she rummaged through the items. *That's so like him. Never met a stranger in his life. No wonder he's such a good businessman and why everyone comes to him with their problems.*

She helped dish out the breakfast meal and set the steaming potatoes and fresh eggs down in front of the bewildered man. Rory looked at him with a smile. "Come on, dig in. We'll never get through this paperwork with your stomach growling. Perrin, pour the man a drink."

It went on like that until the meal had been consumed and everyone was satiated. Perrin excused herself from the table and carried her plate and utensils over to a wooden bucket on the nearby table to be washed later. Rory reached out and cleaned off a corner of the table and spread the parchment in front of him. He motioned the older man closer and began reading the first paragraph to him. She walked out of the kitchen, shaking her head in an amused fashion.

She unlocked the front door and grabbed her bucket and cleaning rags. Attacking the windows, she hurried to get everything done before the bells on the cathedral tolled the hour. All along the street she could see the other shopkeepers sweeping out their stores or setting out items to lure passersby inside. She waved to a few of the ones she knew before turning and giving the door window one last wipe. She carried everything to the back of the store and put the cleaning supplies in a closet. Perrin grabbed her broom to give the porch one last going over before starting to set all the new books out.

Working with more enthusiasm than she felt, she managed to get the porch into decent shape. She had to admit, even though it was a lot of work, she took pride in her father's store. One of the favorite parts of it was the large sign that hung outside on the porch, proclaiming this to be STARBRIDGE

Books And Scrolls. It featured two children walking across a bridge made of stars and had been painted by one of the artists in the Royal Quarter in return for a set of books. She had loved the painting as a little girl and its simple picture conveyed what books meant to her. More than just a source of knowledge, they could take her away to other places, teach her about other cultures and relive the stories of the heroes and legends of the past.

She started to head inside when she saw her friend, Tamara, heading toward her store. She started to call out to her, but from the way Tamara's shoulders were humped forward, there was no doubting the mood her friend was in. She started up the steps, and Perrin saw that the scowl on her face matched the rest of her body language. Tamara navigated the wooden steps and stopped just outside the door. "Can you get away for a bit?"

"Father's reading for someone. I might be able to once he's finished. You want to come inside and talk?"

Her friend started to say something and thought better of it. Her defiant attitude seemed to melt and she looked at Perrin with tears forming in her eyes. "Sure. I have to talk to someone about this."

"You know you can talk to me about anything, Tamara. What's all the mystery?"

"I'll tell you once we're inside."

Perrin moved into the store and propped the door open for any customers. *If I'm going to be here, I might as well look like we're open for business. Although I think those books will have to wait for a bit before I can get to them.* Perrin reached over and tapped Tamara on the shoulder. "All right, what's going on?"

"I'm having problems with Bishop Marius again."

"He just doesn't seem to get the message, does he? I know you've got a great location down in the lower Merchants' Quarter and you've got a full house every time I go to visit you, but what's his problem? I mean, it's not like the Cathedral's schools aren't full also."

"He's still going on about how the Cathedral should be

the only organization that educates the youth of Sagras."

"I've seen their schools. I can't fault them for their buildings, their equipment, or the quality of their books—that is, if you can afford the appropriate donations to the Cathedral *and* you don't mind a bunch of dour-faced priests and laypeople teaching you all day. To be honest, Tamara, yours is the only school in the region that doesn't charge a fee, and you actually seem to care if the kids learn something or not."

"Thanks. I do love my kids, even when they're little hellions. I'd guess half of my students come from the Barrens and, let's face it, no one lives there or in Lowtown if they can avoid it."

"I wonder if he's threatened by the idea of free education."

"I think he's more upset that I'm a follower of Dashin than Arran."

"Now, wait a minute. Sure, the Emperor is a dyed-in-the-wool Arranite, but the church has never actively gone after the old faiths before. I think there are more followers of Dashin and Selmus here than anywhere else in the Empire."

Tamara stared out the window, a bit of her old fighting spirit coming back as she thought about her school. "Well, it seems King Marcus has decided to get on Emperor Stephan's good side, so he's currying favor with the Cathedral and the bishop wants my school closed."

"Isn't getting his majesty to close your school sort of like trying to shoot a fly with a ballista? I mean, it doesn't seem like something he'd want to spend his time dealing with."

Tamara's face went a little pale at that comment. "He's not, and the bishop knows there'd be a backlash if the church guards just marched in and took over the school, so they've hired Bloody Douglas to handle it."

Perrin's hand rose to her mouth in spite of her efforts to remain calm. "Oh, that's bad. I've heard rumors about him and none of them are good."

"Be glad you live up here on the Hill, Perrin. Douglas Valio doesn't prey on many people this close to the wall. However, he's well known down the Hill, it's like he reserves all his evil for those who can't or won't fight back. Let's face it: If there's a way to make money in this town, he's involved somehow. Murder, blackmail, extortion, loan sharking, fencing stolen goods, smuggling? He does it all."

Perrin had to remember that although Raven might be quite familiar with Bloody Douglas, the shopkeeper's daughter should not be. Therefore, she had to ask questions she already knew the answers to in order to keep up the illusion. "If Douglas is so well known, why doesn't the king do anything?"

"Oh, Perrin, you lead such a sheltered life. The city watch is a joke and the Royal Guards don't care about anything that happens below the Old Wall. Besides, everyone knows Valio is a favorite of the king's youngest son. As long as Douglas doesn't fleece the nobles to the point it becomes an issue, nothing is ever going to happen to him."

Isn't that the truth? We've butted heads many times. So far, he's the biggest single contributor to my travel funds here in the city-state. I don't feel guilty stealing from his operations and whenever I can mess up one of his operations, well, I sleep better at night. He's donated the most money toward keeping Tamara's school open, although that would be a big surprise to him.

Perrin gave a quick glance toward the kitchen. She could hear the old man and her father still discussing something, so she motioned Tamara to move a little closer. "You say Douglas is after you. How did you find out? Has he approached you yet?"

"When I went out after school yesterday, I saw a couple of his men standing near the corner of the school building. As I passed them, one of them looked up at my building and said, 'You know, it's too bad. These old wooden buildings burn so quickly. Not like those old brick ones. Now *those* are some fine architecture.' The other looked at me and then at him and replied, 'Yeah, and the doors on these old buildings are notorious for sticking.' It was obvious they were passing a warning to me."

"What are you going to do?"

"I don't know, Perrin. They've already scared two of my assistant teachers away. Only Agnes and Paul are still with me. I don't want to knuckle in to their threats, but I don't want something to happen to the school, especially if the children are there. I'm afraid they might get hurt or killed just because I'm being stubborn."

"Look, the Cathedral has tried to shut you down before and you've always been able to wait them out. Face it, Bishop Marius has the attention span of a gnat. He'll get upset with someone else and start a new crusade soon."

"I don't know, Perrin. If Douglas has already accepted a royal commission, he's not going to forget, even if the bishop does." Tamara's brows furrowed as she stared off into the distance. "He's got a reputation to uphold."

Perrin gave her friend a wistful smile. "I wish I could do something to help."

"I know, Perrin, but I don't think even your dad has enough pull to get me out of this. I just appreciate you being here and letting me vent."

The sound of footsteps brought their conversation to a close. The old man thanked Rory profusely before scurrying out of the store. Rory spotted Tamara and got a big smile on his face. "Ah, and how's my favorite teacher? Trying to give Perrin a few pointers?"'

Tamara noticeably forced a smile before answering the big storekeeper. "Things are well. The children really appreciate the books you've donated to the school, and so do I."

"Well, be sure to come back soon. I just received a shipment and as soon as someone puts them out" —he gave Perrin the evil eye before continuing—"there'll be some more to donate. I ordered a few extras for you."

"You really don't have to do that. I can't possibly repay you for everything you've done so far."

"And I told you, there'll be no more talk about payment." Rory laughed before turning around and heading back toward the kitchen. "Besides, you teaching all those kids to read is good for my business. Get them interested in reading and

I'll sell them all the books they want."

Tamara turned and gave Perrin a big smile. "You've got a good dad, Perrin."

"Yes, I do." Perrin smiled at his retreating form before turning back to her friend. "But he's right; I do have to get to work here. I'll stop by tomorrow. If you get too worried, you know you can stay here at night. We've got an extra room upstairs."

"No, I don't want to get your family involved in this. But thanks for the offer." Tamara walked toward the door but paused for a second in the doorway, looking back over her shoulder. "He's got a good daughter also."

"That'll be enough of that. Go, you've got a school to run."

Tamara nodded and disappeared down the porch steps. Perrin turned and went to work on the book crates. She could hear the sounds of Rory doing the breakfast dishes and the noise of people walking outside the shop. Normally, those were comforting sounds, but today, her thoughts were troubled as she felt a cold rage building up inside her.

Save it, she told herself. *You'll need that edge if you're going to play that game.* Raven had never directly challenged Bloody Douglas before, but he'd never given the thief a reason to before, either. Perrin frowned. *There has to be something I can do to hurt him bad without having it tracked back to Tamara—or me, for that matter.* Quentin would have her hide if he found out Raven had broken the truce between his guild and Douglas, so there would be no help from that direction. *I won't ask Jerek to help if I don't have to; I don't want to drag his clan into this if something goes wrong.* Perhaps Bertok might have some advice for her. She'd go see him tonight.

One way or the other, though, this is going to be settled. Up to now, Douglas, I was only interested in possibly going to go after you because you're a bloated, self-confident, arrogant pig, and that made you such a great target. That was then.

Now, it's personal.

Chapter Three

The day passed slowly for Perrin as she thought of how she was going to deal with Tamara's situation. As she escorted out the last customer of the day and locked the door, her father rubbed his hands with delight.

"Now *that* was a day. We must have sold two dozen books! I knew that new edition would be popular." He scanned the store and frowned. "'Course, now I have to do something to fill those gaps. Can't have the shelves looking bare. I won't get another shipment for two weeks."

"You can worry about that while you're cleaning up. I'll get dinner started."

"Are you going to be in this evening, Perrin?"

"Dad, you know I'm tutoring those kids for Tamara. She's running five different directions during the day. The least I can do is help her out now and then."

"Now and then wouldn't be so bad, but I'm trying to remember the last time you were home."

Perrin tried to maintain her calm, but she could see from the look on her dad's face her emotions were pretty obvious. She waited a few seconds and then said, "Dad, you know this is important to me."

"I know, I know. I just feel like we're becoming strangers. We hardly spend any time together."

"We're in the store all day together. At least I'm not out running around like some of the kids down the Hill." Every time she used that lie Perrin died a bit inside, but better that than breaking his heart if he knew the truth.

"No, no, you're a good kid. I'm proud of you, Perrin. I just wish you would find a good man and settle down. You shouldn't be stuck here taking care of me. You've got your own life to get started on."

Two steps later, she wrapped her arms around him. "It's no trouble helping you out, Dad. You know that. You've had to be Mom and Dad for too long."

"Well, I worry about you when you're out at night. With the rash of thefts and such I've been hearing about, I'm afraid someone will do something stupid."

Perrin laughed. "I can take care of myself, Dad."

* * *

After dinner, Perrin let herself out the back door and headed down to Lowtown where her "student" was waiting. A quick trip to the sanctuary and Perrin's alter ego emerged, celebrating the freedom of the darkened streets. A few minutes later, she was near the bottom of the Hill, watching the shadowy shapes that moved atop the wall, briefly silhouetted against the lamps strategically placed along the wall. She watched as they met at various spots, their long pole arms nearly invisible against the dark sky. Luckily for her, the guards were more interested in what was going on outside the city walls.

She glanced at the tall stone walls. King Francis II had built these a hundred years ago, separating the city proper from the dock area. The associated businesses, warehouses, taverns, and inns that lay beyond were part of the city in name only. According to the city guard, everything beyond the Great Gate was expendable. That included the people who chose to live there.

Raven needed to get out there, though, but it wasn't going to be easy. The Great Gate was too well guarded, but there were several smaller gates used for transporting goods to and from the docks. There would still be guards there, of course. Even though Sagras hadn't faced an enemy in years,

King Marcus was a stickler for protocol. The guards would verify every person who passed through the gates and the last thing she wanted was for some overzealous guard to recognize her and start something.

A noise up the street drew Raven's attention. It took a second, but she identified it as the sound of an iron-shod wheel moving along the damp cobblestone streets. It wasn't a sound she was used to—only a few streets in Lowtown were paved—but count on the merchants' guild to cough up the money to get their goods delivered with the minimal amount of mud on them. As the wagon approached, she could see the driver appeared half-asleep as he mechanically moved the reins just enough to keep the old mare in motion. It looked as though they were headed home after a long day, and that was perfect for Raven's needs.

She hid in the darkness until the wagon slowed to negotiate the corner, then eased over the tail of the wagon and found a grimy tarpaulin to hide beneath. One whiff of the tarp and she resigned herself to breathing as shallowly as possible. The stench was impressive.

Please, oh please, be a short trip.

After a few bumpy minutes, she felt the wagon slow to a halt. Risking a quick look, she could see she was in one of the smaller barbicans. The sight of the huge portcullis hanging over the wagon, its iron-shod wheels ready to dig into the ground if it was released suddenly, made her skin crawl. She'd never heard of one falling by accident, but she had trouble making herself look away and pay attention to what was going on around her.

"Phew! What have you been hauling, old man? That smells worse than the latrine." A pained voice sounded just on the other side of the wagon wall and she pulled the tarp back over her head.

The old man cackled at the guard. "Heh, you think that's bad, wait 'til I come through here in the summer. Now *that's* a smell that'll curl your toes!"

"I'll pass. Coming back in tonight?"

"Nope. Buela and I made our last delivery for the night. Time for dinner and bed." The old man's gravelly voice carried in the stillness of the night. Clucking to the horse to get it moving again, he started whistling a tuneless ditty as they made their way into Shantytown.

Raven began to hear the waves lapping against the docks and the unmistakable barking of the sea lions in the distance. She remained under the covers, waiting for the old man to reach his destination and unhitch Buela. After several turns, she felt the wagon slowing to a stop. *Not a moment too soon. I may never get this smell out of my clothes.*

The old man's soft voice caught her by surprise. "You can come out, missy. No way the guards can spot you now."

Raising a corner of the tarpaulin, she could see he was still sitting on the bench, turned just enough that he could watch her. His eyes were hidden in the shadows, but she knew, without a doubt, they were twinkling at the sheepish expression on her face. She flipped the tarp off herself and sat up with as much dignity as she could muster. She grabbed the edge of the wagon and vaulted into the street, adjusting her clothes once she was safely away from the smell.

"If you knew I was back there, why didn't you turn me in to the guard?"

"Hell, I knew you weren't gonna rob me. First off, I ain't got nothing worth robbin' and you're smart enough to know that. Second, if you were gonna do that, you'd have done it back in town. Better chance of escaping in town than out here. 'Sides, I have a feelin' I know who you are."

"You do, hmmm?" she asked, curious to hear his response.

The old man looked at her intently, head cocked to one side for a bit. She could see the lines etched deep on his face as he contemplated her challenge. A few loose strands of white hair rustled in the breeze beneath his hat. After a few moments of staring into her eyes, he threw back his head and laughed. "If I weren't sure before, I am now. You're that Raven person. Heard quite a bit about you at the taverns. You're just too damn cocky to be anyone else."

She gave him a mock bow. "Guilty as charged. But, now that you've caught me, what are you going to do with me? Go call that young guardsman? I hear there's quite a price on my head."

The old man hooted again. "That young popinjay? He'd probably pee all over himself if he ever faced a real threat. 'Sides, he seemed like a nice kid. Less'n you were gonna turn yourself in, you'd wind up skewering him 'cause he ain't gonna outfight you."

"I'll defer to your decision there."

"Aw, come on, Raven. You must have a reason to come to Shantytown and twern't no bother you hitchin' a ride like that. I doubt Buela even knew you were there. You just take care though, this ain't a good place for a young, good-lookin' woman like you to be wandering around by herself."

Raven patted the rapier on her hip and smiled up at him. "I'll try to stay out of trouble." She reached into a pouch on her hip and pulled out a double crown. She flipped it through the air toward him. "Have a little something for the ride and the company."

As he was watching the coin flicker in the air, she took advantage of the opportunity to slip into the shadows of a nearby alley. He caught the coin and turned to say something but stopped when he realized she was gone. She muffled a laugh at his expression, then watched as he coaxed his horse into motion, heading toward one of the still-open taverns.

She hung out in the alley for a bit to ensure no one else had noted her arrival, but the streets were empty. In Shantytown, once darkness fell, people were either in their houses or in the taverns. She ghosted down a few streets until she got her bearings and then headed into the dark mazelike streets toward her destination.

She narrowly avoided being spotted a couple of times when a rapidly opening door spilled light into an alley to be followed by a body being flung into the dirt from a makeshift tavern. She didn't have to hide here; the city watch never came into Shantytown with less than a squad during the day and never after dark. Still, where she was going, the fewer people who saw her, the more comfortable she was.

After she was certain no one had followed her, she made her way to her destination. Slipping through a hole in a wall, she made her way through an unkempt yard of what might have been a fancy house years ago. Reaching a shed behind the building, she removed a key from a pouch on her belt and inserted it into the rust-covered iron lock on the door. The lock might have been rusty, but the workings were well oiled. The lock fell open into her hands without a sound.

She slipped inside and then threw the interior bolt to lock the door behind her. Moving a stained rug on the floor revealed a trapdoor. A short descent into darkness down a metal ladder led to a narrow passageway. Another ladder led up there and she eased the trapdoor open and entered the house.

Letting her eyes adjust to the dim light, she paused in what had probably been a kitchen. Age and decay had destroyed whatever functionality it might have had; now it was just another room filled with trash. Moving past the carelessly piled junk, she entered the main room and let out a small sigh.

A series of small lamps were burning within, providing dim light to the room. The soot-blackened walls and ceiling, dark and gray with the passage of time, could not hide that once this had been a grand house. Now, mismatched furniture, piled high with books and scrolls, dominated the room. There was no discernible order to the room, but Raven knew the occupant knew where everything was in this mayhem — or claimed he did. Against the far wall stood a rude bed, its linens and blankets strewn about. It appeared the occupant had recently vacated the bed, which meant he was probably upstairs. She picked out the strongest looking chair and gingerly sat down to wait.

She pulled out one of her daggers and a whetstone and began sharpening the finely balanced weapon. Heavy footsteps came to the top of the stairs and paused. She gave the dagger a few more scrapes before she called out, "Come downstairs, you old goat. If I meant to harm you, would I be making all this noise?"

"Raven! How many times have I told you to let me know when you arrive?"

"I did let you know. You heard me sharpening my dagger."

"I swear, girl, one of these days, I'm not going to recognize you and turn you into a dragonfly or something."

"Bertok, if you could turn me into a dragonfly, I'd make you turn yourself into one and come visit me on the Hill instead. You're a hard man to get a hold of on short notice." She smiled slightly as they fell into a familiar banter, which meant Bertok was getting over being startled. He had never said why he was living in this squalid condition, but given his jumpiness, he was hiding from someone.

He clomped down the stairs, muttering to himself as he descended. He was an older man but would never admit to his actual age. His stringy black hair and long beard were streaked with gray, but his ice-blue eyes were clear and still had the power to stare a hole right through you. Raven used to love how aggravated he would get because she was several inches taller than he, but he made up for it by being nearly as round as he was tall.

"Young woman, show the proper respect for your elders," he said as he slid into his usual chair in the corner. "Just because I choose not to reveal all my powers, do not presume I am powerless."

"So you claim, Bertok. Looking at the luxury you live in, your clientele obviously can afford the best magic can offer." She slid the dagger back into its sheath on her neck, her fingers resting lightly on the soft leather wrapped around the handle. It was one of a pair of specially made throwing knives she'd had ordered from the best weaponsmith in Sagras and they had been worth every shilling she'd paid for them.

Bertok bit back a retort and then set his mouth in a tight grin. "You didn't come all this way just to insult me, so there's obviously something you need."

"Provided you can work me into your busy schedule."

"I'll have you know I do a rather thriving business when you're not around. Other people take my assistance seriously, whether you do or not," the wizard snapped at her. "You're aptly named, you know. You bring me about as much luck as your namesake." His eyes narrowed. "Ah, you're up to something. You're beating around the bush, hoping I'll do something to show you I'm not incompetent. That way, you'll get out of paying for it."

Raven gave him her most disarming smile, but he merely harumphed at her. She had hoped he might get wound up and do just that, but he was getting harder to fool these days. Bertok took her silence as a confession and shifted in his chair, ignoring its protest.

His face grew serious. "Show me something from your last lesson."

"What do you want me to do?" The sudden turn in the conversation startled her.

"Impress me."

Raven took a breath and stared at one of the smoky lamps hanging from a wall sconce, letting her body relax. She began to speak, her voice barely audible in the stillness. As she concentrated, the lamps in the room almost imperceptibly began to dim. There was nothing affecting her vision and the flames still flickered, but she knew the room was growing darker. Speaking the final word, she stood up and moved about the totally blackened room, easily avoiding the debris and clutter to reach the stairwell. Turning around, she spoke the counter word, reversing the spell. The room slowly became brighter until it returned to normal.

"Splendid. I'm impressed. I could barely see you and I knew what you were doing. Anyone else would have thought the lights had been extinguished." Bertok smiled at his student. "You need to practice more. You should be able to darken a room much faster than that, although the slow fade was a dramatic touch."

"That's the effect I was going for. If I bring the lights down a bit at a time, a guard shouldn't notice something's wrong until it's too late. Then I can strike before his eyes can adjust."

Bertok frowned. "Well, I shouldn't be surprised. You're practical as always. However, there's more to magic than as an aid to your thievery. Still, you did well. What do you need?"

"An acquaintance of mine is having issues with a certain bishop. Is there anything you've heard of, something that if it were to turn up missing—or even better, just turn up—that might get him to back off? Oh, and he's hired the best leg breaker in Sagras, so I need to deal with Bloody Douglas, too."

"An interesting proposal. You're not asking for much, though, are you?" Bertok's eyes brightened as he appeared to recall something. A sly smile ran across his face, making him seem more vulpine than usual. "Under normal circumstances, I disapprove of tangling with the church. Most of the priests I've met are reasonable fellows, even if they're not crazy about the practitioners of magic. However, I've noted the higher up in the hierarchy some get, the more they need the air taken out of them from time to time ..." He continued muttering in this vein as he began shifting books from one pile to another, obviously looking for something.

Raven waited patiently as he searched. She'd been around him long enough to know once he got his teeth into a problem, the building could burn down and he'd never notice until he finished. She leaned back in her chair and got comfortable. While she watched him work, her mind wandered back to their first meeting.

She hadn't been working as a thief very long, but she was having a run of luck. She was on her way home from relieving one of the king's warehouses of some choice objects when she saw two head breakers attacking an old man. She was never sure why she got involved, but she watched as the older man fell beneath their blows and something snapped in her. As one bent over to do something, she kicked him in the privates. He fell forward, striking the nearby stone wall with his face. The other turned to find himself staring at the point of her rapier. Deciding the odds were not in his favor, he grabbed his dazed partner and disappeared down the alley, calling back curses at her.

Helping the older man to his feet, she saw he wasn't injured too badly. He seemed to be nothing more than a down-on-his-luck drunkard, but head breakers didn't usually waste their time on people like that. Raven had a suspicion there was more to this man than met the eye. She escorted him to his hut and made certain his wounds were treated and he went to bed before she made her way home.

The next morning, she came down to the dock to pick up something for her father and stopped by to see how the man was. To her surprise, he seemed to have no sign of the wounds he'd received the night before. He also recognized her immediately and thanked her for aiding him. As they talked, they soon discovered they had a lot in common. He was well read, articulate, familiar with the imperial capital, and had a quick mind. He recognized a kindred spirit in her, someone who wasn't satisfied by being merely swept along by life.

She started coming by his place to check on him. While cleaning it one day, she stumbled across a pile of old leather-bound books hidden beneath a pile of well-worn clothes. Leafing through them, she realized they were magical tomes. She was trying to work out how some of the words in one were pronounced when he suddenly appeared, snatching the book out of her hand. He was furious about her going through his things, but after he calmed down he admitted he was a hedge wizard—a self-trained magician. He was impressed she was able to read anything in them. Normally, only those gifted with some talent could decipher the writing.

Since she knew his secret, he decided to help her with her own. Her vibrant red hair and blue eyes were going to make it virtually impossible to avoid being recognized. She admitted she'd tried several things to disguise herself, but either they were unwieldy cosmetic tricks or dyes that were too hard to wash out of her hair, which brought up some awkward questions in the morning.

A few days later, he presented her with a small package—a token of his appreciation for saving his life, he said. It was a small medallion made of white gold. She tried it on and then he taught her a phrase to use. Once she had memorized it, he had her hold the necklace in both hands and say the words aloud. As she did, she felt strange—it was as though the world had gone out of focus and then snapped back into place. Once she had her balance back, he handed her a small mirror.

One glance and she nearly dropped the mirror. Deep brown eyes gazed back at her and a lock of raven hair hung down between her eyes. Her freckles and light complexion had been replaced with olive-colored skin and her fine cheekbones were thickened and squared slightly. She was still an attractive woman, but it was a complete stranger looking back at her. Bertok gave her a careful going over and pointed out she was also several inches shorter than normal. He said she was now more of a raven than the cardinal who'd entered. She liked that and had been using that nom de guerre ever since.

A sudden exclamation from Bertok interfused her reverie. "Here we go. I knew I'd read something in these dispatches." He waved a parchment a few inches in front of her nose. "Go ahead, read it. This may be just the thing."

She tried to focus on the paper, but finally had to reach out and grab his arm to hold the paper in place. "What might be the thing? What are you going on about?"

"The Dragonstone. They're keeping the Dragonstone at the cathedral in Sagras."

Raven favored him with the same look she gave to little kids who came into the store to get "some book" they'd heard about. "And, pray tell, what is a dragon stone?"

"Not *a* dragon stone," he thundered. "*The* Dragonstone. It's a huge ruby with the image of an ancient dragon inside. Is it a flaw? A magical creation? A god's whimsy? The soul of an ancient dragon? Who knows? Who cares? What's important is it's supposed to be magical and it certainly is priceless. According to my, ahem, sources, it belongs to the Imperial College of Wizards. For some reason, it's being stored in the Grand Cathedral of Praxil as we speak."

"Well, that's no problem, then. I'll just slip in, avoid the ecclesiastical guards, the city watch, and probably the Imperial Guard and just glide out with an unfenceable gem." Raven's voice rose, sarcasm dripping off her words. "While I'm at it, why don't I steal the cardinal's best stole and cassock, too?"

"You can take whatever else suits your fancy, but if you can get ahold of the Dragonstone, you can force the church to leave your friend alone. They're not going to want word of the gem's disappearance to get back to Wolf River. The Church and the Imperial College have an uneasy truce on good days. Something like this could cause a real rupture. In fact, I'm certain there would be a quiet offer of a reward for the return of the gem."

He looked up at the ceiling and then back to her with a hungry fire visible in his eyes. "Think about it: You'd accomplish what no other thief in the entire empire would dare, and you'd probably have enough money to finally leave Sagras for good."

She was torn. It was a huge risk, but there it was, the answer to her problems if she had the courage to take it. *Damn him for appealing to my vanity. But, he's right. I know he's right.*

She closed her eyes, took a deep breath, and then opened them, a similar fire burning within her.

"All right. When do we get started?"

Chapter Four

Two men moved with quiet determination down a dim passageway, barely noting the cobwebs and dust on the stone walls and floors. Only the occasional torch burning in its sconce fought off the encroaching darkness. There was a feeling the passage of time and the events of man meant little here.

A small spiral staircase rose at the end of the hall and the younger motioned for the other to proceed. His steel-gray eyes took in the surroundings with a practiced air and his physical presence denoted a martial background. He glanced down the hall to see if anyone had noted their passing.

"Wulfric, come on, man!" The peeved voice of the elder man echoed down the stairs. "We're running late enough as is. You know he hates to be kept waiting."

"Be that as it may, Gerhard, it's important no one sees us. The prudent course is to be a little late and undetected rather than on-time and observed."

"Oh, very well." Wulfric heard Gerhard's pained sigh in the quiet of the stairwell and smiled to himself. The elder man's aristocratic airs rubbed against his military bearing. There was a fire in his eyes that matched Wulfric's, though.

Satisfied no one had noted their passage, Wulfric bounded up the stairs two at a time to catch up with Gerhard. Only the sound of their steps and their breathing broke the tomb-like atmosphere of the deserted stairway. Fewer torches hung in the spiraling staircase and the darkness made climbing the marble stairs treacherous. Wulfric shook off the feeling that the passage was getting narrower as they made their way to the top.

A small landing appeared and Wulfric walked up to the ironbound door. He raised the brass ring attached to the heavy door and let it drop. The ring struck the brass plate with a loud *clack* that echoed through the stairway. Gerhard glared at him but held his tongue.

Wulfric repressed a shudder as he looked at the small, wizened man who opened the door. His back stooped with age, Bela stood there smiling and motioned them into the room. The mute servant was a constant presence at the king's side, carrying out minor tasks for his master. His lack of speech made him invaluable at private gatherings such as these.

It's unnatural how devoted Bela is to King Marcus. He acts as if he's part of the family rather than a mere servant. Marcus had granted him privileges he never should have had. Thus, the palace staff lived in fear of him because Bela knew he wouldn't be punished for anything he did as long as he kept Marcus happy.

The room beyond Bela was austere. The walls and floor of the chamber were carved from a pale rosy marble and lined with vertical columns of onyx. Tapestries depicting ancient battles of the old Kingdom of Sagras hung from ceiling to floor. A large mahogany table and heavy chairs dominated the circular room, but these affectations only added to the heavy atmosphere of the room.

Around the table, three men were deep in conversation. One was an older man, thin and parsimonious-looking, his thinning white hair standing out in all directions. Wulfric knew at a glance it was Fraser, the master of the exchequer. The man responsible for the king's treasury. Wulfric had held many tempestuous discussions regarding military funding with him. *You'd think the dribbles of money doled out to the military of Sagras were coming out of his own fortune the way he howled at every request.*

The second man there seemed sculpted from the same marble that made up the room. A large, muscular man, his light green eyes stared ahead as he let Fraser rant about something. Hugh was the chamberlain of the king's court. He was the most powerful non-noble in Sagras and many resented his family's humble beginnings. As chamberlain, he was in charge of everything that went on within the palace walls. He determined who received an audience with the king, he ran the royal staff, and he was responsible for the palace guards.

King Phillip had elevated Hugh's father after he saved the king's life at the Battle of Black Lion Pass nearly fifty years ago. Hugh served underneath Wulfric, rising to be the captain of a light cavalry unit, before assuming his father's position as chamberlain nearly twenty years ago. Hugh served King Phillip and then King Marcus when he had assumed the throne three years later.

The third member of the trio was King Marcus himself. From the second Marcus walked into the room, there was no questioning he was in control of any situation. The king not only had strength of personality, but he had a powerful physique. Wulfric's weapons master called the king "sneaky strong." Many of the king's sparing partners would agree.

A large parchment had been rolled out on top of the table, its corners held down by large onyx paperweights. King Marcus was pointing to something on the parchment and from the look of things, Fraser was attempting to talk him out of it. As usual, Hugh's expression was inscrutable.

His majesty must want to spend some money. Fraser never gets that emotional over ordinary items.

Gerhard and he waited at the door until Bela made their presence known to the king. With an impatient wave, King Marcus beckoned them over. The two men hurried across the room and joined the others at the table.

"So glad you two saw fit to join us." The king's tone was frosted with impatience as he ran a hand through his deep brown hair.

"We apologize for the delay, your majesty," Wulfric began, cutting Gerhard off. "Your message suggested discretion, so we took a more circuitous route to ensure privacy." The king waved his hand in boredom, so Wulfric lapsed into silence.

"Fraser, you have made your point," the king said, turning back to the other two. "In fact, you have more than made your point. However, your job is to determine how best to fund this task, ensure sufficient funds are available, and that they continue to arrive until the task is completed. You will dole them out to whomever I so choose in whatever amount I so choose. Are we in agreement or should the crown entertain a new minister of the exchequer?" Fraser stared into the king's piercing brown eyes and paled. To Wulfric's amazement, he showed some wisdom and swallowed whatever comment he had been about to make.

The king turned to his chamberlain. "Hugh, you know what needs to be done. Set the ambassadors to their tasks. I need to get as much information from them as soon as possible. Also, ensure the guards are on alert. This cannot leak out."

Hugh nodded, his black hair making his pale skin stand out. "It will be done, your majesty."

With a wave of his hand, he dismissed the two men. Exiting past Wulfric and Gerhard, Fraser left the room in a foul humor, looking neither right nor left. Hugh paused for a moment to exchange pleasantries with the two men before disappearing down the stairs in Fraser's wake.

"Come on, gentlemen, we don't have all day." The king motioned with his arm, drawing their attention to the table.

Looking down, Wulfric could see a map of the Empire of Taleronda and the adjoining lands. Emperor Stephan's lands were outlined in red and a large star on the map identified the city-state of Sagras far to the south of the Imperial capital. Looking closer at the map, Wulfric could see it identified lands within the borders of the empire Stephen did not control—independent cities and kingdoms neutral enough that Stephan was content to ignore them. The map was filled with pins bearing small flags in different colors. To Wulfric, it resembled a campaign map.

The king had been watching his face and as Wulfric's eyes rose to meet his, the king smiled. "Yes, General Wulfric, it's what you think it is. It's time Sagras reclaimed its glory and took its rightful place within the Empire."

"And to achieve these goals, the king will require absolute obedience." A soft voice carried through the room and Wulfric spun around. A large man stood beside a tapestry he held to one side, revealing an alcove there. His dark skin hid his features beneath his hooded robes, but there was no mistaking the malice that lurked within those dark eyes.

Kazmer.

Kazmer was the leader of the Black Leopards, the king's secret police. The Leopards were fighters, assassins, and wizards who operated outside the laws of the city. They answered only to Kazmer and he answered only to the king.

The Leopards had served Sagras well for generations, winning battles before the army needed to be mobilized and eliminating threats to the throne before the king knew they existed. But they changed ever since Kazmer assumed leadership. There was something unwholesome about the man, Wulfric thought. He destroyed not from necessity but because he enjoyed it.

Turning to face the assassin, the general kept his voice steady. "That goes without saying, Kazmer."

"One would think so, but I'm not convinced," the man said, his voice dripping with insinuation. "The minister does not appear to have the proper enthusiasm for this plan. That concerns me."

Wulfric's blood ran cold at the offhand comment, but he kept his military bearing. "That would fall under your office, not mine." Wulfric turned to the king. "What would you have our army do, my liege?"

"I'm looking years into the future, Wulfric." The king rubbed his hands together in a self-satisfied manner. "I intend to leave my sons a land worthy of their heritage. The red flags designate independent lands within the Empire. Since they see fit to ignore the benefits of being under the emperor's benevolent rule, I shall help them come to their senses. Some we will conquer, others will appeal to the emperor for protection. Either way, Stephan should be grateful for their addition."

The king picked up a stiletto he had been using as a pointer and indicated several spots on the map. "These lands with the green flags are beyond the Empire's boundaries. However, they sit on strategic land or have resources of which the emperor could make good use."

"And these areas designated with the blue flags, sire?" Wulfric already knew the answer, but knew the king wanted him to ask.

"Why, Wulfric, these are our primary targets. We'll need to secure these lands to provide supply routes between Sagras and these new additions to my kingdom. Of course, they're vassals of the emperor, but if they fall fast enough …" The king paused for dramatic effect and then continued in a rush, "Well, it's unlikely he'll get involved. It takes too long to raise the imperial levies to deal with emergencies. Besides, an enlarged Sagras is more valuable than a collection of tiny states."

"What does your majesty require of me?" Gerhard asked while the king was admiring his own plans.

The king turned his head toward Gerhard, a look of annoyance visible on his still-youthful face. "You, my good ambassador, are to keep Emperor Stephan as neutral as possible. I don't care if you have to obfuscate, flatter, cajole, or keep the poor man drunk. Keep him and the imperial levy near Wolf River as long as possible. What I do not want is my rivals making him think that I'm a threat to the imperial throne."

Turning his head to Kazmer, he smiled. "At least, not yet."

Wulfric's face froze in place. *What has Kazmer been putting in King Marcus's head? Taking over a few small city-states and rural communities is one thing. But challenging the emperor is treason!*

45

A knock interrupted Marcus's gloating. Bela looked at his master, a look of confusion on his face, and then walked over to the heavy door. The wizened man opened the door a crack and Wulfric could tell by the way his body stiffened it was someone not welcome.

"I'll only say this one more time, Bela: I will see my father, so you can move or be moved," came a familiar voice from the other side of the door.

Kazmer lifted two of the paperweights, letting the map roll up on itself as Prince Geoffrey pushed past Bela and entered the room. Geoffrey was the king's eldest son, but he was nothing like Marcus in temperament. Tall and handsome, Geoffrey favored his mother with his long blond hair and clear blue eyes, although he had inherited Marcus's strong nose and chin. "I was told you could be found here, Father."

"And you have found me. What wouldn't wait until I finished with my meeting?" The king's voice carried a mixture of contempt and disappointment.

Marcus's feelings toward Geoffrey was the palace's worst-kept secret. The two were a complete mismatch—the warrior king and the scholar son. Geoffrey was more comfortable with the palace's scholars than the fencing masters. He would spend hours hunting through the palace archives in search of old, forgotten books. He didn't neglect his martial training, but it was not a driving interest of his, whereas Marcus prided his skill with sword and bow over most everything else he could do.

"The ambassador from Helion has arrived. You asked to be notified the instant his ship docked." Geoffrey's voice matched his father's in tone, but he was still a prince. His eyes remained looking at a point below his father's gaze in deference to his father's status.

"Why did *you* come to inform me? Wouldn't any of the servants have sufficed?"

"I decided not to rely on anyone else with the interest you showed when you made the request." A smile appeared on his face as he continued, "It's obvious we're negotiating a new treaty with Helion. Our current trade agreement is profitable, but I knew there was a reason you were inviting them so I did some research. The demand for Pilgaia wine is at an all-time high and with the poor crop of grapes this year, the prices will rise soon. Helion is the gateway to the Pilgaian hills, so it makes sense to lock in a favorable trade rate before the reports of the weak harvest get out."

"Ah, gentlemen, this is why he is my heir. He sees opportunities and finds ways for Sagras to profit from them. Go, my son, meet the ambassador and see to his entertainment. I shall join you soon."

Geoffrey's smile beamed at his father. Compliments from Marcus were rare; compliments in front of the court were even rarer. "At once, Father. I will ensure they are in the proper mood for negotiations by the time you are available."

Receiving a nod of dismissal from his father, the young man rushed from the room. With the sound of the door latching into place, the smile fled Marcus's face and darkness descended on it, making the warrior's heart in Wulfric pause for a second.

"What did I do to be cursed with such an idiot child? There's not a noble bone in his body. Too much time with his head stuck in a book and not enough time in the real world. His brother, Owen, would make such a better ruler than he. Now *there's* a lad who knows what he wants and how to get it, and Fashadi take the hindmost."

Wulfric saw the expression on Marcus's face change as his rant drew to a close. Marcus picked up the stiletto again as Kazmer unrolled the map. "Helion is on our list of targets, gentlemen. We can use this as an opportunity to position troops there to 'guard' the shipments of valuable wine. Once the time is right, we can swoop down on the undefended city. Helion may not be valuable, but its strategic importance cannot be overlooked."

"You know, Your Majesty, accidents do happen from time to time." Kazmer's soft voice cut into the silence as the men stared at the map. Wulfric started to object to the implied threat, but the king waved him off.

"Kazmer, I know many things, but regicide is not on my list of things to do." The assassin lifted his hands in front of him, until the fingertips touched as he bowed to the king, acknowledging the rebuke. "Besides, that son of mine did make a good suggestion, albeit inadvertently. Let us take a look at the map and see what would be the best way to make a *strategic alliance* with Helion."

With an understanding laugh among them, the four men closed around the table, their voices dropping into conspiratorial tones.

Chapter Five

"It's getting really intolerable, Perrin. Those men were outside the school again today."

Perrin poured Tamara another cup of tea as she sat at the kitchen table. Rory was watching the store while she talked to her friend, but she knew her father was hovering close by. He was unaware of Tamara's situation, but he had a strong sense of what was right and wrong and wasn't averse to getting into the middle of something. If he thought Perrin or her friends needed backup, he'd be right there. Unfortunately, when dealing with someone like Douglas, that was probably the wrong thing to do.

Perrin sat down next to her. "Surely it's not that bad. I think they're just trying to scare you into quitting."

"No, it's gotten worse than that, Perrin. A couple of the men actually came into the school today. They didn't do anything, just sat at the back of the classroom and watched. I'm afraid they're going to start targeting my students' families soon."

"That's incredible. Did the students see them?"

"I don't think so. They were pretty quiet. I tried to act like nothing unusual was happening."

Perrin poured some more tea into her own cup as she thought about the situation. This was going way beyond intimidation now. In fact, if they were being this blatant, something was getting ready to happen before Tamara could rally any support. If Perrin was going to help, she needed to do it before more well-meaning people got dragged into this conflict. Douglas's leg breakers wouldn't care if they were the intended target or not. Anyone getting in their way would be dealt with savagely and efficiently. It was going to take someone who could meet them head-on to get their attention.

"Are you okay, Perrin?"

"Oh, I'm sorry, Tamara. Just trying to think of something I could do to help you out. Have you gone to the guards? There's got to be something they can do."

Tamara made a snorting noise before breaking into the first smile she'd had since she walked into the store. "The guards? And what are they going to do ... provide aid to an unlicensed school teaching guttersnipes and future dock-workers how to read and think? They'd be more likely to smack me around for trying to make people think they're better than where they were born. Besides, you've seen them. The only real men in armor are the ones in the army. The city guards are good for shaking down merchants and occasionally catching someone who falls right at their feet. No, they'd take one look at Douglas's men and decide it was time to visit the nearest tavern."

"Given how poorly King Marcus pays them, I'm surprised they do as well as they do."

"I have noticed he isn't sparing any expenses on his army, though. Have you noticed they're expanding the Red Quarter again? If they keep this up, they'll be moving the city walls again."

"Or driving the people out of the Barrens to make room. There's plenty of room in Lowtown, I guess." Perrin tried to keep her face still, but she couldn't help remembering her last passage through the Barrens. Two more families had been burned out because there was sickness in the house. It was cruel, but the only way to prevent a return of the Red Death from forty years ago.

Perrin stood up. "Let me walk you home, Tamara."

"You really don't have to."

"I know, but I'd feel better. I can stop and get some items

I've wanted to buy for a while. Please?"

Tamara gave her a familiar grin. "All right. Mainly because I know you're not going to take no for an answer. Just make sure your father's all right with that."

Rory's voice rumbled in from the main room. "Of course. It's a little slow today. No sense both of us being stuck in here."

Perrin escorted Tamara out the kitchen door and down the alleyway toward her home. They talked about different subjects and paused at a few shops to look around, all the time slowly making their way down the Hill. Reaching the borderlands between the Merchants' Quarter and the Barrens, they turned down a cobblestone path that led to Tamara's house. Two men rose in a graceful motion from her steps and disappeared into the alley as the two women approached. Tamara hesitated, but Perrin nudged her forward and they went inside. Nothing seemed amiss, but Perrin could see all the tension that had been in Tamara's body return with a vengeance.

Tamara took a deep breath and then leaned against a chair. "I never expected to see them outside my door. What's going on? What should I do?"

"First thing, you're going straight back to my place. I need to stop and see someone about a favor. Let's see if we can't get this solved one way or another."

* * *

Raven watched from a rooftop near Tamara's house as the moons rose over Sagras. Below, a young woman made her way down the street and unlocked the door to Tamara's house. A faint light appeared inside and then began moving through the house. After a while, the light appeared in a window on the second floor and then went out. Raven knelt in the shadows of a chimney and waited.

The streets darkened below and only a few gas lights burned on the nearby streets. Raven noted with grim amusement the lights nearest to Tamara's house didn't respond to the lamplighter's attempts to ignite them. After a few halfhearted tries, the lamplighter climbed down his ladder and disappeared into the gloom. The streets were deserted except for the occasional animal rummaging around for something to eat.

She was beginning to think she had wasted her time when a group of shadows began detaching themselves from various buildings and moving into the street. They moved quietly and if she hadn't been expecting them, she might not have noticed them. She saw two of them produce small barrels and it became obvious what they were getting ready to do.

She let them mill about a bit more before she struck her flint to the tinderbox next to her. Once she had a flame going, she lit one of her torches and tossed it into the street among them. They scattered at the sudden burst of light and the two men with the kegs retreated fastest. She tossed several more torches among them, sending them running with each flaming projectile. While they were distracted, she lowered herself to the street on a rope and walked over toward Tamara's house.

She took up a stance in the middle of the street, one hand on her rapier. "You're not wanted around here. In fact, tell Douglas this is a mark he's going to have to return unclaimed. This person and all her friends are under my protection."

One of the larger figures walked closer, his masked face covered in flickering shadows. "Yeah, and who the hell are you?"

"Someone who knows who your boss is. If Douglas wants a war, then I guess you can start it right here and now. Personally, I think it would be a lot cheaper for him if he backed off. Likely to save a lot of lives."

Raven could feel the others beginning to move closer to her, their courage returning as they realized how outnumbered she was. She gave the largest one an insolent smile as she drew her rapier. "I guess you're going to ignore my suggestion. A pity. Do you really want to die that badly?"

The large man looked her up and down as he drew a blade from its sheath. "And just what do you think you're going to do about it? Looks like we have a playmate, boys. I hope she likes it rough."

"Oh, I like it rough, but I'm afraid you're going to be too busy poking your guts back inside your stomach when I get finished." As the mass of bodies began to surge toward her, she gave out a loud whistle. The on-rushers paused to look at her and then turned to follow her now upward pointing finger. Behind her on Tamara's roof, five figures rose from the shadows, arrows pointed at the crowd below. Another whistle and four more archers rose from an adjoining roof-top. As their eyes continued to follow Raven's upstretched hand, more and more archers appeared. Another whistle and two of the houses nearby opened up and more bodies came pouring out, all armed with swords or clubs.

"Now, as I was saying, you can leave here on your own, or you can leave when the body cart comes by in the morning. But, my dear friends, you are going to leave. And when you leave, you are not going to be coming back. Tell Douglas whatever you have to, but make it clear that any attempt against Tamara, Tamara's friends, Tamara's students, or Tamara's school will be met with escalating force. I have nothing against Douglas but Tamara is under my protection and I will fulfill my contract."

Raven lowered her rapier at the apparent leader of the group. She could see the sweat beads forming on his forehead as the others looked to him to decide what to do. "You have until I get to ten before someone's going to be real dead." She let the silence settle in on the milling crowd. "Six …"

The leg breakers' nerve broke and they began shoving and pushing as they tried to find a means of escape. By the time she had gotten to nine, the sound of running feet faded into the night, leaving only the large one still on the street. "Get over it, girl. You're not going to just shoot me down. If you were, you wouldn't have given us a chance to run. You'd have laid all of us out while you had the chance. I'm calling your bluff. Either order your men to shoot me or else come face me. It's not like I can go back to Douglas anyway, so give me some satisfaction."

"Are you crazy? Why should I just have you shot and dragged off into the alley?"

"Because the Raven isn't a cold-blooded murderer and that's what this would be."

She saluted him with her rapier. "So, me putting a foot of steel into your belly wouldn't be murder?"

"Not if I get you first. Although I would like your word that if I win, your buddies here let me walk."

One of the figures started to move forward, but Raven motioned him back. She turned and began circling the large man. "It's your funeral, but you have my word."

She feinted and watched how he reacted, closing and then dancing back. Even in the poor light, she could see he was a competent fighter. Raven noticed the large man was in good shape and had reach on her. If she was going to win this fight, she was going to have to remember everything her sword master had been teaching her.

They continued to circle, trying to spot a weakness in each other's defenses. Raven noticed he was keeping his left hand slightly behind his hip instead of resting on it. That was an unorthodox stance. There were only a couple of reasons she could figure out why he would do that and none of them were good for her.

She decided to push the issue and see how he would react. With a sudden flurry, she advanced to try and take him high on his shoulder. It wasn't a killing stroke, but if he was hiding something, hopefully he'd expose himself.

He flinched as her blade slipped past his and awkwardly parried her attack. In the next instant, he lunged forward with a long dagger in his off-hand and she had to skip backward out of reach. She moved out of easy striking range and pulled a heavy stiletto from her boot. She turned her body more to the side and stood with the stiletto poised above her head. Her instructor had called it the scorpion style. It wasn't her favorite, but she doubted her opponent had ever seen it before. If he was going to cheat, then she had no compulsions against making his life miserable.

They stared at each other in the gloom as they continued their dance. Now that his dagger was exposed, he led with it, holding his rapier down toward his hip to take advantage of any opportunity that might appear. Raven glanced away from her opponent from time to time to orient herself with the street. There were stairs going into buildings and the cobblestones that lined the road in front of Tamara's were getting slippery as the night breeze began blowing in off of the bay. Raven suspected a fog could begin rolling in if that light breeze kept up.

They made a few more passes, but neither was quite ready to commit to a full-out attack. Raven was pretty sure he might be able to beat down her guard if he committed himself to it, but he recognized she was faster. Neither of them had a clear advantage, though. Still, she couldn't stay out here all night. Unlike him, she did have a deadline to meet. The dawn was several hours away, but it was coming.

She moved in quickly, trying to lure him into an attack. He flicked the dagger toward her rapier and then thrust the rapier at her stomach. She caught the dagger deep on her rapier's blade and shoved it to the side, deflecting his rapier in the same motion. As his blade slid just beside her ribs, her left arm shot out, driving the point of the stiletto into his left arm. He let out a small cry of pain and retreated. He managed to hang on to the dagger, but his grip was loosened. That gave her an opportunity to press the attack. He thrust again with the rapier, but she caught this attack with her stiletto and turned it. She drove the tip of her rapier into his right shoulder before he could get the dagger up to deflect her attack.

He reeled backward, trying to shrug off her attack. She held her ground, letting him retreat and take up a defensive position. "I think we both know how this fight is going to end. I have no desire to kill you. If you leave now, you can be miles away before Douglas knows you've left town."

"And how the hell do you expect me to do that? It's not like Douglas paid up front."

"You have family?"

The large man stopped and the tips of his weapons dropped as he stared at her. "What the hell does that matter?"

Raven slid her stiletto back into her boot and then reached to a pouch on the back of her belt. She tossed it at him and the sound of coins clinking echoed in the silent street. He glanced down at it and then back at her. "Who're you kidding?"

"No kidding. I told you, I don't want to kill you. Take the money, get your family and get the hell out of town. You'd have left with the others if you weren't worried about feeding your family … or worried Bloody Douglas would take tonight out on them. Four of my friends will escort you to the city wall. Where you all go after that is your business, just be long gone by morning."

The man sheathed his dagger and warily bent down to pick up the pouch. "I don't understand it."

"What's to understand? How many times can I say I don't want to kill you? I don't want to kill anyone. I'm a thief, not a butcher. I'll defend myself and I'll defend my friends, though." Raven motioned to one of the shadowy figures who'd been watching the fight. "See he gets all the help he needs leaving town. If he needs a cart, then find one for him. I just want him gone." The shadowy figure nodded and motioned for her opponent to follow.

"Wait. Before I go, let me say Jack Sharkey doesn't forget when someone does him a favor. I don't know when we'll cross paths again, but I will remember this."

"Well, Jack Sharkey, let's hope for both our sakes we don't meet again. Now be off with you. Dawn's coming quicker than you think."

Jack nodded his head and walked away; moments later he disappeared around a corner.

One of the shadowy figures came over and stood in front of her. "You let him leave alive—*and* you gave him money?"

Another figure joined them. "Dimitri, this is Raven's way.

56

She asked us here to help, not to tell her how to handle it."

"Jerek, this is madness. How does she stay alive? She's too soft to be a good thief."

Jerek waved a hand over his head and the shadowy figures began to disappear into the darkness of the city. He turned to Dimitri. "We'll discuss this back at camp. When a friend of the Corconti asks for help, we do not turn them down. She has done many favors for our clan. She's one of the few *nabarja* who give a damn about our tribe. Let's not give her reasons to wonder why she puts up with *uritaki* like you."

"Be careful, Jerek. You may be in love with this city, but the tribe comes first. If push comes to shove, will she support the city or the tribe?"

Raven walked in front of Dimitri. "Why would I have to choose? I have no loyalty to this city, but never forget, Dimitri, I have no loyalty to the Corconti, either. The only person I am loyal to is me. That's how I stay alive. I protect my friends, and I consider the Corconti friends, but my friends do not take advantage of my good nature. I don't expect the Corconti to tell me how to live my life."

Dimitri gave her a cold look and then turned back to Jerek. "We will talk in the camp."

Jerek stood beside Raven until Dimitri was a small shadow in the distance. "I know Dimitri can be a jerk, Raven, but you must be careful about how you talk around my brothers. The clans know the *nabarja* would love to have excuses to drive us out of their realms. If Dimitri makes the others think you're just like the rest we've met, you may have a hard time getting our support the next time you ask for it."

Raven rested a hand on his shoulder, "I'm sorry. It's just people like Dimitri get on my nerves. I can't tell if he is upset because I'm not Corconti or because I'm a woman. Would you have made the same decision I just did?"

"Probably not. Then again, I would have simply shot that Sharkey in both legs and dumped him in an alley."

"So you wouldn't have killed him, either?"

"Again, probably not. But I wouldn't have given him a

chance to kill me, either. You are too nice sometimes."

She put an arm around his neck. "I can be nicer."

He gave her a quick kiss. "I know you can be. However, I know this routine. It's time for you to pull your disappearing act and I do need to get back. My father has a full day's worth of work on my list for tomorrow. I suspect it will be a few days before I can get back into town again."

"Three nights from tonight, the Black Boar tavern?"

"If I cannot be there, I will send someone carrying my regrets."

"If you cannot be there, you will have regrets for missing a good time with me."

"Indeed I will. Now off with you, my vanishing storm crow."

Raven gave him another kiss and then hurried off down the street. As she reached an alleyway, she looked back to see Jerek knock on Tamara's door and the young woman who'd taken the teacher's place come out, adjusting a sword. The Corconti woman waved in Raven's direction before Jerek and she headed toward the Great Gate and to the Corconti camp outside of town.

Raven paused at the mouth of the alley for a bit, watching as they disappeared into the gloom before hurrying off to her lair and the trip to her own home where she'd find Tamara still sleeping in their spare room. She wouldn't know what had happened here, but hopefully this was the last she'd have to worry about Bloody Douglas. The time to deal with Bishop Marius once and for all would come soon enough.

Chapter Six

Raven made herself comfortable at a table in the back of the Black Boar. It was only an hour after sunset, so Jerek's absence was not worrying her ... yet. Leave it to that fool Corconti to probably do something that would have a pack of the city guards chasing him around the city. The barmaid brought another mug of ale over to her along with a tray of bread and cheeses. Raven thanked her and tossed a small handful of silver coins onto the tray. The maid gave her a smile and deftly made the coins disappear as she turned from the table.

A few moments later, Jerek came through the door and made his way toward the back table. He called out something to the bartender that Raven couldn't quite make out over the buzz of the noisy room, and then he danced past a couple of chairs and vaulted over the railing to land just in front of Raven's table.

"Very nice and unobtrusive entrance, Jerek. I think the three drunks who're passed out under the table over there might not have noticed you."

"I'm obviously slipping, then. Used to be, the ladies said my presence would wake the dead, much less a few drunks."

She smacked him on the arm. "You're obviously a humble person."

"Why, yes, I am. You ensure my ego gets pierced every chance you get."

"Yet it refills itself nightly."

He looked hurt for a moment, but his good nature never

let him stay angry with her for very long. He leaned a little closer and stage-whispered, "I'll never understand how you can remain inside these walls at night. How do you live not being able to see the stars?"

She smiled at the young man. "I could ask you a similar question. How do the Corconti survive in the wild with no walls to protect them from an enemy?"

A self-indulgent smile spread across his face, making his dark brown eyes twinkle in the dim light. "That's easy. The Corconti don't have enemies, therefore we don't have to hide."

"No, your tribe of wanderers and thieves are welcomed everywhere they go." She liked Jerek, but sometimes he brought out her snippy side.

"True, but we are noted musicians, healers, and horse traders. Also, we know where we are and are not welcomed. We've learned not to go where we are not appreciated."

Raven fought down the urge to drop something heavy on the smirking Corconti. Luckily for Jerek, the barmaid arrived with fresh ale for Raven and a smoking green drink for Jerek. Raven eyed the thin glass warily. "That does not look healthy."

Jerek picked up the drink and downed it in one long pull. His face flushed and his eyes bulged as the alcohol hit him; a small gasp of air escaped from his lips. "No, no, it is not healthy at all." A second or two later, he sat back in his chair with a satisfied smile on his face. "But not everything that is enjoyable is necessarily good for you."

"Like our current lifestyle."

"Like that, for instance. You have to admit there are things we could do that are certainly a lot safer than making money the way we do. Like, say, raising good horses and traveling the byways your people don't seem to appreciate."

"Don't get stupid, Jerek. I told you: We've got a good working relationship here. Let's not spoil it by you going all mooncalved on me."

"Mooncalved? Me? Why, you wound me to the core."

"I'll wound you a little bit lower if you don't get those thoughts off your face and back into that dark little space you call a brain."

Jerek gave a dramatic gulp and leapt backward out of her reach. "By the gods, give a girl a pair of pants and a sword and she becomes dangerous."

"Watch it, wanderer."

Raven felt the person rushing toward her before she heard the rustling of feet and clothes. She turned and spotted Ginny seconds before she nearly bowled Raven out of her chair. Raven slid the blade in her hand back into its sheath before returning the hug. "Glad to see you up and about, Ginny. How're you feeling?"

"I'm doing better, thanks to you. Well, you and that creepy guy Bertok."

Raven's forehead wrinkled slightly as she drew her eyebrows together. She hadn't thought Ginny would mention him being around, so she decided to act as if she didn't know he'd been there. "Bertok. He stopped by to see you?"

"Well, sure. He said you'd asked him to stop by and deliver some medicines. The doctor who was seeing me wasn't going to let him at first, but Bertok had a talk with him outside my room. A few minutes later, he came in and gave me some nasty-tasting liquid and I fell asleep. When I woke up, my broken arm and cheekbone were healed. Oh, Raven, how can I ever thank you enough?"

The "doctor" was actually a local Raven had paid a few coins to, to act like one. Until she and Jerek had hit that young nobleman, there was no way she could have afforded a real doctor. The ones who hung around in the Barrens were doctors in name only—incompetent at best and damn deadly at worst.

Raven had Ginny hold out her arm so Raven could examine it. She traced a line down Ginny's forearm; her friend giggled. Not only could Raven not see that both forearm bones had been shattered, but there was no sign of bruising. Even given the time between the beating and today, there still should have been some evidence of damage. She wasn't sure what Bertok had given Ginny, but hoped he hadn't paid too much for it. She hated being in debt to him.

"I don't know why you hang around an old letch like Bertok, Raven. He's ugly and he smells of bad beer. But thank you again for the medicine."

"You really want to repay me, Ginny?"

"Oh, yes, Raven." The blond girl nodded her head so hard, Raven was afraid her tight curls would smack her in the face. She rested a hand on Ginny's bare shoulder and looked her in the eyes. "Quit seeing that loser. He's never going to change and he's never going to quit hitting you. The next time, he might not stop at just breaking your arm."

"But, Raven, I know he was just—"

"No. Listen to yourself. He's not a good guy. He's not going to change. You have to take care of yourself or the next time, you're likely to be dead."

Tears welled up in Ginny's eyes. "You just don't understand."

"Understand? No, I don't understand. Why would someone like you—someone as beautiful and wonderful as you—put up with crap from guys? You can find a guy who wants you for you. But you have to convince yourself that you're worth treating right."

"That's easy for you to say, Raven. You're beautiful, you're brave, and you've got Jerek."

"Well, she's right about that, Raven."

She shot him a look of disgust. "You're not helping."

Jerek stood up, spun his chair around and then sat in it backward, leaning his chest up against the back. "She's right, Ginny. You're a good person. You don't have to put up with his crap. You've got enough money to keep you off the streets a few more days. Why not rest up and think about what Raven's said. Heck, if you need a new job, maybe Hendrik, here, can give you some tips on who's hiring."

"Damn, I thought I could sneak up on the two of you. Should have known you'd be paying attention." Turning toward the gruff voice, she saw Hendrik, his scarred arms interlaced across his burly chest, leaning on the rail separating this section of the tavern from the main floor. Of all the bouncers around town, Hendrik was probably her favorite. Built like a beer barrel on legs, he kept the chaos in the Black Boar down to manageable levels and had no trouble evicting the most boisterous of drunks. "I might not have seen you come in, but I did notice you didn't stop by to say hi. You haven't been around here for a while. Where have you been hiding?"

"I've been busy." Raven stood up and grabbed another chair for their table. "You have a few minutes, or do you have to get back to the door?"

Hendrik looked around and turned back to her with a grin. "Nah. That fight's over. I think I can sit here for a minute or two."

"Fight?" Confused, Jerek turned around to survey the tavern. "What fight?"

"Exactly," Hendrik replied with a sly grin.

Raven motioned for Ginny to sit down and then turned her chair so she could easily see the two of them. Jerek stood up, attempting to catch the barmaid's attention. "So, is there anything interesting going on this evening?"

Hendrik's laugh matched his rough exterior. "Interesting? In the Black Boar? Nothing interesting ever happens here. A few murders, a few bar fights, the occasional theft. Pretty slow night."

"Glad to see you have it under control."

Hendrik moved his chair so he could lean back against the wall and still keep an eye on the place. "So, I wasn't trying to eavesdrop …"

Jerek poked at him with his glass. "But you weren't *not* trying to eavesdrop, either."

Hendrik gave him a dirty look and then continued. "But I have to agree with Raven here, lass. I don't care whoever this blackguard is, if he'll put a hand on you in anger, he'll keep doing it. I see it happen all the time here."

Ginny's eyes welled up with tears. "You're all ganging up on me. It's not fair."

"It's not fair that he hits you. What's it going to take to get it through your head? If Jerek were to ever lay a hand on me, he'd be looking for his fingers for a week. Not because I'm stronger than him, but because I won't take that crap from him—or anyone. Neither should you. Hendrik, do you know anyone who's hiring right now? We have to get Ginny out of that house she's working in."

"Are you still working at Old Lady Verine's? Ginny, I thought you said you were going to give that up." Hendrick frowned at her and Ginny's lower lip started to quiver again.

"I was. But Caliphar didn't want me to go and he's the lady's enforcer. He's got a bad temper, too. I saw him take a lash to one of the girls before. He never left a mark, but she couldn't stand up for almost two days. He's going to expect me back there soon. Besides, that's where Byron will be looking for me."

Raven ran her hand down her face, half in shock and half in amazement. "Okay, now we have two really good reasons for you not to go back there. Hendrik, can you find a place for her to stay and find her a job? Actually, Hendrik, do you have any friends who *aren't* in this town who could put her up?"

"I can say yes to all three questions. An old friend, retired like me, is opening a place about forty miles south of here. It's a way station/tavern. He's going to need good dependable help and I hear he's got a son just about Ginny's age who's not hard on the eyes ... if you're female, that is."

"But I have to—"

"You have to listen to Hendrik here. This is for your own good." Raven turned to Hendrik and nodded toward the back door. "Are there any rooms here that Ginny could stay in tonight?"

"Aye, lass. Not been much call for rooms. Most people prefer to sleep their drunks off at home or in the street. Much cheaper."

"Then could you escort Ginny up to one and see she's

secure for the night?"

Ginny stood up, "Raven, I am not a child. You don't have to—"

"Ginny, you're going with Hendrik. You're going to spend the night here and then you're going to do what he tells you to do in the morning. I will make sure that Caliphar does not give you any trouble between now and then. In a few weeks of not being in that hellhole, you'll find things look quite a bit different. But if you're incapable of helping yourself, then by the goddesses, I will help you."

Ginny stared at the three faces across the table from her and Raven watched as her resolve crumbled. "You're all being so mean."

"Yes. Yes, we are. And if being mean to you means you're going to live a life where you don't get beat up or killed, then I'm going to keep being mean to you. Now, go with Hendrik. I'll check in on you later."

Hendrik held out his hand and his big mitt engulfed the young girl's. She followed him meekly toward the door and they disappeared to some catcalls from the semi-sober patrons. Raven felt her body begin to relax and she collapsed backward into her chair. "Oh, goddess, please protect me from people who won't take care of themselves."

Jerek stared at the back door for a while before turning his chair around to face Raven. "You really care about her, don't you?"

"Yeah. She's been put down and used all her life. I guess moving to the Barrens after being raised in Lowtown was a big step up for her. Unfortunately, she had to hook up with that idiot Byron instead of a good man. It was his idea for her to work at Verine's, too. I understand what little money she gets to keep, she spends on stuff to make herself look good for him. She's got nothing and is never going to have anything if she doesn't change—and soon."

"The question is, why? Why do you care?"

Raven leaned back and picked up her mug of ale. "I care because sometimes I think no one else in this world does,

Jerek. I don't know. Maybe I'm just a sucker for a sob story. Maybe because someone ought to give a damn about someone other than themself once in a while."

"We look after our tribe. It's beyond our capabilities to look after the entire world."

"I know, Jerek, and that's one of the things I like best about you. The Corconti are like a big family—even when you have knuckleheads like Dimitri, he's mostly worried about the tribe. Ginny needs someone like that to watch after her. I do what I can, but I'm not taking her in to raise, so she's going to have to figure it out one way or another."

"And Byron?"

"He's an idiot. If he doesn't die from some disease soon, he'll get stabbed by a jealous lover or her boyfriend."

"Caliphar?"

"That's another matter. I don't believe he's that skilled with a lash, so it's probably enchanted somehow. That means someone with some serious connections is interested in the girls at Verine's. I hadn't heard anything about that before, but I hadn't really been looking for it. If I get Ginny out of there, I'm still not sure I'm that interested. Like you said, I can't babysit the entire city."

"So you don't think Caliphar is likely to be a threat?"

"It all depends on Ginny. Does she stay out of town? If so, he's not going to waste a lot of time looking for her. If she comes back into town, then it's just a matter of time before either Byron or Caliphar kills her first."

"Do you think she'll come back?"

Raven leaned forward. "I don't know, Jerek. I wouldn't, but I'm not her."

Two mugs of ale later, Hendrik reappeared at their table. "She wasn't happy about being put in that room, but I managed to persuade her it was for the best. She does look up to you, Raven."

"I'd rather she did less looking and more listening."

He gazed around the room and then spoke to them in a lower voice. "Speaking of listening, the question is, have either of *you* noticed anything interesting this evening?"

Jerek leaned closer. "No, nothing too out of the ordinary. Why?"

"Just a rumor floating around. Don't know who's behind it, but I hear there's some who've taken a dislike to your pretty companion there. What I hear, they're a bit aggravated that she's a freelancer and they'd like nothing better than for the city watch to stumble onto her lair."

Raven's voice took on a dangerous tone as she tried to keep her emotions still. "And do you have any names to go along with these rumors?"

"Lass, if I did, that'd have been the first thing I told you. All I know is what I overheard from a couple of drunks as they stumbled past me the other night. Don't know how long these people have been hunting you, if they are hunting you at all. It could be just drunk talk, but I figure it's better to have you a little worried than surprised."

She leaned over and gave Hendrik a hug. He smiled at her, then reached down and fished out the gold coins she'd slipped into his pouch. "Lass, you're not quite good enough to fool an old retired thief like me yet. No, I'll not be taking your money. Now, go on and enjoy yourselves. I'll keep an eye out for any trouble."

Once Hendrik walked away, she turned and glared at Jerek. "I'll be damned if someone's going to violate my sanctuary just like that."

Jerek raised his hands in defense. "Hold on there. I'm on your side, Raven. Don't get too worked up about this. Like Hendrik said, we don't know if there's something to this or not. Let me look into this. Tell you what: I'll talk to Quentin about this. I'm still in good standing with the guild." He pushed a dingy pewter tankard filled with dark ale toward her. "Here, take a drink and get yourself together."

She took a big draught from the mug and slammed the stein down on the table. "By all the gods, if Quentin and I can work out our problems, why the hell can't the others leave me alone? I tell you, Jerek, if I find there is some truth in this, I'll skin someone alive."

Jerek waved his hands downward in front of her. "Raven, please, keep it down. You're playing right into their hands acting like this. You go out of here half-cocked and you'll just be painting a big target on your back. Give me a little time, then you can turn the town upside down if you choose."

She was about to start another blistering rant but something brought her up short. *Damn it, I hate it when he's right. Why does he have to be all logical when I want to rage?*

She caught Jerek's worried expression as he watched her. After a while, he seemed satisfied the storm had passed. A cautious smile crept across his face and his shoulders visibly relaxed. "So, what should we do for the rest of the evening?"

"I think I'll let you buy me a few more ales and then I'm going to retire for the evening."

"You always seem to call it an early evening."

"What can I say? I need my beauty sleep."

"You realize, even beyond this, you've drawn a lot of interest, Raven. Among the thieves, I mean."

Raven flipped a hand through her hair like she'd seen some of the noblemen's daughters do at her father's store. "When there are only three female thieves in the guild, I'd be more surprised if there wasn't."

Jerek ignored the flippant tone and pushed on. "Look, I'm serious. You're a mystery and people love to solve mysteries. No one knows where you came from, where you live, or even your real name. Hell, they know more about the Corconti than they do you and we're notorious for keeping to ourselves. Did you know, no one has ever seen you in the daylight?"

"Gasp! You've discovered my secret. I'm a vampire." She took a playful nip at his throat as he withdrew in mock fear.

"I'm just saying, you've draw attention. You're young, female, successful, and a mystery woman. It's become a cottage industry to figure out who you are. I hear there's a pot of money set aside for the person who discovers your real name."

"Well, warn them it could be very dangerous to try and

collect that money. I'm not serious about much, but who I am or what I do is none of the guild's business. If I want them to know, I'll let them know."

Jerek took a sip of his ale. "I'll be sure to pass that on to them."

"So will I. I need to see Quentin anyway. Might as well nip this in the bud before it gets out of hand."

Chapter Seven

Perrin turned the sea bass frying in the cast-iron skillet and prepared the platter sitting next to her. The smell curled through the kitchen, luring her father back yet again to ask how much longer until dinner. She laughed and shooed him out, asking who was supposed to be closing the store if he was back here getting in her way.

A dockworker had sent the sea bass as payment for her father's help. The messenger pointed out they'd only go to waste if Rory didn't take them, so her father accepted the gift in the spirit it had been offered. Perrin knew he'd do something to reimburse the man in the next few weeks. Her father was embarrassed when people did things for him, no matter how much he deserved it.

Not that I can blame Father for nosing around back here. They do smell delicious. Besides, the quicker we get through dinner, the sooner I can leave. I'd like to get home at a reasonable hour one of these nights.

"Are those fish about done?" came a plaintive voice from the bookstore.

"I'm taking them off the stove right now. All I have to do is finish setting the table and wait for you to finish closing the store."

"I can be done in a few minutes. No nibbling until I get there."

She heard the sound of sweeping cease and then the familiar sound of the door shutting and locking. Rory's heavy footsteps echoed through the store as he hurried back to the kitchen. Before she had finished dishing out the potatoes and cutting the bread, he had slid into his chair and grabbed his knife and fork.

"If you put half as much effort into selling books as you do in getting ready for dinner, Father, you'd own the Royal Quarter."

"I'll have you know, I'm a great salesman. It's out of deference to the king I'm not the richest man in town. No need to make the poor man feel bad." Rory chuckled before digging into his plate.

They enjoyed the time to just sit and visit, discussing the events of the day and the characters who'd visited the store. Perrin reminisced about the man who came in looking for a specific book and was not going to accept the fact that it was not available. Rory nodded and pointed out that happened more often than you'd think. It was as though people thought they were hiding "the good stuff" in a back room somewhere. The conversation waned as they concentrated on their food and Perrin relaxed. Her father hadn't brought up her status as a single woman yet and Perrin wasn't going to, either. She appreciated that he seemed more intent on his sea bass than his lack of grandchildren for the moment.

"So, how's the tutoring going?" Rory asked, looking up from his plate and wiping the corner of his mouth with his napkin.

Perrin was caught off-guard by the question for a second. She *did* tutor a couple of children in the Laborers Quarter, so the stories she'd been telling him weren't a lie. However, they only met a couple of hours a week rather than every night.

"Jochim's reading is improving. Marissa is having a little problem with the arithmetic problems, but she's getting better. She might be working for you before too long. She loves books." Perrin felt a touch of pride as she reported on her students. She enjoyed the time she spent working with the children. It was unfortunate they couldn't attend Tamara's school full time, but their parents needed them to work.

"I'm glad to hear that. Let me know when their birthdays are coming up. I imagine I can find some books they'd enjoy."

Perrin got up and gave her father a hug. These were the moments she felt closest to him. He hugged her for a bit and then shrugged her off, his ears turning pink with embarrassment. He wasn't a demonstrative person and affectionate displays made him uncomfortable, even from his daughter. She knew, deep down, he enjoyed it just the same.

Perrin carried her plate over to the washtub and began to get ready to draw the water to wash the dishes, when Rory spoke up. "Leave them. You've got stuff to do tonight. I'll get to them in a bit."

Guilt washed over Perrin. She hated taking advantage of her father's good nature, but this was too good of an opportunity to pass up. She grabbed a cloak, then slipped out the back door and headed off in the direction of the Laborers' Quarter.

Making her way down the wooden sidewalks, she saw the city stretching out before her. However, unlike most mornings while she swept the walk in front of the store, these streets were empty. The long shadows of the dying day were met with only quiet and solitude. When she was certain she couldn't be seen from the bookstore, she veered to the north and made her way to the Commons.

As she approached her sanctuary, she was pleased with her efforts to ensure it appeared to be an abandoned building, the wood scarred and weathered with age. The only possible hint someone might live there was the windows on the first level, which were boarded up. Perrin had gone to great lengths to disguise her sanctuary, adding heavy drapes and barricades to keep curious passersby from trying to take a peek inside.

After another short trip through the sewers, she entered the dilapidated building. She wasted no time changing her outfit. Slipping the leather jerkin over her shoulders, she fastened the ties and buckles holding it in place with practiced ease. Once she was certain everything was correct, she activated the medallion.

When the room came back into focus, she smiled. Perrin looked at herself in the mirror, at her now raven-black hair hanging over part of her face, obscuring her features. It was almost as though Raven was a different person from Perrin. Whereas Perrin was the dutiful daughter, Raven was the wild adventurer, a kind of younger, more carefree sister.

She rummaged through the armoire, debating which potions or powders to bring along with her on tonight's soiree before turning to her weapons. She inspected each to ensure they were in good shape. Slipping the throwing knives, daggers, and rapier into their scabbards, she returned to the sewers and made her way deeper into the city, following the maze of tubes and ladders until she reached a point where several tunnels converged. She found the ladder she was seeking and climbed up. About halfway, she found a loose tile hidden beneath some mossy growth. Moving it revealed a switch that opened a hidden doorway in the wall next to the ladder. The doorway revealed a small landing and she stepped through, into the dark tunnel leading toward the heart of the hill.

Raven removed the small gem from her pouch and summoned the spell that made the gem glow with a cold light. Pausing to examine the gem, she recalled a conversation she'd once had with Bertok. He told her she had an affinity for magic, but lacked dedication. Unless she gave up being a thief, he warned, he wouldn't teach her anything more than "harmless" magicks because stronger spells might backfire on her … or worse. Raven frowned at the memory. *Like a hedge wizard would know anything about real magic.*

"It's dangerous to daydream while holding a light. You make a great target." A familiar voice sounded from down the tunnel.

Raven saw Jerek standing against the tunnel wall at the edge of the ball of light she'd created. "You again? Do you have a tracking spell on me?"

"Of course I do. What's the point to being the Corconti's

chief's eldest son if I don't take advantage of it? I had one of the wise women create a charm just for you."

She knew the Corconti did have their own magic. Bertok was suspicious of it and had said so enough times. He was constantly warning her about spending too much time around Jerek. "All right, you caught me. What are you going to do with me?"

"Why, what else? Take you home and add you to my harem." He fell into the familiar banter that had been going on since they'd met.

"I'm afraid you'd find me a poor addition. I don't share well."

"Oh, really?"

"Really." Raven moved forward and put a hand on his shoulder, giving him a seductive look. "I'm afraid for the other ladies of your harem. It would be unfortunate, all those accidents occurring so soon after my arrival." She gave him a knowing look and he retreated in mock fear.

The young Corconti stepped aside to let her pass. "Oh, well. In the interests of my harem's safety, I grant you liberty again."

Her voice became more serious. "Have you seen Quentin this evening?"

Jerek paused, not anticipating the change in conversation. "Yes, he's back in his room—or at least he was the last time I saw him. You've got something on your mind, don't you?"

"You remember the conversation with Hendrik the other night? I want him to warn the others to leave me alone." She plowed on before her courage failed her. "There is another reason, but I'm not certain I want anyone else involved … yet. If, and I repeat, *if*, I decide to take this job, there's a thousand ways it can go wrong."

"Wait just a minute, Raven. If there's a chance something could go wrong then I have to be there to help you."

"If I need assistance, you're the first one I'd ask."

Jerek cocked his head to one side and put on his best puppy dog eyes. "You promise?"

"I promise to beat you about the head and shoulders if you don't pretend to have some sense in that pea-sized object you claim is a brain." Raven gave him a threatening look before breaking into a smile. "If things start to get interesting, you're the only one here I trust to back me up." Raven pretended not to notice that he was fishing for information. She didn't want to talk about the Dragonstone with anyone in the guild if she could avoid it.

She walked down the tunnel with Jerek. She could feel the concern coming from him. "Look, Jerek, I know I'm not really welcome here, but Quentin's word is law in the guild. If he tells them to leave me alone, then they'll leave me alone."

"I don't know how Quentin does it."

Raven looked at him. "Does what?"

"Keeps this group of thugs and murderers in line. If Quentin didn't have such a tight grip on them, the merchants would have been screaming to the king a long time ago."

"You and I both know the king runs things up there and Quentin runs things down here. Besides, the merchants are quick enough to hire Quentin when they need a rival hit, and the nobles are more than happy to hire us to acquire what they can't buy, whether that's information or goods. No, the king may not like the guild, but he's not going to get rid of it anytime soon."

Jerek paused and looked at her. "No, I suppose not. Even the Corconti give the guild a nominal take to ensure we have access to the fences and black market. It's not safe to go alone, as I'm sure you know."

Raven just nodded as they resumed their walk through the tunnel. This is why she was not looking forward to her meeting the Quentin. Every thief in Sagras was supposed to belong to the guild and follow the guidelines. Only a few, like Raven, operated on the fringes, and she knew better than to push her "independent" status. Those who refused to acknowledge the guild's authority tended to disappear—or worse.

Reaching the end of the tunnel, they came to a wooden

door set into the wall. Jerek opened the door and revealed an iron gate on the other side. They waited for someone to come and recognize them before they entered a large room lit by several lanterns hanging from the ceiling. The room was filled with crates and boxes scattered everywhere. People dressed in all manners of styles wandered through the room. Some called out occasional greetings as they recognized Raven, while others gave her dirty looks or turned their backs as she passed.

She followed Jerek to the far wall. The short hallway there led to a number of additional doors, but there was only one she was interested in. She knocked on it.

A rough growl came from the other side. "Go away! I'm busy!"

"Busy getting drunk if I know you," Raven called, then stepped to the side.

She counted to five and the door came flying open as a wild-eyed man stepped into the hall. His tunic was askew and his gray boots weren't tied and flapped as he moved. What Raven noted most was the short thrusting sword he held in his right hand.

Feeling a tap on his shoulder, he spun around to find Raven's rapier pointed at his Adam's apple. "Now, now, Quentin, is that any way to greet an old friend?"

He stared down the length of steel pointed at his throat. After a moment's confusion, he recognized Raven and a crafty grin settled onto his face. "Ah, lass, it's good to see you again. What say you put that pigsticker down and come in?"

She ignored the smooth-as-honey tone in his voice. "As soon as you sheathe that toothpick you're carrying."

"Oh this? With this group lounging around here, eating me out of house and home … well, it's good to be prepared." The guild master sheathed the short sword. "What brings you around these parts, Raven?"

"I need to talk to you but the hallway isn't high on my list of where to conduct this meeting. Too many observers for my taste." She risked a quick glance over his shoulder into the main room. The altercation hadn't gone unnoticed and a few of the onlookers were drifting toward them.

He pushed his door open, motioning for her to go ahead. She shook her head and motioned him forward with her rapier. The grin wavered for just a moment but he shrugged his shoulders and went back into the room. Raven waited until he reached his desk and sat down. She whispered over her shoulder to Jerek before entering. "Please stay outside and ensure no one listens at the door."

"You mean no one else."

She gave him a dirty look before she eased the door shut in his face. Sheathing her rapier, she took the seat opposite Quentin. His room was cluttered with papers, weapons, and clothing. His desk was the only organized section of the room. He leaned forward, resting his elbows on the hard cherrywood surface, his bearded chin resting on his fingertips. She could see he was beside himself with curiosity was waiting for her to make the first move. Since Raven was not a member of the guild, he owed her no special privileges. Still, she donated a portion of her profit to the guild. Quentin considered her "loyal enough."

"First, some of your guild members have taken an unhealthy interest in my personal affairs. I would suggest you try to discourage them."

"You don't say? You come and go like a shadow. You let no one inside your council. Yet you're upset people are curious about you? I thought you were smarter than that."

"Don't play stupid, Quentin. You know I don't like to kill, but you know I will to protect what is important to me. That includes my privacy."

Quentin threw his hands into the air in surrender. "I'll do what I can, lass, but I'm not their father. They're grown men and women. They'll do what they think best."

"They listen to you, Quentin. If you say you'll speak to them, then that's good enough for me and I do appreciate it. However, there was another reason I came to see you tonight. I need information. I have a potential job lined up and if anyone knows what's going on in Sagras, it would be you." Raven hoped her story would appeal both to Quentin's position and vanity.

The guild master smiled and waved his hand around in an expansive gesture. "Lass, you have come to the right place. If there is anything in this town that's worth acquiring, I either know about it or can find out about it."

"I knew I could count on you. I have a client—an exclusive client," she added, to cut off Quentin's unasked question, "who collects unusual gems and jewelry. I have viewed the inventories of the city's jewelers at one time or another. My client is looking for something more unusual."

"A most delicate problem." Quentin enjoyed the word-play as much as the question itself. "So your client, being a connoisseur, would not be satisfied by just any gem or jewel. He … or she," he added before Raven could comment, "prefers something unique."

Raven crossed her legs and leaned back in the chair, smiling at Quentin. "I think unique would be better than rare."

Quentin leaned back and closed his eyes. His voice resembled a cat's purr. "Unique items are more than just valuable, although I *do* have some knowledge that might help with your search. Of course, there would be a small fee for this information."

"Of course." Raven matched him purr for purr. "I would never dream of asking you to provide assistance without some form of recompense."

"Twenty-five percent of your commission," he said, still facing the ceiling.

"Five percent."

Quentin's head snapped forward and his eyes locked with hers. He knew he had her now. It was only a matter of how desperate she was to meet this commission. They stared at each other, feeling for weak points. After what seemed an eternity, Quentin spoke again. "Ten percent."

Raven gave him her most winning smile. "Done."

Quentin smiled at her and she could tell he considered

this free money. If he gave Raven information, she would be honor-bound to make the agreed payment. He had no compunction using her reputation against her. Besides, the threat of the guild hunting her hung over her head if she reneged on her pledge.

Reaching into his desk, he pulled out some parchments, ruffled through them, and pulled out a sheet that he consulted before looking over the edge of the paper. "There are three items of interest. All have entered the city within the past three weeks. You can decide which one to go after, or you can go after all three. It makes little difference to me as long as I get my cut."

He lowered his eyes to the paper and cleared his throat. "The first is a diamond necklace reputed to be almost a thousand years old. Rumor says it contains a huge, flawless stone, surrounded by fourteen additional stones, all set in platinum filigree. To say it is priceless would be an understatement. Some adventurers found it in an old tomb in the Kingdom of Avione far to the south. Istvan Dacian owns it. He serves the minister of the exchequer. I can't say how much longer he'll possess it, though. Rumors of a cult dedicated to returning the necklace to the tomb of the ancient king have surfaced. Your client might not live long enough to pay you if you decide on this item."

He paused, trying to gauge her interest, but Raven tried to keep her face neutral. If Quentin thought she was interested in any of the items, odds were he wouldn't provide her with the rest of the information. She almost could hear him thinking, *Why give away good information?*

When she didn't give any indication of her interest, Quentin sighed and began again. "Another item is a huge sapphire carved into the shape of a falcon. They say this gem comes to life when the proper command is spoken. Of course, as is so often the case, the command word has been lost to antiquity. A young noblewoman, Rebecca Buchan, came into possession of this item last week. A new paramour from the city state of Arii gave it to her. He is, alas, but one of many young gentlemen vying for her attention. Such are the foibles of love." He let out a dramatic sigh and then plowed ahead with the remaining item.

"Finally, we have a renowned item. The Dragonstone, a huge ruby with the shape of a dragon within, arrived three days ago from Wolf River. It is rumored to possess mystic qualities." He looked at her over the top of the paper. "I tend to believe this particular rumor since it was owned by the Imperial College of Wizards."

He looked back down at the paper. "Ah, here we are. It is at the Grand Cathedral of Praxil, under the care of Bishop Marius. According to my informant, he is holding it for his majesty. Why it's in the cathedral rather than the palace is a mystery." He paused and a distressed look crossed his face. "Most unfortunate. The Black Leopards, the king's secret police, are guarding it, as well as the usual guards. Too bad, it's the rarest of the items on the list."

Raven kept her composure and began to question Quentin more about the sapphire bird. However, her mind was racing. *The Black Leopards. The elite of the elite. How am I supposed to slip past* them? She half-listened to Quentin as he told her what he knew about Lady Rebecca, which wasn't much more than he'd already said. After a bit, she thanked him for providing the information for her.

"It was my pleasure, Raven," Quentin said. "I don't know exactly what you have in mind, but be careful. All of these are heavily guarded. Do your homework and have a backup plan. No commission is worth losing your life over."

She shot him a pitying look. "Oh, stop it, Quentin. You'll make me think you've gone soft."

The look he gave her reminded her too much of her father. "Not at all, lass. I've taken a liking to you. You've got a fire I wish half the brothers had. Besides, if you pull this off, I can retire on my share of the commission alone. So don't get caught."

"Now, that's the Quentin I've come to know and love."

"See, lass, if you'd just give me a chance to ..." he started, but she slipped out of the room and shut the door, cutting off his lecherous advances in mid-sentence.

Jerek was leaning against the opposite wall waiting for her. She grabbed his sleeve and hurried off before Quentin got any more "ideas." They were halfway to the entrance before Jerek managed to gather his wits and speak.

"Did you find out what you needed?"

"What did I need?"

"Look, Raven, if *you're* making deals with Quentin, you're involved in something big."

Raven stopped at the tunnel leading out and gave Jerek a sad smile. "I told you, I can't ask you to help me yet. I've got a lot of planning and research to do. I don't know if it *can* be done, whether one person, a team, or the entire guild goes after the target. I may decide to pass on the entire thing. How can I ask you to help when I don't know what *I'm* going to do?"

She patted him on the cheek. "Besides, I wouldn't want anything to happen to you if something goes wrong. You're going to be the next leader of the Corconti. A lot of people are relying on you. I've only got myself." She felt a twinge at that lie, thinking about her father.

"I knew something was going on." He started to go on, but she raised her hand and held it over his mouth.

"You'll be the first person that I ask for help." She smiled at him again and slipped out the door, leaving him standing there, staring at her retreating form.

Chapter Eight

The moon hadn't risen before a small shadow slipped out of the darkness surrounding the Grand Cathedral of Praxil. Raven eased down an alley until she reached the back of a two-story building facing the cathedral. She unfolded her grapnel hook and tossed her line up, wincing as the hook made a soft *thunk* as it caught on a protuberance. Once it was secure, she made her way up as fast as she could climb.

She pulled the line up after her, but left the hook set in the roof. Kneeling at the edge of the roof, she shrugged off her backpack, then crawled along the roof, pulling the pack along as she tried to keep a low profile. She used the faux parapet for cover, staying deep in the shadows until she reached a secluded site.

She began scanning the side of the cathedral with the telescope she'd acquired from a ship captain when she'd stolen a chest of pearls he'd been carrying. Starting at the highest point of the bell towers, she worked her way down to ground level, examining every square inch she could.

The cathedral looked the same as it had the past four nights. The ecclesiastical guards were conducting their rounds outside the cathedral. Focusing the telescope on the windows, she saw they'd been augmented by the Royal Guards inside. What worried her the most was she hadn't spotted any Black Leopards. *For all I know, there's one on this roof right beside me and I just can't spot him.*

Rolling on her side, she pulled out a parchment and a

charcoal stick and set them beside her head. She checked the rough map she'd made of the cathedral. She had spent hours each night improving her diagram based on her observations. She knew the layout of the cathedral, but what troubled her was that she still hadn't determined where the Dragonstone was being kept. She had identified three places where it might be held based on the guards assigned to each, but there was no way to verify any of her suspicions from a rooftop.

She had been inside the cathedral twice during the day. However, the guards had been alert and she wasn't able to slip off to investigate. The most aggravating thing was having to be polite to Bishop Marius when she bumped into him. The way he had looked at her hadn't seemed very bishop-like, either. She decided he had to be a political appointee rather than an ecclesiastical one.

She pulled out a minute glass filled with sand and sat it beside her as she watched the guard passing beneath her. As he made the turn around the corner, she flipped it so the sand began to fall. She continued to rotate the glass until she reached the ninth turn when he appeared around the far corner and began another circuit of the large building.

He's a little slower than the others. She made some additional notations on her paper. *When it's time to make my move, I need to be certain to do it on his shift.*

Shifting her body, she gave her target another going over with her telescope. The moon was rising and the light began casting shadows along the face of the cathedral. She changed position, ensuring the strengthening moonlight didn't glint off the glass in the telescope. *There! What was that?*

Training her telescope on the roof, she noted an enlarged shadow next to a gargoyle on the northeast corner. Focusing the telescope, she saw a man dressed in black crouching beside the gargoyle, watching the streets approaching the cathedral with catlike patience.

Gotcha!

She shifted her focus and spotted two more black shapes near gargoyles at the northwest and southeast corners, also watching the streets. She marked their positions on the map and began scanning the surrounding roofs looking for their backups. For one of the few times in her life, she appreciated the moonlight. Dangerous as it was, it worked against the Black Leopards since they had to remain in position to protect the Dragonstone.

She identified three more spots that were probable hiding places that overlooked alleyways. It appeared they wanted a thief to think they could approach the cathedral unseen. Annoying as it was, she admitted they'd done their work well. Looking at her map, she couldn't identify a single means of egress. She wasn't willing to say this was an impossible task, but the Leopards had made it damn difficult.

Closing her telescope and gathering her maps, she made her way over to where her rope was waiting. She lowered it, then herself, to the alley below, then flicked the rope to loosen her grapnel hook and caught it before it hit the ground. She stowed everything away and retreated down the alley until she was out of sight from the cathedral.

All right, the direct route isn't going to work. There must be something I'm overlooking. Entering the Commons, she spotted the Black Boar Tavern and decided to stop. She was greeted by a cacophony of noise and lights as the bodies and conversations swirled past her. The smell of cheap alcohol and unwashed bodies hit her like a physical wall.

"Well, well, well. You're becoming quite the regular." Turning, she saw Hendrik sitting by the door.

"You having a party here tonight?"

"Nah, same old drunks we have every night." Hendrik pushed a stray lock of his thinning blond hair out of his eyes. "Only had to toss three guys out of here tonight."

Raven nodded. "Slow night. Any word on Ginny?"

"Last I heard, she was doing well at the Iron Wheel. My friend says she's made a few friends there, both male and female. Seems to be fittin' in just fine."

"That's good to hear. Let's hope it stays that way."

"I feel the same as you. 'Course, this evening's likely to

get a lot more interesting once the group over by the window gets a few more ales in them."

"Oh?"

"Yeah, a bunch of nobles slumming. They're dressed down, but I can spot nobles almost every time. For one thing, they take baths on a regular basis. I expect a number of people here will exit just about the time they wrap up for the night." Raven exchanged a knowing look with him and headed over to the worn mahogany bar.

She made her way through the crowd until one of the patrons stepped in front of her, blocking her path. She gave him a quick glance. From the studded leather jerkin to the wear on the leather wrapping his dagger's handle, she could see he was one of the local toughs. The smell of ale rolled off him as his bloodshot eyes gazed at her with undisguised lust. Ten years, thirty pounds, and maybe eight hundred ales ago, he might have been handsome. Now, with the accumulated scars and missing teeth, he was merely annoying.

"Hey, what's your hurry?" He reached out with a meaty paw to grab her, only to find she'd ducked beneath his arm and slipped past. She circled a pockmarked table and listened to the guffaws of his companions. Then a sharp thud, a cry of pain, and the sound of a chair turning over caught her attention.

I was hoping it wouldn't come to this. I'm not in the mood tonight.

She turned around once she reached the bar and saw the man who'd accosted her standing there, his face flushed bright red. One of his companions was lying on the floor, trying to get his chair off him. The rest of the bar patrons were backing away, trying not to get between him and her.

Thanks for the assistance. No, seriously. I can take it from here.

"Hey! What's your problem? You too good to talk to me?" The veins in his neck and forehead stood out against his ruddy skin as he waited for her reply, his jaw jutting forward.

Realizing he was determined to make a scene, she gave him a careful going-over with her eyes. She noted how his dark brown hair was cut, the bangs trimmed to not fall into his eyes. He was weaving, but his weight was forward on the balls of his feet. He had a large dagger on his right hip and a rapier on his left. All of these were the signs of someone who knew how to fight. Even though he'd been drinking, he wasn't any less dangerous. She was going to have to be careful. She was no slouch as a fighter, but she remembered her weapon master's lessons well. *Never fight someone on their terms. Get them off balance. Make them fight on your terms.*

She noted his left foot inching forward. That and the placement of his rapier told her that he was right-handed. He was much larger than she was, so she'd have to overcome his reach and strength advantages. She couldn't let him get her cornered.

"Hey, I asked you a question! I said, do you think you're too good to talk to me?" His voice was even louder this time. The crowd drew back farther, trying to avoid meeting his gaze. A confrontation seemed inevitable.

She leaned back, determined to seize control of the situation, rather than be swept along. She glanced over the tough's shoulder and saw Hendrik getting out of his seat, a large sap in his right hand. She shook her head and he slipped the sap into his pocket. She gave the drunk a sad smile. "No, I don't think I'm too good to talk to you. I just don't *want* to talk to you."

The tough stared at her, confused, uncertain whether she was mocking him or not. Taking a step forward, he began again. "You may want to rethink that attitude of yours. When I want to talk to a woman, I talk to her." He tugged at his sword belt and nodded at the crowd, as if looking for affirmation.

"Well, you're talking to a woman now. What did you want to say?" She turned to the bartender and motioned for a stein of ale. He set it on the counter next to her and beat a hasty retreat. She kept her eyes on the man, reaching back along the bar with her right hand for the stein.

She could see he was flummoxed now. Most people

backed off when he blustered and she was acting like he wasn't even there. She watched as he realized everyone in the tavern was staring at him. She could see the more he thought about it, the more enraged he got.

He tried a new tack to get her off balance. Wiping the back of his hand across his mouth, he smirked at her. "Well, seein' how you're all dolled up like a guy yourself, you must be one of those girls who don't care much for men. Right?" He laughed at her, looking at his companions who gave a weak chuckle.

She lifted the stein to her mouth and took a sip as if she didn't have a care. She watched the tension building in his frame before she answered. "No, I like men. When you see one, send him my way." At that, the entire bar started laughing.

With an inarticulate scream, he lowered his head and rushed at her, arms spread wide to sweep her into a bear hug. She waited until the last possible second. Just as he reached her, she spun to the left and ducked low, letting him run into the bar. Unable to check his forward momentum, he hit the bar just below his sternum. Folding almost in half, his head and arms slammed onto the mahogany top of the bar. The entire bar shuddered from the impact.

Raven brought her right hand down, slamming the earthenware stein on the back of his head. The stein, still filled with ale, landed with a solid *thunk* but failed to break. The showering ale encouraged everyone still in the area to move away from the rumpus.

The tough was dazed but not knocked out. It appeared his head was harder than she thought. He lay stretched out across the bar, his mouth opening and closing like a fish out of water. With deliberate slowness, he reached up and touched the back of his head. Rolling over onto his side to face her, he looked at the blood covering his hand dumbfounded.

The sight of his own blood seemed to further enrage him. He forced himself back upon his feet, looking for her. She stood about ten feet away, with her left hand behind her back, holding the stein in her right. Rising up to his full height, he towered over her like a brown bear on a rampage. "I'm going to kill you for that."

"No, I don't think so."

The blow seemed to have cleared the alcohol haze and his movement was slow and deliberate. He began to move forward, a cold look of malice in his eyes, but he pulled up after two steps when he found himself facing the rapier she held in her left hand. The steel reflected the flickering tavern light as if followed his every move.

"The way I see it, you have two choices. You can leave now and we'll have a nice laugh about this someday, preferably in different taverns. Or, you can try to draw your sword and defend yourself before I can run my steel through your throat. I'll give you a bit to think it over." Raven stared down the length of her blade, still holding the stein in her right hand.

He was caught in no-man's-land and he knew it. He was too far away to rush her and too close to draw his rapier in time. She could almost see the thoughts going through his head. Indecision flickered over his face as alcohol and machismo tried to overrule logic. Then a smile crossed his face and she tensed, thinking he was going to push his luck.

A loud thud sounded behind her. She risked a quick glance over her shoulder and spotted Hendrik standing over a body a short distance away. He was tapping his sap in his open palm and frowning at the fallen man. *Hmm, I guess one of his friends wanted to get involved. Thank goodness Hendrik kept it a fair fight.* Turning around, Raven saw resignation has settled on her opponent's face.

She made a small motion with her rapier and the tough walked over to the table where he'd been. Gathering his cap and gloves, he and his companions headed toward the door. Raven followed behind them, rapier held loosely in front of her.

He looked back at her when he reached the door. "This isn't the end of this, wench. You'd better spend some time praying with your priest, because if I find you, they'll be burying you." Acid dripped from his voice as he made one last attempt at intimidating her. She gave him a wan smile and flicked the tip of her rapier at him. With a snarl, he slipped out the door into the darkness. Hendrik pulled the unconscious man to the door and tossed him into the street to join his companions.

The crowd stood in hushed silence, staring at Raven and Hendrik. Raven stared back until they retook their seats and conversations began to buzz around the tavern again. After a bit, it was as if the incident had never taken place.

"You've made a bad enemy, Raven, my dear." Hendrik motioned for the bartender to bring them two ales. His concern was obvious, but she ignored it, knowing he'd be embarrassed about showing that much emotion.

"If he's the worst of my problems, then life is good. Thanks for the backup there."

"My pleasure. You know, something good came out of it."

"Really? And what good could come of this?"

Hendrik took another drink from his stein. "With all this excitement, it appears our young nobles escaped without drawing attention. And they spent a lot of money tonight."

"*So* glad to be of service." She took a deep draught of the amber liquid herself. After a few seconds of staring at the door, she continued. "By the way, who was that lunkhead?"

"Goes by the name of Robert. Robert Marjory, if I remember correctly. Got a surname, must have some noble blood in him somewhere. I doubt he got it honestly, if you know what I mean, lass." Hendrik winked at Raven. "Anyway, he and his friends are new to Sagras. The word on the street is ol' Bloody Douglas recruited them himself. They're mean fighters. Not a speck of decency among 'em."

Raven nodded and filed the information away. So apparently Douglas wasn't going to give up on Tamara's school after all. Still, if Douglas was bringing in help from out of town, he was getting a healthy payment from the bishop. Another reason to figure out how to get to the Dragonstone.

She thought about the fight. Marjory wasn't very impressive, but she noticed the others let him do the fighting. Was he their stalking horse? She resolved to find out more about him and his friends.

Still, something Robert had said was rattling around in her brain. She took another drink and brooded while Hendrik wandered back to the front door. The combination of the adrenaline pumping through her and the ale made it difficult to make sense of her thoughts. She retreated toward a side table and leaned against the smoke-stained wall, still keeping an eye on the door. Something said her dance partner wasn't the type to quit.

An hour and two more steins of ale later, she was no closer to an answer than when she'd started. The noise in the tavern rose as the night crowd filtered in. A shadow fell across her table and a small dagger appeared in her hand. She started to lunge until she saw the shadow belonged to a familiar face.

"Ian, what the hell are you doing slipping up on me like that? I could have killed you."

The young man smiled at her. "I'm glad to see you, too. May I join you?"

She waited until her heartbeat quit racing before she motioned to the empty chair at her table. She knew Ian from the thieves' guild. He wouldn't have been the first person she would have invited to have an ale with her. There was something about Ian that didn't set well with her. After the altercation with Marjory, any familiar face was welcome, though.

"So I heard you bearded Quentin in his own room the other day." The blond thief gave her a smile and she repressed a shudder. He reminded her of a shark preparing to bite. "Must have been something important?"

"You've got bad sources, Ian. Quentin and I just caught up on some old times and I paid a few debts I owed him."

He leaned his elbows on the table, waiting for the barmaid to make another pass. "So *you* say. *I'd* say you're planning something big. I'd like to get in on the action. I mean, you do pretty well for yourself."

Raven leaned back, giving herself a little more room. She fixed a small smile on her face and steeled herself to deal with him. "'Fraid you're barking up the wrong tree, Ian. I don't have anything special going on. I just find it's a good idea to keep Quentin happy. I drop by, give him a little money and some information, and he doesn't interfere with me."

"But you have to admit, you've got quite a reputation. And you're always dressed pretty well. You're making some good scores somewhere." Ian leaned back to let the barmaid put his ale on the table. "How'd you and Jerek do the last time you went out?"

"Can't complain. Paid for an evening of drinking."

"I was wondering, are you and Jerek a team?"

Raven tried hard not to spit her ale all over the table. There was little question in her mind what Ian meant by "team." "No, we work together on occasion, but we don't have a formal agreement or anything like that. Why do you ask?"

"Well, I was hoping we could go out some evening and see what happens." There was something in Ian's voice that told her he wasn't thinking about burglary.

She felt uncomfortable the way Ian looked at her, but decided to try and extract herself from the situation without making it worse. "We'll see. Things change so fast in this city. Who knows what's going to happen in an hour, much less a week or so from now."

She could tell Ian wanted to say something else, so she beat him to the punch. She sat her stein of ale down and stood up, catching him off guard. "Tell you what, I need to check up on something, I'll catch up with you and we'll figure something out."

Ian attempted to grab her arm, but pulled his hand back just ahead of Raven's dagger digging into the table. "Hey! What the hell's wrong with you?"

Raven's eyes flashed at him. She pulled the tip of the dagger out of the table and turned the point toward Ian. "Don't ever try that again, you little weasel. I decide who touches me and when. You haven't earned that right yet."

"Oh, and you're so high and mighty you get to make those calls?"

"I'll trim your fingers all the way up to your elbows if you try that again."

Ian sat there, anger and embarrassment fighting for control of his face. She stared at him, keeping a loose grip on the dagger. If he flinched, she intended to drive it into his chest before he could clear the table. After what seemed an eternity, he spread his hands out on the table and relaxed, an unpleasant smile crossing his face.

"All right, take your little toy there and go. I may not be the fighter Jerek is, but you can't just push me around. Crossing me was a bad mistake. I'll see you put in the ground before I'll let you insult me like this."

Raven flipped the dagger over and reinserted it into its sheath strapped to the inside of her right arm. "Take your best shot, weasel. I've been threatened by better than you."

She backed away from Ian until she knew she was out of range and then made her way across the quiet room. She wasn't going to give Ian the satisfaction of turning to keep an eye on him. She focused on Hendrik, who was watching Ian for her.

"Well, lass, you've made another lifelong friend tonight. Keep this up and they'll be beating the doors down to see you."

"And I'll be manning the parapets, dumping boiling oil on the lot of them. Sorry for the disturbances, Hendrik."

"Nonsense, lass. A spot of excitement is good for the place. Keep the customers entertained and tomorrow night we'll have even more people wondering what'll happen. I think Ol' Rausch should put you on the payroll after tonight's performances."

Raven rolled her eyes and slipped out of the tavern, into the cool night air. Glancing both directions, she convinced herself no one was waiting for her and slipped off into the darkness to get changed and go home.

As if tonight couldn't have gotten any worse. First the damn Black Leopards have the cathedral under observation, then I run into the hunters, and now Ian has to prove to be an idiot. Put me into the ground, indeed. I've seen his swordwork; I'm not too ... A sudden thought brought her up short. *Into the ground. That's it! I can't approach the cathedral above the ground, might as well see what lurks beneath. It's one of the oldest buildings in Sagras. There has to be someone who knows what's beneath it.*

Feeling better than she had all night, she made her way across the Commons and into her sanctuary. She glanced around before ducking inside the building that led toward the sewers. In her haste to get inside and change, she never noticed a small black shadow detach itself from the alley and disappear into the darkness.

Chapter Nine

Night settled over the city of Sagras like a comfortable blanket. Once the merchants had closed and the workmen made their way home, the city's roar settled into a quiet murmur. Only the city watchman's footsteps or a sea lion's bark in the distance intruded into this interlude. The watchman checked the door on a warehouse and found it locked, as it had been on the four other rounds he had made. He disappeared around the corner and a small shadow detached itself from one of the alleyways.

Raven crept from alley to alley to avoid detection, constantly moving up the Hill toward the Royal Quarter of Sagras. Unlike her usual ventures, tonight she had a specific mission in mind. After the events in the tavern, she needed to settle something soon. She did not need Douglas's men getting in her way, especially if he'd brought them in specifically to hunt for her.

She paused to let a group of revelers pour out of one tavern and stumble down the street toward another. She waited until the way was clear again and then continued gliding up the Hill.

Turning a corner, she froze in place as a sudden light shone into the alley. She pressed against a building to avoid being spotted as a prostitute led a young nobleman into her room. That caught her attention for a moment. *I know him, but I've never seen him here before. If he's going to leave the Hill to visit my part of town, then he's moving up on my list of inter-*

esting people.

Raven approached the old wall at the midpoint of the hill. *This might slow some, but it's my favorite way to reach the nobles. The City Watch still hasn't figured out how I get in without going through their guarded gates. I almost feel sorry for them.*

The shadowy figure removed her backpack and threaded a silk rope into a folding grapnel with practiced fingers. Shrugging the pack back on, she moved up next to the wall and lofted the line skyward. She waited to see if anyone reacted to the sound of the hook catching. When there was no response, Raven tested the line to ensure it was secure before ascending the wall with catlike grace and then descending the other side. Once everything was in back in the backpack, Raven headed up the Hill. After a bit, she stopped in front of a walled residence in the shadows of the Great Keep.

Leaping upward, Raven caught the top of the low wall and climbed up, lying prone atop the wall. Squinting into the darkness, she listened for any sign she had been detected. Hearing nothing disconcerting, the lithe figure eased onto the manicured lawn. Approaching the house, she peered into the darkened double windows where a hint of movement caught her eye. She remained motionless as two mastiffs came snuffling into the room. One came to the window, the hackles on its back raising as it noted something unusual. After a few moments sniffing near the window, the two great beasts turned toward the door and disappeared from sight.

Raven examined the windows, paying particular attention to the frames and the windows themselves. She pressed a small piece of clay with a fine piece of string to the windowpane above the latch and fixed the other end of the string to her left wrist. The hand inside the right black leather glove flexed and the mechanism within released four small blades, extending from the finger tips.

The dark apparition etched an ever-deepening groove into the glass, pausing from time to time to ensure the patrolling hounds weren't returning. After a few minutes, a rap against the windowpane sent a piece of glass tumbling into the room to be brought up short by the attached string. She drew the string upward and inched the glass out, setting it aside for use later.

Raven pulled out a small paper tube from one of the belt pouches. Using the clay, she molded it into a ring around the tube and then unfolded one end of the paper with care. Setting the tube into the hole, she used more clay to seal the hole.

Careful ... now is not the time to get in a hurry.

Once the tube was secure, the ebon figure unfolded the other end of the paper, tapped on the window, and waited. The sound of paws scurrying its way was her reward. Drawn by the noise, the two huge canines came back into the room.

Well-trained dogs. Nothing but the best. Just what I expected. They're not going to bark until they're certain someone's out here. That should work out just fine.

The dark gray dogs moved through the room, low growls emanating from their throats. As they approached the window, Raven rose up and blew hard into the tube, spraying a light-blue powder into the faces of the two canines. Before they had a chance to howl, they collapsed, their tongues lolling out of their mouths. She watched for a few moments to see if anyone had been aroused, but the house remained black as a tomb. The dogs' chests rose and fell in a steady rhythm. The sleeping powder had done its job once again.

Removing the items from the window and slipping them back into its pouch, Raven reached through the hole and worked the latch loose, slid one of the windows upward, and crept into the house. Stepping past the slumbering animals, she reached the doorway and scanned the house. Looking down a narrow hallway, the light of a fire in the kitchen caught her attention. Women's voices emanated from there but the kitchen was not the target, so their presence was noted and ignored. Skirting the firelight spilling into the hall, she took sure but quiet steps toward a stairway and began to climb.

Nearing the upper landing, Raven paused and listened.

Only the sound of snoring and tossing bodies was audible in the quiet house. Easing around the corner, Raven checked for guards standing watch. Tonight, fortune seemed to be smiling; the hallway was bare except for a few paintings and five doors. Only one of them was of interest.

The lithe figure approached the door, lock picks in hand, but it was unlocked. Pocketing the tools, she eased the door open and entered the room. A cacophony of snoring greeted her, filling the oversized bedroom. The large figure in the bed tossed and turned, its corpulent body winding its silken sheets around it.

Probably having a nightmare about all the people he's cheated this past week alone.

A look of disgust ran across her face as she stared at the overweight merchant. Douglas Valio. The only good thing about him was that his fleet of merchant ships brought rare and exotic items to the Royal Quarter on a regular basis. Several of them now decorated the inside of Raven's sanctuary.

Still, she was here getting ready to challenge Bloody Douglas himself. This should be a new experience for him. After all, word on the street was if you fell afoul of Douglas, you'd be better off killing yourself rather than letting him get his hands on you.

That's a laugh. It wouldn't be his hands. Ol' Doug here is too fat and out of shape to collect his own debts. His head knockers collect for him, although I hear he's at every inquiry. I've also heard he's pretty tough when he has six or seven toughs backing him up and his victim is tied to his chair. Damn ruddy-skinned demon. If you can't get your pound of flesh from your current "guest," you'll get it by selling them or their family into slavery, armed with royal writs, no less.

Raven fingered the hilt of one of her daggers and stared at the sleeping merchant. *It would be too easy to simply gut you right here, you foul-smelling pig. Unfortunately, I need you alive … at least a bit longer.*

Reaching the far wall, she removed an oversized portrait

of Douglas, revealing an ironbound safe mounted in the wall. A sudden noise froze Raven in her tracks. Turning her head, she could see Douglas squirming in bed, seeking that elusive comfortable spot in the mattress.

Perhaps I should have saved a little of the powder for him. At least his snoring will hide any noise I make. I could pull the safe out of the wall and no one would ever notice over that racket. At least it's where it's supposed to be. Finding who built this safe and where it was cost me good money. Glad to see it was well spent.

Retrieving her lock picks, Raven inspected the safe for a few minutes before settling on two of her picks. With practiced ease, she inserted them into the lock and manipulated the oversized tumblers. After a few minutes, the lock surrendered and with a gentle tug the well-oiled door opened without a sound.

Of course Douglas would keep something this close to his heart in good working order.

Raven put the tools back in the pouch and set the backpack on the floor next to the wall. A velvet pouch and a crystal vial filled with amber liquid were set on a nearby table with care. She took one more glance at Valio and began inspecting the contents of the safe. *Hmm, very nice, Douglas. You've got a good eye for gems, I'll give you that. And Imperial Crowns? I can think of some people who could use them more than you.* She held up a bracelet with a look of disdain. *Feh. Cheap baubles. Must be for your courtesans. No self-respecting thief would waste time on these.*

Moving with deliberate haste, Raven withdrew a small gem from another pouch and spoke a soft word. The gem began to glow in a cold blue light. Cupping her hand around the gem, she allowed only a small beam to project into the room. The light was dim but it was more than sufficient to make out what was on the papers. *Perfect. This is what I was hoping to find. Going to be hard to collect those debts without a list of who owes you what, eh, Doug? What's this …? Royal warrants? I think those'll go with me also.*

Satisfied, Raven returned the discarded items to the safe.

Setting the crystal vial in the safe, she eased the safe's heavy iron door shut. The liquid was highly flammable. If everything went right, the vial would fall the next time the door was opened, consuming everything within the safe.

That should make it hard to know what I took. With a little luck, it just might scare him a bit also.

Locking the safe, Raven drew a black dagger out of its sheath and moved closer to the bed. With a sudden move, she placed a hand over Douglas's mouth and rested the edge of the knife on his neck. His eyes shot open but the prick of cold steel against his neck told him to lie still. After a few seconds, she took her hand away from his mouth and motioned for him to be quiet. She pulled up a chair and eased into it, still keeping her dagger aimed at his heart.

A deep, gravelly voice rumbled out of him. "All right, you're obviously not here to kill me, so you must want to talk. So talk."

"Are you always so gracious to your house guests?"

"Only the uninvited ones."

Raven allowed herself a slight smile. Douglas might be a fat pig, but he recovered quickly from his surprise. "We need to talk about a certain job you've accepted. I'm here to tell you it's going to cost you a lot more than you're going to make on it if you keep after it."

"You're Raven, aren't you?"

"Who I am is not important. However, there's a certain young schoolteacher who's under my watch and I'm determined nothing is going to happen to her."

Douglas let out a small laugh. "If that's what I owe this unexpected encounter to, then I'm afraid you've interrupted my sleep for nothing. Your little stunt the other night cost me enough as it was. Although, I'm impressed. I always thought you worked alone or with only a couple of people."

"Let's say I called in a whole bunch of favors. I can do it again if need be."

Douglas motioned with his hand and Raven nodded. He pulled the covers off and sat up in the bed, staring at the shadowy figure. She was reasonably sure he couldn't see her against the blackness of the room, but she wasn't going to let him get closer, either. "No, I don't think lighting a candle would be a good idea."

"I didn't think you would. Still, if that's why you're here, you're wasting your time. I returned the money to the bishop. I don't need the headaches. Besides, the merchants' guild had a meeting the other day and they're taking up a collection to hire guards for the school and the teacher. Seems some people both on the Hill and just below it like this young woman. Being an upstanding member of the guild, of course I contributed toward the guards."

"Of course you did. If you've called off the hit on her school, then why are you bringing in out-of-town thugs?"

"Ah, you met the boys the other night, didn't you?"

"Perhaps."

"I'm glad. I hope you paid a lot of attention to them. They're not here to deal with your precious schoolteacher — they're here to deal with *you*. You see, I can let the teacher go. However, I cannot allow you to challenge me and live. Bad for my reputation."

"You know I could kill you right here and now."

"No, you won't. You're Raven and you seem to have an aversion to killing. An aversion, I am happy to say, that I do not share. So unless you are going to kill me right now, I'd plan on leaving in a hurry. I'll give you one minute to get off of my property before I call for my guards."

"You are a fat, disgusting pig."

"And a very powerful and wealthy one. And power and wealth mean nothing if you're not willing to use them. That's what separates us, Raven. I'm willing to do whatever it takes to achieve my goals. You're a pretender and you'll be swept into the gutter soon enough. Your own good nature will be your downfall."

"I wouldn't count on that."

"I would. And you now have thirty seconds before I sound the alarm. Let the games begin."

Raven glided out of his room and hurried down the stairs, ignoring the sounds of alarm in the kitchen. She made her way out the window and used the clay from earlier to reseal the piece of glass into the windowpane. The cut in the window would be discovered in a thorough inspection, but it would delay discovery for a while. She might need to break in again and there was no sense in giving away her methods.

Raven hurried off the grounds. The thin moonlight deepened the shadows, making it easier to avoid the occasional city watchman. Leaving the Royal Quarter, she descended into the Laborers' Quarter, flitting from alleyway to alleyway until it reached a poorer section of town. She thought about dropping by the Black Boar and then immediately changed her mind. *If Douglas has hired hunters, it's time for Raven to change her habits. I also need to warn Jerek. If word gets back to Douglas that it was the Corconti backing me up, it could get bad for them, too.*

She spotted a familiar face coming out of one of the taverns and decided to follow him for a bit. She climbed up a rainspout to the roof and then bounded from building to building behind him. Finally, the figure paused outside a store and she watched as he leaned his back against the door. He looked for all the world like he was bored, but she knew he was jimmying the lock with a set of picks.

She hurried ahead and found the back door to the store and quickly picked the lock. She slipped in and shut her door just as he eased the front open. Hiding behind a dressmaker's dummy, she let him get a few steps into the store before she spoke. "You know, Kristof, you might want to make sure a building is empty before you break in. What if I had been the owner?"

The figure froze in place and then relaxed when he realized who was speaking. "For the goddess's sake, Raven, don't do that. I nearly threw this dagger into your heart."

She shifted the full-length mirror with her rapier. Kristof turned his head and realized she was much closer than he'd imagined. "No, you would have thrown your dagger into this mirror and then I would have stabbed you in the hand to make you quit being foolish. Now, listen to me. I need you to get a message to Jerek."

The Corconti paused, his head leaning to one side as he tried to focus on her in the dark. "He's not with you?"

Raven waved her arms around. "Do you see him?"

"No."

"Then he's not with me." Raven tried to keep the worried sound out of her voice. "Douglas has hired people to hunt for me. I need to figure out what they're up to—and soon."

Kristof leaned back against one of the counters, with a nonchalant look on his face. "I thought you already knew how good they were?"

"What do you mean by that?"

"The one you fought the other night, Robert Marjory?"

Raven ticked off some points on her fingers. "Big ox, no technique, just puts his head down and charges. Yeah, he's not the one I'm worried about."

"I should say not. He was found dead last night in the alley behind the Black Boar. The back of his head had been crushed in."

"What? I hadn't heard anything about that."

Kristof nodded, brushing some imaginary dust off his shoulder. "Jerek says you've been pretty preoccupied lately. Some say you did it. Some say you'd never kill someone from behind. Some don't know what to believe. Lots of rumors running around. I hear the rest of the hunters are pretty aggravated with you."

"Oh, that's just wonderful. Look, tell Jerek to keep the Corconti out of town for a few days. I don't want Douglas to know you all helped me the other night. He's got connections with the king and he may decide to take out his frustrations on you. Give me a day or two to see what's going on and how good these guys really are."

"You know he's not going to agree to that."

"Tell him I'm not worried about him. Tell him I'm worried about the women and children in your camp. Douglas is not adverse to selling people into slavery. I know what that would do to a Corconti."

Raven heard Kristof's sharp intake of breath. Slavery was anathema to the Corconti tribes. "All right, I'll tell him when I see him. However, he came looking for you this evening. Did you not talk to him?"

Raven shook her head. "No, but we don't always plan on seeing each other. We tend to run into each other. Perhaps he's visiting the guild?"

"Perhaps. I'll do what I can. By the way, were you planning on robbing this place?"

"No, I just stopped in to speak to you. Help yourself."

Kristof grinned. "Thank you, I will."

Raven returned the grin and then made her way to the back door. As she let herself out, she turned and called back over her shoulder. "I'm sure the ladies back in your camp will appreciate the fineries. You do know this is a dressmaker's shop?"

Before Kristof could answer, she had slipped out the door and disappeared into the darkness. A few moments later, a dark figure slipped out of where it had been hiding and made its way down the alley.

Chapter Ten

Perrin swept the floor, pushing the dust around more than getting it out of the store. A slow day was coming to a close and she was just killing time until night fell. She'd been reviewing the events of the last few nights over and over again. She was upset at herself over the incident with Ian.

I need to be careful. I shouldn't let him get to me. But, damn it, he takes a lot of liberties just because he's Jerek's friend. She gave the broom a sudden violent swish, raising a cloud of dust in the middle of the room.

"Hey, watch what you're doing in there! People don't want their books all dirty before they buy them!" Rory's disapproving voice rang out from the back room. Embarrassed, she ducked her head and concentrated on finishing sweeping before he came in to inspect her work.

"Are you about done with the ledger?"

"Yes, we need to make a few more sales to be in the black." There was a worried tone in his voice he was trying to hide. "I wasn't expecting that last order of books to be so expensive. There's no questioning the quality of the books Pietor produces but he raised his prices again. Either I need to find some new patrons or I need to find a new supplier."

"Do we have any books to deliver up the Hill?" She wanted an excuse to visit the Royal Quarter in daylight. *After all, no one would be suspicious of a young bookseller making a delivery, would they?*

"Actually, we do." He stuck his head in the door, his

voice brightening. "Thank you for reminding me. Old Tybalt ordered some books from the Imperial College on alchemy. They arrived a few days ago but I'd forgotten about it. I should run that up there right away."

"Let me take care of it. I could use a breath of fresh air." She set the broom down in the corner before he could think about it. "I'll run upstairs and grab my walking shoes while you get the bill ready."

Before he could respond, she passed him in the entryway and hurried up the stairs. Removing the slippers she wore around the store, she slipped into her boots and tied her hair back into a long ponytail. Re-entering the store, she saw her father standing behind the counter with a package and a small piece of paper. He stared at her with his head cocked to one side.

"It's all right, Father. I just want to make up for being gone so often in the evening. It's the least I can do." She bowed her head slightly and looked up at him.

"Oh, no, you don't. Don't even try that look on me. You've been getting away with murder ever since you turned six with that fake pout. Go on, get out of here." He turned away with a dismissive wave of his hand. "But don't dawdle. It'll be dark soon and I'd rather you were home. Strange things are afoot these days."

Something in her father's voice made her pause at the door. "You never objected before when I was tutoring." She watched his reaction, wondering what had brought this on.

"I've heard some dark talk down at Liam's." Perrin knew Liam ran a freight business down near the city wall right on the border of the Merchants' Quarter and the Commons.

"There's always talk down at Liam's. His customers aren't the kind who're usually found this far up the Hill. "

"Well, according to Liam, someone or something hit the thieves' guild like a plague over the past couple of days. Bodies are turning up all over the place."

Perrin felt her stomach tighten, but she put a skeptical look on her face. "Father, please, thieves turn up dead all the time. I thought you were talking about something serious."

"Laugh all you want, Daughter. I'm telling you Liam is scared. It appears some of these thieves didn't die easy. It looks like someone had tortured them. He says they've been finding bodies out in the open, almost like a warning for other thieves." There was no questioning the concern on her father's face.

"Have you seen any of these 'warnings,' Father? It sounds horrible, if it's true." She phrased her question to show him she was concerned.

"No, and I'm not in any hurry to do so. According to Liam, most of the bodies have turned up in the Laborers' Quarter, the Commons, or Lowtown. I don't do much business down there outside of doing some readings. But whatever is happening out there, I don't want you to get caught up in it, either. I want you home before dark, young lady." She could tell from the tone in his voice that this was not a suggestion.

"All right, Father, I'll be home before dark. You *do* realize I'm not ten anymore? I can take care of myself." Before he could reply, she disappeared down the wooden sidewalk that went along the front of the stores before turning up the hill toward the Old Wall.

As she walked, her mind raced. *I thought this was between Douglas and me. Surely he knows Quentin would never authorize the guild to take him on directly. It has to be those hunters trying to get a lead on me. I need to warn Quentin, but he's likely to take it out on me anyway. At least I hope this is just related to the hunter. I hope the king or the merchants haven't declared war on the guild.*

She made her way through the winding streets until she reached the Royal Quarters. After explaining her presence to the guards, they allowed her to pass. She began to take a roundabout path through the quarter, looking for items of interest. She noted three new merchants opening up for business and several new houses being constructed, to include a construction crew working on the upper floors of Douglas Valio's place.

She stopped one of the workers who was carrying in some lumber through the main gate. "What happened here?"

"Not sure. Some sort of explosion. Whole bedroom caught fire. Seems the owner just got out with some minor burns, but we have to repair about five rooms up there. Just lucky the whole house didn't catch on fire."

Perrin let the shock she was feeling in the pit of her stomach reflect in her face. "That's horrible. Any ideas what happened?"

"Nah. Some people are blaming that newfangled gas heater he had in his house. Apparently the Royal Quarter is pumping natural gas from the salt marshes for cooking and heating. Me? I'd stick with good ol' firewood. Much safer. Funny thing is, Lord Valio wouldn't talk to the Royal Guard when they came by earlier. Said he didn't need their help to deal with it."

Perrin made some more small talk and then continued on her way. *Bertok, you swore that vial would cause a minor explosion at best. Just burn up what's in the safe. Now Douglas thinks I tried to kill him, after all. This is not going to help my reputation here or with Quentin.*

She passed a few people who knew her from her father's store and paused to speak to each of them. She kept her conversation light, but listened to their stories, looking for tips. These people could come and go because they were beneath the notice of the nobles and the courtiers who lived on this side of the Old Wall.

She canvassed one portion of the quarter before she decided to make her way to Tybalt's. He had a great reputation in Sagras, not only because of his skills as an alchemist, but because his potions and powders had saved the lives of many of the poorer folk. Tybalt never took payment from those who couldn't pay. The thieves' guild had placed a permanent ban on his property. Even non-guild thieves, such as Perrin, respected this.

She knocked on the open door, noticing the unoccupied sitting room. "Hello? Is anyone home?"

"I'll be there in a bit." A strong voice came from the opening on the far wall. "Just take a seat; I'll be with you as soon as I can. Bit busy now."

"I'll be right here. I have a delivery for you." She entered and noted the aura of order and calm the room presented. A large table and a padded chair stood at the far end of the room, covered in neatly stacked papers and books. A small stone gargoyle stood atop the papers. She set her package down on one of the wooden chairs that lined the walls and sauntered around the room, admiring some of the paintings on the walls. Her practiced eye could tell they weren't extremely valuable but they were competently done. She guessed they were a payment from one of his less wealthy customers.

She approached the table, curious to see what books lay there. She extended a hand to move the topmost book to read the title of the one beneath when the small gargoyle turned its head and hissed at her, baring its small but sharp-looking teeth. She withdrew her hand and stepped away, keeping a close eye on the little creature. The gargoyle turned its head to track her movements. Its head nodded slightly when she was apparently far enough back and its expression softened into a pseudo-smile.

"I see you've met Zluty." Tybalt stuck his head through the doorway, his long gray hair going in fourteen different directions. "He tends to be overprotective of my things. He's more bluster than bite, though." He pushed his glasses up on his nose and stared at her. "You're Rory's daughter, aren't you? I recognize the hair. You're the spitting image of your mother."

"He startled me. I've never seen a live gargoyle before … He is alive, isn't he?" Perrin circled the desk, staring at the strange little creature.

"Not in the same way that you and I are, but yes, he's alive. You'd need to spend some time with Alaric the Sage. He specializes in rare creatures like Zluty." Tybalt sat at the table and extended a thin hand. The small gargoyle half-walked, half-hopped over to him, its wings slowly opening and closing. It climbed into the proffered hand, wrapping his small pointed tail around the alchemist's thumb. Tybalt lifted the creature up to his shoulder where it hopped off, and then settled into a resting position, looking for all the world like a small stone statue again.

"What an amazing creature!" Shaking herself out of her befuddled state, she picked up the package she'd brought. "Here are the books you ordered. Father asked me to bring them to you as soon as we got them." She decided to gloss over the fact they'd been at the store for a few days.

He opened the wrapped package carefully, untying the string and placing it in a jar with other similar pieces. Once the books were exposed, he held them aloft in triumph. "Ah, very good. Very good. I've been waiting for these new texts." He set the stack down on the table and pointed at Perrin with one of the books in his hand. "Istavan of Wulfberg has been proposing some interesting theories for years. Well, I now possess a copy of the book he claims his discoveries are based on. We'll see if he knows what he's talking about or if he's as big a blowhard as I believe him to be."

"A competitor?" Perrin's curiosity woke at the vehemence of the outburst.

"He should wish he could be considered to be a competitor." She could almost see the alchemist staring right through the unknown rival. "He's claims he's found a new method for rendering objects invisible—one that last longer and resists normal means of detection. Now that I have the book he based his work on, we'll see how effective his new method is."

"Turning things invisible? Can you do that?" Perrin tried to keep the excitement out of her voice.

"Pfah! Child's play if you have the proper components, patience, and skills. I could even teach you how to do it," the alchemist said with a dismissive wave.

"Now, that's something I would have to see to believe. Me? An alchemist?" A plan began forming in her mind and she began to play up to his ego. "I've read about these things in books Father has at his store. They claim a wizard has to cast a spell, though. You mean alchemists can do it also?"

"Young woman, I'll have you know alchemy is a noble calling. Our results are more reliable than those wizards. In fact, why don't I prove it to you. You could work on a standard powder while I investigate Istavan's so-called miracle. This way, when I present my findings at the Imperial University, we'll have independent confirmation." He ran his hand through his goatee as he became lost in thought. Perrin could see by the expression in his eyes he was standing before that council in triumph.

"Tybalt, I'm honored you'd consider teaching me about alchemy, but my father needs me at the store. I'm not certain he'd let me come up here to work full time with you." Perrin hated passing on such an intriguing opportunity.

Tybalt gazed through her like he was staring at something a thousand miles away and began walking around the room, the words coming in a staccato delivery. "Nonsense. I'm certain he could spare you for a few hours a day. I'm sure we'll make great progress. It's a simple process. Nothing complicated. Any first-year student can do it. You'll pick it up in no time. Wait right there." He pointed to a chair as he set out like a man on a mission.

Perrin sighed and sat down. She had no clue what was going on, but she could see he'd made up his mind and a herd of wild dragons wouldn't deter him. Perrin watched in amusement as he alternated between chewing on the end of a feathered pen and lowering his head to write furiously. After a bit, he sanded and blotted the ink before rolling it up and sealing it with a small ribbon.

"Please give this to your father. I believe the offer I made in there to hire you will more than make up for any lost time at the store. You'll be my assistant for the next three weeks. Also, please take this." He handed her a silver bracelet from the drawer. "This bears my mark and will allow you to come and go from the Royal Quarter without question."

Perrin was torn between not wanting to take advantage of the alchemist's generosity and the thief thinking she'd been given the keys to the royal treasury. After a moment's indecision, she managed to shove the thief back into her hiding place and accepted the bracelet. After all, with the invisibility powder she would learn to make, she wouldn't need a special pass to get past the guards.

Tybalt looked pleased. "Very well, return here tomorrow after lunch. We'll get started then." The alchemist busied himself unwrapping his books and beginning to page through them. After a bit, he looked up to see Perrin still standing there. "Were my instructions not clear? I'll see you tomorrow."

"No, they were quite clear and unless my father has any objection, I'll certainly be here."

"Then why are you still here?" She noted the hint of annoyance in his voice.

She fixed a smile on her face to soften her response. "You need to pay for the books."

Tybalt's face turned a deep shade of red and he excused himself to retreat into his workshop to retrieve the funds. Perrin made certain not to let out the tiniest hint of a laugh until she was well away from the store and heading out the gate to the Merchants' Quarter.

Chapter Eleven

Slipping out of her sanctuary, the darkness surrounded Raven like a welcoming blanket. She decided there was no point in waiting after hearing about the attacks on the thieves' guild. Between the hunters and Ian's snooping the other night, there were too many people getting interested in her activities. Moving through the darkened streets toward the Cathedral of Praxis, she shrugged her shoulders to adjust the straps of her backpack.

I hope I don't regret packing all this extra stuff. If I was sure where they had stashed the Dragonstone, this would be simpler. I prefer to custom-tailor my tools to the job, but I have no clue what I'm going to run into. Better to carry a little extra weight rather than realizing I left the tool I needed behind. There are just too many variables to make me comfortable. I hope I'm right because I'm only going to get one shot at this.

Hiding in the shadows, Raven could see the bell tower of the cathedral rising into the night sky. In the day, the tower glistened with its myriad stained-glass windows. At night, though, the windows loomed down over the city like so many eyes, dark and unfathomable. The windows made her feel uncomfortable, as if she was being watched by something not quite human.

Several streets from the cathedral, she pried open a cover leading into the city sewers. Once she was certain no one noticed the noise, she lowered herself into the depths and pulled the cover over her head. The all-encompassing darkness pressed against her like a physical object. Seconds later, the blue light from her gem flared to life, filling the area with a soft glow. The sudden light startled the regular denizens and she heard rat feet pattering deeper into the shadows.

She climbed down the rough wooden ladder and noted the direction the water was flowing. Pulling out one of the maps she'd made over the past week, she aligned it to match the sewer system and began heading toward the cathedral. She moved through the labyrinthine corridors of the sewers, checking her map every so often to ensure she was still on course. She doubted anyone had a complete map of these corridors, not even Quentin. She'd spent a lot of time mapping out sections over the past year and she'd paid good money to get maps of areas she hadn't visited yet. The cathedral district set cost her the most to acquire. Tonight, she'd find out whether or not she'd gotten her money's worth.

According to the map there were three openings beneath the main building and one in the rectory just outside the cathedral. She'd try the ones beneath her target first. It would be nice if they were unguarded and unlocked, but she was prepared for the worst ... or so she hoped.

She placed one hand against the wall to steady herself, noting the slimy feel of the tile even through her gloved fingers. The fetid air permeated the sewers, making everything feel damp. The walkway itself was slick from the constant moisture, making her progress treacherous. She heard movement in the water flowing beside her and wondered what animal could live in the streams flowing below the city. Then again, she wasn't sure she wanted to know.

She walked down the path with ginger steps, trying to ensure her footing before she committed to the next step. Every so often she doused her light to return the sewers to total darkness. She stood still, letting her eyes and ears adjust, while she searched for any indication of light or movement ahead. She knew guards might be stationed below the cathedral, but they couldn't remain in pitch-blackness for too long without losing their edge.

The walkway began a gradual descent. Checking her map, she saw the slope would drop almost twenty feet. When she reached the bottom, she would be about fifty steps away from being underneath the cathedral. She held the gem tight in her right fist, spreading her fingers apart to let the light strike the walkway ahead of her. A sudden flicker ahead made her pause, clenching her fist tight to cut off the light. Waiting in the darkness, she counted to thirty, but the flicker didn't reappear. She unmasked her gem again, letting a thin stream of light illuminate the ground ahead of her.

There!

She knelt down and examined what she'd found. A small thread was suspended about four inches above the floor. Its dust coating made it almost indistinguishable from the walkway. She traced it to a bell hidden against the ceiling. The other end was suspended across the water and tied to the wall.

So much for "I hope they don't know about the sewers."

She examined the bell and noted from the lack of corrosion that the well-hidden device hadn't been placed in the damp sewers long ago. However, the bell's mere presence was another problem. If a noise-making device was in the sewers, someone had to be there to hear it.

Stepping over the string, she loosened two of her pouches. Using her fingertips, she checked the collection of clay balls within each. *I hope Bertok knew what he was doing when he made these.*

She took off her backpack and set it on the ground ahead of her, being careful not to set off any other alarms. If there were guards, she needed to be armed. However, the footing was too slick. If she tried to walk with her rapier drawn, she might scrape it against the wall and expose her position. It was time to try out Bertok's device.

Withdrawing a device from her pack, she slipped it onto her arm. She locked a metal cuff into place on her right wrist before securing leather straps on her arm. The device contained a katar, a punch dagger favored by assassins from the

Eagle Islands far to the south. A rare weapon in these lands, its thick triangular blade reached almost nine inches. Bertok had designed the elaborate scabbard to be held tight against the inside of her right forearm. Moving her right hand upward would release the catch, letting the katar slide forward into place. This way, she avoided any delay in drawing the blade. She'd never used the weapon outside of practice with her swords master and she hoped she could keep that streak intact tonight.

Resecuring her backpack, she moved forward with caution. According to her map, the first entrance should be around the bend in the sewer. That would be the first place a guard might be also. Cupping the gem in her hand to let out the least amount of light, she edged her way forward, checking the walkway for more trip wires.

When she reached the beginning of the curve, she found another string tied higher than the first. She started to step over it and then paused. *That's too easy. No one even tried to hide this string. Someone wanted me to find it.*

Reaching into a different pouch, she pulled out a small blue vial. She poured a sparkling dust into her hand and recapped the vial. Kneeling, she lowered her head and gave a small puff into her hand. The dust swirled in the air and wafted down the walkway. The glistening dust settled on a second wire just beyond the first. Almost hair like, it was virtually invisible. Without the quartz dust, she wouldn't have seen it even if she knew where it was. If she had stepped across like she intended to do, she would have broken the string for certain.

Following the first string led to nothing. As she feared, it was a ruse, just there to draw her attention. She loosened the first string and lowered it to the ground. She traced the second wire, moving with studied caution. She didn't find anything on her side, so she followed the string with her light. When it reached the ceiling, she came to an abrupt halt. There, pointed right at her, was a bolt thrower with four missiles, set to fire the second anyone tripped the wire. An oily fluid glistened from the tips of the bolts. At this range, it wouldn't have missed.

Raven could feel a cold sweat break out on her forehead. *Damn, bolts* and *poison? This feels like the Black Leopards' work. I don't think the City Watch is smart enough to set a dead-fall trap.* She took out four copper coins and set them beneath the wire. If she came back this way in a hurry, she wanted to avoid this trap.

Once she determined there weren't any other trip wires beyond the one she'd just marked, Raven continued to the apex of the curve in the tunnel. Dousing her light again, she let her body relax. Concentrating on the gem in her hand, she entered a light trance Bertok had taught her. She tuned out her breathing and heartbeat and listened for any signs ahead. She needed to be certain her light hadn't been spotted while avoiding that last trap.

After a while, she heard something rustling in the tunnel ahead of her. Raven knew it was too big to be a rat. What she couldn't determine was whether it was on her side of the water or not.

If it's on the other side, I can slip past in the darkness. Even cats need some light to see. Of course, if it's on my side, I'm going to trip over it. It might be able to track me by scent. Then again, I doubt it'd detect much of anything right now. A side effect of the concentration trance was her heightened sense of smell. This was not proving to be an advantage in the sewers.

Everything said she needed to stay still, but she also was conscious of the passage of time. If she didn't get the Dragonstone and get out of the sewers by morning, she might never have another chance. Plus, if she was late, it'd be impossible to explain to her father where she'd been when he awoke in the morning.

Easing forward, she kept her back to the wall to minimize her exposure. Slipping her hand into the pouches she'd prepared earlier, she took out two small clay balls. She felt the ground ahead with her boot before putting her weight on it. Once past the curve, she tossed one of the balls down the sewer and shut her eyes.

She heard it clack against the tiles and then a bright flare lit the tunnel, visible even through her closed eyelids. Cracking her eyes open, she saw a stumbling dark shape up ahead, holding a hand up to its eyes. Taking the second ball, she tossed it as hard as she could at the figure's feet.

Sensing her movement, the figure attempted to point something at her. The thin walls of the clay ball cracked upon impact, releasing a reddish-gray smoke. The cloud enveloped the figure and it collapsed, its momentum carrying it into the water. The light from the flare faded and she relit her gem to examine the scene.

Raven approached the figure and hauled him out of the water. It was a man dressed in black leather from head to toe. Only small eye slits and an opening for the mouth exposed any skin to her light and a small hand crossbow lay on the walkway beside him. Checking for a pulse, she noted there was a slow but steady one and his breathing was shallow and rhythmic. Bertok's improved sleeping powder had done its job again. She checked him over and found a scimitar and several pouches filled with nasty sorts of weapons. Raven slipped a couple of the pouches onto her belt and picked up the crossbow and a supply of bolts, just in case.

If Bertok was right, the effects of the powder wouldn't wear off for about eight hours. She'd be long gone, but his relief would be here before then. She'd hoped to slip in and out unnoticed, but there was no chance of that now.

When no one responded to the flare, Raven commanded her gem to its full light. Looking at the ceiling, she spotted a section of tiles a different color than the rest. So far, her source of information was earning his money. Now it was time to find out how accurate the rest of his information was.

She found a series of small tiles set in the wall that slid to one side, creating a rough ladder. Climbing up, she pushed a tile next to the discolored area up and to the side, revealing a small lever. She pulled down on the lever and a section of the ceiling swung down on noiseless hinges, revealing a metal plate above her. She examined the grate to determine how and where it opened, then braced her back against the tiles hanging down and placed her gem inside one of her pouches, plunging the area into darkness. Pushing with both hands, she was pleased to find it came free of its mooring without a sound. The dim light above flooded down the opening. She climbed higher until she could peer into the room. No one was around, so she climbed into the room and secured the lid. A flickering light shone beneath the heavy wooden door in front of her. She crossed the room and listened at the door, but no sounds came from the hallway.

Easing the door open, she found herself in an ornate hallway. One end ended at a huge, dimly lit chapel. Past a series of doors, a stairway led upward at the other end. She headed toward the stairs, knowing the bishop's chambers were the obvious hiding place for the Dragonstone.

And, without a doubt, the most likely to be guarded, too.

She hurried as fast as she could without making noise. It would be hard to explain her presence should one of the acolytes serving the bishop discover her. She had the clay balls with sleeping powder, but there weren't many of them. No sense in wasting them.

She knew the bishop's living area was on the third floor. Using her light only when she had to, Raven avoided the few wandering guards and acolytes moving through the cathedral and made it to the top floor. She crept down the hallway leading to a huge set of double doors. To her surprise, there were no guards in the hallway. Maybe the Dragonstone was not here after all.

Deciding to check anyway, she listened at the doors and could hear soft noises. She drew back and checked the door on the right. She didn't hear anything, so she tried the handle and found the door unlocked. She opened the door with care and let herself into the room.

It was a large bedroom. From the window on the far wall, she could see a small ledge leading to the bishop's bedroom window, which was ajar. She eased herself onto the ledge, pressing her chest against the wall and spreading her arms out to maintain her balance on the narrow precipice. She knew if she slipped here, the cobblestones below would break more than just her fall.

Inching along, she reached the window. Craning her head to the side, she glanced into the room and saw only the occupant of the grand bed. She reached out and eased the window open enough to fit her lithe frame through.

Catlike, she dropped to the floor. The figure snorted in his sleep and continued to make the small wheezes of a man carrying more weight than was good for him. She had caught glimpses of this room during her observations. Since there were large, ornate windows on three of the walls, she knew if the Dragonstone was in this room, there weren't many places it could be. A quick glance narrowed the possible hiding places. Unless it was tucked under Bishop Marius's pillow or hidden under his bed, the most logical place would be a hidden safe.

She paused long enough for her eyes to become accustomed to the dark and then began searching, checking the walls for anything out of the ordinary. The timer in her head was counting the minutes she'd been inside the cathedral. She knew the guard in the sewers would be discovered unless she found it soon. She felt her heart begin to race faster and forced herself to stop and relax before continuing her search.

A good thief is a confident thief, Sean had always said when he was training her those years ago before he died. Shaking her head, she continued her search. Now was not the time to be thinking about her old lover. However, she felt her confidence returning and resumed her search with renewed vigor.

Completing her first circuit of the room, she realized there was no sign of a hidden panel or door anywhere in the room. Could she have made a mistake? She headed toward the window to check the other two rooms when she stopped. A silly grin crossed her face. *Tell me they aren't that incompetent.*

Marius tossed and turned in his sleep and Raven hoped he was dreaming of the punishment waiting for him for his deeds. A lot of poor people could have used his mentoring and stewardship but, under his reign, the church only cared for those who could afford to tithe the proper amounts. She had no use for hypocrites like him.

She made her way over to the bed and shrugged out of her backpack. Easing down onto her hands and knees, she crawled beneath the bed. The sagging mattress made it a tight fit. Taking a chance, she lit her gem and used the light to inspect the floor. Near the head of the bed there was a small section of boards that seemed different. She wiggled up to it, desperate not to bump the sleeper above her. Using a dagger, she worked the tip underneath the faint seam and pried upward. As the wood shifted, she could see a small depression beneath the floorboards. After a bit of a struggle, she worked her fingers underneath and lifted the lid.

She could see a metal lockbox resting within the small opening. Reaching in, she lifted it out and set the heavy box beside her. She extracted her lock picks from their pouch and the lock surrendered to her attack after a few twists. She was able to lift the lid without poking the mattress above her and saw a large velvet sack. Pulling on the strings, she opened the sack and saw a large red gem. She didn't dare expose much light, but she could swear she saw something lurking within the gem.

Damn, Bertok could have warned me how lifelike that flaw looked. I swear it turned its head when I looked at it.

She pulled the drawstring shut and placed the sack into one of her pouches. She relocked the lockbox and slipped it back into its resting place. Carefully aligning the lid to its original orientation, she eased it back into the hole. Once she was certain no one would notice anything, she backed out from beneath the bed.

Marius had rolled over and was facing away from the window. Deciding not to waste the opportunity, she gathered her things and let herself out the window. She eased it back into place and worked her way down the ledge. Now was not the time to make a mistake. She was relieved to find the other room still unoccupied and made her way through the room and down the hallway to the stairs.

Her journey back to the storeroom was uneventful and soon she found herself working her way through the sewers and slipping past the fallen guard. She recovered the coins she'd left and then retreated to a different point from where she'd entered the sewers. Making her way to the surface, she wandered through the town, stopping every so often to ensure no one was following her. Once she was comfortable, she made her way toward her final destination of the evening.

She patted the Dragonstone in her pouch. *I know exactly where you need to be kept. And I know who'll be taking a bath before they head home. There's no way in the world I could get past Father smelling like this.* A big grin fixed itself on her face as the magnitude of what she'd just done hit her. She took a few dance steps down the street before calming down and rejoining the shadows that called to her.

Chapter Twelve

The morning sunlight streamed through a crack in the curtains, shining like a spotlight on Perrin's face. Wrinkling up her nose in disgust, she rolled over to escape the offending light and pulled her down-filled pillow over her head. The damage was done, though, and she forced herself upright in her bed, red hair falling like a fiery cascade over her face.

She slipped into a dark green dress and paused. She heard her father in his room across the hall. A frown creased her face, realizing he wasn't downstairs. Either he was getting a late start or she was up earlier than usual. The events of last night were fresh in her mind. She knew the Black Leopards would be out in force trying to find the thief.

She pulled back the offending curtains to look outside. Pulling up a chair, she stared at the city and harbor below while she brushed her hair. She saw the buzz of activity down at the docks as the laborers began to gather in the cool morning air.

Looking to the east, she made out Hunter's Wood across the river. Fog rising from the river made it look more mysterious than usual. The leaves were turning colors as the season progressed. Placing her hand against the window, she could feel the chill on the glass. In a few more months, the winter storms would start to blow in from the north. *Ah, but with any luck, I'll miss the ice and snow and be in the Southern Islands.*

Going into the bookstore, she picked up her feather duster and attacked the dust that had accumulated overnight. She noted the worn feathers on her duster and reminded herself to pick up a new one as soon as possible. She spied several new crates over in the corner. *Looks like Father received a new shipment of books. Must have come in while I was preparing dinner last night. Guess he forgot to mention them.*

She called up the stairs with a teasing tone. "Father, are you going to lounge in bed all day or are you going to get started with breakfast?"

"I'll be down in a bit. Why don't you get some fresh water while you're waiting? I've got something special I want to make for dinner tonight—something to celebrate your new position with Tybalt. And, by the way, it's already paying off. He's referred four new customers to us already."

Perrin looked at the empty stairwell with a look of consternation. *He's acting peculiar this morning. This isn't like him at all. I've heard people trying to act like nothing's wrong. It takes an accomplished actor—someone fearless or a complete fool—to maintain their composure when they're threatened. Father is neither of those things.*

She shrugged before stepping into the kitchen to grab the two oaken water pails. A small breeze caught at her hair as she shut the back door behind her. Brushing it out of her face, she glanced both ways in the alley, scanning for any sign of observation before she walked down the steps behind the house. She shook her head in disbelief. That was a Raven act, not the actions of a storekeeper's daughter.

What's the matter with you, Perrin? Are you expecting the Black Leopards to materialize from between the buildings and spirit you off? Just go get the water.

She had just gotten to the bottom of the stairs when a voice startled her. "Well, hello! How are you this—AWUP!" A well-swung pail cut off the owner of the voice as he went sprawling to avoid having his head taken off.

Perrin used the momentum from her swing to spin around and bring up the other pail. Without thinking, she took aim at the prostrate figure before she realized who was lying in the dust. She just managed to halt her swing while

123

he scrambled out of the way.

Jerek!

She let her adrenaline rush mix with her initial anger and gave him a fierce glare. "Just what the hell do you think you're doing, sneaking up behind someone like that? And what are you doing in our alley? You don't live around here." She could see the last accusation hit him like she'd struck him across the face with a whip.

He started to get back to his feet, but a quick motion from her pail convinced him to remain still. The bright blue of his shirt and doe-colored leather pants were quite a contrast against the gray dust of the alleyway. He raised a hand to protect himself from the pail. Once he realized she wasn't going to brain him, he lowered his arm and pushed himself up into a sitting position. "Hey, take it easy. I just said hello. I wasn't trying to scare you." His face clouded over as he pondered her earlier statements. "And no, I don't live around here, but last time I checked the alleys were owned by the king. Who are you to tell me where I can't go?"

She saw she'd hurt Jerek's feelings with her comment. She was relying on the fact the Corconti were sensitive about being wanderers. As much as it bothered her, she wanted him upset and not thinking straight. She wanted him thinking about anything except the person standing in front of him.

"Well, you should know better than to scare people like that." Her blue eyes flashed at him in the morning light. "I didn't see you when I came out. What are you, some kind of magician who comes and goes in a puff of smoke?"

Jerek's mischievous grin appeared on his face. "No magician, lass, although it would be a useful trick if I could learn how to do that." Sobering as she raised the pail to threaten him again, he pushed on. "I was just cutting between the buildings. I turned the corner and, like a vision, there you were."

Perrin knew he was calming down if he was starting to turn on the Corconti charm. Jerek was as silver-tongued as they came. Plus, as much as she hated to admit it, he was handsome in a devilish kind of way. He always said Raven was the only woman who never fell for his charms, which made her so damn interesting to him.

Perrin decided to regain the initiative. "Well, you can just go back through that gap and get on about your business. I've honest work to do and it doesn't include you."

"And why would you assume I'm not doing honest work? You judge me far too harshly, I fear." Jerek lifted himself off the ground and brushed himself off when she didn't make a threatening move.

Perrin mentally slapped herself on the forehead. *You've never met him before as Perrin. There's no reason to think he's up to no good. I have got to get out of this situation before I give myself away.*

He stepped forward, hands outstretched. "To make up for frightening you, may I please carry those pails for you?"

"You're not concerned about me carrying too much weight. You're just worried about me smacking you with one of them." Perrin stepped back from the young Corconti and shook one at him in a threatening manner.

He brought up a hand in a fainthearted attempt to shield himself. "As you wish. At least may I escort you to the well? That was your destination, was it not?"

"You may not. I am not in the habit of being accosted by strange men and then letting them escort me anywhere." Perrin's eyes narrowed but she found herself relenting at Jerek's crestfallen face. "However, if you happen to be walking that way I can't stop you. These are the king's streets, as you pointed out."

His face brightened but he held his tongue at the cold look she gave him. She moved to one side of the alley and gestured for him to stay on the other. She let Jerek stay one pace ahead of her so she could keep an eye on him. He brushed the dust from his clothing as they walked.

I've never seen him in anything other than his work clothes. That's a look more befitting the son of a tribal leader than the dark leathers he wears at night. Who knew he cleaned up so nice? Stop that, Perrin. Don't screw it up by getting all fluttery now.

As they emerged from the alley, she saw merchants and their families gathered at the well at Silver Heron Way and Black Prince Road. Getting the morning water was a great excuse to catch up with gossip and talk shop before work started, often with more deals taking place here in one morning than in fifty merchants' guild meetings.

I should have known there'd be a crowd. Oh, no, here comes Brigitte.

Brigitte, who ran one of the clothing shops nearby, was heading straight toward her. Brigitte's speed was impressive; she was faster than her round shape led one to believe. To Perrin's chagrin, she was also a notorious gossip and Perrin could see she was giving Jerek the once-over.

"Perrin, so good to see you. I was expecting to see your father, though. Is he all right?" Perrin knew Brigitte was spending more time at the bookstore lately. She was a recent widow, but she was determined she wouldn't remain one long. Rory said he felt like a cow being sized up by a butcher every time she cornered him. Perrin had begun bringing up Brigitte every time he started talking about her unwed status. That was usually sufficient to bring the topic to a screeching halt.

"He's fine, Brigitte. Just thought I'd fetch the water for a change." Perrin walked toward the well, taking the older woman by the elbow to steer her in that direction. However, Brigitte slipped out of her grasp and turned back around to face Jerek.

"Why, Perrin. Aren't you going to introduce me to your *friend*?" Perrin could hear the quiver of anticipation in her voice.

Perrin winced at the way she had said *friend. Aauugh! Jerek, why, of all days, did you have to be here?* Composing herself, she looked at Brigitte. "We haven't been introduced. We happened to bump into each other en route to the well." She left the statement hanging, hoping Jerek would avoid saying anything about how they met. It was going to be difficult enough as was.

"You're right and curse my inexcusable manners!" Jerek bowed, sweeping his right hand across his boot tops in a flourish. "I am Jerek, son of Dominick, of the Black Wolf Corconti. At your service, ladies."

Brigitte turned pink and brought her hand up to her mouth to hide the smile. "Oh my, Perrin. You do find the most entertaining gentlemen, don't you?"

Perrin felt a blush creeping up her cheeks and threatening to merge with her fiery hair. She most *certainly* did not find gentlemen, entertaining or not, on a regular basis and didn't want Jerek thinking that for a second. She tried to compose herself, but the twinkle in Jerek's deep brown eyes told her he'd noticed her embarrassment.

"Brigitte!" Her voice rose and extended the last syllable of the older lady's name. "I don't consider bumping into a person walking by the back door as 'finding' someone."

Jerek broke in before Brigitte could speak. "Truth be told, I bumped into her. I wasn't paying attention when she came down the stairs. The least I could do was offer to carry the pails to make up for my clumsiness." With that, he stepped forward and made a small gap in the crowd of people. He motioned for Perrin to begin filling her pails.

With a smile to Brigitte, she hurried through the throng and set her pails on the edge of the well. Jerek turned the well-worn handle and raised a scarred wooden bucket from the depths. He filled her pails without wasting a drop and then lowered the bucket into the water for the next person in line.

Leaning forward to pick up the pails, he whispered to Perrin, "So, is she always this blunt?"

Trying hard not to laugh, Perrin whispered back, "No, she likes me. You should see how she is with some of the others."

Giving Perrin a knowing look, he grabbed the pails and started carving a path through the milling merchants. Perrin looked over her shoulder and waved good-bye to Brigitte, who was still standing there agog. Brigitte wasn't used to people extracting themselves from her conversations so deftly. Catching up to Jerek, she fell into step and was almost back to the alley before she realized this was *not* what she had in mind.

"You know some interesting people, Perrin." She realized it was the first time he'd used her name the entire conversation.

"Believe me, that was a mild dose. If she thought there was something spicy, she'd still be with us. I swear she's part snapping turtle." She motioned for him to give her the pails, but he smiled and kept on walking.

Once they were out of sight of the well, he slowed his pace and waited for Perrin to catch up with him. "I see. In that case, it's a good thing she doesn't know about me. Or you, for that matter."

Perrin stumbled as she realized what he'd just said. She glared at the pails he was carrying as if accusing them for her sudden clumsiness. "I think what bothers her is I'm a boring person. There's so little to gossip about me."

"Oh, I think you're a lot more interesting person than you let on." The young Corconti continued, not looking at her. "After all, we're more alike than people would guess."

With a sudden sick feeling in her stomach, she slowed down. "And what do you mean by that?"

Jerek came to a halt, resting the pails on the ground. He paused and flexed his fingers. "Being a bookseller's daughter, you're well read, have an insatiable curiosity about the world beyond these city walls, and are very intelligent. I like to think the same things of myself. As the future leader of my tribe, I have to be a very good reader of people."

Perrin found herself relaxing. Running a hand through her hair, she saw an opening to distract this entirely too observant man. "Well, I like to think I'm well read. It's hard to sell books you haven't at least looked through. I enjoy ones about exploration and travel the most. Tell me, why haven't the Corconti written about themselves or their travels? They're noted musicians, poets, and storytellers. People are curious about you and your customs."

Jerek gave a knowing nod. "Storytelling is a very noble calling. While we love to tell *your* customs, legends, and myths, it's not easy to share *ours* with outsiders. We have no desire to be the objects of idle curiosity. If people are interested in us, there are ways to learn."

"I can appreciate that. But wouldn't a wider understanding of your tribes be beneficial? I mean, it might lead to fewer misunderstandings between your people and mine."

"You act as if we want to be incorporated into your people. Even with the misunderstandings, sometimes it is better to be outside looking in. The Corconti do not make war. We do not fight over food or precious rocks. If there is no food, we leave and go elsewhere. If we need money for things, we find ways to get it. If not, we make what we need or go without. If we are not wanted, we leave. It's a very simple life." Jerek picked up the pails and began walking toward her home again.

"You make it sound as if it's a bad thing being who I am." An accusatory tone crept into her voice. The Corconti were looked down on by many of the townspeople as vagrants and thieves. That the Corconti might be as prejudiced about city dwellers was disconcerting.

"That begs the question." Jerek stopped again, facing her. "Who are you?"

"Who am I? I am Perrin, daughter of Rory the Bookseller of Sagras." She used the same singsong voice he'd used on Brigitte and gave him a mock curtsy.

"Ah, so you're a shopkeeper's daughter. That explains why Raven never comes out except at night." He dropped that bombshell into the conversation without hesitation.

Perrin tried not to turn white at Jerek's comments. He continued looking at her apparently waiting for a comment from her. She tried to bluff it out, adopting a mocking tone. "Raven? I've heard that name before, but I'm not sure where."

"You can pretend if you wish. It doesn't change facts. You *are* Raven."

Perrin gave him a stern look. "And how did you reach

that erroneous conclusion?"

Jerek spoke to her like a headmaster might talk to a recalcitrant youth. "I suspected you might be Raven the second you swung that pail at me. Trust me, I wasn't just watching you because you're beautiful ... which you are, by the way. I've spent many evenings learning your tendencies. Your reaction was a move I've seen her make before when surprised. You walk like her. Your weight is on the balls of your feet. The way you hold your arms, it's as if you're ready to draw a rapier, even though you're unarmed. A mere shopkeeper's daughter would never act like that. Even the expression on your face right now is the same expression I've seen you give me countless evenings when I've annoyed you."

His smile softened as he saw her cringing at the overwhelming list of flaws in her disguise. "Don't feel bad. I doubt anyone else knows Raven well enough to note these tells. But if I were you, I'd never play cards against me. You'd never get out of debt. You can no more hide the way your body reacts than you can prevent the sun from rising."

"So, if I am Raven, then what?" She'd been dreading this moment ever since she'd taken on her nighttime persona.

"If I am right, I wish you wouldn't keep me at arm's distance. I've wanted to get to know you better for quite some time, but you never let me get that close to you." He scanned her over with an experienced eye. "I must admit, I like your hair like this much better than black. I don't know if this is the wig or the other is, but either way, you're an attractive woman. I'm fond of Raven, but I wouldn't mind getting to know you better, also."

"I'd prefer you didn't get to know her at all," a gruff voice sounded from behind them.

Looking up in horror, Perrin realized they'd stopped a few feet away from the back door to the store. Rory was standing on the back steps, his arms folded across his chest. *Oh, goddess, how much did he hear?*

She stared at her father, but he was busy staring at the young Corconti holding the water pails. Perrin knew from that expression, of all the young men she could have chosen to talk to, Jerek was at the bottom of her father's list. Jerek flashed his most disarming smile and handed Rory the pails. Her father snatched them away and set them just inside the door.

"I was getting worried when you hadn't returned. I see now why you were delayed." Rory's icy tone left nothing to the imagination.

"I was intercepted by Brigitte, but Jerek managed to extricate me, otherwise I might *still* be at the well. She hinted she'd love to be invited over some evening. Shall I have this gentleman pass a message to her? If you don't want him here, I'm certain he'd be happy to go to back to the well."

Rory visibly blanched at the thought of spending an entire evening fending off Brigitte's none-too-subtle advances. "Err, um, no, that won't be necessary." Turning to Jerek, he mustered up as much politeness as he could. "Thank you for assisting my daughter. That was most gracious of you."

"Think nothing of it. You've done a fine job raising your daughter. Her grace and manners reflect well upon your family," Jerek said, almost by rote. The Corconti had a habit of speaking formally when dealing with townspeople. He'd told Raven it made townspeople uncomfortable when the barbarians spoke their language better than they did. *"Besides, a person who feels guilty is easier to guile than an equal."*

Perrin almost snorted out loud at Jerek's compliment. Grace was not an attribute people associated with her. She'd been gangly growing up and most people thought she was as graceful as a two-day-old colt learning how to stand. However, Jerek's speech had the desired effect on her father. He began to grin at the young man in spite of his anger and unfolded his arms, relaxing his body.

Rory's voice was still gruff, but it softened by the moment. "Well, it was a nice thing to do, carrying the pails like that. Tell you what, we're about to have breakfast. Would you care to join us?"

Jerek bowed his head in deference. "I am afraid I have

business in the city. I understand you received a shipment of books my father ordered from you. If you don't object, may I stop by later and pick them up?"

Perrin saw a transformation go through her father. In seconds, he went from aggrieved father to businessman. "So, you're Dominick's kid? Yes, they arrived yesterday. I hadn't had a chance to send word, but I'm not surprised you knew they were here. Your father always seems to know what's going on in town."

"As a merchant, you understand the need to keep one's ear to the ground. We are traders and knowledge is the most valuable of commodities." Jerek gave Rory a knowing wink.

"Indeed, I pay good money to know about new books long before they are finished."

Perrin wasn't certain if she should be happy that her father and Jerek were getting along, or if she was going to be sick over the abundance of smugness in the air. The moment passed as Jerek looked up at the sky and then bowed at the waist to the two of them. "I shall be back this afternoon to claim my books. Until then, good merchant." He tuned and disappeared between two buildings, moving in the direction of the Royal Quarter.

Perrin entered the house, still worrying about how much of their conversation Rory had overheard. *Damn that Jerek! If his loose talk made Father suspicious, I won't be able to get out of this house for months.*

"So, you know Dominick's boy? Seems like a nice enough kid for a Corconti." Her father placed her breakfast on the table in front of her. "A little too forward and a little too glib for my taste, but Dominick speaks well of him. Supposed to be a hardworking kid."

Perrin stared at her father. It wasn't like him to hand out empty praise. He must have been impressed with what he'd heard. That was not the reaction she'd expected when he'd discovered them in the alley.

He lifted a large pot and poured steaming hot chocolate into two cups and handed her one. Perrin looked up at him in surprise. Chocolate was an expensive treat. He must have been in a good mood this morning to splurge like this. This was reserved for special days and holidays.

"Well, this is a pleasant surprise! What's the occasion?" Perrin smiled at him, holding her hands over the steam rising from the earthenware cup in front of her.

"Oh, just in a really good mood today."

"Uh-huh. And did anything happen to put you in a 'really good mood'?" Perrin noted he was not acting like himself today. He was acting more like a schoolboy than …

Perrin sat straight up in her chair as a suspicion ran through her mind. He was looking insufferably pleased with himself. "Is there something I should know about, Father?"

"This is a rather awkward topic to talk about with one's daughter. Since you've been out so much, I've been hanging out at the Golden Gryphon Inn. It's been too quiet at night with no one here but me."

"Yes?"

"Well, uh, I had been going to the inn, you know, just to visit with people down there. Don't get out much with the shop and all, so it's nice to get a chance to catch up on all the happenings." He paused, fumbling with some sentences he was trying to get out.

"Going to the inn?" she asked, pausing on the last word to get him back on track.

Gathering up his courage, Rory began again, his words tumbling out like a broken fountain. "Yes, going to the inn, and … well, I met someone. Her name is Fiana. I want you to meet her. She's really a nice person. I think you'd like her."

Perrin sat there half in shock. Father was seeing someone? That … didn't seem right. True, he had been alone ever since her mother had died, but this was …

Stop. It's been nineteen years, he has a right to have a life. But … how could he?

"I've wanted to talk to you about this, but you're always so busy, getting home late. It's been a real godsend to have someone like Fiana to talk to in the evenings. Anyway, I'd like you to stay home tomorrow night so you could meet her."

Perrin sat there dumbfounded while Rory waited for some reaction. Pulling herself together, she gave him a weak smile. "That's really nice, Father. I'd like to get a chance to meet ... her." She'd started to say Fiana but couldn't bring herself to do it. Naming her would make this too real. Right now, she preferred to stay in the abstract where it was safe.

They finished their breakfast in awkward silence. Perrin mechanically went through the steps of cleaning the shop to get it ready for the upcoming day, but her heart wasn't in it. The bells from the cathedral rang the hour and she opened the door to the shop. Her father was cleaning up in the kitchen, whistling as he scrubbed their breakfast dishes. She stared into the shop, imagining sharing the place with someone other than her father.

Stop it! You're acting like a silly schoolgirl. Is it so wrong for him to find happiness after all this time? It's not like Mother died last week. But the more she argued with herself, the more despondent she felt. "Father, are you going to be much longer?"

"Just a few more minutes. Why?"

"I need to go see Yolande for a bit." Yolande ran a green grocery a few doors down from the store. She'd been a surrogate mother for Perrin for many years, a cross between the grandmother who spoiled her when Rory wasn't looking and the aunt who helped her understand things when the world got too hard to bear.

"I'll be out in a moment. How long do you think you'll be?" She noted the worried tone in his voice.

Perrin didn't respond, staring at one of the ships leaving the dock, heading out into the open sea beyond the bay and wishing she was on it. The morning sun turned the water in the bay a sparkling white. *The waves are bright this morning. That must be the reason my eyes are tearing up.*

Chapter Thirteen

Slipping out of her sanctuary, Raven headed toward the Green Gryphon tavern to meet Jerek. She was a little nervous after their encounter the other day. Even though she trusted him, she felt more vulnerable than she ever had in her disguise. It had been tough keeping her mind on Tybalt's instructions today.

I guess it's a good thing I only blew up two glass vials today. Tybalt could tell my mind wasn't in the lessons. I just hope he doesn't get too disgusted with me before I finish the vanishing powder. I have big plans for it if I can get it to work right.

Moving through town, she noticed the streets were emptier than usual. The few people she did encounter took one look at her light cloak and gave her a wide berth. She didn't know if the stories her father heard at Liam's were true or not, but something had spooked the regulars.

Strange. I heard the thieves' guild got hit, but if it was just those few hunters I met the other night, Quentin should have dealt with that by now. He's not going to maintain control of the guild if they feel he's gotten too weak to deal with a few bounty hunters. This feels bad, but I can't just go to him and ask what's going on.

Entering the Green Gryphon, she noticed there were only four patrons sitting at separate tables with their backs to the wall, watching the doorway over their cups. It was as though they were waiting for something to happen. Waving to the bouncer as she entered, she walked up to the bar with a casual air and waited for the bartender.

"Business seems a little off tonight, Andre. You been watering the ale again?"

The large man grinned at her as they shared an old joke. "Aye, it's been a bad couple of days all around." He pushed a large wooden stein filled with ale toward her. "And, I'll have you know, I never water the ale. I save that for the whiskey."

Andre waited for her to enjoy her ale while he wiped down the counter with a stained rag. His shirt was about as stained as the rag and his apron barely hid his waistline. There was no questioning his strength. You didn't lug beer barrels around all day without developing upper-body strength, as a few rowdy patrons had found out to their chagrin. Andre had been a soldier before retiring after one too many wounds. His scarred face hid the kind streak hidden within, but if you took the time to get to know him he was a valuable friend. He was one of Raven's trusted sources of information.

She took another drink from the stein and turned to look at him. "I've been out of the area. I hear there have been strange happenings in the Commons. Any idea what's going on?"

He glanced around the room and leaned forward. "I've got a few theories, but there are those who think keeping one's thoughts to themself leads to a longer life."

Raven favored him with a sympathetic look and then took a deep draught. "I understand. Of course, there are those who don't mind taking a few risks if the potential profit is tempting enough." Wiping her hand across her mouth, she pulled a small pouch off her belt and dropped three ten-crown coins from it into her left palm, as if the money meant nothing to her. Andre's eyes widened at the sight of that much money. "I mean, I wouldn't want you to feel you were helping out an old friend and not being thanked for it." She set her ale stein on top of one of the coins and slid it back across the bar toward him.

"Here lass, let me refill that for you." He slid the stein off the bar and let the coin drop into his outstretched hand. As he returned with the freshly filled stein, he leaned forward.

"From what I've heard, and mind you I haven't heard a lot, someone's hitting the thieves' guild hard. Four of my best customers turned up dead within blocks of here. It's not bad enough they're scaring away my customers. They're killing off the paying ones."

Raven's voice dropped even softer and she lifted her stein almost to her mouth before speaking. "Who's behind this and why? Come on, Andre. Thirty crowns are a lot of money, I expect to hear something I don't already know for that amount."

Andre saw from her expression she was not in the mood to be messed with this evening. His voice dropped to a low whisper. "Be right back." He went to deal with one of the few patrons. Raven looked around and wondered what was keeping Jerek. *I hope nothing has happened to him. The big goof needs to get his head out of the clouds and pay attention to the world around him.*

After filling the man's drink order, he came back to the bar and stood near her. He began dipping some of the steins into a pail of hot water his assistant had just brought out of the back room and drying them with one of the bar rags. He looked miserable but she knew he wanted the rest of the gold coins.

Raven turned and rested her back against the bar to survey the tavern. She had the distinct feeling someone was watching her, but couldn't spot anyone. Lifting her stein up to hide her mouth again, she stage-whispered, "I'm listening, Andre."

"I have it on good authority the Black Leopards are behind the mayhem. I'm not certain why King Marcus set them on the thieves but they're looking for something or someone. They haven't killed anyone important yet. Word on the street is they've taken out a score or more but they're all grunts. Hell, half of the dead weren't even full members, just guys down on their luck who were doing some second-story work to feed their families. Quentin and the other leaders are all hiding somewhere. People are trying to figure out how the

Leopards found so many." He paused to exchange pleasantries with a new patron who had walked in.

Raven stared at the newcomer over her stein. He appeared to be a young nobleman out slumming. He was trying to blend in by dressing down, but it was obvious by the way he carried himself he wasn't from the Commons. He flashed Raven a questioning smile, wondering if she was looking for a little companionship. The look she gave him encouraged him to retreat to the far end of the bar and keep his thoughts to himself.

Andre returned from talking to the chastened young man and picked up his story. "Also, I hear they're snagging people off the streets, both thieves and regular people. It's like the Leopards are trying to make a point. From what people say, the kidnappers don't come right out and say what they're looking for. Instead, it's something like, 'whoever took it will know what we're looking for and they should return it very soon.' That's an odd way to get information, don't you think?"

"I don't think they're trying to *get* information. They want the word to get out they're looking for something. The question is, whom are they trying to get the word to?" The fact the Leopards were "looking for something" meant it was related to her.

Andre continued, with an ominous tone in his voice. "I can't answer that but I can tell you this: Whoever the person the Black Leopards are after, I hope he's got eyes in the back of his head. Quentin's put a bounty on their head—preferably on their *severed* head. He knows the Leopards are going to 'stay busy' until they find what they're looking for, and he knows the quickest way to get the Leopards off his back is to turn the person over to them."

Raven slowly sat her stein down and slid the other two coins over to Andre. "It might be worth my while to see what's going on for myself. Wonder how much money I could squeeze out of Quentin if I play my cards right?"

Andre gave her a disapproving look. "I don't want you

getting into something you might regret."

"Me? Get into something? I don't have any idea what you're talking about." She flashed Andre a disarming smile just as Jerek walked in the door. The Corconti waved to the two of them and then bounded over to the bar.

"Sorry I'm late. It took longer than usual to convince the city guard to let me inside this evening. Something's put a little more starch in their backbones. Not certain I care much for that. It's going to get expensive to keep coming in after dark."

"Well, son, if you came into the city before dark, you could enter like anyone else."

"But, Andre, where's the challenge in that?" He tossed a couple of coins on the bar and motioned to the far end of the tavern. "Bring a bottle of your best and send it to my ... excuse me, our table." Before Raven could react, he'd grabbed her by the hand and was leading her through the maze of chairs and tables to a secluded booth in the back.

"Jerek, what's come over you?" She managed to slip her hand out of his.

"Why, the full moon, the beautiful stars, and even the heavens themselves weep in shame at being compared to you."

"All right, you. How much have you had to drink tonight?"

"Not a drop of liquor, although if Andre will shake his stumps I'll take care of that. I've been looking forward to this evening ever since we talked the other morning."

Raven felt herself flush and thanked the gods the lights were low. "Jerek! What is the matter with you?" She waved her hands, trying to make him lower his voice.

He sobered for a bit, turning to face her. "I'm sorry. Ever since our conversation the other morning, I've been thinking about this opportunity. I want you to come to the camp with me. My father has asked to meet you."

Raven stared at him as if he'd begun spouting Karatanese. "Your father ... wants to meet me? Why?"

"I told him about you but he is old-fashioned. It is his prerogative as the elder of our tribe to meet any outsider who will be spending time with us. You *did* say you wanted to learn about the Corconti."

Before Raven could answer, Andre showed up with a bottle of his finest wine. He gave Jerek a knowing wink before turning to Raven. "Look, lass, if this one gets out of line, you just let me know. I'll toss him out on his ear if he treats you wrong."

"Andre!" Now she knew no amount of darkness could hide the blush running all the way to her hairline. The grizzled old bartender chuckled as he walked away.

"All right, Jerek, if you're done acting like a mooncalf, perhaps you'll tell me what the hell is going on?"

A serious look settled on his face. "Are you playing with me, Raven, or are you really this dense tonight?"

"I guess I've had a lot on my mind. You know, something about thieves turning up dead all over the city? Maybe you heard something about it?"

Jerek nodded and moved closer. "Oh, we've heard about it. Never heard of the Black Leopards hunting thieves before. I always figured we were a tad beneath them. Times do change, though. The tribal council has declared this city off limits for the time being. Only Eirik and I are allowed to enter. In fact, I had to get special permission to come here this evening, but I knew this is the only time I could see you."

"So, what was so important that you had to see me?"

"I told you: My father wishes to meet you." Jerek leaned closer and dropped his voice. "You, you. Not your daytime you."

"And again: Why?"

"If we are going to be seeing each other, he wants to determine what kind of woman you are."

Raven couldn't believe what she was hearing. She repeated his last statement out of shock. "If we're going to be seeing each other?"

"We'll talk more about that later." He finished his wine

140

and stood up. "We'll expect to see you five nights from now. Please do not disappoint my father. I'd hate for him to get one of the wisewomen to cast a curse on you. Well, enjoy the rest of the bottle." With that, he bowed and rushed through the door into the darkness beyond, leaving Raven sitting there with her mouth hanging open.

She sat there staring at the empty doorway, trying to figure out what had happened. Jerek must have gotten something out of carrying the pails from the well that she hadn't. Either that or he'd been drinking from some wells she didn't know about out there in the woods. Either way, she was going to have to try and rein him in. If he kept spouting off, he was going to compromise Perrin and she was not ready for the world to know that bit of information quite yet.

She decided there was nothing to be gained puzzling about *that* in a public tavern. She corked the bottle and tucked it into her backpack for later and headed toward the door. She stepped into the shadows as soon as she cleared the doorway and waited for her eyes to adjust to the dim light. Once she could see, she hurried to the corner of the tavern and stepped into the shadows to wait.

The feeling of being watched had intensified. A few minutes later, the young nobleman came outside. Squinting into the darkness, he scanned the street, looking for something … or someone. He stumbled descending the stairs and began walking toward her. She wrapped her cloak about her and drew farther back into the shadows. She let him pass and then slipped out to follow him. She wasn't sure if he was just young and stupid or had sinister intents. Either way, there was no sense in taking chances.

He wandered the Commons until he made his way to another tavern. Peering in the window, she noted he turned his attention to the lone barmaid and realized he was simply on the make. However, she still had the uncomfortable feeling she was being watched. She tried to attribute it to nerves, but the feeling wouldn't go away.

She waited as long as she possibly could before making

her way through the dark streets. Raven became even more disconcerted when she realized even the daughters of the night were missing from their usual haunts. If *they* were afraid to ply their trade, the city was more dangerous than even the stories had led her to believe.

After slipping through a few more alleys, she decided to call it an evening. It was obvious there was nothing to be accomplished by wandering the streets. *I wish I could talk to Quentin, but I have no idea where to find him. If someone's hunting thieves, the last place he's going to go is the lair.*

The feeling of being followed was still strong. She'd doubled back on her path several times, lying in wait for her mysterious pursuer, but never spotted them. The shadows were normally her friends, but tonight, they seemed to mock her.

She retreated through the winding alleyways of the Commons until she neared her sanctuary. She descended into the sewer several streets away from her normal approach. She crept forward and listened for any signs of pursuit. Only after she was convinced she hadn't been followed did she dare use the hidden switch to open the chamber and ascend into her sanctuary.

Raven shone the light from the lamp around the storeroom to ensure her sanctuary had not been violated. Entering the main chamber, she hung her cloak on its hook and placed her weapons into their rack. She shrugged out of her armor and draped the sword belt over its hook. Catching a glimpse of her face in the mirror made her pause. There was no questioning the stress she'd been under tonight.

And it's only going to get worse. What with the Dragonstone, the thieves' guild murders, Douglas's hunters, the Black Leopards, and now Jerek losing his mind, I'm thinking a long trip sounds like a good idea. She poured herself a small shot of brandy. *Bertok and I need to talk, and soon. I need to know what we're going to do with this bloody jewel. After all, it was his idea. I should have known if a wizard was involved, it would be more trouble than it was worth.*

She finished the brandy and returned to the armoire. She

pulled the medallion out and examined the symbols that lined its edges. She recognized a few from the bits of arcana she'd wheedled out of Bertok. There was so much she didn't know and a wave of frustration washed over her. She could still hear his repeated admonitions that he wouldn't teach her magic ... yet. She knew Bertok had his reasons and she'd never had cause to doubt him.

She checked herself over in the mirror again. It was still bizarre to see Raven in Perrin's clothing after all this time. As she raised the medallion to speak the spell, a flicker in the mirror caught her eye. She spun around, a hidden dagger appearing almost without her realizing it, but the blade never left her hand.

A young woman, probably not much older than fifteen, stood by the now-open storeroom door, her arms crossed insolently across her chest. "I was wondering when you were going to notice me." The cynicism in the girl's voice was at odds with the young face staring at Raven.

For the second time that night, Raven was speechless. But then she forced herself to say, "Why are you here?"

Raven kept her dagger trained on the young woman. Examining her uninvited visitor, she noticed the intruder was unarmed and didn't seem to be much of a threat. She was dressed in a light-blue peasant blouse and leather pants. Raven noted the girl's boots had been repaired a number of times, but they had been well made and expensive once. Blond hair fell in soft curls over her face in a cascade, hiding her features, but the ice-blue eyes staring at Raven were unforgettable. There was an intensity in them that made Raven nervous.

The girl walked over and flopped down on Raven's chair. "I'm here because I wanted to talk with you undisturbed." She crossed her legs and reached for the bottle of brandy — only to find a dagger now imbedded in the table a fraction of an inch from her outstretched fingertips.

"If you're trying to get on my bad side, you're doing a damn good job of it." Raven realized the girl had her at a disadvantage, but she was damned if she'd give her that satisfaction. Carefully retrieving another dagger from the armoire, she continued, "You were the one following me tonight."

The blonde glanced from the knife to Raven and back to the knife. With a deliberate motion, she pulled it out of the tabletop and checked its weight. "Yeah, and believe me, it wasn't easy. You're pretty damn hard to track when you're nervous. I've been trying to find this place for a month."

"A month? What's so important that you couldn't approach me and make arrangements to meet? What's so important about finding this place?" The violation of her sanctuary angered her, but there was something about the girl's story that intrigued her. If there was any truth in it, she was more tenacious than Raven would have suspected.

"I needed to find this place without you spotting me. I figured it was the only way to convince you to let me be your apprentice." A cocky smile crossed her face as she tossed the knife back to Raven.

Raven caught the knife without thinking and started to put it away when the girl's words sank in. "Let you become what?"

"Your apprentice. I want you to train me." She sat up, uncrossing her legs. "I've been keeping track of you for a while and I want to be your apprentice."

Caught off guard, Raven tried to buy some time as she paced back and forth in front of the fireplace. "What's your name?"

"Alexis."

"So, Alexis … if you've been tracking me, you know I don't work with a partner on a regular basis. I'm happy with that and I don't see any reason to change."

"Look, Raven, I'm not a bad thief in my own right. If you could teach me the tricks of the trade, I could be awesome. Why, between the two of us, we could pick the town clean." She paused for a moment, then a sly tone crept into her voice. "I notice you don't mind teaming up with Jerek from time to time."

Raven felt herself blushing at the insinuation. "You'll notice I'm not the 'pick the town clean' type. That's how I've survived so long. Thieves with a reputation draw the attention of professional hunters. I prefer to deal with the amateurs, otherwise known as the City Watch. Besides, you can't be a day over fifteen."

"I turned sixteen a few months ago. That's why I need a new place to stay. The guys at the last place thought I should start 'paying' for the privilege. The last one who said that only needed thirty stitches for *his* 'payment.'" A savage look crossed her face at the memory.

Raven was caught off-guard by the fragile person who peeked out from behind Alexis's mask of bravado. *Not quite as tough and brave as you act, hmm? There has to be some way to get out of this.*

"So what do you say? When do we start?" Alexis's voice broke in on her reverie.

Raven whirled around to face her, a frown fixed on her face. "When do we start? Are you kidding me? Okay, you're sixteen. You have been on the streets, picking a few pockets and breaking into a few houses in the Commons or even the Laborers Quarter. That's a long way from the world I inhabit. I'm not into penny-ante stuff that'll get you killed for a couple of coppers."

"You don't think I know that?" Alexis shot back, her face now a mask of cold fury. "Why do you think I've been tracking you for a month? Come on, Raven, you're the best thief in town and I want to learn from the best."

"I want a million crowns and a flying ship, too, but I don't see it happening anytime soon." Raven's lip curled into a snarl. She saw too much of herself in Alexis. She was not going to be responsible for another person's life. "Besides, you're too young to be admitted into the thieves' guild."

"Oh, like you're in such good standing with them. I've done my homework, Raven. I know you operate on the fringes. They haven't gone out of their way to hunt you down yet. I don't know if you've got something on the guildmaster or if you've got a special deal with him. I don't care either way, but don't throw guild membership at me."

Raven tried taking a reasoning tone with the intruder. "You may have noticed it's not a really good time to be a thief. There are a lot of bodies turning up these days. What if I just refuse to be responsible for your death and kick you out on your scrawny butt?"

"I thought you might respond this way. I don't think you have much of a choice in the matter." Alexis stretched in the chair much like a cat toying with its prey.

That comment brought Raven up short. "You *are* a cocky thing. I'll give you credit for that. Get out of my chair and take that one over there." She pointed to a small straight-backed chair across the room. Alexis shot her a pained look before rising and lowering herself into the uncomfortable seat. Raven took her place in the padded chair and poured a snifter of the brandy.

Swirling the amber liquid, she peered at Alexis over the top of the glass. Looking closer, Raven noted she had the look of a kid who'd been on the streets way too long. She'd seen too many of them since she'd become Raven. "You say I don't have much choice in this matter? What could you have to hold over my head?"

Alexis grinned at her, her youth showing through the facade of maturity she tried to project. Extending her hand, she started ticking off comments on her fingers. "You're a popular person. Some merchants have put a fifty-crown reward for the location of your lair and two hundred crowns for you. I know a couple of thieves are upset you beat them to that shipment of jewels a month ago. Also, I hear some in the thieves' guild are interested where you go every day. They've offered a nice reward for information." She looked around, pretending to be bored. Raven noticed, though, she was tensed to jump if the older thief even flinched. "The way I see it, staying on my good side would be in your best interest."

Raven sipped her brandy and stared at the young woman sitting across from her. A cruel grin crossed her lips as she continued to stare over the snifter's edge. Alexis began to squirm at her unrelenting gaze. She let the young girl sweat for a while, before continuing in a soft, deliberate manner. "There's no guarantee you'll leave here. That, too, might be in my best interest. From what you've said, who'd notice if you … disappeared?"

Alexis's smile faltered but she kept her composure. "Mind if I have a drink?"

"All you had to do was remember you were a guest here and ask. After all, I didn't invite you."

Alexis poured herself a small shot of the brandy and took a drink. From the look on her face, the strong alcohol burned as it went down but she tried to brave it out. Raven tried not to smile at the girl's attempt to match her intensity. After a few seconds, she set the glass down. "I said I did my homework. You've killed before but never killed in cold blood. In fact, you've gone out of your way not to kill someone even if they deserved it, like that one thug working for Douglas. You even paid for him to leave town with his family rather than killing him when you had the chance. That's why people don't turn you over to the watch. Goddess knows, most people could use that kind of reward money." She leaned forward and Raven noticed she was eyeing how far she was from the exit, despite her bravado.

"It's true. I'm not a cutthroat. I like to conduct my business with a minimum of fuss. However, I don't like to deal with people threatening me." The dark-haired thief twirled a knife between her fingers. "This could be an exception to the rule."

"It could be. There's more to you than most people know, Raven."

Raven gave the blond girl a careful glance. It was possible Alexis was a plant. The Black Leopards could be using her, or she could be one herself. However, that wasn't the feeling she was getting from the intense young woman.

Well, you've gotten yourself into a fine mess. She knew her threat was a bluff. *Damn, Alexis has done her homework. I have killed before, but I've never set out to kill someone. That's not a road I want to go down. But what do I do with her?*

She stood up and grabbed the lamp off of the table, startling Alexis. Striding across the room, she opened a door, revealing a small hall and a stairway. "Come here!" Her voice cracked like a whip in the silence and Alexis nearly overturned her chair in her haste to get across the room.

Raven made her way down the hallway and up the stairs, raising a small cloud of dust with every step. She reached the second floor and opened one of the doors there. Alexis was close behind, curiosity getting the better of her.

The open door led to a huge bedroom. Pulling the dust covers off the furniture revealed a four-poster bed covered with silk sheets and a beautiful quilt, while the rest of the stored pieces were made of the finest woods. Raven heard Alexis's sudden intake of breath as she gaped at the opulence.

"This is where you'll stay tonight," Raven said after she lit a couple of the oil lamps. The warm light brought out the richness of the fabrics and woods even more. "Where are the rest of your belongings?"

Alexis walked around the room, gazing at the finery there. She noticed several dresses hanging within the chiffonier. "Belongings? I'm wearing what I own.' She ran her hands over some of the dresses before the import of what Raven had said sank in. She looked over her shoulder at the dark-haired thief standing by the door. "Where I'll stay tonight?"

"Where you'll stay tonight. Until I return tomorrow evening, you will remain on this floor of the house. There is a small kitchen here on this floor as well as a privy. Do not descend the stairs until I summon you. Consider this your first test. If you can do this, I will *consider* training you." Raven waved a hand in front of her, cutting off an excited reply from Alexis. "If I find any evidence you've descended during the day, your training will cease. Above all, if you hear me below, you will not come downstairs until I call for you. Is that understood?"

"But what if—"

"Is that understood?"

"Understood."

"There will be things I ask you to do in the future you may not understand. If I tell you to do something, *do* it, right then, without thinking. I'll explain when there's opportunity to go into more detail. However, if you want to train with me, you have to learn to trust my judgement. If I tell you to do something, it's because I'm trying to save your life. If you hesitate, if you argue, if you disobey, you'll be dead or worse. Do you understand that?"

"Understood."

"Get some rest. We'll begin a few hours after sundown … *apprentice*."

Chapter Fourteen

Perrin leaned on the counter in the bookstore, watching the ocean through the open door. It had been a few days since her visit to the cathedral. Keeping a low profile seemed like a good idea, but still, she was dying to know what the word on the street was.

With the guild in disarray, she wasn't certain about who she could go to for information. Raven still had good connections at the various taverns in the Commons and the Red Quarter, but contacting any this evening might put them at risk. If the Leopards were hunting thieves, they might also be hunting the people who associated with them.

There was nothing to do but wait until nightfall, although in the meantime she could at least see how Alexis was doing. She'd done well the past two nights, demonstrated she actually had some skill. Perrin just hoped the girl had enough sense and good luck to stay alive long enough to use them.

I wish Jerek would stop by, though. If anyone knows what's going on, he would.

She hadn't seen him in the past couple of days. She was supposed to meet his father in a few nights and that frightened her worse than the Black Leopards did. She wasn't sure what he'd told Dominick and she didn't want to embarrass Jerek in front of his father.

Damn that Jerek. How dare he make any plans for the two of us without talking to me! I'm not even sure there is a "two of us" yet. His father sent him to fetch me so he can decide whether or not to approve of me? Am I a horse and he needs to check my teeth? What if I don't approve of him or Jerek? I don't recall agreeing to anything. What was he thinking?

She smiled, thinking about how Jerek and her father had met, but her emotions sank when she remembered the evening afterward. Her father had introduced her to Fiana over dinner. She seemed pleasant enough, although she was a lot younger than Perrin thought she'd be; couldn't be more than ten years older than she. Fiana had got a cute kid, though—thirteen-year-old Ronan would be breaking the girl's hearts in a year or so. Surprisingly, he'd fallen in love with the bookstore the second he saw it. Rory told Perrin that Ronan had acted just like she had when she first started working here—couldn't wait to come back and get some reading in.

Fiana and Perrin tried to be polite, but it was tough. Rory, bless his heart, was oblivious to their awkward interaction the entire evening. However, there was no question he was in love with Fiana; he hadn't even seemed to notice when Perrin retired for the evening.

Speaking of Father, where is he? I thought he was getting our lunch? Probably got caught in a conversation and lost all track of time … again.

She wandered to the front of the store and stuck her head outside. Glancing along the street, she didn't spot him among the townspeople wandering about. Her lips pursed as she contemplated taking the afternoon off to go wandering about herself. It would serve him right. Returning to the counter, she heard footsteps rushing up the steps. She spun about, preparing a proper welcome for her father, when she saw it was Angelina.

Perrin smiled as her friend entered out of breath. "Well, hello. What can I do for you?"

"Oh, Perrin, I just can't believe it!"

"You can't believe … what?" Perrin wondered what new gossip Angelina had brought.

"Well, these men came to my father's shop. Your father was there, too. I think he had your lunch in that basket he was carrying ..."

Perrin cut her off before she could get too far afield. "What was said that you couldn't believe?" While she waited for her friend to compose herself, she relaxed now that she knew where her father was.

"Marauders. They struck the Corconti camp last night. They say you can still see the smoke rising from Hunter's Wood if you know where to look ..." Angelina gave a small yip as Perrin rushed past her to peer across the river, searching for a sign of the Corconti camp. There was a faint column of smoke rising in the afternoon sky as Angelina had said.

Jerek!

"My dad and yours went rushing out as soon as they heard about it. I was supposed to tell you that he'd be back soon and not to worry about him." Angelina continued speaking, oblivious to the panicked look on Perrin's face. "I can't believe anyone would attack the Corconti. It's not like they have anything worth stealing. Maybe someone got tired of having a band of thieves around town."

Perrin wheeled on her friend, but caught herself before she said something that *Perrin* would never say. Most merchants thought the Corconti were nothing more than vagabonds and thieves. Angelina had never spent any time with someone like Jerek; neither had Perrin, as far as anyone knew.

"Who were the men talking to your dad? Did they say anything else about the attack?"

"I think one of them was a guardsman but he wasn't in uniform. I remember him near the gate that leads to Hunter's Wood before. He's been there when Mother and I go mushrooming. The other person was the old guy who runs the stables down by the gate. He'd taken some horses to trade and found the camp. He came back to alert the town in case any marauders were still out there."

Perrin wondered why they were at Bryan's jewelry store until Angelina continued with her story. "It was strange. Before Father left, the guard asked if he had any dealings with the Corconti. Had they tried to sell him any gold statues, gems, jewels, or anything like that? I mean, is he stupid or what? Where would they get jewels or gold objects?"

Perrin's blood ran cold as Angelina continued prattling on about the Corconti. *Oh please, don't let this have anything to do with my visit to the cathedral. I never thought someone might think the Corconti were involved with the Dragonstone's disappearance, much less that they'd attack the camp.*

After listening to Angelina a bit longer, Perrin couldn't take it anymore. "Watch the store for a second, Angelina. I've got to get something." She hurried upstairs and put on her boots. She came down and grabbed an iron key from behind the counter. She carried her father's strong box to a chamber hidden beneath the stairs and secured it. Then she grabbed a shawl, wrapped it around her shoulders, and headed toward the door with Angelina in her wake.

"Angelina, if my father comes back, I've gone to the Corconti camp. Here's the key to the front door. Please lock up and take the key to your father's store. Either my father or I will pick it up there."

"Why would you want to go there?"

"I have a friend in the camp and I want to see if he's all right."

The young girl's grew wide and a silly grin found its way to her face. "Perrin's got a boyfriend." Perrin started to say something, but there wasn't time to play these kind of games.

And Jerek *was* out there.

She hurried through the city, dodging in and out of the throngs of people on the streets. Approaching the city gate, Perrin slowed her pace and tried to blend in with the flow of people entering and leaving the city. Spotting a group of farmers, she slipped into step with them and struck up a conversation with one of the women. Once they'd crossed over the bridge, she took her leave and turned north along the river bank. After a short walk, she turned and disappeared into the wood, finding familiar trails. She had mapped out sections of the forest long ago, just in case she had to flee the city guards.

A twinge of pain hit as she thought about those days. It was just after Sean's execution. Sean had been her first lover and first mentor. He had trained her, back when she was in love not only with him but the adrenaline rush of being a thief. His capture and execution had led to days of blind panic. She was afraid whoever had turned him in knew who she was, too. That fear drove her to learn everything she could about the sewers and the woods. She wanted to be certain if she *had* to disappear, she could. That was before she'd met Bertok. The amulet felt cold against her skin, hidden beneath her dress, but it was a comforting feeling just the same.

Nearing the Corconti camp, she couldn't miss the acrid scent of smoke. It wasn't the typical scent she would have expected to encounter. That smoke carried the spicy scents of their cooking. There was something terribly wrong about this smoke.

She stood at the edge of the clearing, almost afraid to leave the shelter of the woods. Scanning the camp, she was shocked by the scale of the destruction. The Corconti's tents had been burned in the fight. Only a handful of the twenty or so still stood. The survivors were carrying bodies off to one side, and most of the survivors bore wounds of some kind.

Across the clearing, a number of Olghar stallions lay on their side, their throats slit. Perrin's eyebrows rose as she stared at the senseless slaughter. The Corconti were renowned for raising and training these powerful horses. *Marauders wouldn't kill valuable horses. So, if it wasn't marauders, who did this?* Tears welled up in her eyes and she blamed herself again for the death and destruction she saw.

She glanced around, searching for any sign of her father or Bryan. After a while, she spotted one of the men who'd picked up the books at her father's store with Jerek. He was directing two other men sifting through the remains of a tent. Coming out of the woods, she called out, "Dushan! What happened? Where's Jerek?"

The man spun around, a large knife appearing in one hand. Recognition set in and he gave her a sheepish look.

"Ah, the bookseller's daughter. Come with me." She followed him to one of the semi-intact tents where the Corconti women tended to several wounded men. She recognized Dominick, Jerek's father, sitting on a bed. He had a bandage wrapped around his right shoulder and another blood-soaked one on his forehead. He gazed at the bed next to him, the tears making his gruff face seem all too vulnerable.

Dushan motioned her into the tent and then returned to his work. She hurried over to see Jerek lying in the bed next to Dominick. From the pallor on his face, she knew he'd lost a lot of blood. One of the Corconti women had finished changing his bandage and looked at Perrin. She had seen that look of resignation before. The pain in her eyes was easy to read.

Perrin began to leave when Jerek's weak voice stopped her in mid-stride. "This must be heaven, because an angel has appeared to guide me." She turned to see him lifting his head from the rolled-up blanket that served as his pillow.

She rushed back and knelt beside his bed. "Jerek, what happened? How … why … I don't understand. I'm so sorry …" Her words tumbled out as if someone had opened a dike and let the water just pour out.

"Hold on. I'd love to answer you. You have to give me a chance. I'm not quite myself today." He rested his hand on her arm. Perrin bit her lip and tried to slow her emotions down.

Jerek lowered his head and coughed a couple of times. "I think they were from the city. They hit us at night … took out the guards before we had a clue. We made a stand while Dushan and the others rescued as many kids as possible."

Perrin lifted her eyes and looked to Dominick. The leader of the Corconti appeared to have aged overnight, his strong, powerful frame shrunken and his shoulders slumped in defeat. "I think there were around twenty of them; in the darkness, it was hard to tell. I've never seen marauders like them before. They cut down most of our warriors before they could defend themselves. They never had a chance."

"What did they want? You've lived here for years." Perrin feared the answer that was coming.

"They were looking for gems. Didn't say why but they were certain we had some." Dominick looked up, shaking his head. "We gathered up all we had but that only seemed to make them madder. It was like they were looking for something in particular. They grabbed Tereza to encourage us to tell where the others were hidden. That's when Jerek got hurt. He dropped three before one of them got him from behind. At least Tereza got into the woods before they could go after her again."

Jerek opened his eyes and gave her a weak smile. "You always told me women would be the death of me."

"Shhhh. Don't talk." Perrin picked up a cloth and wiped his brow. She could tell he was running a fever and his breathing was shallow.

"No, I need to talk to you. Dom, could we have a little privacy?" He turned his head toward his father and the older Corconti sighed. With a little help from Perrin, Dominick managed to get to his feet and shuffled away.

Jerek grabbed her hand and pulled her closer before she realized what was happening. "Perrin, listen to me. It's not our way to share problems with outsiders, but I know you. Dominick didn't want to tell you they were after the Dragonstone. You're the only one with the skill and courage to beard the church like that. If you took it, be careful."

"Hush now, Jerek. Even if I did take it, why would they come after your people?"

"I don't know. Guess our reputation preceded us. I imagine that's why they're after the thieves' guild also." Jerek laid back on the blanket roll, his eyes staring up at the top of the tent. "They looked like marauders but were too good." She had to lean closer as his voice trailed off. "Had to be Black Leopards. King Marcus is in this … up to his neck."

A spasm of coughing ran through his frame. Perrin rushed to get him a cup of water, but when she returned she knew Jerek wouldn't need it. She ran her hands over his face, closing his unseeing eyes before turning and running out of the tent, tears streaming down her face.

Stopping outside, she tried to pull herself together. She looked around and saw Dominick directing some men to bring the remaining horses to the clearing. The women and children were loading four carts that hadn't burned with whatever they salvaged. Dominick saw her and hurried over to her.

"He's gone, Dominick." She managed to get that out before collapsing into his arms. She was grateful for Dominick's presence but she also felt guilty using him for comfort. *If I hadn't been so stupid, Jerek and all the others might still be alive. It's all my fault.*

Dominick's voice broke through her tears. It was strong and clear, even though it was just above a whisper. "It's all right, Perrin. He wasn't going to last much longer. Honestly, I thought he wouldn't survive the night, but he knew you'd come. Don't know why he thought that. No one had been sent to fetch you. He just knew you'd be here."

Perrin looked around and saw the wounded being led to the carts. "What's going on, Dominick?"

"We are leaving, Perrin. It's time for us to go. We'll take Jerek and the others back to our ancestral lands to bury them. After that? Only the goddess knows. All I know is our time here has come to an end. We may return. We may not. Know this, though, your father and you will always be welcome in our camp."

He paused and then called to one of the young boys in a language Perrin couldn't understand. He ran into the woods and returned with a small box. The boy handed the box to Dominick, then rushed off to help load one of the carts. Dominick shook his head, a smile crossing his lips in spite of his injuries and loss.

"Ah, that Alois. He's my great-nephew. He's got a lot of my sister in him. He's young, but he'll start training to take Jerek's place. He's about all the family I have left." Dominick wiped a hand across his eyes and then handed Perrin the box. "Jerek picked this out for you."

Perrin wanted to push the box away but it was as though

her hands belonged to a different person. She watched her hands untie the small string holding the box lid on and open it. Inside was a wide golden bracelet with a small obsidian raven inlaid in the gold.

She looked up at Dominick, who gave her a sad smile. "Wear that and you will be welcome in any Corconti camp, no matter the tribe. It was to be a wedding present for you." He paused again before continuing. "Besides, I agree with him. Red hair is much more attractive on you than black. Good-bye, Perrin. I do not believe we will ever meet again."

She stood there as the leader of the Corconti motioned for everyone to finish loading the wagons. She tried to speak, but nothing came out. She saw movement in the tent near her and knew they would be bringing Jerek's body out any moment. She turned and fled the camp, unable to face Dominick any longer. As she ran blindly through the woods, she kept seeing the smile Jerek would get when he'd gotten the best of her.

It's not fair.

This wasn't supposed to happen.

It's all my fault.

She had no recollection of her flight through the forest. She didn't know how long or how far she had been running until she stopped and realized she had reached the river. Staring up at the city walls across the river, a flame rushed through her mind.

Her eyes focused on the palace atop the Hill, half hidden behind the old city walls. *No, this is not my fault. Nothing I did made Marcus turn the Black Leopards loose on an unsuspecting people. This is his doing and his alone. By the gods, he will pay for what he's done. Like my namesake, I will bring darkness and ill fortune to them before I am done. If the Royal House did not fear the Raven before, they will now.*

Chapter Fifteen

A sudden knock on the door drew King Marcus's eyes from the sheaf of papers he had been reading. *I thought I told Bela I didn't want to be disturbed. This had better be important.* He placed the papers back inside the leather pouch and secured it in a hidden compartment in his desk. He gazed around the library to ensure there was no evidence of what he'd been researching and then ordered whomever to come in.

Bela opened the door, his gray hair falling over his face as he kept his eyes downcast. He waited for the king to tell him to come in before he pushed the door all the way open. The wizened man led two men dressed in black leathers into the room and motioned for them to wait over by the fireplace. Bela turned to the king for further instructions and Marcus casually waved him out of the room. Bela scurried out of the room and Marcus had a sudden vision of a spider disappearing into its web.

He took his place in a comfortable chair, placing the men between him and the fire. He took his time straightening his shirt, finding a few flaws in a long, flowing sleeve that demanded his immediate attention. He knew from experience that standing in front of the fireplace was uncomfortable. His father had stood him there on more than one occasion. He stared at the two men, watching the sweat become visible on their brows. The Black Leopards' training served them well; no sign of discomfort made it to their faces.

Turning to the one standing on the right, he began, "So,

tell me of your efforts at the Corconti camp."

The first Black Leopard knelt in front of the king and made his report, his voice neutral. "Sire, there was evidence of some thefts. However, we were not able to prove they were involved in the theft of the Dragonstone."

"Survivors?"

"We eliminated most of the males, but some were able to elude us in Hunter's Wood. They are leaving the region, but we are tracking them. We can mount a second expedition against them if you so wish it." Marcus noticed the faintest of quivers in the assassin's voice.

"I see. So our information was incorrect. Make note of that." King Marcus kept his face still as he turned to the second one. "And *your* mission?"

"I contacted our informant in the thieves' guild. He doesn't believe anyone in the guild was responsible, but he will continue to check. He believes the guildmaster has information he keeps from the rest of the guild. That is in keeping with our profile on Quentin. He had no information regarding the attack on Douglas Valio."

"So, in your opinion, should we continue thinning out the thieves to encourage whoever did take the Dragonstone to return it?"

"Sire, I am one of your servants. I have no opinion. I follow whatever orders you give me." The Black Leopard straightened his posture, eyes staring straight ahead.

"I see." The king's eyes narrowed as his voice almost purred. "Very well." He turned to the first Black Leopard. "You may leave."

"Yes, Your Majesty." He bowed and left. Even this close, Marcus found it difficult to hear the assassin's footsteps on the hardwood floor.

The king stared at the retreating Black Leopard before turning around to face the remaining one. "I have two missions for you and your team. I want you to strike the thieves' guild hard. Don't kill the leader but put out the word that if the Dragonstone is not returned soon, it will be unhealthy for any thief in the town, guild member or otherwise."

The king stopped and stared at the ceiling. After a lengthy pause, the Black Leopard prompted, "And the other mission, Sire?"

"The man who just left. His team failed and left witnesses who can warn the real thief. If they cannot carry out a simple task, they're useless to me. Assemble your team and kill them."

Marcus's command was no more impassioned than if he had ordered the cook to prepare a goose for dinner, but there was no questioning the meaning behind the casual tone. The assassin's eyes tightened at the order but his face remained impassive. He bowed his head to the king. "It shall be as you ordered, Sire."

"It had better be. You've shown a lot of promise. I'd hate to have to order your execution also." His smile pinned the Black Leopard in place like a pin through a butterfly. Once Marcus was certain the young man understood him, he released him and sent him on his way.

"Well played, Your Majesty," a soft voice came from behind him.

"Damn you, Kazmer!" Marcus spun around to find his spymaster standing near the doorway. "Someday you are going to presume too much."

Kazmer leaned against the wall, the hood of his cloak pushed back onto his shoulders. His black hair was nearly invisible against his dark skin. It was cropped so close he might as well have been bald. He tapped a dagger against his right wrist, an indolent smile on his face. "My lord, I only have your best interests at heart. I am pleased how you decided to handle the incident with Fridrik. He was marked for death with his failure. You give Osman a chance to prove himself and raise his standing within the Leopards. As I said, well played."

Marcus smiled at Kazmer, although the smile didn't reach his eyes. "I'm so glad you approve. Do you have any information for me?"

"Indeed I do, but what we need to speak of is too important for a place such as this. May I recommend we retire to a more *secure* place?" The large man made a sweeping motion toward the door with his arms.

The king followed the spymaster until they reached a spot halfway down the hall. Kazmer reached up and pulled down on a torch sconce. King Marcus stood agog as a panel in the hallway slid to one side, revealing a stairwell descending into darkness. He'd grown up in this palace and had no idea this passageway existed. His eyes flickered to Kazmer, wondering how many other "surprises" were in store for him. Kazmer was busy lighting the torch and pretended not to notice Marcus's stare.

"This leads down to one of our training areas, Sire." Marcus couldn't help noticing Kazmer's voice failed to cover his pleasure at disconcerting the king. "Spiridon already is waiting down there for us."

Marcus's eyes widened even more. Kazmer had contacted the court magician? Something was afoot tonight. He followed Kazmer down the spiral staircase, passing several passageways that split off from the main stairs. He resolved to investigate this section of the castle now that he was aware of its existence. He was certain the Black Leopards did not value this area, else Kazmer would never have revealed it to him.

Reaching the lowest level, Kazmer led him to a doorway at the end of a short passageway. Removing a large key from around his neck, he unlocked the door and motioned with one hand. "Please, Your Majesty, after you."

Marcus knew the assassin was up to something. He had an annoying habit of acting more subservient the more he was in control of a situation. Sighing, the king decided to play along for now and entered the chamber. As he stepped through, he saw he was on a small landing. Below him, the weapon masters were putting several of the Black Leopards through an obstacle course that seemed to involve gymnastics as much as it did knowledge of weaponry.

He allowed himself a few minutes to enjoy the deadly

grace of his assassins before turning back to Kazmer. "This is all very entertaining, but I believe you brought me down to meet with Spiridon?"

The tone in his voice was not lost on the assassin. He hurried forward, wringing his hands in a feigned apology. "Of course, Your Majesty. He's waiting at the bottom of the stairs." Kazmer glided across the landing and began descending a shadowy stairwell. Marcus followed, amazed as always how the assassin moved without any obvious effort.

A doorway stood open at the bottom of the stairs and the wizened shape of Spiridon was visible through it. The court wizard stood up and motioned to them. "Ah, you've arrived, Kazmer. Good evening, Your Majesty. There are important things we must discuss. Our time is limited."

"What do you mean, old man? Come to the point." Marcus felt the hackles rising on the back of his neck. Spiridon was not his favorite retainer, always talking in possibilities and probabilities. Pinning him down on a subject was like trying to catch a will-o'-the-wisp with your bare hands.

Spiridon didn't reply to the king's nudge. He shuffled over to a table where an object lay beneath a rough blanket. With a quick motion, he pulled the blanket aside and revealed a strange device. If stood upright, it would rest on the three attached legs. A series of dials and gears were visible in the strange metal box atop the legs.

"And this would be …?" Kazmer phrased his question to prod Spiridon along. Marcus glanced to his right and saw the faintest hint of curiosity on the assassin's face. He knew Kazmer was intrigued by the device if he let that much emotion show.

"This would be the device to provide our king the edge he needs in his upcoming battles. Or it would be, except for the fact it's missing the single most important item needed: the Dragonstone!" The wizard's voice rose in volume as his frustration became visible.

Marcus tried to calm the wizard down. "The loss of the Dragonstone is unfortunate. However, we are attempting to resolve that situation. In the meantime, our plans are progressing. With or without the Dragonstone, Helion will fall to us."

"What you say may be true. I am not an expert in the art of war or in the dark arts that Kazmer knows. However, your advisors tell me the battle will be close and the battles beyond may be even closer. This device would guarantee your victory. However, with the Dragonstone's disappearance, time grows short."

"Yes, you said something about time being limited when we arrived, Spiridon. What do you mean?" Marcus read Kazmer's bored tone as a bad sign.

"The magicks holding this device together are fragile. If we have not recovered the Dragonstone by the dark of the moon, I will have to start over from scratch. That means we would have to wait seven months before the device was rebuilt." The wizard scurried over to one of the cabinets in the back of the room like a spider.

"Seven months! Unacceptable."

"I thought Your Majesty would object, which is why I brought this." Spiridon walked to the king with a glass jar and two vials in his hands. He set them on the table beside the device. "The jar contains a resin from a tree that can only be found in one region in the known world. If a rider left today, it would take him three months to reach it. The vials contain magical crystals I have grown in the caverns beneath the castle. Again, it takes time to create powerful components like these. Being powerful, they begin to decay after a certain amount of time."

"There must be another source for these items?" Kazmer held one of the vials up to the light to examine what lay inside.

To King Marcus's surprise, Spiridon stepped forward and snatched the vial out of Kazmer's hands and returned it to its rack. The old wizard had moved faster than either man thought him able to. Marcus filed that bit of information under things to be investigated further and then listened closer to the wizard as he continued. "There is … if I were to requisition them from the College of Wizards. However, questions would be raised—questions we do not want to answer at this time. These are not common items, Kazmer. I can't just walk down to the farmer's market and purchase them."

"I'm certain he wasn't implying you could, Spiridon." Marcus stepped forward to draw the wizard's attention to himself. "So, there are no other items that could replace these ingredients?"

"Gentlemen, we have a little more than three weeks to recover the Dragonstone or else there's no point searching any longer. Either you will have the weapon to ensure your victory or you will not, Your Majesty. There is no middle ground."

The wizard's pronouncement was met by silence. As the seconds stretched on, ideas were thought of and discarded in Marcus's mind until a soft cough caught his attention. Turning, he saw a small smile cross the assassin's face. He noted that it wasn't a very comforting smile.

"Your Majesty," Kazmer said, "I have an idea ..."

Chapter Sixteen

"So, what's on tap for tonight?" Alexis descended the stairs and stretched her arms over her head. Raven noticed the rest and food seemed to be working. She seemed much more relaxed these days than when they'd first met.

"Wait a minute. Have you been changing clothes? Those look like you've slept in them."

"What part of 'I'm wearing all of my belongings' didn't you get?"

Raven gave her a look of disgust. "I would expect you to at least get out of your clothes and into one of those night-gowns upstairs so your clothing can air out."

Alexis put a hand on top of her head and then moved it toward Raven's chin. "You'll pardon me for not being as tall as you."

"All right, that tells me what's on tap for tonight's train-ing. We need to acquire some more fresh food if you're go-ing to stay here for any length of time. Same goes for fresh water. Speaking of fresh, might as well get you some new clothes." She wrinkled her nose as Alexis passed. "And you need a bath."

"What's wrong with the way I smell?"

"Nothing if you enjoy smelling like you rolled off an offal wagon. Here's your first official lesson. A thief avoids draw-ing attention to herself. Strong body odor can be noticed by guards and guard dogs. You are required to change clothes, clean your hair, body, and nails and clean all your gear on a regular basis. Once a day would be optimal."

"Damn, now you sound like my mom." Alexis flumped down in the straight-backed chair. Raven smiled as she noted her protégé left the nice chair for her. As Alexis looked up, she steeled her face into a disapproving look.

"There are some rules if you are going to continue to live here. Remember, this was my sanctuary before you invaded it. By the time I am done with you, apprentice, you'll think your mom was the greatest saint ever to walk on the earth. But, by the gods, you'll be a damn good thief, or you'll be a dead one." She paused to let her words sink in before she continued. "If you remember our earlier conversation, you must remain within this house if I am not with you. I made some mistakes if you were able to track me here. If we are going in and out all the time, I believe a third person will duplicate your success."

"How long do you intend to keep me locked up?"

"You are not locked up. You're free to leave at any time but if you do leave, you'll never be allowed in here again. Again, you sought me out. Either you live by my rules or you don't get trained. It's that simple."

Alexis didn't say anything, but her body language spoke volumes to Raven. She let Alexis stew for a bit before continuing. "We'll be going out every evening for training. I was hoping to keep a low profile for a while. That is no longer an option. However, since you're going to trail along whether I forbade you or not, we need to train you so I'm not wet-nursing you. That'd just get us both killed."

"Thanks for the vote of confidence … Hey, what do you mean, *we're* going to have to train you?" A suspicious look crossed Alexis's face. "Who's this 'we'?"

"What weapons do you use?" Raven continued as if Alexis hadn't said anything.

"I can handle a knife and I throw a mean rock. I've never had much reason to carry a weapon. Are you going to answer my question?"

"In good time. Stand up and extend your arms." Alexis

did as she was told and Raven got up from her chair and walked around her. "Lower your arms and follow me."

The puzzled girl followed Raven to the storeroom. Raven raised the lid on a chest in the far corner, exposing a jumbled mass of weapons. She rummaged around and emerged with a rapier with a black lacquered scabbard, two throwing knives, and a leather blackjack. She set those aside before standing up. Turning around, she noticed Alexis made no move to pick up the weapons.

Alexis pointed at the rapier. "Look, I said I know how to use a knife. If I tried to use that overgrown meat spit there, I'd just wind up stabbing myself."

"That's where the 'we' comes in. Nights you are not training with me, you will begin training with my sword master on the rapier and any other weapons you're interested in learning. You won't be an expert when we begin our mission but at least you won't stab yourself. In fact, I want you to wear the rapier during all your training. You need to learn how to maneuver without banging it into things."

"What do you want me to do with this?" Alexis pulled the left sleeve of her blouse up, exposing an ivory-hilted dagger in a scabbard strapped to the inside of her forearm. Raven berated herself for not noticing it earlier. To give Alexis credit, the flowing sleeve of the blouse provided perfect camouflage. There was more to her apprentice than she'd thought.

"You might as well keep it. I'm assuming you know how to use it?" Raven fought to keep the admiration for her apprentice out of her voice.

"There's a guy over on Black Dog Lane who'll vouch for it. A couple of inches lower and he'd be singing in the choir at the cathedral."

Raven laughed along, but when Alexis mentioned the cathedral, a hint of suspicion reared its head. *She said she's been looking for me for a month. Did she see me staking out the cathedral? Does she know about the Dragonstone? She's going to bear watching for a while.*

Alexis strapped the rapier onto her waist with an awkward motion and slipped it into position. Raven had her practice until she could draw and sheathe the blade without hurting herself before returning to the main room. "So, now that we have you armed, let's take a look at your tools."

"My tools? I'm not a carpenter, I'm a thief."

Raven ran her hand down her face, trying not to show her frustration. "What do you use when you're breaking into someone's house? How do you get past the locks on a chest?"

"For a house, I find a place that's not locked or else I use a rock to knock out a window. If the chest is small, I take it with me and use a crowbar later. Otherwise, I ignore it and grab something else."

"We've got a lot of work ahead of us. All right, come with me. We've got to get you cleaned up and properly equipped, and start an intensive training program. If you're going to be of any use, you're going to have to be as adaptable as I think you are."

Alexis grinned at her. "Let's get going."

"I hope you're this enthusiastic by the end of the evening."

* * *

A short trip through the city's sewers led them to the edge of the Merchants' Quarter. The ladder to the surface led into a dilapidated building. Raven helped Alexis through the trapdoor and secured it, putting a worn rug over the top. Slipping past the broken furniture Raven edged up to the window to check out the street. There were a few people wandering around. Still, if they timed it right, they should be able to slip out without being spotted.

Alexis joined her at the window. "You use the sewers a lot, don't you?"

"You know a better way to get around without people spotting you? Come on, our first stop isn't far from here." She waited until a city watchman disappeared around the corner before she slipped out and moved into the shadows. She was pleased to find Alexis right behind her. She led

Alexis down the alley until they reached the back door of a dressmaker's shop.

She motioned for the young thief to move up next to her. She took out her tools and a small glowing gem. She handed the gem to Alexis and showed her how to cup her hand around it. Then she showed her apprentice the tool to use to pick the lock on the back door and why she didn't use the others in her small pack. She knew it was taking longer to show Alexis what she was doing than it would take to pick the lock, but a dressmaker's shop was a better place to practice than say a jewelry shop.

A quick twist and she felt the tumblers shift. She gave the door a soft tug and it slid open a crack. Alexis reached for it but Raven stopped her hand just short of the handle. A shake of her head told the young thief she needed to relax and watch. It wasn't her turn yet.

Raven opened the door a bit wider and waited for any response. When she was certain no one had noticed, she eased the door open enough for Alexis and her to slip through, then pulled it shut behind her. She pulled a second gem out of her pouch and commanded it to give off light.

Alexis moved up close to her. "What do we do now?"

Raven winced and replied in a whisper. "We're going to try and find something that you like. We'll get the material from here and I'll commission a dressmaker in the Laborers' Quarter to make you some clothes."

"Oh."

"Now, if we can concentrate? I credit my success to minimizing time on site. Get in and get out as soon as possible. What colors do you like?" Raven gave her a look designed to impress her point.

"Blue, rose, maybe a purple if it's not a wine color." Alexis raised her eyes toward the ceiling as she thought. "I remember having clothes like that when I was little."

"We'll see what we can find." Raven sent Alexis off in one direction while she went the other. The two canvassed the shop, picking out items they wanted. She could almost see the hands on the Great Clock on Abraham's Tower moving. After locating several bolts of cloth and other accessories, Raven tapped Alexis on the shoulder and pointed toward the doorway. Raven could feel Alexis's eyes boring into her as she counted out a few coins and left them on the counter. The dark-haired thief joined her at the door and opened it an inch or so. Alexis started to say something but Raven cut her off with a swift move.

Looking through the crack between the open door and the jam, Raven saw a city watchman making his way up the alley. Raven watched him as long as she could through the small opening. After he passed beyond view, she counted to ten and opened the door, looking for any sign of him. She spotted him at the far end of the alley.

Raven motioned for Alexis to take their goods and hide behind a small barrel a few feet away. Once Alexis reached the barrel, she flattened against the wall before sliding down behind it. Her fluid movement and tactics impressed Raven. She might be raw on technical skills, but her basic technique was very smooth.

Stepping into the alley, Raven eased the door shut and locked it. Hiding in the shadows next to the door, she waited until the watchman moved around the corner. They made their way back to the ramshackle building and Raven peeked in to ensure it was still unoccupied before the two slipped inside.

"There are a few bags in the bottom dresser drawer. I keep a few here, just in case." Raven peered through the windows for any sign of the city watch. "Go put your stuff in there and I'll get us something to drink."

"A drink sounds good. What the heck was that back in the shop?"

"What was what?" Raven opened a concealed panel on one wall and pulled out a clay jug. She brought it over to a table and sat it down, halfway between the two women.

"Why did you pay for the stuff we stole? If you were going to pay for it, why didn't we go out and just buy it when they were open?" Alexis paced back and forth and then spun around to face Raven. "I don't like feeling like someone's making a fool of me."

"Apprentice, pay attention. You sought me out. I didn't go looking for you. Everything we have done this evening has been training; you don't know the sewers, so I showed them to you. I hope you were paying attention since you're guiding us back to the lair. You don't know how to pick locks or properly enter a building without exposing yourself. I'm trying to teach you how to stay alive. You need to get that chip off your shoulder and realize there's a reason for everything I do."

Raven paused to open the bottle and pass it to Alexis. Her apprentice took the bottle, trying to hide her trembling fingers. It seemed Raven's outburst startled her more than she wanted to admit. Raven paused to let the words sink in before continuing. "There's no need to make an enemy of that dressmaker. She didn't make as much money on that cloth as she wanted but at least she got something. Now she's less motivated to contact the watch tomorrow. That's another lesson. There are merchants who deserve to been taken and there are those who're not bad people. The requirement is to know who they are."

"You make it sound so easy. I can't just go into the Merchants' Quarter or the Royal Quarter to see who's who."

"You can and you will once I know you can be trusted out by yourself. We'll deal with that another night. However, you've got one more test tonight. I hope you were paying attention."

"Trusted out by myself?" Alexis's response gave Raven a vision of a cat arching its back. "I've been taking care of myself for a while, thank you very much."

"Now is not the time for this conversation. You seem to enjoy jewelry from the way you were looking at mine."

"Yeah, what of it? Jewels are not only beautiful, they're small and portable and on occasion, they're enchanted like this one. Pound for pound, it's almost always better to grab a jewel or a piece of jewelry than a sack of gold coins."

Raven found herself nodding. "Almost always is the correct answer. What would be some reasons against taking jewelry?"

Alexis ticked off on her fingers. "Some pieces are too distinctive. Sometimes, it's more trouble than it's worth to tear a piece apart and separate the good gems from the decorative ones. In addition, jewelry isn't easy to spend. You have to find someone you trust to give you a good price for it. Even then, they're going to give you about half of what it's worth."

"Spoken like someone who's dealt with fences before." Even though Alexis was cocky and sported a bit more attitude than she liked, Raven saw definite possibilities. She took the jug back and resealed the cabinet before motioning for Alexis to follow.

They slipped out the door and headed toward the nicer part of the Merchants' Quarter. Raven had considered taking Alexis to a specific jewelry store, but her protégé wasn't up to the Royal Quarter yet. Instead, the one she had picked out for Alexis had just received a shipment from a neighboring kingdom. There should be some choice pieces still there. Moreover, the jeweler was a rude, obnoxious man who went out of his way to belittle her father's bookstore. A little payback never hurt, either.

They moved through the streets and alleys, using hand signals when there was enough light to see each other. Unlike the Commons, this part of town had a few streetlamps here and there to help the City Watch. It was nice being able to see where they were going, but it slowed them down, having to select better hiding places to avoid the watch.

Moving down an alley, Raven spotted a familiar shape in the shadows ahead. She motioned for Alexis to stay where she was and advanced on the shadowy figure. After a short wait, the figure tensed up, realizing someone was right behind him. He spun around to find Raven's rapier already pointed at him. The sight of thirty inches of steel aimed at his throat arrested his motion. His dagger dropped from his nerveless fingers as his eyes followed the thin steel blade to see whose hand held it. A small smile made its way to his swarthy face unbidden.

"Glad to see it's you, Raven. I was afraid you'd been caught up in all the ugliness going on with my fellow thieves." The man's thin voice carried in the alleyway.

"Save it, Cedric. First off, they're not your fellow thieves. If I recall, you were expelled from the guild for shorting them on their cut. How long did it take for those wounds to heal?"

The small man winced at Raven's words. "That's all water under the bridge. Quentin and I decided to let bygones be bygones. No reason to bring up ancient history."

"You know, I imagine Quentin would be interested to hear I'd seen you this evening. You know, word on the street says someone ratted the thieves' guild out. Know any ex-members of the guild who might harbor a grudge?"

"Now, Raven, let's not be hasty." He reached up to guide the tip of her sword just off-line. "I had nothing to do with that. If I had, don't you think I'd be long gone from Sagras? I'm one of the first people they'd suspect. Besides you, that is." His last comment was followed by a large gulp as the tip of Raven's sword pushed slightly into the skin of his throat.

"What did you say?" There was no questioning the dangerous quality of her voice. His forehead broke out in sweat as he fumbled for the right thing to say.

"You know, I would never think of such a thing. You heard the thieves' guild got hammered last night? Word is you and that Jerek guy were an item. Well, he got killed and then the guild got gutted. Some are saying you might have ratted out the guild to get back at whoever set Jerek up."

Raven felt the rapier go limp in her grasp as the enormity of what Cedric said hit her. He scrambled several feet from her before she regained her senses. From the expression on his face, Cedric recognized he'd said too much. She began advancing on him, rapier at the ready.

"Sometimes I think you talk too much, Cedric, but now you're going to keep talking. What did you mean, 'get back at whoever set Jerek up'?"

Cedric gulped and then answered, his voice almost a squeak as the words escaped. "Did I say that?"

"You did and it may be the last thing you say if you don't come up with the right answer in the next couple of seconds."

Cedric stared at the tip of the rapier and then answered in a slow calming voice. "I heard someone didn't care much for Jerek, so he put out the word that whatever the king's looking for, the Corconti might have it. And before you ask, I don't know who. I got the word from a guy at the bar who'd heard it from someone else. It's not like people keep me up to date with stuff."

"Mainly because you'd sell the information to the first guard for a drink and a place to sleep."

"Nah, I'd spend it all on the drink. Sleeping you can do anywhere."

"That's probably the first honest thing you've said to me all night. Now, perhaps you want to keep being honest and tell me who is implying I'm behind the thieves' guild's problems. I'd love to see what they'd say to my face." A small smile settled on her face but it just made Cedric feel more uncomfortable.

"Now, look, Raven ... let's be reasonable. I said *I* didn't believe them. I just thought you should know what some people are saying." He tried to back down the alley without tripping on something.

"So, who *are* these people?" She drew a dagger with her right hand, while the tip of her rapier made little clockwise motions.

The cowering thief's voice was almost incomprehensible through his sobbing. "I don't know. I never saw them before. You know I got kicked out of the guild a while ago. They've added a buncha new guys since then. You can't kill me because I don't know someone's name!"

"Get out of here, Cedric; you disgust me. If I see you in the Merchants' Quarter again, I'll kill you on the spot." She paused to let her warning sink in. Cedric's eyes opened wide as he realized she wasn't going to kill him, at least not right then. As he started to rise, her voice cut him like a whip. "If you were smart, and I know you're not, you'd leave town as soon as the city gates open. I hear there's a market for incompetent thieves in Tongra. It's about a two-week journey, but a change of scenery might do you good."

Cedric scrambled toward the entrance to the alley. As he reached the opening, he looked back over his shoulder. "Some guy was asking about you at the Cup and Crown tonight. Said if any of us ran across you to let him know. Said he'd make it worth our while."

"And this is supposed to frighten me?"

"You said a lot of hurtful things tonight, Raven. Still, nothing you said is a lie and Dashin knows I deserve worse. Since you're sparing my life, I'll try to return the favor. Stay away from that one. There was something wrong about the way he was asking about you. *Dead* wrong, if you follow my meaning."

Cedric disappeared around the corner of the building before Raven could question him about the stranger. She approached the entrance, but the small man was gone by the time she got there. She saw a watchman approaching with a lantern and retreated back to where Alexis waited.

She felt the hot stare of the young thief on her. "Whoa, you gave that guy the business. Was he as bad a thief as you made him out to be?"

"Actually, Cedric was a good burglar. There are advantages to being thin and wiry. However, he's greedy and a coward—two bad qualities in this line of work. He deserved to be expelled from the guild." She sheathed her rapier, surprised at how shaky her hand was.

"But *you're* not in the guild ... " Confusion was evident in Alexis's voice.

"No, I'm not. If I joined, I'd be honor-bound to follow their rules. Quentin knows I can't and he respects my honesty. That's why he allows me to operate without interference." The dark-haired thief leaned against the wall, trying to get her emotions under control. She was too keyed up to take

Alexis on her test as it was.

Alexis waited a few moments and then plunged ahead. "I see. So, was he right about that Jerek guy?" Raven shot her a dirty look and she changed the subject. "Okay, bad question. Do you think he'll leave town?"

"I hope so, for both of our sakes." Raven glanced up the alley and saw the watchman's lantern light growing stronger as he approached the entrance. Raven and Alexis found more secure hiding places and waited until darkness settled over them once more. Once she was certain the watchman wasn't standing there with his lantern covered, she motioned for Alexis to come over.

"Are you ready to continue?"

Alexis checked herself over and tugged the rapier back into place. "I think so, if I can leave this overgrown pigsticker outside with you." She turned to make room for Raven to take the lead, but touched Raven on the shoulder. "You're not going to check up on that person, are you? Smells like a trap to me." There was an awkward pause when Raven didn't answer. Alexis ran a hand through her curls and looked back at Raven. "You *are* thinking about it, aren't you?"

"Yes, I am." A guilty expression settled on Raven's face. "I have a reputation in this town. I can't afford to just ignore him."

"There's more to it." Alexis's voice was alive with conviction. "You're up to something."

"As I said, I have a reputation in this town. My reputation is what keeps people from turning me into the guards when I'm hiding. My reputation is I may be a thief, but I'm an honorable thief. I've gone to a great deal of trouble to ensure people can trust me and someone is out there trying to ruin me. This man might be a lead to find out who's behind this smear campaign. Whoever's behind that is probably involved in the attacks on the Corconti and the guild."

Raven paused, getting a grip on her emotions, and then turned to Alexis with a smile. "But that can wait for another evening."

Chapter Seventeen

"All right, tell me again, why the hell are we here?"

Alexis's questions rang in Raven's ears for what seemed the thousandth time. She looked back over her shoulder at her young companion. "Remember last night when I said I can't lay low? Well, this is it. The Black Leopards killed Jerek and they don't do anything unless the king says so. We're scouting the palace because he owes me and I intend to make him pay."

"But it's the *palace*. It's not like we're breaking into a little mom-and-pop jewelry store."

"Why do you think I've been driving you so hard? There's no margin for error, but I need a partner. Like it or not, you volunteered."

Raven came to a halt at a corner of an alleyway and made a downward motion with her palm. Alexis stepped back without a second's hesitation and pulled her cloak up around her face and hair to hide them. Raven withdrew into the shadows, watching as a Royal Guard patrol passed by their hiding place.

By the gods, the guards are thick as fog tonight. Something stirred them up. We've been running into them ever since we reached the Royal Quarter. Alexis is right, though. She's further along in her studies than I could have hoped, but this is no place for a half-trained thief. Still, she'd have tagged along anyway. At least, this way I can keep her out of trouble. I hope.

"What's down this alley that's so important anyway,

Raven?"

"I found a spot for a base camp. There's a secluded garden near the back wall of the keep. I can bring a few items at a time we might need and store them there. Less suspicious than hauling everything at once."

Besides, I need to do some on-site reconnaissance. All of those days working for Tybalt are starting to pay off. I've almost mastered the vanishing powder, but there's not enough time to make more than a couple of doses. I want to save it for the actual strike. Let's see how well just good old thieving pays off. Somewhere in there is something I can steal that'll hurt King Marcus more than just killing him would.

I wish I knew what was going on with Bertok. I've sent three messages to him and he hasn't responded yet. I hope the old fool hasn't gotten himself in trouble.

Focus, Raven, focus! Worry about what you're doing now and worry about other things back at the lair over a nice brandy. Otherwise, you're not going to get home to worry about them.

Alexis slipped over to where she was standing. "I think they're gone. Should we get going again?"

Raven nodded, a grim smile on her face. Without a word, she began flitting from one building to another. Keeping her movements smooth, exposing herself for a few seconds at a time, she made her way down one of the main thoroughfares until she disappeared down a narrow alleyway. She slowed to ensure Alexis saw where she'd gone. Once her apprentice turned the corner, she picked up her pace again.

The alley reeked from the accumulation of garbage. The remains of crates, barrels, and other unidentified items made transiting the alley tricky. It wasn't the alley's cleanliness that attracted Raven, though, it was its location. She had spotted this alley while she was "clearing her head" from the fumes at the alchemist's shop. This alley led to a gap between two buildings. On the other side was a deserted lane running behind the palace. If there was a way in, that was where she'd find it.

She waited for Alexis at the end, taking shallow breaths to

avoid the overwhelming stench. Once her apprentice was in sight, she turned sideways and began the torturous passage between the two stone buildings. The opening wasn't blocked by a gate or some standard obstacle, probably because it was so narrow. The average man would never fit but Raven was just thin enough. By keeping her back against one wall, she managed to sidestep down the passageway.

She turned her head and saw Alexis pause at the opening before taking a big gulp and following her mentor. Raven smiled with pride in her student. She knew it wasn't easy for Alexis to trust her without question, after growing up on the street as she had. If they both survived, Alexis might be the better thief in a few years.

Raven winced when projections dug into her back or legs but she forced herself to keep moving. These stones were much rougher-hewn than ones down the Hill. After an eternity, the passageway widened and they were able to step out into the cobblestone lane. One side was lined with large hedges surrounding the yards. The other side was the back wall of the palace. They'd reached their destination.

A sudden noise sent them scurrying back into the passageway. They waited as a guard patrol made its way down the lane. As the light from the torches faded, Raven motioned Alexis to follow her to the back of the palace wall.

Raven noted the lane was several feet lower than the back wall, and the area beneath the wall was lined with cut stones and mossed over. She ran her hand over the moss and noticed it wasn't secure on the rocks. *Oh, they're good. This stuff will scuff and come loose the second a boot hits it. I might be able to get a line up to the top of the wall, but even with a running start, there's no way I'd clear the moss. The guard would have to be blind not to note my passage.*

"All right, you dragged me here. What's the plan?" Alexis stared up at the imposing wall rising into the night sky in front of her.

"There is no plan, current or otherwise. That's why we're here. We're going to devise one." Raven pulled out her small telescope and examined the crenellation at the top of the wall, looking for anything that might give her inspiration.

Raven pointed to a two-story house down the lane. "I need you to climb up to the top of that house. That should be a good place to watch the top of the wall through the telescope. Try and spot every guard and note whether they're on patrol or stationed up there. If they're patrolling, I need to know how long it takes for them to complete one trip. Also, note how many different guards you see."

Alexis's face pinched into a frown. "That's going to take a while." A quick look at Raven's expression halted her follow-up comment and she secured the telescope and scurried away before her mentor could explain reality to the apprentice thief.

She's got potential, but she's got to learn discipline. You can't waltz into some place like this. This is going to be the toughest thing I've ever done in my life.

She continued to examine the grounds outside the castle walls. There were no guards stationed at the back wall of the castle. It soon became clear why: there were no openings of any kind that she could find. The more she looked at the wall, the more convinced she was this was *not* the way to get into the castle.

She found a secluded spot and settled in to watch for patrols. She began a count in her head after the first one passed by. Every patrol was made of six guardsmen and she noted one of them checked the mossy wall. Her instincts had been right regarding the moss. It wouldn't surprise her if it had been specifically cultivated just for that purpose. Her father knew most of the people who handled landscaping up in the Royal Quarter. Odds were that if she asked just right, she could find out who'd done this—not so much for getting into the castle, but if she ran into it again somewhere else here in town.

She counted to 600 before the next patrol passed. She knew before it arrived it was a different patrol since they were walking in the same direction. There was no way they could have circled the palace. From their shuffling gait and downcast expressions, they had a while to go before they were relieved. She filed that information away with the rest of tonight's discoveries. Even though it looked as though this was a wasted trip, it might pay off another night.

Several patrols passed by, all maintaining about the same pace, before she saw Alexis creeping down the lane. If she hadn't known Alexis was there, she might have missed her altogether. Calling out in a stage whisper, Raven drew her into the shadows and waited for her report.

"The guards remain on station positioned about every thirty feet apart. I watched for an hour and they were not relieved in that time. It would be a miracle if anyone could scale that wall, period. I don't have any idea how you could do it without being detected. In fact, if I was a guard, I'd let them climb most of the way up before cutting their line. I imagine these cobblestones would halt a falling body rather well." Her sardonic tone was unmistakable as she rubbed her arms against the chill of the night air.

"I agree. This is not the way to get into the palace. We'll have to research some other options."

Making their way back down the lane, Alexis turned to her. "Are you certain there's no way to reach the palace through the sewers?"

"That's not what I said. The sewers begin at the palace and work their way toward the sea. It's simple to reach the palace via the sewers. I said we *can't* get there through the sewers."

"But if the sewers go all the way to the palace ... Oh, you're saying it's not safe to go to the palace via the sewers."

"I'm saying the sewers near the palace are crawling with guards, Black Leopards, traps, alarms, and even a few creatures the Black Leopards don't want to fight."

"Well, if we can't go under and we can't go over, that pretty much leaves going through, and I think they'll notice the battering ram." Alexis ducked to avoid being hit by Raven.

"I thought about it. Not like that, don't be ridiculous. I

meant stowing away and being taken inside. However, the guards inspect everything. They even open barrels and crates before they are admitted. No, there must be another way. There is no such thing as an impenetrable fortress. There's always a crack somewhere."

They were approaching the Royal Quarter's wall when a rustling in a hedge caused them to freeze in place. Raven flexed her left hand and small needles extended from the fingertips of her glove. Liquid glistened in the dim light from these claws. After a few moments, a young boy stuck his head out of the foliage and looked up the street at her.

"Excuse me, but are you Raven?"

"Why would I admit to it, even if I was?" She hated being off-balance like this.

"I have a message for a dark-haired woman named Raven from Quentin. If you're not her, I'll be on my way." He withdrew his head into the hedge. Raven rushed up, only to see him laying where she'd last seen him. "Ah, I thought you were her."

Cheeky little guttersnipe. She forced a smile onto her face. "All right, you said you have a message for me?"

"Indeed I do," he said, holding out an empty hand.

For a split second Raven was tempted to grab the kid by the collar and pin him against a tree. The moment passed and she fished out a silver half-crown and handed it to the kid. He stared at it for a second before it vanished inside his shirt. "Quentin says meet him in the small room behind the Brown Bear. Said you'll know how to get there. Said he has information you might find useful."

"Quentin says a lot, doesn't he? Since when does Quentin volunteer information?"

"Hey, no skin off of my nose, lady. Quentin does what he wants when he wants. I don't care as long as I get paid." The kid looked up at her with the coldest eyes she'd ever seen. He nodded to Raven, stared at Alexis for a second, then stepped back into the hedge. Within seconds, there was no sign he'd ever been there.

If not for the memory of the child's eyes, Raven might have believed it was a daydream, so completely did he disappear. She resolved to avoid this kid when he got older; he seemed like the perfect candidate for the Black Leopards if they found him.

"Wow, that kid was a little intense."

Raven turned and nodded her head at her apprentice. "Just a little. Let's go. I'm curious to see what Quentin wants. I guess the Leopards haven't gotten him yet."

"You think it's safe? His seeking you out seems too convenient."

Raven could only shrug. "Who knows with Quentin? He didn't get to be the leader of the thieves' guild by playing it safe. If he's going to all the trouble to summon me, the least I can do is see what's on his mind."

* * *

Reaching the alley behind the Brown Bear tavern, Raven stopped short and pulled Alexis into the shadows. Letting her eyes adjust, she scanned the alley and the rooftops for any signs of watchers. After a few minutes, she was satisfied that either there was no ambush or it was too well concealed for her to spot.

"You see that building there, the one with the false front on it? No, don't look at it. Just casually look around and tell me if you see it."

Alexis made a show of stooping down to pick up a rock and then stood up. "Yes, I can see it."

"Good. I need you to climb up there. Find a good spot where you can watch the meeting place. You've still got my telescope, don't you?"

"Yes. What do you want me to do when I get there?"

"With any luck, you won't have to do anything but not fall asleep. Be certain you're not spotted and that you're alone up there. If there's someone up there, keep a close eye on them. Don't do anything unless you think he's a threat. If something starts to happen, scream and then run like hell. I can take care of myself, but I'll feel better if you're out of the area."

"I couldn't desert you like that." She started to continue, but Raven held a hand up to her lips and stared into her eyes.

"That's not a request. That's an order. If you don't follow these instructions to the letter, then don't come back. You won't be allowed in. Remember our agreement." Alexis stepped back, raising a hand to her cheek as if Raven had slapped her.

"All right now, let's go," Raven said, her voice lightening as if nothing had transpired. She headed down the alley, confident that Alexis would follow her instructions. Even though she was expected, she found herself hugging one of the walls in the alley and keeping an eye on the rooftops.

Reaching the back door to the Brown Bear, she stepped to the side. Placing her back against the building, she reached out and knocked on the door with the back of her right hand. Her left hand rested lightly on her rapier, even though she knew she'd be cut down before she could draw it if this was an ambush.

A rough voice called out, "Come on in. It's unlocked."

Taking a deep breath, she set a nonchalant look on her face and swung the door open. A small fire burned in the fireplace and there were three shadowy figures in the room. Raven entered and then stepped to the side, shutting the door behind her. As her eyes adjusted to the light, she could see Quentin sitting behind a desk, flanked by two large men. From their armor and scars, Quentin had acquired some heavy-duty guardians. She spotted a chair and waited until Quentin nodded. She brought the chair to the desk and sat down, making certain her hands went nowhere near any of her weapons.

Once she was comfortable, she waited for Quentin's next move. He sat there with his fingertips forming an inverted V in front of his mouth, making it hard for her to read his emotions. Once he was certain he had her attention, he lowered his hands to the desk and leaned forward. "No doubt you've heard of the guild's problems?"

"Yes." She decided not to volunteer information until she saw where he was going.

"Would you happen to know anything about it?"

"Only what I've heard on the streets. A rumor here, a snippet of conversation there. Nothing I can put my finger on."

"I thought so. Perhaps we should hold this conversation in private?"

Quentin motioned for her to follow him. The first of the enforcers walked over to the fireplace and tugged on one of the bricks. A section of the floor slid back, exposing a darkened stairwell. The other enforcer brought him a lamp and Quentin motioned for the guards to stay there. The two guards took positions on either side of the door as Raven and he went below.

The spiral stairwell led to a comfortable room below the original one. Quentin used the lamp to light others around the room, giving the room a warm glow. He sat down in one of the overstuffed chairs and poured himself a drink. "Please sit down, Raven. We have much to talk about tonight."

She accepted the drink Quentin poured for her and looked around the room. A few paintings adorned the walls and some exquisite figurines and pottery were arranged in the room. The room was disconcerting given his rough-and-tumble image. She leaned back in her chair, waiting for him to make the first move.

Quentin noticed her examining the room. "Yes, it's a nice place. Too bad it isn't mine. I have a friend who lets me borrow this place for delicate negotiations."

"Ah, this didn't seem quite your style of decor." The whiskey was smooth and quite appropriate for the room.

"Oh, don't get me wrong, I have my collection of baubles also. One doesn't become the head of a guild, even a guild of thieves and cutthroats, without acquiring a taste for finer things. I don't intend to be a thief forever, although I hadn't planned on retiring quite this soon. That brings us to why I summoned you. By the way, I appreciate your promptness. I know you're not in the guild, lass, but there are times we have to cooperate to save all our skins."

Raven set the whiskey down on the small table next to her chair. Quentin was acting peculiar and there was no reason to let the whiskey screw up her senses also. "You mentioned the troubles the guild has run into, upstairs?"

"Indeed. The Black Leopards hit the guild hard. We had thirty-seven people turn up dead in three nights. Also, I heard about what happened to Jerek's camp. There were six members of the guild killed there. I think there are only twelve of us left in the entire town."

"That's horrible. I knew something was wrong when even the Daughters of the Night were hiding."

"They've been leaving a cryptic message around town. They say the thief who stole it—whatever *it* is—knows what they're looking for. Very interesting, wouldn't you say?"

Raven picked up her glass and held it in front of her face, watching the light reflect off the cut crystal. "Yes, quite cryptic."

"In fact, considering a conversation I held with someone a few nights before this happened … well, the timing is peculiar, don't you think?" Quentin leaned forward and rested his elbows on his knees.

"Could be a coincidence." She kept her eyes on him, trying to figure out where this conversation was going. If he suspected her, why not just come out and say it?

"You're right, it could be. However, the Black Leopards took something important from both of us. They destroyed my guild. It would take years to rebuild it and I'm too old and set in my ways to start over. On the other hand, they took Jerek from you, which I suspect hurts you a lot more than losing the guild haunts me." There was no doubt. Quentin *knew* Raven was the source of his problems.

She lowered her hand near a throwing dagger. "So where do we go from here?"

"Why, my dear, we take our revenge. You started this

mess so you get to clean it up. I want you to hurt King Marcus, humiliate him, do something so dramatic it'll keep him up at night wondering if you're coming back to finish the job. After tonight, I doubt you and I will ever meet again, but I will know whether you succeed or not. But if you fail to follow the only order I've ever given you, I *swear* every thief within one hundred miles will know you were the one."

"You know I didn't betray the guild. I never did anything to hurt the guild!" Raven tossed the now-empty glass across the room. The sound of glass shattering did not change the cold smile on Quentin's face.

"No. I know that. I knew the Black Leopards had been infiltrating the guild for years. We've arranged some *accidents* but we were never certain we'd taken care of them all. Call it unfair if you wish but you *will* be my instrument of revenge …" Quentin's voice trailed off, but Raven could hear the "or else," at the end.

"Damn you, Quentin, just because you don't have the guts …" She halted in mid-sentence as he raised a hand.

"I have made arrangements. In two days, be at the Golden Eagle tavern in the Merchants' Quarter. A man name of Galen will meet you there. It would be useful to be your charming self when dealing with him. He's retired but don't let that fool you. He's forgotten more about thievery than both of us will ever know."

Raven crossed her arms and stared at Quentin again. "So, what information will this sage be imparting to me?"

A most unpleasant smile crossed the guildmaster's face. "You'll want to listen to his stories, lass. As far as I know, he's the only person who ever found a way into the Great Keep and returned to tell the tale."

Chapter Eighteen

"Bertok! Get your ugly face downstairs!" Raven's voice rang out in the wizard's hovel. Alexis tried to find a clean spot to sit down while Raven paced through the room, trying not to trip over the junk on the floor.

Bertok's voice thundered down the stairs. "Is that any way to speak to your mentor, Raven?"

"I have questions and you better have answers, old man. You got me into this and, by Praxil, you're going to get me out of this." Raven's reply matched him decibel for decibel.

"Praxil? I thought you a follower of Santi the way you act. And just what have I 'gotten you into'?" Bertok appeared at the bottom of the stairwell, his grayish-brown robes askew and his hair flying in all directions. "Last I checked, you got into enough trouble without my assistance. And who is this person you've dragged into my home without so much as a by-your-leave? What if I hadn't been expecting company?"

"What, your place would be even filthier?"

Bertok's lip curled in a snarl as he dropped into his chair. The small cloud of dust that rose only seemed to infuriate him more. Raven leaned back in her chair and interlaced her fingers across her raised knee. Alexis's gaze flickered between the two. "Should I wait outside?"

"So, have you been keeping up with your lessons?" Bertok leaned forward, resting his elbows on his knees.

"As much as I've been able to. You see, there's this little matter of the Black Leopards hunting me. Also, if you haven't noticed, bodies are piling up in the city faster than you can clear them away."

"Fine. We'll dispense with the lesson until later. Again I ask who is this person you've brought with you? Why is she here? Does she have a clue what we're talking about?"

"Bertok, this is Alexis, my apprentice. Alexis, this is Bertok. He's a hedge wizard of dubious qualifications, and my mentor." A dry chuckle halted her. "Did I say something humorous, Bertok?"

"Your apprentice? What happened to the 'I never want to be responsible for anyone but myself' Raven?"

"For your information, I didn't choose my apprentice. She sought me out and had an effective argument for taking her on."

"I'm sorry for the interruption. Please continue. How much does she know? Before I can help you, I need to know how freely I can speak."

"Alexis knows something is wrong in the city, but she doesn't know I'm at the heart of the storm—at least she didn't until right now. If she's to be my apprentice and be of any use to me, though, she's going to be brought up to speed in a hurry." Raven turned to see a confused look on Alexis's face.

A red flush extended up the young thief's cheeks. "Hold on a minute. When you told me the other night you were upset at the king, somehow you forgot to mention the Black Leopards were hunting *you*. I knew they'd hit the thieves' guild, but this is a little different. Is there anything else you'd like to share?"

"I've been testing you these past few days. I had to see how much I could trust you, Alexis. You appeared out of nowhere just as this started. You could have been a Black Leopard for all I knew."

She saw Alexis struggling to keep her temper under control. "And now ...?"

Raven turned to Bertok. "So, what do you think?"

"Unless she's well trained, magically masked, or a pathological liar—none of which she appears to be—I'd say I got a good reading from her. She's hurt, angry, confused, and thinking things best left unsaid. But, no, she is not a threat to you … or me. In fact, she probably needs some training. Her thoughts are crystal clear to me."

"If you're reading my mind, old man, read this."

Bertok's grin grew wide. "Anatomically impossible, but your sentiment is understood. I *will* get out of your head …" Alexis cut him off with a sudden intake of breath and he gave her a kind smile before continuing. "Ah, excuse me, *Alexis*. That's a subject I'll let you bring up with Raven when you choose." He leaned back in his chair as Alexis tried to regain her composure. "So, we all have little secrets. This is good. A certain amount of illusion is useful."

Raven frowned at Bertok. The old fool had a habit of saying the wrong thing at the worst possible times. He was right, though. If Alexis was going to help, she deserved to know the truth.

"The Black Leopards, the Royal Guardsmen, and the City Watch are up in arms because I stole the Dragonstone from the Grand Cathedral of Praxil. It appears to be more valuable than I was led to believe by a certain hedge wizard. The king turned the Leopards loose on the thieves' guild to pressure me into returning the gem. They don't know it was me but others have started putting the pieces together. Plus, as I said, the Leopards hit the Corconti camp. So, I'm going to make King Marcus pay."

Alexis sounded shocked as she moved in front of Raven and stared at her. "*You* hit the cathedral? Do you realize the king banished an entire contingent of the Royal Guard because of that fiasco? Everyone thinks a team of thieves had to be involved in something that big."

"No, it just took a lot of planning and a lot of luck. That's why I'm pushing you so hard. Why do you think we spend all that time practicing every night? We're only going to get one shot at the Great Keep. When we go after the king, we're going for a big score. You realize we'll have to clear town afterwards."

Alexis scoffed, "Like I have anything holding me here."

A guilty thought about her own family stopped Raven for a second before she turned to Bertok. "But that still brings us to the main question: What is so damn important about the Dragonstone that Marcus would send the Black Leopards against the thieves' guild?"

"I've been researching, Raven, but I don't have any answers yet. I'm waiting on some information from the Imperial capital. I still have some friends back there with connections."

"You ... have connections ... in the Imperial capital?"

Bertok bristled. "Young woman, do not presume you know everything. You know little about my life before you met me."

Raven waved her hands at him. "All right, all right, don't get your back up. You mentioned it might have some magical properties when we decided to go after it."

"As I said, I haven't learned much. What I have discovered makes me think it's tied to the lunar cycle. According to legend, its powers are at their height at the dark of the moon. I have no idea what that means, though. It's not something you have to worry about. Your grasp of magic is still too fundamental to attempt to use it."

"Thank you for that note of confidence."

Alex was unable to remain quiet. "So, when do we go after the Great Keep?"

Raven saw the anticipation in her apprentice's eyes. "When I think you're ready. Until then, you will continue your lessons and help with the scrut work involved in planning a mission. And do not think about impressing me by trying to get in by yourself. There won't be enough of you left to bury—and that's if I get a hold of you." From the crestfallen look on her apprentice's face, she was sure the message was clear.

Bertok's voice broke the awkward silence. "How are you going to get into the keep? Compared to that, the cathedral was wide open."

Raven thought back to her conversation with Quentin.

"I have a lead, but I'll have to check it out on my own. If I'm going to catch him, I need to leave soon."

Alexis spoke up. "Are you certain you don't need me to come? If nothing else, I can keep an eye on things."

Raven tried to soften her reply. She knew Alexis was uncomfortable with how the evening had gone. "Not this time, Alexis. You need to get some sleep. I have an important mission for you tomorrow. Remember how you said you couldn't just go into the Royal Quarter and look around? That's exactly what you're going to be doing during the day tomorrow. I'll leave detailed instructions for you when I get back. Just be certain to be upstairs before dark. That rule still stands, understood? Why don't you head home now? I need to speak to Bertok in private before I leave."

Raven could tell her apprentice was excited about the special mission, but disappointed about not tagging along. Alexis mustered up as much good nature as she could and said good-bye to Bertok. Raven made certain she left before she turned to Bertok. Almost as if he was reading her mind, Bertok began chanting a small spell.

"A silence spell, just in case your friend is listening beneath the trapdoor. So, you haven't told your apprentice who you are?"

"No more than you've told me who *you* are."

"Ah, but you are not my apprentice. If you were willing to give up this silly thievery and concentrate on learning a true art, *then* you might become my apprentice."

"Let's not start that again. I don't have time this evening. I wasn't kidding when I told Alexis I needed to speak to you. You saw something inside her tonight. Can I trust her or not?"

"So the old hedge wizard is washed up and useless except when you need information?" She could tell his heart wasn't in the bantering. "But in this case, I do have something useful for you. You can trust her. I don't know what she's told you about her past. She's earnest in her desire to be taught by you. She is desperate to earn your respect. If anything, she needs to be given more praise so she doesn't do anything stupid to try and impress you. There's no sign she's working for the Black Leopards or for Quentin. More than that, I will not say."

* * *

Music filtered down the darkened streets from the Golden Eagle tavern. The front area was well lit with footmen waiting to assist people from their carriages or to take their steeds to a nearby stable. Its clientele consisted of young noblemen, junior officers and wealthy merchants. It had become the place to see and be seen in Sagras. And tonight, it had another visitor.

Raven lurked in the shadows, watching who came in and out of the place. Quentin had told her to meet Galen tomorrow night. However, she wanted to get the lay of the land before she tried to approach him. She saw familiar faces in the tavern, people who frequented her father's store or the sons of other merchants on their street. She would have to be careful when she met with Galen not to appear to recognize them. Sometimes it was hard to keep everyone she knew straight since Perrin and Raven traveled in such different circles.

As she watched, a movement on a rooftop caught her attention. The figure moved along the crest of the building across from the Golden Eagle. It paused from time to time to scan the streets below, staying low against the roofline. Raven pulled back into the alley, confident she hadn't been spotted.

Strange. I've never seen a burglar work like that. Wonder what they're doing up there?

Scanning the alley to ensure she was alone, Raven used her grapnel and rope to scale the neighboring building. Hiding in the shadow of a chimney, she scanned the rooftops with her telescope for the mysterious figure. After a few minutes, she spotted a small hump in the darkness near the center point of the roof across the street from her. She watched for a while before getting bored. *Doesn't seem too threatening. They're just lying there, peeking over the edge of the roof watching the Golden Eagle. If they want to scout out the tavern for a possible mission, who am I to complain?*

She started to leave when she noticed the figure had turned its back to the tavern and was doing something in the shadows. *Okay, now* that's *odd. Maybe I should check this out.* There was a six-foot span between the tavern and the next building over, but with a running start she reached the roof of the tavern with room to spare. She landed on her hands and feet, crouching in the darkness until she had her balance back. Once she was sure of her footing, she found a suitable hiding place near the edge of the roof. She could see the street in front of the tavern as well as the figure across the street. She brought her telescope up and was relieved to see the shadow hadn't reacted to her mad dash across the rooftops.

What are they doing over there? Waiting for someone? Waiting for their partners to join them? They're too far away from the tavern to be planning a strike. You'd never see any details from there. About all you can do is see the street in front.

She scanned the other rooftops but didn't observe any movement. If the figure had any partners, they were better at hiding than it was. Something she'd thought a few seconds ago stuck in her head.

Almost as if they were waiting for someone …

Her eyes widened as she realized who it might be. Even if she was wrong, she couldn't take the chance. She scooted back until she was out of the shadowy figure's line of sight before lowering herself to the ground. She made her way to a side door and let herself into the tavern.

"Can I be helpin' you now, miss?" The bartender gave her an uncomfortable stare as she reached his station behind the smooth, polished bar.

"I'm looking for a customer, goes by the name of Galen. I hear he likes to stop in once in a while."

"Ah, it be Galen you're lookin' for," the bartender said, *sotto vocce*, as he wiped the bar. "Yer a little early still. He likes to roll in here, oh, about an hour 'fore midnight. Usually got a lady or two with him, the dog. Don't see how he does it. He ain't the most handsome of chaps, but he tips well, that

195

he does."

"An hour before midnight. Thank you." She slid a gold crown across the bar to him. "I think I'll take in some air and return about then."

"Not a bad idea, miss." Caught off-guard by his comment, she watched as he gave a quick nod toward one corner. She gave a casual turn and saw a group of young noblemen, heads down over their drinks. "I'm not familiar with that group, but they seem to be up to something. I'd say it's for the best if you're not here whenever they start whatever they're going to start. Too damn quiet for a young bunch of rowdies."

Raven asked for a small ale and slid another silver coin across the bar to him. She knew that coin was worth six or seven drinks, but the information he gave her was worth it. She took the drink and turned around, resting her back against the strong wood. As she raised the mug to her face, she could see five men nursing their drinks, giving the appearance of having drunk much more than they had.

So, there are five waiting in here and one waiting on the roof across the street. I'd say Galen has more enemies than he knew. So much for being retired. She exchanged some pleasantries with the bartender, then left, using the same side door she'd come in.

She made her way to the end of the alley to see if she could spot which direction Galen might be coming from. She beat a hand against her thigh, wishing Quentin had given her more information. If she had a clue which direction he was coming from, or what he looked like, she would have gone ahead to warn him. She couldn't take the chance of going one direction and him approaching from the other. If she didn't act at just the right moment, though, she knew how he'd be leaving.

After some hesitation, she came to a decision. She slipped back down the alley and cut behind the small warehouse that stood beside the tavern. Taking a deep breath, she rushed across Sea Shadow Lane into the alley across from her. Taking out her grapnel, she climbed to the roof and headed toward the shadowy figure.

The buildings on this side of the street butted up against one another, so she had a straight path to the figure ahead of her. She halted where she was and used her telescope to examine the rooftops. She spotted the figure lying on the roof and knew what they had been so busy with a little while ago. A cocked crossbow rested beside them. This was no sentry, it was a sniper.

She cursed under her breath as she tried to plot a course that would minimize her risk. There just weren't that many things on these roofs to provide shelter. Raven looked up in the sky, but there were no clouds to block the pale light coming from the moon. There was no way she could reach the sniper before she was spotted, unless ...

Thinking back to her visit with Bertok, she calmed her mind and began chanting a spell. She'd never tried using magic on a mission before now. A small ball of darkness began to form around her, growing larger as the spell progressed. The whole world seemed hazy, but she knew she was surrounded by an opaque cover. Reaching into one of the sacks on her belt, she pulled out a small, heavy, leather sack and wrapped its cord around her wrist.

Armed with the bludgeon, she made her way forward. She tested each step before putting her weight on it. She knew the illusion would hold as long as the target wasn't looking for her. After what seemed an eternity, she reached the sniper. They had shifted once or twice, glancing her way as if the figure felt something was wrong. Raven's luck was holding so far.

With a sudden downward blow, Raven slammed the bludgeon onto the back of the figure's head. They gave a soft moan and then lay still, limbs akimbo. Raven checked and found a small, fluttery pulse. She knew the Leopard would wake up with a headache, but would wake up. Rolling the sniper over, Raven was surprised to see their cap slide off, revealing a cascade of hair. Going over the body, Raven relieved the female assassin of all her weapons and anything else she found. She'd examine them in detail later, but for right now, she felt much better knowing her opponent was unarmed.

She tied the assassin up and then went to the edge of the roof and dropped down into the alley below. She inched around a corner of the building until she could see the road in both directions. There were still five Leopards in the tavern, so whatever happened, she had to keep him out with a minimum of fuss. If she drew their attention, she doubted she or Galen would escape.

The clock in the Great Keep chimed the hour and was answered by the faint tolling from the cathedral. She tensed as a small, enclosed carriage appeared on Sea Shadow Lane. A young man was at the reins and she heard the faint laughter of two female voices. Raven began walking down the street toward the carriage, keeping an eye on the tavern as best she could.

Just as she drew even with the carriage, she leapt into the seat with the driver. Before he could react, she'd slid a knife under his neck, the cold steel resting lightly against his skin. "If you want to live, turn around right now and head back where you came from."

"Jarrod!" A man's voice thundered from within the carriage. "What in the name of Donmar is going on? Why did we stop?"

The young man started to reply, but Raven stopped him. "No, don't talk; just do what I told you."

She felt him hesitate and she pressed the knife harder against his neck, a small trickle of blood coating the shiny metal. After a few nerve-racking moments, he wrestled the horses around and headed away from the ambush. As the passengers realized what was happening, she heard the carriage door open. She spun around to see an older man hanging half out the door, pointing a small hand crossbow at her.

"Young woman, would you be so kind to explain yourself? Why are you threatening my manservant?" There was a twinkle in the man's eye, but amused or not, Raven noticed the crossbow never drifted an inch from her heart, even with the bouncing of the carriage.

"Galen, I presume?"

"Perhaps, but that does not answer my question."

"Would the fact you were walking into an ambush and I'm trying to keep you alive mean anything to you?" She kept a close eye on the bolt still aimed at her heart.

"A noble cause, lass, but I'm a hard man to convince. If you'd take your knife away from Jarrod's throat, I'd be happy to listen to your story." She sheathed her knife and Jarrod brought the carriage to a halt. Galen motioned for her to join him inside.

The two young women looked at Raven with wide eyes, their beautiful silk dresses and long gloves in distinct contrast to Raven's armor, leather pants and rough blouse. Galen motioned them to sit with him, while Raven sat across from him by herself. His crossbow was lightly held, but at this range there was no way he could miss.

"So, you're trying to save my life. How do I know you're not leading me into an ambush of your own?"

"Because if I was going to ambush you, I'd wait until after you were drunk. I know enough about you to know I'd never take you sober."

"Reasonable enough."

Raven gave a nervous glance out the window. "Could you have Jarrod start moving again? I think the five Black Leopards waiting at the tavern will notice you haven't shown up at your usual time." Raven tried to scoot in the seat so she could see down the street.

"Black Leopards? Waiting at the Golden Eagle? Totally unacceptable. I'm going to have to scratch that establishment from my list. I seem to have become predictable. I agree with your analysis of this situation." A real smile reached his face now. "Jarrod! Head toward the Blue Star. We haven't been there in a while."

"As you wish, sir."

The older man removed the bolt from the crossbow and uncocked it before sliding it into a small compartment next to the door. "You have to understand my precautions. One does not get to where I am in my line of work without being cautious."

"That stands to reason. Are we free to talk or can I meet you later? A mutual friend suggested I meet with you regarding one of your former … triumphs."

Galen paused for a moment. "Ah yes, I believe I know what you're referring to. Our mutual friend told me he would be sending someone to find me. Your name would be … ?"

"Raven."

"Yes, that does ring a bell. Come with me once we reach the tavern. I'm certain Jarrod can keep these two ladies entertained while we converse. It appears I'm going to have to disappear for a while. I guess his majesty didn't receive word that I've retired."

"Perhaps he's trying to ensure you're permanently retired."

"Indeed."

Chapter Nineteen

After leaving the women and Jarrod, Galen and Raven went to one of the private meeting rooms upstairs. Galen unlocked the door and scanned the room before entering. He motioned for her to sit in one of the velvet chairs while he eased into another. He sat with his back to the wall, casually observing the door and the windows. He might not admit it but her warning about the Black Leopards had shaken him.

"Quentin told me to expect you tomorrow night. Why are you here now? How did you know the Leopards were looking for me? I don't mean to sound ungrateful, but I get nervous when people deviate from what I expect."

Raven related the earlier events, leaving out the part about casting the spell. After she finished, he rose from his seat and tugged on a pull cord in the corner of the room. He returned and spread his hands out on the table in front of him. "I do have some information you might find useful. We'll go into that once Cecil shows up with the bottle I ordered."

"I know I should have finished that sniper rather than just tying her up. Once she was helpless, though, I didn't see the point."

"Nonsense. You're neither an assassin nor a thug. If you were, Quentin would never have mentioned me to you. He'd have turned you in for the bounty on your head. He still might once you're no longer useful to him. I do like the man but he's a bit predictable."

Raven's eyes flew open wide. "Bounty? On me? Why

would anyone be hunting me?"

"We all know there's a sizable bounty on the cathedral thief. No one from the king to the lowest stable boy knows their true identity. I must say, though, there are some who have a good idea who might be behind it."

"That makes sense, but I know of several thieves in the city capable of pulling off such a heist. Why would there be a price on my head?"

"Indeed there are." He pulled a bag from his belt and set it on the table. He removed a pipe and a smaller sack filled with tobacco and packed his pipe. As tendrils of smoke began to rise from the bowl, his gray eyes caught hers. "On the night of the incident, two were in jail, one was so drunk he couldn't move, five have been accounted for, and one arrived in Sagras two days afterwards from overseas. That leaves four possible champions of the thieving world who could have done this. We'll ignore the possibility that it was an outsider. The job required a greater depth of knowledge than someone unfamiliar with the city would have."

Raven nodded in spite of herself, curious to see where he was going with this line of thought.

"That leaves four thieves in the city accomplished enough to pull off a skilled and daring heist. So, who was it? Besides yourself, my dear, the other candidates were Zeki, Theobard, and the Corconti, Jerek. We both know what happened to Jerek when the Black Leopards hit the Corconti camp. No one knows much about Zeki except that he's a cat burglar. Seems he'd be the obvious suspect. However, he specializes in objets d'art. Gems and jewels hold little interest for him. Besides, word is, he's a religious man. He'd never steal something hidden in the cathedral. Theobard was killed the night the Black Leopards hit the thieves' guild. So even if he did do it, we can't give him up to take the heat off."

"That *is* unfortunate." A soft knock at the door halted her follow-up question. She made her way to the door, being careful not to walk in front of it. She loosened one of her daggers, before answering the subsequent knock. "Who's there?"

A gruff voice filtered through the heavy oaken door. "Cecil, with Mr. Grayhill's order." Raven turned toward Galen, who nodded. She opened the door, keeping one foot against it in case someone tried to push through. She saw the bartender standing outside with a bottle and two glasses on a tray. She took the tray from him and shut and locked the door.

The older thief sat there with an amused look on his face, a small stream of smoke rising from the finely carved pipe he clutched in his teeth as Raven poured the wine. She noticed it was an expensive brand and a good year. Perhaps, when she'd retired, she'd enjoy the spoils of her efforts as much as Galen did. She set the glass down in front of him and poured herself one. She raised her glass to him and they sipped the dark red wine in silence.

"Ah, lass, now this is a good life," Galen said, sitting back in his chair. "Good wine, a fine smoke, and a beautiful *and* intelligent woman to share the moment. However, I suppose you'd like to get on with our discussion."

"Well, there are quite a few things I'd like to discuss with you, but Quentin suggested you possessed an elusive piece of information. Could you share it with me?"

"Ah, my truest claim to fame. The knowledge of how to reach the Great Keep without being spotted. I bedeviled Marcus's poor father for years, you know. I never took anything of great value, except for King Duncan's piece of mind. There's nothing like the realization someone knows the way through your defenses to keep you up at night. I'll wager he slept with one eye open, wondering if I was in the shadows next to him." A soft, malevolent chuckle emanated from the old thief.

"King Marcus owes me a great deal, and he owes Quentin, too. I need to get into the Great Keep without being spotted. Can you teach me how to do that?" Her eyes narrowed as she envisioned a hundred different ways to take revenge on King Marcus.

Galen tapped the cooling embers in his pipe with the hilt of a small stiletto. Taking his time, he relit his pipe and then turned to face her. "I can. Knowledge does not come without a price, though. I've lost a lot of friends thanks to the Black Leopards. I know you didn't intend for that to happen. However, since you started it, you're responsible for fixing it."

Thinking Galen sounded a lot like Quentin, she replied with care. "What do you want me to do?"

"My sources tell me those hit squads knew where to find people, what their names were, and where they hung out. Someone inside the guild betrayed them. Find whoever it was and deal with them. I don't care if you do it or someone else does but deal with it."

"I have my own reasons to agree but if that's your price, consider it done."

"That's a good lass. All right, draw close and I'll tell you how I did it. Pay attention. I'm only going to tell you once and you damn sure aren't going to write it down ..."

* * *

Quentin wasn't joking. Galen has forgotten more about being a thief than Quentin and I know combined. He knows more about the city than half the sages. Still, the stories he told tonight weren't for my entertainment. Every anecdote related to my raid on the keep in its own way. He was trying to show me what to do and not to do without just saying "Don't do this." Oh, he's good.

Raven smiled, thinking about that when she heard the cathedral bells chiming three in the morning. She decided a quick stop at the Black Boar would top the night off. She hadn't been in there since the last time with Jerek.

Stepping in, she saw Hendrik sitting in his usual place by the door. "Hendrik! Good to see you. What have you been up to?" She looked around the bar at the dour group of patrons. Everyone seemed subdued this evening, huddled together and whispering among themselves. This wasn't the noisy, raucous tavern she was used to visiting.

"Evening, Raven," Hendrik called back, tapping his sap against his leg as he sat there. Raven noticed he seemed tired and his easy smile was missing. "Been a while since I saw you last. Still impressing all the boys?"

"Isn't it their job to impress me? How's business?"

"Pretty poor. If the old crowds don't start showing up soon, we may not *be* in business. Bills are piling up."

"Sorry to hear that. How's Ginny?"

"She's doing well. Word is that friend of mine's boy is quite taken with her. Seems they're talking about a spring wedding, from what I hear."

"Well, good for her. About time something went right."

Hendrik sighed deeply. "Well, for her, anyway. Sorry to hear about Jerek. Seems there's enough misery 'round here to make someone consider pulling up stakes."

"It wouldn't be the Black Boar without you."

The bouncer turned and she could see he was sporting some new scars on his arms and his face. "You remember Robert Marjory? That gentleman you had a disagreement with here?"

She slid closer to him and kept her voice low. "Yes, I heard he had an unfortunate accident a few nights ago. I seem to remember you tossing one of them out yourself that evening."

"Exactly, well, ol' Douglas, he's still not a hundred percent recovered from that fire at his place. Still, he's recovered enough to start giving orders. Seems that group has taken a shine to this tavern. I hear their leader, Raymond, tried to talk Douglas into buying this place for them. So far, the owner has refused to sell but they're persistent."

"So they still come here?"

"Not much I can do long as they're behaving. I've busted their heads a few times, but let's face it, lass, it's tough to fight four or five hired swords—sober *or* drunk. Maybe twenty years ago, I might have chanced it. These days? I'm happy to go home to the wife and dream about life in the country when we save some money."

"You? In the country? That I'd have to see." A barmaid swung by and Raven ordered a large stein of ale for herself and whatever she, the bartender, and Hendrik wanted. The

205

barmaid smiled and hurried off to fill *that* order.

"What, you don't see me living in the country, or you don't see me retiring?"

"A little of both. Seems a lot of people are considering retirement these days."

"Raven, with what's going on in the city, I'm thinking living in the country would be healthier for my wife and me. Even with the occasional bandit or wild animal, I think the odds of seeing my grandkids would improve." Hendrik accepted the mug of ale the barmaid handed him.

Raven thanked her and looked at Hendrik over the top of her stein. She'd never seen him so disheartened before. Marjory's friends really had worn him down. From the reaction on Hendrik's face, she hadn't hid her expression as well as she'd hoped.

"Hey, now, don't beat yourself up. If it hadn't been you, it'd have been someone else. They were waiting for an incident. The fact Marjory got humiliated just stoked the fires a bit."

A sudden commotion outside drew their attention. The door flew open and a body went rolling into the middle of the barroom. As Hendrik rushed over to see what had happened, Marjory's friends appeared in the doorway, sadistic looks on their faces.

"Look there, Colin. It seems this deadbeat is still refusing to pay Mr. Valio what he owes," the smallest of the three said. His thin, high voice reminded Raven of a weasel's. She couldn't get a good look at him, though. He managed to stay well back from the entryway in the shadows. She pegged him to be the first one to run from a fight and the first to claim a victor's share.

The largest of the group pushed his way into the tavern, his brown eyes focused on the body in the middle of the room. "I'd say this guy needs a lesson on keeping his word. If we make an example of him, others will remember it's a bad idea to owe Mr. Valio money and then not pay."

The third one glided in also. He was a tall, thin man with sharp cheekbones. His voice was smooth but there was no questioning the malice in his tone. "I agree with David. These peasants could use an object lesson." Raven noticed his sword and studded leather jerkin were worn, but well cared for. He was the most dangerous of the group so far.

Hendrik imposed himself between the three in the doorway and their target. "That's enough, boys. I think you've made your point. He'll need a doctor to set those bones as is."

Colin looked at the bouncer with a sneer. "Don't get in our way, old man. You've caused us more trouble than anyone else in town. We'll settle with you soon enough." Raven stepped forward, ready to come to Hendrik's aid if he needed it.

Before she reached the door, a voice from the bar stopped her. "Hey, Colin! There's someone here you ought to meet. She's by the door." Raven saw a blond-haired man leaning against the bar. He must have slipped in the side door while everyone was watching the spectacle at the front. Raven noted he carried two throwing axes on his back along with the sword on his hip.

Colin spun around and a look of recognition crept over his face. "You. I remember you. You're the one who whacked Robbie with that stein. Didn't play fair, taking advantage of him and all. Didn't even give him a chance to defend himself."

"Not my problem. If he wants to pick a fight with someone in a bar or an alley, that's no skin off my nose. If he wants to pick a fight with me, then I intend to win." Raven loosened the strap holding her rapier in its scabbard with her right hand. "That goes for anyone else."

Colin's eyes narrowed as he stared at her. "Perhaps it's time we made a small payment on the hurt we've been planning for you. Philippe, watch the old man here. If he thinks about getting froggy with that sap, let him know that would be a mistake." The tough at the bar moved into the room without a word and sat down where he could keep an eye on Hendrik.

Colin drew a sword and began to advance while the tavern's patrons beat a hasty retreat in all directions. Near the door, the thin man leaned against the wall and relaxed, watching with a faint look of amusement on his face. David, the weasel-like shadow, was nowhere to be seen.

Raven drew her rapier and relaxed, assuming her normal fighting stance. She hated the whole ridiculous situation. She also hated she wasn't engaging the unnamed warrior first. She knew he was the most skilled of the quartet. He would watch her fight and study her technique while Colin took the brunt of the damage.

Colin began pushing tables out of the way to clear as much room as possible. She circled the open area, taking note of everyone's location. For all his bluster, Colin was a good tactician. He continued to cut down their impromptu arena. They sized each other up as they maneuvered for position. Out of the corner of her eye, she caught a glimpse of the barmaid herding people out the back. The toughs didn't even mind when Hendrik helped their earlier victim to his feet and guided him toward the back. Then again, they knew where to find him.

They drew closer until the tips of their swords touched. Colin's sword was heavier than hers, with a stiffer blade. She tapped his sword a few times, but he wasted no time bringing it back on line. Deciding to move the odds into her favor, she drew a long dagger with her right hand and held it at the low ready. It opened up her chest a bit but she was trying to lure him into attacking that area.

On the first pass, they came together, sparks flying as their blades beat against each other's. Colin seemed uncomfortable fighting against Raven's sword-and-dagger technique. She tried to press her advantage but he kept his distance, his sword dancing in the flickering lights of the tavern's lanterns. They continued feinting and parrying, looking for any opening that presented itself.

Her swords master had drilled her for times like this. Morgan might have lost an arm in one of Sagras' wars but he hadn't lost his skills or the ability to teach. He'd drilled her until it seemed time slowed down as she fought. It was an illusion but it let her notice things she didn't see at the start of a fight.

After the last pass, Raven began noticing things about Colin: he favored moving to the right; his right shoulder dipped before he tried a lunge; his heels rose slightly before he advanced. And he was getting frustrated. He wasn't used to fighting a near equal; beating up townspeople and merchants was more his style.

Forcing him to circle left, Raven opened up her stance. She saw how Colin's eyes narrowed as he saw the opening. She let her breath sound a little ragged to give the impression she was tiring. She wanted to end this as soon as possible. She suspected she'd have to fight the unnamed one next and wanted to be fresh if she did.

A sharklike smile crossed Colin's face as he lunged. At the last possible second, Raven slipped to the right, letting her dagger guide Colin's sword away from her. She felt the edge of his sword glide against her ribs, opening a slight wound there.

On the other hand, her rapier was right on target. Colin provided most of the momentum as he rushed upon the point, driving it deep just above his belt. A high-pitched scream ripped out of him as the steel ripped into his guts. She relaxed her grip and let the sword turn in her hand, trying to keep the blade from snapping off as Colin collapsed. She withdrew the blade and stepped back.

"If you hurry, you can probably save his life. There are healers at the cathedral and you can reach it in time, if you leave now." She kept her dagger pointed toward Philippe and her sword toward the unnamed tough.

"Colin always was impatient; I see you figured that out. Well done." The thin man in the doorway gave her a mock salute with his sword. "I suppose we ought to get him to the healers. Our employer would be upset if we lost another member in this tavern."

He nodded to Philippe and the miraculously reappearing David and they grabbed Colin by the shoulders and feet. He watched them carry Colin out with no trace of emotion on his face. He put his sword away with a flourish before speaking one last time to her. "Don't worry; I won't make the same mistake. I look forward to crossing steel with you one day."

Raven didn't say a word to him as he backed out the door. She made her way to the door and watched as they disappeared down Eagle Wing Road toward the cathedral. She cleaned the blood off her blade with a bar rag and sheathed her weapons. She noticed the wound on her side and motioned for Hendrik to come over. He brought her a bottle of whiskey, poured some in a glass for her, and poured some directly into the wound. She hissed through her teeth as the alcohol burned at the wound, but better that than an infection.

Hendrik sent the barmaid after some clean towels from upstairs. As soon as she returned, he made a makeshift bandage for Raven and had her flex her arm and torso a few times to ensure it would stay in place. "Best I can do, given the circumstances, lass. I'd see about getting a new jerkin. This one isn't worth the effort to repair." He leaned up against the bar next to her. "You do have a way with men. You have a whole new group of admirers."

"What can I say? I guess I'm irresistible." She looked down at the jerkin. "I've been meaning to get a new one anyway."

"Want me to walk you home?"

Raven reached over and gave him a peck on the cheek. As Hendrik turned bright red, she smiled. "No, but you're a good man to offer. Now, why don't I get out of here and let you get back to fleecing these customers out of their hard-earned pay."

"That's the Raven I know." Hendrik looked at the wide-eyed patrons still standing at the edge of the bar. "All right, the lot of you! The show's over. Since you're already standing at the bar, place your orders as you come back in."

He turned around to check on Raven one last time, but she was gone.

Chapter Twenty

"I can't believe it, Raven. You got into a fight with four hunters last night? What were you thinking? Are you *trying* to draw a bull's-eye on yourself?"

Raven cut Alexis off with a sideways motion with her arm. "We're changing the subject and I'll pretend this didn't happen. We've got too much to do tonight. Did you pick up the supplies on the list I left you?"

"Tonight? What's happening tonight?"

"Nothing if you didn't complete your assignment."

The young thief tossed her head in aggravation. "Oh, I found what you were looking for. It took me most of the day to finish."

Raven nodded, pleased with her apprentice's accomplishments. Some of those items were obscure. If she found all of them, she knew the city better than Raven had hoped. "Your training isn't complete, but we don't have time to wait. I have a way into the Great Keep and we're going to use it. Every night is another chance something could go wrong."

"Have you decided what you're going to do?"

"No, this is a scouting mission. We're going to see if we can get in and get out without getting caught. Special emphasis on the last part there, apprentice."

"Understood."

Raven paced around the room, internally debating on the best way to take advantage of Galen's instructions. *What am I missing? I've retraced every story he told me last evening. I've repeated the steps to enter the keep until I know it almost as well as I know how to find my own bed. I know I can do this. But it's been so long since he was there last. What's changed since then?*

Coming to a decision, she turned to Alexis. "Grab your cloak and your tools. There's a keep that needs a visit."

* * *

As they reached the outskirts of the keep, a cold wind started blowing off the bay. She saw torches being lit all along the docks. The ships were setting out to sea before the storm could arrive. If they didn't want to get caught, it had to be a serious storm. Raven could almost smell the rain in the air now.

Remembering Galen's instructions, she led Alexis down a series of dark alleyways until they came to a dead end behind the Sword and Gauntlet tavern. Once she was certain no one was watching, she lifted up the covering to the sewers and they crawled into the darkness below.

Taking one of her gems, she summoned the soft light and took some comfort in its familiar glow. The area looked a little more run-down than Galen had described but she chalked that up to the passage of time. At least the water in this branch of the sewer was almost clear.

She reviewed the map in her head and the pair began walking upstream, stopping every so often to ensure nothing was ahead. Raven was determined there would be no mistakes on this journey. If they lost this egress, her dreams of revenge against King Marcus would be over.

Counting in her head, she reached two hundred and began searching the left wall. Nothing. She felt a twinge of panic and then relaxed when she realized her stride and Galen's might be different. Alexis and she began checking for a loose section, about six feet off the floor in both directions.

"Raven, over here."

Raven hurried over to Alexis. She saw Alexis kept her hand on one spot on the wall. She took one of her daggers and tapped on the wall; a hollow *thunk* rewarded her efforts. Turning the dagger around, she chipped mud away from a small groove with a steady stroke, until a small square was revealed on the wall.

Raven motioned toward the spot. "Go ahead. You found it."

By the soft light of her gem, Alexis looked for any sign of traps or alarms. Raven watched with a smile on her face. Before they'd started training together, Alexis would have pushed the switch without thinking. Completing her examination, she gave the exposed square a hard push. Her persistence was rewarded as the section slid inward for a few inches and they heard something click. Alexis withdrew her fingers and Raven saw a section of the wall swing inward.

"Well done, Alexis. Let's see where this passage leads."

Raven noticed the dry, stuffy air as the two entered the dark passageway. She glanced at the walls and spotted a thin layer of dust covering everything. Trusting her instincts, she slowed down and began examining the walls.

"Goddess, the air here reeks of age. What's the matter?" Alexis looked up to see Raven coming back down the corridor toward her.

"I'm checking the dust. The good thing is no one has used this passage in years. Given the lack of air movement and the direction the tunnel is going, I believe it goes straight beneath the keep. That matches what Galen told me."

"You said, 'the good thing.' That implies a bad thing."

"Very good, apprentice. If you'll examine the floor, you'll note it's as dust covered as these walls. We're leaving a perfect trail. If anyone were to come this way, they couldn't miss our presence."

"Unless Bertok taught you how to levitate, I don't see a way to avoid disturbing the dust."

"Unfortunately, he's never offered to teach me that spell. When we get to the end of the passage, wipe your boots with a rag. We don't want to leave dusty prints behind to lead a guard to our passage."

"Yes, Mother. Speaking of that, what exactly *has* he taught you?"

"Well, I can create light and cast darkness—that's about it. Says I need to focus less on the thief business before he'll teach me real magic."

Alexis looked suitably unimpressed. "Unfortunate. Your spells could be useful considering our line of work. It would be nicer, though, if you could put guards to sleep or cloud their minds so they can't see us."

"Nope. We have to do this the hard way." Raven finished inspecting the passageway and took the lead. The pair checked for any hidden exits beneath the layers of dust as they went along. Raven had to concede that Galen was right; it seemed there was only one way in.

Only the echo of their footsteps kept them company. They reached the end of the passageway to find a blank wall in front of them. A well-worn wooden lever stuck out of the left wall.

Alexis stared at the lever with a suspicious air. "I guess that's supposed to open the way?"

"Hidden passages are only hidden from the outside. It makes sense to have an obvious way to leave when you were done using it."

Alexis moved to pull the lever before Raven stopped her. "We might want to be prepared. We don't know what's on the other side."

Alexis looked down at the floor, embarrassed. The pair drew their weapons and doused their gems, plunging the passageway into darkness. She felt the first pangs of fear and did her best to try and master them. *What the hell is taking Alexis so long to open the passageway?*

As the darkness closed in on her, she couldn't take it anymore. "Alexis, open the damned door."

"It's been open for several minutes. I thought you were making certain everything was clear."

Raven felt sheepish. "I never heard the door move." Now that her attention had been drawn to it, she could feel the hint of a breeze and the fresher air. She summoned just enough light from the gem to get a glimpse beyond before calling up its full power.

"Your friend, Galen, has a morbid sense of humor."

Raven didn't respond. The door had slid into the floor, revealing a large cavernous room that held the necropolis for the Great Keep. This chamber had been hewn out of living rock with a long staircase rising at the far end. The walls were honeycombed with openings and she could see small objects lying within. She remembered Galen's instructions and found the mechanism to raise the false wall back into place. Raven made Alexis open and close it to ensure she could find it if she left on her own.

"I wonder how much stuff they buried with all these people? Seems like we could spend time down here and make a small fortune." Her apprentice's eyes gleamed with anticipation.

"I'm not training you to be a grave robber. I have standards, you know."

Alexis started to say something and thought better of it. She fell in behind Raven as they started up the stairs. They could see the small openings in the wall as they climbed and tried not to think about what they represented. Reaching the top, she doused her light and cracked open the door. She saw light flickering from a wall sconce and the passageway led off in two directions. Raven pointed to the right and they set off, Raven taking the right side and Alexis the left. Raven noticed Alexis had her rapier drawn and motioned for her to put it away. It wasn't worth the chance of scraping it across something to save a few seconds drawing it.

Several hallways connected to the dim hallway. Galen's instructions ended where they had entered the keep. From this point on, they were on their own. Raven listened at each corner but stayed with the main passageway. This was *not* the time to get lost. Their search led them to a stone staircase rising in a tight spiral. Raven couldn't determine its height in the dim torchlight ahead of them. Once she was convinced it was safe, she began moving upward, staying close to the right-hand wall.

After a while, they came to an opening and peered out into what Raven believed was the ground floor. They saw two guards standing near a grand staircase and another spiral staircase at the far end.

Raven ducked her head toward Alexis. "I think I have an idea where we are."

"Good for you. I haven't the foggiest notion."

"We're in the southwest tower. Let's see where it leads. Maybe we'll find a floor that doesn't have guards posted."

They waited until a courtier distracted the guards before sneaking past the opening. Approaching the second-floor landing, Raven felt her tunic snag on something. She thought it was a rough spot on the wall until she examined it closer. It was too regular to be an imperfection; it had to be a switch of some kind. Alexis gave her a worried glance. If something drew the guards' attention now, there was no place to go.

Raven screwed up her courage and gave the piece of stone a solid push. A door swung open without a sound, revealing a small passageway leading to a wooden door. The two stepped through and found the opening mechanism inside the small hall. Closing the false wall behind them, they crept down the hall and examined the wooden door, taking careful notice of the large iron lock.

Alexis impressed Raven with the speed and thoroughness of her inspection of the door. A shake of her head told Raven she hadn't detected anything, so Raven pulled out her tools and went to work on the lock. She was working on the last set of tumblers when she froze.

There were voices in the stairwell behind them.

* * *

"I'm telling you, Gerhard, I don't understand why we're meeting *here*." Fraser's nasally voice preceded him down the hallway and Gerhard tried to hide his annoyance. His correspondence lay half unfinished on his desk back in his quarters and his valet needed his input to pack for the trip. However, the message Bela had handed him made it clear his presence was expected.

"Fraser, I don't recall the king needing your permission to hold a meeting. Now hold your tongue and wait for him. Do you have the key to the door?"

"Why would I have it? That damn … I mean, Bela should have it. He has the keys to everything."

"Very well, they shouldn't be much longer."

The two men stood in an uneasy silence as they waited. Gerhard started to say something and caught himself. *If it was anyone other than Fraser, I'd enjoy a conversation to help pass the time. If I have to hear his voice one more time, though, I swear I'll strangle the man. Come to think of it, King Marcus might give me a promotion for that. His majesty's feeling for Fraser is well known. Goddess knows, if the man weren't a wizard with money, the king would have banished him years ago.*

Gerhard brightened as the door opened and Bela appeared, leading Wulfric and Kazmer. Bela shuffled to the door and inserted an iron key. It seemed the ring of heavy keys should be too much for his thin frame but his twisted form hid a powerful strength. The key turned without effort and Gerhard noticed an odd look on Bela's face. Bela pushed opened the door and stepped to the side to let them pass.

I wonder what's caught the old dwarf's attention. Oh well, as long as he's busy with that, he's not in the way or getting offended over some imagined slight. There's something not right about that man.

Gerhard joined the others at the small table. He noted the room was martial in spirit with only a few moth-worn tapestries to decorate the room. *Heh, Wulfric's in his element in here. Now there's a man who needs to learn to enjoy life. He'll be dead by forty if he doesn't learn how to relax.*

Bela gave up on whatever was bothering him about the door and fetched a couple of bottles from a small cart, setting them on the table. Gerhard watched him shuffle to his seat. He watched the group at the table like a human spider examining its prey. Tearing his eyes away from the king's servant, Gerhard poured himself a glass of the wine.

After everyone was settled, Kazmer leaned forward to ensure he had everyone's attention. "I'm glad you all came. Time grows short. We have not recovered the Dragonstone. However, there's another matter we must deal with first."

Wulfric glanced around the room. "We're not waiting for Hugh?"

"No, Hugh will not be attending, nor will the king. We, the *true* members of the king's council, need to agree on this matter before I talk to his majesty."

"I'm not certain I like this." Fraser's voice quavered as he turned toward the master assassin.

"Your likes and dislikes mean nothing, Fraser. All I need is for you to follow orders when I give them."

"When *you* give them? I answer only to his majesty, Kazmer. You may lead the Black Leopards, but we're a council of equals here."

Gerhard saw Kazmer's eyes narrow dangerously. *Fraser picked a poor time to grow a spine.*

The royal assassin straightened in his seat, fixing his gaze on the smaller man. "Fraser, you sit on this council by the whim of the king. You know the kingdom's finances better than any four men alive. However, never believe you're the equal of me. His majesty would regret your loss but you can be replaced. Sit down, shut up, and listen for once."

Fraser started to continue, but a kick in the shins from Gerhard stopped him. He seemed to realize the danger he was in and stared down at the table.

"Now, if there are no more interruptions, I'll continue."

Silence met the assassin's statement and an evil smile spread across his face.

"Excellent. There is a matter more pressing than even the Dragonstone. What are we to do about the king's son, Geoffrey?"

"Why should we do anything?" Wulfric's question was

echoed on several of the faces. "The king's health is not in question."

"Our upcoming campaign against Helion worries me. I have counseled the king against leading the troops but he believes he should be at any major battles. 'It improves the troops' morale,' he says."

Wulfric's head snapped around at the implications of the assassin's rant. His hand clenched into a fist as he turned and spoke. "Kazmer, the odds of anything happening to the king are remote with Helion's undermanned army."

"It doesn't matter whether we're facing Helion's farmers and vintners or if we're up against the Imperial Levy. We must consider the future. Helion is only the first of many campaigns before King Marcus takes his rightful place. It's time we cleared the way for Owen's accession."

Gerhard leaned forward, resting his elbows on the table. "I thought the king said regicide was not on his current agenda?"

"He did and it's not. He's never forbidden me from acting in the kingdom's best interests, though." Kazmer let a more collegial tone creep into his voice. "Gentlemen, let's be frank. Geoffrey assuming the throne would be a disaster for Sagras. King Marcus might say how disappointed he is, but he's a father. Geoffrey would have to lead a rebellion for Marcus to take action."

Gerhard brought his fingers together in front of his face to hide his expression. He was uncomfortable discussing Geoffrey's potential murder. Still, there was no question Owen would be a better king. If only there was some way to convince Marcus to skip Geoffrey in the succession …

The ambassador looked at Bela. The king's servant was the wild card here. Was his loyalty to the city higher than his personal devotion to King Marcus? The feral look on the mute's face confirmed Gerhard's worst fears. Bela was allied with Kazmer. For some reason, that worried him more than Kazmer's attitude. After all, if one could remove a prince, why not a king? Where was Kazmer's ambition taking him?

"I see our ambassador to the Imperial Court has been holding his tongue. What is your opinion, Gerhard?"

He stared at the plain stone ceiling before answering. "I agree Owen would make a better king than Geoffrey. I think even Hugh would agree if you pressed him hard enough. Is there no other way than killing the prince?"

"Killing him is one way to be certain he doesn't reappear on the scene later and bollix something up. I am open to suggestions … ?"

"None at this moment. Let me ponder it and I'll get word to you. I leave for Wolf River on tomorrow's tide."

"Don't take too long, Ambassador. Are we agreed that something must be done with Geoffrey, one way or another?"

The members of the council nodded in agreement. Kazmer stood up, his cold smile returning to his face. "Then gentlemen, ponder what we've talked about. The future of Sagras relies on what you decide over the next few days."

The council members rose and, one by one, slipped out down the hidden passageway and exited into the stairwell, until only Gerhard and Bela were left. Gerhard watched as the servant stuck his key into the lock, locking and unlocking it several times before pulling the door shut. Bela stared at the lock a little longer before following Gerhard into the stairway. He trudged upstairs while the older man made his way to the first floor to prepare for his voyage.

First thing though, I need to take a bath. For some reason, I feel dirty.

* * *

The darkened chamber was bathed in a soft glow from behind one of the tapestries. Raven poked her head out, then motioned for Alexis to join her. They leaned on the table, taking a few moments to gather their wits.

Alexis rubbed her nose. "I'm glad they left. I thought I was going to sneeze if we'd stayed there much longer." The young apprentice turned to face Raven. "Wow, that guy sure sounded scary."

"Believe me, he *is* scary. That was the leader of the Black Leopards."

Alexis paled as she realized how narrow their escape had been. "When you decide to mix it up with people, you don't waste time with small fry, do you? I can't get over what we just heard. It was like they were talking about taking out a pile of trash instead of killing the prince."

Raven's voice sounded harsh in the small room as she pulled her lock picks out of a pouch. "That's none of our concern. We came here to steal something and get out of town. It doesn't matter if the entire royal family gets killed off, just as long as it doesn't happen before they realize what we've done." The lock's tumblers turned with a decisive click. "Let's get out of here. We're lucky they didn't notice the door was unlocked."

Reaching the end of the short passageway, Alexis worked the lever. Cracking open the concealed doorway, Raven gazed out, but couldn't see anyone. She noticed the lights farther up the stairs were out. *That's strange. I thought they were lit earlier.*

She turned to descend the stairs when something stuck her hard on the side of her head and her right shoulder. Slumping against a wall, she saw a small man with a wild look in his eyes. He lifted the mace and took another swing at her, just missing her. Her vision swam from the effects of the strike and the stone stairs provided almost no footing. If he hadn't been in a hurry to attack her, she'd be dead right now. As it was, she couldn't move her right arm and her eyes refused to focus as she dodged from side to side to avoid getting hit again.

She retreated down the stairs, resting her left hand on the wall for balance. The thin man gave her an evil smile as he pursued her. Her feet scrambled for purchase as he faked an attack at her head. If she hadn't been flailing, his true attack would have landed her left arm, leaving her defenseless.

Raven blinked, trying to get her eyes to focus. All she could do was keep moving and try to avoid taking more blows from her attacker. Moving in for the kill, something caught his attention at the last second. He spun around and deflected Alexis's thrust with her rapier, but it still scored in his left shoulder.

He turned to attack the younger thief. Alexis tried to avoid meeting his attacks with her thin blade, letting him press his attack. Since she was retreating upstairs, she used her height and the curve of the stair to protect herself. As he concentrated on Alexis, he seemed to lose track of Raven. She forced herself back into the fight and drew one of her daggers. She motioned for Alexis to attack the strange little man. Alexis became more aggressive, forcing him to concentrate on parrying her attacks. Raven squinted to focus on him and then lashed out, ramming her dagger into his lower back.

The small man's body went rigid and his head shot back. His mouth was opened in a scream but nothing came out. Raven rammed her body into his, keeping him upright with her damaged right arm while she continued to stab him, inflicting horrific damage. She felt him collapse onto the steps, his mace clattering on the steps behind him. Alexis hurried to stop it as Raven slumped down beside the dead man.

"Raven, are you all right?" Alexis's voice sounded like it was coming from across the river.

She forced herself to be lucid for a moment. "No. Listen. Hide him. Use the alcove. Lock the door. Go to Bertok's."

After that, everything was a blur to Raven. She had no idea how they got out of the keep. All she remembered was everything hurting: her head, her shoulder, her ribs, her knee. Her vision would clear for a few moments and then get progressively fuzzier. She had vague recollections of the sewers and then a rainstorm. She remembered a small wagon, blankets, and a smelly tarp. The rest of the trip to Bertok's was painful, but in her half-conscious state, she didn't notice the passage of time, just the number of potholes in the streets of Sagras. She saw Bertok's face when the old wizard pulled the tarp off her and carried her into his house.

She heard Bertok and Alexis talking and then Bertok

forced a nasty drink down her. She fought with him and then she fought the sudden urge to upchuck everything she'd eaten in the past week. As fast as that sensation had hit her, it went away—and so did the fog in her head.

"Goddess, Bertok. I don't know what you shoved down me, but that was some vile-tasting crap," she blurted out, once she regained control of her stomach.

"Well, you didn't give me much time to flavor it. Next time you decide to go into convulsions, you could give me some warning first."

"I'll try to keep that in mind. It's not every day I get whacked in the head."

"Maybe if it *did* happen more often, you'd give up this foolish idea of being a thief and settle down to a more honorable profession."

"What? Hedge wizard?"

"You don't see people trying to whack me on the head, do you?"

"Excuse me, you two," Alexis broke in. "This is neither the time nor place for this argument."

Something about the pitch of Alexis's voice made Raven feel like someone had just stuck a stiletto through her temples. "Please, Alexis, a little softer. If you keep that up, I'm going to need another shot of that … whatever it was."

"I can't give you any more until tomorrow night. That took all of the artemisia I had on hand. Come by tomorrow—I want to examine you closer and I can give you another dose. I'll even add flavoring to kill the taste. Now, let me look at that shoulder."

"Who *was* that little guy, Raven? It was like he couldn't speak."

Before she could answer, Bertok broke in. "Little guy, couldn't speak? Lords of Fire and Ice, Raven. If you thought they were upset over the Dragonstone, that was only a taste of what they're going to do now. The man you killed was Bela, the king's personal servant. Tell me, did anyone, *anyone*, get a hint you were there?"

"No. We don't think he saw us, either. We were surprised in a small hallway and I didn't have time to lock the door before hiding. I guess he noticed the door was unlocked but didn't make a big deal about it. He must have been coming back to check when he spotted us. Thank goodness he was mute. If he had called out for help, we would never have gotten out of there alive."

Alexis cut off Bertok's next question. "And don't worry; they're not going to find him anytime soon. Where I hid his body, it shouldn't turn up for quite a while."

"Let's hope you're right, dear child, let's hope you're right."

Chapter Twenty-One

Raven made her way through the darkened streets of Sagras toward the Royal Quarter. It had been three days since her fight with Valio's thugs and she hadn't seen any sign of them in town. She didn't know what they were up to but their silence was more nerve-racking than their blustering.

She patted her waist to assure herself the vial of blue powder was secure in the sack on her hip once again. She had completed her project just as Tybalt had been successful in his attempt to refute his rival's theories this afternoon. He acted as pleased with her accomplishment as his own and had given her this vial to show her father her work.

As she negotiated the familiar alleyways, her mind wandered back to earlier in the afternoon. Tybalt reminded her of Bertok in his own way. In fact, their conversation today had been reminiscent of several she'd had with the old hedge wizard.

* * *

The small gargoyle landed on the table in front of Perrin, startling her into dropping a small vial she had been putting in her pouch. It pounced on the vial, wrapping its hands and tail around it protectively.

"Now, Zluty, what did I say about startling Perrin? I taught you better manners than that!" Tybalt's voice boomed from the darkened back room, chastising his mystical creation. "That is hers and she's free to take it with her. Let her have it." Zluty stared into the darkness before chirping a few times and carefully handing the vial to Perrin. Its glassy eyes stared at her and he gave her what might have generously been called a smile before hopping down the table, unconcerned by the alchemist's tone of voice.

Perrin hid a smile behind one of her hands. She found the creature a little disconcerting but it acted like a cat whenever it wasn't "on duty." Perrin watched it play with one of the spare vials on her table. Tybalt emerged from his inner sanctum, brushing some dust off his robes, and joined her at her workbench, his ever-present staff in his hand. His clear blue eyes watched her closely as he lowered himself into a nearby chair.

"You have the makings of a great alchemist, Perrin."

"Coming from you, that's a high honor. I watched you work on that last batch of potions. You measure and pour so fast; I could only identify a few of the components."

"Years of practice and a desire to keep my business. If you know what I am mixing and in what amounts, why would you pay me to make potions for you? A great alchemist is part charlatan. Sleight of hand comes in handy. Besides, it's best if my apprentices don't learn all my tricks yet."

Perrin's laugh sounded almost foreign to her. She hadn't felt this relaxed in days. "I guess I hadn't thought about it that way."

"No, I don't expect you would, Perrin. You have a good heart, like your father." Tybalt summoned his creature to him and gazed out one of the laboratory's windows, his face growing more serious. "Speaking of your father, I have a question for you."

"I'll answer if I can."

"Fair enough. Do you intend to take over the bookstore when he gets older?"

Perrin felt her body stiffen. "We haven't decided yet. I know he wanted me to, but he's decided to remarry. His wife-to-be has a younger son. He may decide to leave the store to him."

Tybalt packed the bowl of his pipe with tobacco, watching her with a measured gaze. "I see." He lit the pipe and let a wreath of smoke rise toward the ceiling. "But you were never interested in being a shop owner."

She felt her face flush. "Is it that obvious?"

"You're a dutiful daughter, Perrin. You've taken care of your father as much as he's taken care of you all these years. You have the makings of a successful bookseller. But even I can't see you working in a store the rest of your life."

She favored him with a bittersweet smile. "It'll break his heart, though. That's all he's talked about for years, passing the shop on to me … and my husband."

"Ah, I see! The shop threatens both your time and your freedom."

"Yes … no … I don't know … I have nothing against getting married. There's so much of the world out there to see, though. I've read about the wonders of the world since I was old enough to hold a book. It's not fair to learn about things and never get a chance to see if they're true."

"And the bookstore is the anchor holding you in Sagras?"

Perrin paused and then faced Tybalt. "Yes."

"Would you consider becoming my apprentice full time?"

He asked it so matter-of-factly she had to stop to be sure she'd heard him right. She started to jump at the chance, but the cold medallion beneath her blouse brought her up short. "I have some business I have to deal with first. If the offer is available after I settle my affairs, I'd love to talk to you about it then."

She thought for a moment she'd angered the old alche-mist. Tybalt's eyes narrowed and she found herself scooting back to get away from his intense gaze. After a small eternity, his body relaxed and he nodded. "I understand. If matters are that pressing, you'd never be able to give the dedication and concentration I will *demand* as your mentor."

* * *

"Would you consider becoming my apprentice?"

As Raven waited at the Royal Quarter wall for the City Watch to pass, she thought hard on Tybalt's offer. Becoming his apprentice would be a great opportunity. As an alchemist, she'd be free to travel about the empire.

Besides, it would give me time to study under Bertok also. That'd make the old goat happy, having me to torture on a regular basis. Combine magic with alchemy and I could be set for life. And if things got bad, I'd always have Raven to fall back on. Provided I survive tonight.

She scaled the wall without a second's thought and headed down familiar streets. At the end of her trek, a familiar house loomed in front of her, still showing signs of fresh construction. From the shadows of a large tree she took out her telescope and scanned the grounds. She was looking for any sign of the person she intended to settle things with tonight: Bloody Douglas Valio.

I hate being this vulnerable but as much as it disgusts me, I have to strike a deal with Valio. I'd rather cut out his heart, if he had one, than cut a deal with him, but I can't afford to have his bloodhounds on my trail right now. Provided they let me get close enough to talk to him, that is.

She decided she couldn't wait any longer. While the City Watch was inept, even they might find her if she stayed in one place too long. Valio's hunters, on the other hand, were anything but inept. Slipping through the shadows, she approached Valio's house from the rear. She discovered a section of the stone wall where the iron spikes were missing at one of the corners. She pulled her grapnel out of her backpack and gave the rope a gentle swing, just enough to get the grapnel over the top of the wall. It made a small *thunk* when it landed and she waited to see if anyone reacted. Convinced no one had heard it, she climbed up the wall.

Hmm, no glass? No spikes? I can't believe he didn't take basic precautions after my last visit. Either he's got a lot of confidence in his hunters ... or else he wants me to try again. Somehow, neither of those options makes me feel comfortable. Thank Praxil, Bertok's medicine is working.

She let herself fall to the ground and rolled into the deeper shadows at the foot of the wall. She lay on the grass and let her eyes adjust to the shadows. There was no sign she'd been observed. Nothing stirred in the yard except for a few branches moving in the evening breeze. She crawled over to a clump of bushes and then sprinted toward the house, staying as low as possible to the ground.

Before she reached her destination, something seemed to strike her, making her stumble to the left. She flattened herself against the wall and then lowered herself to the ground. She didn't know what had struck her, but she knew she wasn't alone.

"Now that's no way to greet an old friend, Raven. Sneaking around in the shadows like that, you'd think you didn't have any manners. Come on out and say hello." The nameless hunter's voice cut through the darkness.

"How can I greet an old friend if we haven't been introduced? Your friends' manners are somewhat lacking."

"Tch-tch. You're right. My name's Raymond of Bedford and I am a mere sword-for-hire. Nobody important like the mysterious thief known as Raven." He stepped from one of the shadows near the back door.

She left the shadows near the wall to hide next to a tree on the lawn. "I believe you overstate my importance, but no matter. I don't mind having a pleasant conversation with you, but I'd rather not have David or Philippe sneaking up behind me. I think you understand my concerns."

"Of course. Colin, Philippe, David, leave us. Go inside and wait."

"But, Raymond!" Colin's voice rang out from a different section of the yard. "You promised I'd have first shot at that—"

Raymond's sharp voice cut him off. "Colin, when you become the leader you can do whatever the hell you want. Until then, you'll follow my orders or you'll be dead before you can draw your sword. Your choice."

"I'm going, I'm going." Colin sounded like a petulant three-year-old as he stomped up the stairs and went in the front door. Another door opened and closed twice and she had to assume Philippe and David had retreated also. She shrugged out of her backpack and hid it next to the tree near her. As she ran her hand down the leather, she found a dart sticking out of it only an inch from her neck. She realized how close she had come to death already.

"I'm waiting, Raven."

"Give me a moment. You wouldn't want a girl to meet you not looking her best."

"I expect nothing but your best tonight—that is, if you wish to live more than a few seconds."

She didn't bother responding. She knew he was trying to get under her skin but she wasn't going to give him the satisfaction. She slipped a few items out of one of her pouches and wedged them into her belt before stepping out to face him.

Light began pouring onto the lawn as curtains were drawn back, casting strange shadows all through the yard. *I know Douglas is hiding behind one of those curtains. He'd enjoy watching me die for his entertainment. Not going to happen tonight, Douglas.*

Raymond and she began moving forward, trying to force the other to have to face the lights. They shifted position, moving from darkness to light and back again. Raven kept her rapier trained on Raymond while holding her right hand behind her back. She knew he'd seen her fight rapier-and-dagger before and she wanted him wondering what she was hiding there.

They began their first pass when Raven stopped and threw a small clay ball at Raymond just before closing her eyes. He slashed at it out of instinct and was bathed in a large explosion of light from the flash powder inside. He stumbled back, temporarily blinded. Raven took advantage, rushing forward. He heard her coming and struck out blindly, forcing Raven to drop into a slide to duck beneath his swing before she stabbed him in the upper thigh with her rapier. She rolled to the side to escape his follow-up attack and regained her feet. She stood still while he shifted back and forth, trying to hear her next approach.

Reaching into her belt again, she came up with another small clay ball. This was a special set Bertok had prepared just for tonight's mission and ones she'd hoped she wouldn't have to use. She tossed it beyond Raymond and closed her eyes. The clay ball burst in an explosion that rocked the house, shattering some of the windows. Raymond stumbled toward her from the blast and she rushed past him, sinking her blade deep into his right shoulder. His sword dropped from nerveless fingers. He tried a roundhouse punch where her attack had come from, but connected with air.

Dropping to a knee, he found his weapon and lifted it in his left hand. *I was afraid of this. He's not worried about using his off-hand. I knew he was going to be a difficult opponent to beat. From the way he's blinking, he's not going to be blinded much longer.* She glanced around at the damage from the explosion. *Damn that Bertok, he overdid it again. That'll bring the Royal Guard for sure. I'm going to have to end this now.*

Reaching behind her back a third time, she pulled out another clay ball. Taking careful aim, she tossed it at his feet. The explosion lifted him into the air, depositing him in a pool of light several feet away. He lay in a heap, blood pooling beneath him. He was staring up as she approached with care.

"What … what did you do? You didn't give me a chance."

"I couldn't afford to give you a fair fight. You're too good, Raymond."

"If I survive, I'll hunt you down and kill you."

She rested the tip of her sword against his chest. "I know that, too."

She wiped Raymond's blood off her rapier and then sheathed it. She faced the now darkened house, trying to project an unconcerned look. "Douglas, I know you're in there."

It took a bit, but a harsh voice rang out. "All right, witch, what do you want?"

"It's simple, Douglas. I want you and your hunters out of

town. I was going to negotiate with you but I see that's out of the question. So now I'm giving you an ultimatum. You have two options: You can leave, or you can die. I don't care about the men with you. They can leave or stick around and die. It's up to them. You, though, have two days to leave or I will be back and I will finish what I started. And there isn't a damn thing you can do about it."

"Two days? That's impossible. You're crazy."

"That's been said so much I'm starting to believe it, Douglas. Two days and I'll be back. You could have Kazmer himself standing next to you and I'll find you, Douglas."

"I'll turn the town upside down to find you."

"No. No, you won't. You'll scramble around, get all the money you have available, not just that money in the safe in your bedroom, and then you'll be gone. Let some other town deal with you. I don't care. Just be gone two days from now."

She stepped into the shadows. She heard the arguing coming from inside the house and the sound of a fist striking someone. She knew the rats were starting to desert Valio, which is why she mentioned the safe. With any luck the hunters would insist on looting it before leaving. She wished she could stick around for the finale, but a commotion was heading toward the estate. That was her cue to leave.

She managed to avoid the cordon of guardsmen around Valio's home and headed deeper into the Royal Quarter. *They'll be expecting me to head for the Old Wall, so I'll find a place to hide and make my escape later.*

She kept to the shadows until she reached the wall separating the Royal Quarter from the Red Citadel. She cut across the quarter, stopping to visit with bartenders and some of the soldiers she knew. After an hour, she left the Red Quarter and made her way clockwise around the Hill through the Barrens, the Laborers' Quarter, and then to the Commons. *Think I'll check on Hendrik. He'll be pleased to know things should start settling down soon.*

A shadow stepped out of an alley as she approached the Black Boar. Raven drew her rapier and whirled to face the threat, only to see Ian's shocked face in the dim light. "By the Death God, Raven, if I had known you were so touchy, I'd have let you know I was here."

"Tonight has not been a good night, Ian. What the hell do you want?"

Ian's face fell at her tone of voice. "I came to apologize for the other night, Raven. I was out of line and I know it."

Ian's apology surprised Raven. She'd known him for a while and humility had never been his strong suit. Something told her he was up to something but she was willing to give him a chance. "Thank you, Ian. That's an unexpected, but welcome, surprise. We'll just pretend the other night never happened."

She turned to go, but the sound of Ian clearing his throat made her stop. "Ah, Raven, before you go, I have something for you."

She looked at Ian. "That's really not necessary."

"C'mon, Raven. I had a good night the other night. When I saw this, I thought of you and, well, I'd like you to have it. You don't *have* to take it."

She hated it when he got that three-year-old's sound in his voice. She decided to humor him, though, since he appeared so sincere. "All right, Ian. What do you have?"

He reached into a pouch and removed a diamond necklace with a huge amethyst in the center. Raven took a quick breath in spite of herself. It was gorgeous and would bring a huge price, even after the fence took his cut. The amethyst picked up the faint glow of the streetlights in its facets and sent a sparkle of purple reflections against the wall of the building.

"Ian, I can't accept something like this. You'd be set for a long time when you sold this."

"I told you, I had a great haul the other night. In fact, I'm going to have to go into hiding for a while. Most of the stuff I got is pretty recognizable, so I wouldn't try to fence that yet. I'd hide it somewhere safe and just wait. It'll be worth your while."

"Ian, I don't feel comfortable accepting this."

"Look, Raven, after our 'disagreement' the other night, I understand your hesitation. I'd like you to have this, no strings attached. Look, I liked Jerek a lot, too. He was about as close to a friend as I had in the guild. I know he liked you a lot, so I want you to have it. That's all."

Raven winced on the inside as he said that, but almost against her will she watched her hand reach out and lift the necklace out of Ian's hand. "All right, Ian. I'll accept it." She slipped it into a pouch on her hip and turned back to thank Ian again, but the lithe thief had disappeared into the shadows.

* * *

She wandered through the city a bit longer before deciding to head back to her lair. *With any luck, Alexis didn't follow me tonight. I'm not quite certain how I'd explain my actions this evening.* The weight of the necklace in her pouch made her as uncomfortable as the weight of her rapier did.

She saw Raymond's face as she moved through the tunnels. His last words still rang in her ears: *"You never gave me a chance."* She shook in revulsion and stared down at her hands. *Galen said I'm not a thug, but I set out tonight prepared to kill someone. That's not me. I'm not a cold-blooded killer. Damn that Douglas for putting me in this situation. Tybalt's offer sounds better by the second.*

No! Not until I settle with King Marcus. There will be a reckoning for what he did to Jerek and the others. I can't set Raven aside until Marcus pays for his deeds. There will be retribution … even if it means my life.

Chapter Twenty-Two

"Perrin, did you see where I put that copy of *Bacquer's Theorems*? I'm expecting the purchaser to be here in an hour and I can't find that book."

Perrin stepped behind one of the counters in the bookstore and drew the missing book out of a small drawer. "You set it there earlier this morning so you wouldn't forget it. Does Fiana know how bad your memory is getting?" she added with a smile.

Rory gave the book an accusing look as if it had crept into the drawer on its own and then grinned at her. "Luckily for me, she is still somewhat besotted herself. I'm sure she'll start noticing my warts soon enough." He glanced out the front window as the sun was starting to set over the harbor. "At least the city seems to be settling down. I haven't heard of any new disasters."

"After the past few weeks, it seems strange. It's almost like the city is taking a breath before something else happens."

"I still can't get over what happened to the Corconti." Rory ran a hand through his hair before continuing. "I mean, I can't get too worked up over the thieves' guild—after all, I know quite a few people who'll sleep better at night knowing their goods will be in their stores in the morning. But the Corconti … They're wanderers and horse traders. I can't imagine that camp had enough to interest bandits or marauders. I tell you, this city seems a lot less colorful without them here."

Perrin steeled herself before responding. "They seemed to be good people. I wish I had gotten to know them better."

"I hadn't wanted to say anything, but when Bryan and I got to the Corconti camp, I heard there was a stranger who'd been there before us. Said she had a chance to speak to Jerek before he passed on. Odd thing is, they say she had red hair."

Perrin thought furiously for an answer. "Well, they say the Corconti were popular with the young men and women in town. But *I'd* have had no reason to be there."

Rory gave her a knowing look. "That's not what Angelina told me when I got back here. She said you'd gone to the camp."

Perrin winced. She'd forgotten all about Angelina. "All right, Father, I was there. I hadn't mentioned it because I wasn't certain how you'd feel when you found out."

"Found out what?"

"That the day Jerek escorted me back from the well ... wasn't our first meeting. You see, some of those evenings when you thought I was tutoring, I was actually seeing Jerek. We'd met some months ago, but decided to keep our relationship quiet until we were certain how we felt about each other."

She could see the hurt on her father's face. "Perrin, when have you ever felt like you couldn't tell me something?"

"Father, I remember your reaction when you saw us in the alley. I wanted to tell you, especially after you told me about Fiana, but I wanted to be sure before I presented him to you. After all, you've been after me to find 'the right man' for years now. I realize he might not have been what you had in mind, but Jerek was a good man."

Rory walked over and put his arms around Perrin. "Honey, I am so sorry for your loss. I just want you to know that if you want to talk, I'm here. You don't have to hide anything from me. No matter what happens, I'll always be on your side."

Oh, great. Like I don't feel guilty enough already about hiding Raven from him. "Of course, Father."

The entrance of a customer interrupted their discussion and Perrin took advantage of the opportunity to escape any further questions. She felt the anger and sorrow and every other emotion she'd been suppressing the past few days and savagely fought them down.

Not now. There'll be time to mourn once this is all over. I need my head on straight for what I have planned for tonight.

* * *

"Alexis, get ready. We're going out this evening!" Raven paused at the bottom of the stairs but only silence met her call. Frowning, she climbed the stairs and entered her apprentice's room. The bed was made, everything was in order, but there was no sign of Alexis.

Damn her. She knows the rules.

Raven started to stomp out when a piece of parchment fluttered on the bed near Alexis's pillow. She'd missed seeing it in her cursory glance through the room. Curious, she picked up the paper.

> Raven,
> Received a message from Bertok. He needed to see me about something important.
> Sorry I couldn't wait for you. He said this could take a while, so I don't expect to be back before morning. Good luck with whatever you have planned for tonight.
> Alexis

Steal my apprentice, will he? Oh, the old faker and I are going to have this one out! Raven projected her thoughts as hard as she could, hoping Bertok could pick up on her rage and have an inkling of what was coming his way. She wadded the paper up into a little ball and started to toss it away, but then smoothed it out and folded it into one of her pouches. She wanted to have the evidence handy when she confronted him.

She paused as a sudden thought sent a cold chill through her. *What if the message wasn't from Bertok?* There was an alternative she didn't want to consider. Alexis was a good kid, but she wasn't suspicious enough to look for hidden meanings.

She shook her head. She had to trust Alexis was with Bertok, otherwise she'd never accomplish what she had planned for tonight. It was audacious enough but she had to have her mind clear.

Fine. I'm going solo. I think someone would pay good money for information that might save his life. Might as well make his acquaintance.

* * *

After a cautious passage through the sewers and the necropolis, she reached the entrance to the keep's lower levels. She stepped into the hallway, then retreated quickly, shutting the door most of the way, when a soft light appeared to her right. Two guards passed by, each wearing ornamental armor and carrying a small halberd and torch. They didn't even give the doorway she was hiding behind a second glance. She let them continue ambling down the hallway, listening to snippets of their conversation rumbling in the hallway.

Raven followed close behind, using their fading lights as a guide. Checking hallway doors at random, the guards never realized their band had added a third member. Raven wondered what lay behind these little-used doors, but there was for another night. She hoped these guards would lead her to something interesting.

At the end of the hallway, they turned and she saw a stone stairwell in their torchlight. She gave them a five-second head start and then hurried up the stairs. By their heavy footsteps, she judged they were two turns ahead of her on the spiral staircase.

After a short climb, their footsteps paused and the volume of their voices increased. The increased light told her they'd reached a landing. She retreated a few steps when a sudden click on the stone told her they were resting on their halberds. She inched forward, trying to make sense of the muffled voices above her. They conversed among themselves, grousing about their schedule before pushing on with their rounds.

Raven relaxed as she realized the guards were moving forward instead of heading her way. She crept forward until her eyes reached the edge of the landing. Peering around, she assured herself no one could see her before she stepped out onto it.

She could see they'd reached the main floors. This was a different stairway from what Alexis and she had used the last time. Halfway across the floor, the guardsmen had stopped to talk to a tall, well-dressed man while a group of chambermaids walked by carrying baskets full of clothing. The guards' and maids' deferential manner told Raven this was someone of importance.

He dismissed the guards with a gesture. She saw the guards enter a stairwell on the opposite wall and go downstairs as he began walking toward her position. She hoped he would turn before he reached the stairwell, but he showed no signs of stopping. She retreated a few steps, wondering if she could reach the necropolis before the guards. After a few steps, she noticed there were no footsteps following her downward. She paused and heard the soft tread of the man going up. Never being one to question a gift, she reversed her course and began following her new prey, hoping he might lead her to the royal quarters.

They climbed three floors. Raven noticed the footsteps were slow and measured. This person was in no hurry to get to his destination. She knew the higher she climbed, her chances of escape worsened, but this was too good an opportunity to pass up.

The footsteps faded as she reached the top of the stairwell. She was afraid she'd lost him, but approaching the entrance she saw the tall man walking down the dim hallway, his footsteps muffled by the thick rugs lining the floor. Only a few of the torches lining the walls were lit. He yawned before he could cover his mouth and took out a large key to open the door in front of him.

Raven waited until she was certain his door was shut before making her way down the hall. Large tapestries and banners covered the stone walls between the wooden doors. *This is too nice an area for the servants and too quiet for business. These are personal quarters for someone, but who?*

She began testing doors to see if any were unlocked. The faster she got out of a long, open hall like this, the happier she was going to be. Reaching the halfway point, her light touch on a door handle produced results. She opened the door a few inches and listened. When she couldn't hear anything, she opened it just wide enough to slip inside.

It was a bedroom large enough to hold her father's and hers with space left over. She gave it a cursory going over but couldn't determine who lived there. Two doors led out onto a large stone balcony, so she unlocked one and let herself out. It was surrounded by a three-foot-high wall and there were other balconies to the right and left about five feet away.

She locked the door behind her, not wanting to make the same mistake she'd made the last time she'd entered the keep. Looking off to her left, she could see a row of balconies leading toward the corner of the keep. But to her right, about three balconies over, a light shone through an open door. *At least someone keeps my kind of hours.*

She estimated the distance between the balconies was five feet. She knew she could make the jump between the gaps, but wasn't certain she could without making noise. Yet she'd come too far to quit now. She fished her grapnel and rope out of her backpack and tossed the padded metal hook over to the next balcony and quickly shinnied across to the next balcony. Two more tosses and she found herself outside the open set of doors. She heard angry voices inside and crept forward, trying to find out what was going on.

"I've gone to a great deal of effort to put this treaty together with Helion, Brother. They've agreed to most of our terms and I understand there's going to have to be some compromise on the few remaining points. Why would we go to war with a potential ally?"

"Dear Geoffrey, you miss the point. It's not whether Helion is a good ally; it's that they're still an independent state and could be turned against us. The only way to be certain of their allegiance is to make them a part of Sagras."

"Owen, it's not like Helion is on the other side of Hunter's Wood. We'd have to seize several villages en route to secure our supply lines. Our supply lines still would be dangerously exposed unless we seized Appilon and Raston to protect them."

Muted clapping sounded in the room. "Bravo, Geoffrey. You weren't sleeping in Wulfric's classes on tactics. You're almost correct. We'd have to seize Appilon, Raston, *and* Fallen Timber, but they're mere appetizers compared to the juicy prize Helion is."

"Owen, be reasonable. It took almost a month to hammer out a treaty with them. Why would Father have me do that, if we were going to attack them before the ink was dry?"

"Well, it got you out of his hair for nearly a month."

"That's cheap even for you, Brother."

"I'm certain you'll survive. Don't you think Father would have used his ambassador if this was important? My dear brother, you were a stalking horse. You kept their attention while we finished our preparations. Don't look so upset. You might be the most valuable member of the conquest when all is done."

"Has Father given the command to begin the campaign?"

"Not yet. He's waiting for something, although he won't say what it is. He keeps hinting it'll make our conquest simpler so it must be important."

"Then there is still time. I will talk with him. I will do whatever it takes to stop this madness. This could turn the other city-states against us."

Owen's voice made Raven feel like she needed to take a bath. "Oh, they'll turn against us, but not until they scoop up the remaining villages for themselves. We'll have enough time to consolidate our gains and begin turning one against the other. The only thing these petty rulers have ever agreed on is that they hate each other as much as they hate us."

"You've been planning this for quite a while, haven't you, Owen?"

"Very good again, dear brother. While you were spending your time in the library learning how to run a castle, I was learning how to run a kingdom. But don't worry. If you're concerned about Helion, I'll give it to you once I inherit Father's realm."

Geoffrey's voice became icy. "Getting a little ahead of yourself, Owen? After all, whether Father leaves us a city or an empire, *I* am first in line for the throne."

"A mistake of nature. You may be first by right of birth, but I have no doubt Father will pass you over for someone competent."

Raven winced as she heard the sound of a chair overturning. "You presume too much, Owen."

There was a short pause and she heard the sound of a door opening. Owen's voice dropped in volume, but there was no questioning his intensity. "No, Geoffrey, you imagine too little. There is nothing I won't do to become king, and I want to rule more than this pathetic little town. You'll see what I mean soon enough."

The sound of crockery shattering against something hard was Raven's cue to slip inside. She found a quiet place and took a long look at the elder prince. He had returned to the table, his long blond hair falling over his face. She noted he was a little older than she. Despite Owen's teasing about his time in the library she could tell Geoffrey had also spent time in the training ring.

He turned in his chair until he was facing her. "Are you an assassin sent by my brother?"

His calm demeanor surprised her as she stepped out into the open. *Remind me not to underestimate him again.* She decided to brazen her way out. Trying to assume a nonchalant air, she approached the table and sat down. "No, Your Highness.

Although considering what I'm about to tell you, I'd suggest locking your windows here in the future."

"A messenger, then, and a lovely one at that. I'm curious to hear your tale."

Prince Geoffrey walked over to a cabinet set on the wall and snagged two crystal glasses and a bottle of wine. He set a glass in front of Raven and then took a seat across from her. "So, if you're a messenger, what story do you have to tell?"

"There is something I need to know first, before I pass my information to you."

"You have me at a disadvantage but do not presume too much." He reached out to pour some wine in her glass and then his. He swirled the purple liquid, letting it catch the light. "However, your audacity amuses me. Ask your questions."

"You know of the Corconti?"

"The wanderers? They had a camp in the Hunter's Wood but they left. A couple of my instructors used to study plant lore with them."

"You don't know why they left?"

"No. All I know is they pulled out one evening and haven't been seen since."

"They left because the Black Leopards attacked their camp and killed everyone they could get their hands on."

Geoffrey's hand struck the table, sending small droplets of wine scattering across its marble top. "*What?* My father's elite guard attacked them? Ridiculous."

Raven took a sip of her wine as she watched the prince's face. If he was faking, he was good. She let him run down a bit before she continued.

"Your father believed the Corconti had something he wanted. He was wrong, but the assassins couldn't leave anyone behind to speak of their failure. He's also turned them loose on the thieves' guild. They didn't have the item, either."

"And how do *you* know this?"

"Because they killed the man I loved." Raven surprised herself at how strong that statement came out. She took a deep breath before continuing. "Also, I know what they were looking for because I took it."

"You stole something belonging to my father and then come to the royal keep? Why?"

Raven tipped her glass, indicating she needed a refill. She was still weighing why she was getting involved in the first place and was stalling for time. She took a small sip and enjoyed the warm, rich taste. "Ah, this is wonderful. I might have to pick some up one of these evenings."

"That might be a problem since I have the only supply in the city."

"Sounds like a challenge."

The prince's laughter rang out and Raven found herself smiling in spite of herself. She saw his body relax as he lifted his wineglass to her in salute. Once he stopped laughing, she decided to get to the heart of the matter.

"Your Highness, as you learned, your father intends to begin a war with Helion. A decision you seem to disagree with." She looked over the edge of her glass, waiting for his reaction.

"If I disagree with my father, that's between him and me. What has that to do with your message?"

"There are some who support this war, but"—she held up a hand to stop his retort—"they support the idea of Owen as the successor even more."

Geoffrey set his glass down, his smile disappearing. "So Owen's threats were not just his usual boasting."

"All I know is most of the Privy Council agreed to support removing you from succession. Most opposed killing you outright, but I think they're more afraid of your father than you."

Geoffrey gave off a sharp bark of a laugh. "Father has never hidden his feelings toward me from them. He's a warrior first and a king second. That's how people like Bela and Kazmer gained the power they have."

"Have no doubt, Your Highness, Kazmer *is* the power behind them. I don't know what the council is going to decide, but it's going to happen soon. It seems to be tied into the campaign against Helion."

"You have evidence I can use against the Privy Council?"

"No, Your Highness, I have no physical evidence. This wasn't the sort of thing they would write down. I overheard them plotting, which means it's the word of a thief against five of the highest ranking men in the kingdom. I thought *you* should know so you could rally your allies. From what I know about your brother, I think Sagras would be better off with you on the throne."

"Be careful how you speak about Owen, messenger. He may be many things, but he is still a prince of the realm."

Raven's cheeks flushed red as she choked down an angry retort. Hadn't she just warned Geoffrey that others were plotting to kill him, yet he was defending his brother? Thinking back on the conversation, she realized Owen had been mentioned as a possible successor, but Kazmer never said Owen wanted his brother dead.

"Forgive me, Your Highness. Oh, one of the council was not present. I believe he's called Hugh?"

"That doesn't surprise me." Geoffrey refilled his wineglass, a fond look on his face. "Hugh is the only commoner in the council. None can argue with his devotion but the councilors resent his presence more than they resent mine. He's as close a friend as I have in the keep."

An idea occurred to her and before she realized what she had done, she blurted it out. "There is a way we might be able to stop this war, Your Highness."

Silence descended on the room as Geoffrey stared at her, his eyebrows knitted together in thought. He brought his elbow down on the table and rested his chin on his fist. Raven became uncomfortable at his intense gaze, not certain if he was upset, curious, or thought she was a madwoman. She felt herself squirming under his stare, wishing he would either say something or look away, at least.

"There is a way we could stop this war." His mocking tone parroted her words back at her. "You arrive on my balcony; tell me my father's pet assassins have been eliminating the

Corconti and the thieves' guild; that the Privy Council wants to depose me; that you have stolen something that belongs to the royal family; and now you're going to help me stop a war, in defiance of my father, *the king*."

She stared him in the eye and said only one word in a soft voice. "Yes."

The prince's mouth widened into a smile. "By the gods, you're serious. All right, thief and rebel, you've caught my attention. What did you have in mind?"

"Your father needs the Dragonstone. Legend says it's a powerful weapon in the right hands. Without the Dragonstone, he is hesitating to attack Helion. This gives you more time to reason with him."

"And you just happen to know where this Dragonstone is?"

"I stole it from the cathedral several weeks ago."

Geoffrey sat up and stared at her. "So you're the thief who got everyone so stirred up. I'm honored to be in your presence. Twenty Leopards were reassigned to the silver mines or the punishment galleys because they failed to stop you."

"And that doesn't bother you?" Raven had seen the galleys before. She never thought anyone would be sent to them over something she'd done. She gave a small shudder and then turned her mind back to the problem at hand.

"My personal feelings are immaterial. Kazmer runs the Leopards as he sees fit. Even if I *were* king, I'm not certain I could interfere in what the Leopards consider an internal matter."

"There is another reason I came to the castle tonight. Your father's pet assassins killed the man I loved, remember? There must be retribution."

Geoffrey stared at her, an unpleasant expression settling on his face. "I thought you came to warn me. Was this ploy to win my trust?"

"I came tonight to warn you, but in all honesty, meeting you was serendipity. I had no clue how to contact you."

"So why warn me? You have no reason to love any of my

family if your story is true."

"Honestly, I'm still asking myself that question. However, you're going to have to trust someone who should hate your family by all rights, because it doesn't look like you can trust anyone else around here. I have no desire for power and I'm not a murderer."

"What do you intend to do to get your retribution?"

"Take your father's peace of mind. I intend to steal something right out from underneath his nose. He's going to spend a lot of sleepless nights wondering how I got in and if I'll be back. If word of the theft leaks out, it will embarrass him among his peers. While it's not an eye for an eye, I'm not going to lower myself to murder to take my revenge. I think he'd have a harder time living with being embarrassed and afraid."

"If I understand you, you want me to help you steal something valuable from the royal treasury to embarrass my father?"

"It depends, Your Highness. Do you want to stop this war?"

"How does stealing something from the keep stop a war?"

"It doesn't. The note left on his pillow saying it would be unwise to march against any city when *he* is so undefended should get his attention."

"Brilliant, yet subtle. It'll definitely cause him to doubt Kazmer, and the army won't move until the council is settled. By then, I may be able to rouse enough support to halt the war before it gets started."

"Plus, a certain thief who's no longer in Sagras might send warning to Helion, giving them a chance to muster support. Sagras might attack an unsuspecting Helion, but not one that's prepared with potential enemies all along the path of march, as you said to your brother."

"Wait, I'm not so comfortable with that thought."

"Kazmer's plans fall apart if the Dragonstone is not found and Helion is prepared. Wulfric will not commit the army without some assurance of winning; neither will your father unless he's lost all his senses."

"Speaking of the Dragonstone, what is your plan for it and this 'item' you liberate from the castle?" The prince looked over steepled fingers at her, his elbows resting on the table. She felt the power of his personality in his gaze. If the council members thought Geoffrey was soft, they'd never spent time with him.

Raven considered various answers before deciding to tell him most of the truth. "The Dragonstone I intend to sell to leave this city once and for all. The other item I would sell also. Of course, for the right price a certain prince I know might be able to purchase both of them in secret." She gave him a coy smile and then picked up her drink again.

Geoffrey's stare bore into her eyes, cold and inscrutable. After a few moments, she began to worry she'd overplayed her hand. As she watched, he lowered his hands, revealing a broad smile on his face.

"I know who you are. Unlike my brother, Owen, I've spent time in the city beyond the Royal Quarter. You are Raven, are you not?"

She nodded, pleased her reputation had penetrated the Great Keep. "I have been called that, Your Highness, among other things."

"The people I talk to seem to have a high opinion of you. There is a gem the ruler of Sagras must have to be crowned king. It is invaluable and there's only one place I can imagine where Father would keep it: the private family armory. There are two routes to reach it, but only one way *you* could have any chance of reaching it unobserved."

He walked over to a desk in a far corner of his chamber and returned with a roll of blank parchment and set a quill and ink beside it. He roughed in a sketch of the lowermost level of the keep that corresponded with the map Galen taught her. However, a few quick strokes of the goose quill showed a hidden passage the master thief had missed.

After a few minutes, Geoffrey finished. It was crude but clear and Raven could see why there was only one way she could reach the armory unseen: The standard route led through the dungeon, but Geoffrey's map showed a much narrower way from an adjoining passageway that would dump her out across the hall from the armory.

The prince began writing in a strong, steady hand. As he finished one set of details, he paused, looking up at her. "You can read, can't you?"

"Yes, I can read."

"That's useful. So many in the city cannot."

Raven thought she heard a note of sadness as he turned back to his work. There was intenseness without the arrogance of his younger brother. He wanted to succeed and he wanted his people to succeed. There was much to like about this man.

He began to explain the drawings when there was a loud knock on the door. Raven's eyes widened at the sudden interruption. She'd been so intent on watching the prince, she hadn't heard anyone approaching. Her head pivoted from side to side as she tried to find a place to hide.

The prince shoved the rolled-up map into her hand and pushed her toward the balcony door. "Go now," he whispered.

She rushed toward the door but stopped. *Slow down! What if there are guards on the adjoining balconies? You'd be running right into a trap. Hide now, escape later.* She slipped behind the heavy curtains next to the open door. Geoffrey waited until she was hidden before responding to the insistent knocking. He strode across the room and snatched the door open. "And what, pray tell, is so bloody important you would disturb me at this time of night!"

The guardsmen on the other side of the door drew back from the vehemence of the prince's advance. Before the prince could slam the door shut, a familiar voice filtered into the room. "Prince Geoffrey, why so harsh with your father's *loyal* servants? They were concerned when you didn't respond."

"Kazmer. I might have known. Please come in." The prince's voice took on a flat, emotionless tone. There was something about the way Kazmer had accentuated the word "loyal" that worried Raven. The master assassin seemed too pleased with himself for her comfort.

"You'll pardon us for being brusque, Your Highness, but I'm afraid this isn't a social call. You are hereby placed under arrest for plotting treason against his majesty, King Marcus. These guards are here to escort you to the dungeon. I'd prefer that you came along peacefully, but you *will* be coming along."

Geoffrey stood there with his mouth hanging open before lowering himself into his chair. "Oh, that's rich, Kazmer. You had me going for a moment."

Kazmer eased into the seat across the table from the prince. "Let me assure you, Your Highness, this is no joke."

"You have some proof of these charges?" Prince Geoffrey waved his hand around in a small circle as he leaned back in the chair.

"Indeed we do." Kazmer's voice lowered into a whisper. "Your own words betray you. You were quite explicit in your conversation with your brother. 'I will do whatever it takes to stop this madness.' I believe that's what you told Prince Owen?"

"Kazmer, I have the right to speak to my father about any subject unless *he* decides I cannot."

"True, Prince Geoffrey, you have that right. However, since your brother swore out the complaint against you, we can take his word on this. You can make your arguments before the high court."

"Provided I live to see the high court."

"That, dear prince, is up to you."

Geoffrey rose to his feet as the guards fell in on either side. Kazmer's eyes scanned the room one last time and his gaze paused on the table. "So, Geoffrey, are you in the habit of drinking from two wineglasses? Or did we just miss a late-night paramour?"

"One was dirty so I poured out the wine and chose another. It's not like I was expecting anyone this evening."

"No, I suppose not. If you'll be so kind to come along now, Your Highness." Kazmer bowed to Geoffrey as the prince gathered up what dignity he had and let the guards escort him from the room. Kazmer hung behind, his gaze moving about the room.

Raven held her breath, trying to be as inconspicuous as she could. She could see the frown on the assassin's face as he debated what the second wineglass meant. She loosened one of her throwing daggers, just in case. To her relief, he turned with a flourish and left.

There should be a servant coming along any minute to extinguish the lights. It would be best if I was long gone by then. But what do I do now?

Chapter Twenty-Three

Perrin pulled her cloak closer as she made her way through the dark alley leading to her sanctuary. *One of these evenings, I'm going to get into trouble. Raven might be able to wander these streets with impunity but a shopkeeper's daughter is fair game.*

Reaching the burned remains hiding the entrance to the sewers, she paused and did a visual sweep of the area. *Something's wrong tonight, the streets are never this quiet. Whatever's happening, the regulars want nothing to do with it.* She waited a bit longer, but the regular ebb and flow of the city streets seemed off this evening. There were few people out and they hurried to get to their destinations.

I don't know what's going on. What I do know is this is no place for me to be wandering around. The quicker I get home, the happier I'll be.

She lowered herself into the sewers and then paused, listening for signs anyone was down there. Certain she was alone, she crept down the walkway and opened the hidden door in the sewer wall. She closed the door and climbed the ladder to her sanctuary. She couldn't seem to shake the feeling that something was wrong, though.

She made her way to the armoire and changed. Reaching up, she took the medallion in hand and spoke the words of the spell. She felt the magic take effect and as soon as her conversion was complete, she relaxed. Strapping on her sword belt and knives, she glanced into the full-length mirror and noted the change in her posture. Where Perrin had been hunched over, trying to make herself invisible, Raven stood upright with a cocky stance, daring the world not to notice her.

I have to talk to Bertok about this magic. There's something strange about the way it's affecting me. Looking in the mirror, she noticed the worried look on her face and shook her head. *Stop that. If you're going back to the keep tonight, you have to stay focused. Worry about stuff you can't solve later.*

She went through her gear, trying to decide what to take with her. Opening one of the cabinets against the wall, she examined the various tools in the drawers. She selected several items before discarding them for others. After deliberating over several of her options, she moved to the table and placed them into her pouches and the backpack. On a mission like this, she couldn't leave anything to chance.

She turned to leave, but a small noise in the hallway caught her attention. She crept to the door and pressed her ear to it. It sounded like soft footsteps on the stairs but as she listened closer, they stopped. *Damn, I'm getting jumpy with Alexis gone. Now I'm starting to hear things. Still, this is* my *sanctuary. I'm not taking any chances. Not here.*

She eased one of her throwing daggers out of its sheath and prepared to open the door. *There it is again. They're getting closer. Wait, they've stopped again. It's now or never.* She yanked the door open and threw in one fluid motion.

If the shadowy figure had been standing, Raven's toss would have taken it just above the belt buckle. However, the seated figure threw itself backward and the dagger imbedded itself in the stairs just a few inches above its face. Raven rushed to engage the intruder only to stop dead in her tracks when familiar laughter rang out.

"If I had known this was the welcome I would get, I might have changed my mind."

Raven stared in shock as Alexis eased out from beneath the still-quivering blade. The young thief pulled the deadly piece of steel out of the wood and handed it back to her. She cocked her head to one side and smiled. "So, did you miss me?"

A thousand thoughts ran through Raven's head, but before she could stop herself, the old sarcastic mentor broke through. "Not by much."

"True enough. That was impressive. Morgan hasn't started teaching me how to throw weapons. He's convinced I can't draw a sword without tripping over my own feet."

"Don't feel bad. He still thinks I'm going to stab myself every time I try to sheathe mine."

"He is a bit of a worrier."

The conversation trailed off into an awkward silence as they tried to find a safe line of conversation. They started to speak a few times, laughed nervously, and then Raven motioned for Alexis to follow her into the sitting room. The young thief noticed all the open cabinets and drawers and her mouth fell open.

"All right, Raven, what's going on? I've never seen you pack like this before leaving. Something's going down, isn't it?"

"Got a few minutes? Grab a seat—your seat, this time. Now, first off, where the hell have you been?"

"Bertok sent me a message, so I went to his place. He felt bad about playing around in my mind so he offered to help me find something I've been looking for."

"And did he?"

Alexis paused for a moment. After a while, she swallowed hard before answering. "Yes. Yes, he did. Let's just say something that's been bothering me for a long time was settled."

Raven suspected there was more than Alexis was saying, but this wasn't the time or place for a long discussion. That could come after their mission this evening. *Provided either of us survive, that is.* She continued packing while she filled Alexis in. When she got to the part where she'd confronted Prince Geoffrey, an incredulous look crossed Alexis's face.

"You went into the prince's bedroom? Are you nuts? What if he'd called the guards?"

"Let's just say having a private conversation with him hadn't been part of the plan. He's a lot more intuitive than

254

his family gives him credit. After seeing him and his brother, I think he'd make a much better king. There's something about Owen that's just slimy."

"But, still, he's a noble. They're good to their peasants because a happy and well-fed peasant works better than a discontented and starving one. They're not concerned because the peasant's not healthy; they're concerned because of a lack of production."

Raven gave her a look to remind her to concentrate on the here and now. "Nevertheless, he's still the best option for peace around here. You heard the Privy Council. Hellion would only be the start of Marcus's or Owen's conquests."

Alexis crossed her arms over her chest, not ready to give up her opinions. "If he's in the dungeon, then I wouldn't put much hope in that option."

"It doesn't look good, I admit. He doesn't have a lot of official support. However, I believe he's got a lot more support than people give him credit for. That's why Kazmer had to seize him in the middle of the night."

"You told him about us being there?"

"No, I told him about *me* being there. I didn't figure you wanted to be a topic of conversation."

"At least you showed some sense there. You say he gave you a map to where this gem was?"

"Where it might be. He wasn't certain where it was, but that's not important now. The map also shows the way to the dungeon. If we can spring the prince from under his father's nose that would be even more effective."

"Uh-huh, and just how much time did you spend with him before he got arrested? C'mon, is he that cute in person?"

Raven felt herself blushing. "Alexis! No … Well, I mean, yeah, he is handsome and all, but think about it. Wouldn't it be a good thing to have the next king in our debt?"

"Provided he doesn't try to cancel that debt before we can collect."

"Do you always see the worst in everyone?"

"Only if they're nobles."

Raven gave Alexis a much put-upon look and was rewarded with the old cocky grin she'd come to expect. She turned away to compose herself and then looked back at her apprentice with a stern look on her face. "If you're coming with me, you'll need to get equipped. Your stuff is upstairs, isn't it?"

"Yeah, I left it up there. I was up there until I heard you come in."

Raven moved toward the hallway when she heard a loud banging at the house's front door and the sounds of shouting filtered into the room. Raven wasn't worried since the door was bricked from the inside but something was wrong. No one had ever approached this house before. Alexis slipped into the storeroom and peeked through a hole in the boards covering the window.

"Raven, it's the City Watch! What are they doing here?"

"No clue. Get your stuff. There's an exit from the room next to yours that leads to the house next door. We can slip out that way."

Raven paused at the door, waiting for Alexis to reappear. The banging outside was getting louder. It sounded like the watchmen were beating on the door with their weapons, for all the good it would do them. She made her way toward the stairwell when something made her stop. There it was again … a soft noise, almost like a padded footfall on the floor above them. She glanced up the stairs, but didn't see anything amiss. Still, something felt wrong.

"Alexis, were the guardsmen surrounding the house or all bunched up by the door?"

"By the door. Why?"

Raven's voice lowered into a whisper. "Back into the sitting room. We're going out the other way."

She retreated into the sitting room, never taking her eyes off the stairwell. She shut the door, then placed a chair beneath the handle, wedging it into place. Only then did she turn to face her confused apprentice. "Someone was upstairs. We were supposed to rush up into a trap."

"Leopards?"

"I wouldn't want to bet my life against it. We need to leave *now*."

Raven secured a few bags of gems from one of her hiding places and joined Alexis in the storeroom. She opened one of the chests and handed Alexis a handful of weapons to take with her. While her apprentice secured them, she moved the rug off the trapdoor and lifted. Unlike earlier this evening, the door refused to budge. Straining, Raven lifted the edge of the door a few inches while Alexis used one of the gems for light to look beneath it.

"Raven, it's tied to the ladder!"

"Damn, can you get a knife through that gap?" Raven clenched her teeth as she pulled against the handle. It was taking all her strength to budge the trapdoor even that much.

"Maybe."

"No time for 'maybe.' Either you can or you can't."

"I can."

Just then, there was a thud on the sitting room door. Raven and Alexis rushed back in as the edge of an ax cleaved through the thin wood. Knowing it was only a matter of seconds before their opponents would be inside, Raven doused the lamps in the room and waited.

With a crash, the door parted and a swarm of bodies charged into the room. The sudden darkness caught them off-guard, giving Raven and Alexis the opportunity to strike first. Raven felt her rapier strike something soft and the high-pitched scream that followed told her she'd hit something vital.

Raven had to let Alexis watch after herself, she was too busy keeping herself alive. She struck at least two more opponents in the darkness and only sheer luck had saved her from being struck in return. She heard a *thunk* just inches above her head as someone's weapon struck the wall and wedged there. Her katar found the stomach of that opponent and he fell against her, pinning her to the wall for a moment.

A sudden burst of light illuminated the room. Someone

had brought down a lamp from upstairs and lit it. Only the body between her and the light kept Raven from being momentarily blinded. Shoving her dying opponent to the side, she stepped to her right, drew, and threw one of her daggers in the same motion. Her aim was true and the dagger struck the lamp carrier in the neck. He fell backward but the lamp dropped from his hand and landed on the floor.

The splattered oil ignited and flames danced across the old dry wooden floor. The black-clothed figures dashed back through the door to avoid the flames. One of them screamed as a dagger appeared in his back and he fell across the mantle, holding the door open. It seemed Alexis wasn't as bad at throwing weapons as she'd let on.

Raven rushed toward the still-open door, determined not to be trapped by the flames, but a crossbow bolt whizzed past her ear. She ducked back, giving the Leopards time to drag their wounded companion through and slam the door shut. Raven turned to see Alexis standing there, bleeding from wounds on her shoulder and left thigh. She had a worried look on her face as she waited for Raven to make a decision.

Raven rushed to the storeroom, motioning for Alexis to follow. She shut the door and stuffed an old blanket in the gap at the bottom of the door. She turned to her apprentice and motioned toward the trapdoor. "Can't go out there. You've got to cut that rope so we can get into the sewers."

"But what if they're waiting for us in the sewers?"

"What if they are? I'd rather face them in the sewers than burn to death."

Raven spotted an old piece of metal she'd found when she had first occupied the house. Using it as a wedge, she pushed on it, forcing the trapdoor up as far as she could. Alexis drew out her longest dagger and began sawing on the rope.

Raven could hear the crackling as the fire raced through the house and felt the heat pulsing through the walls. The old blanket was holding out the worst of the smoke but thin tendrils still curled beneath the door, making it hard to breathe. A grim smile crossed Raven's face as she pushed harder on the old chunk of metal. At least they were getting a little fresh air. Looking up, she saw the door to the sitting room starting to smoulder.

"Any time now, Alexis."

"If you think you can do better, you're welcome to try."

Raven started to respond but decided against distracting her apprentice's frantic strokes. She could feel the door lifting as she put more pressure on the piece of metal. However, she could also see a glow in the ceiling above them as the fire engulfed the upper floors. It wouldn't be much longer before the room they were in was an inferno.

With a sudden snap, the rope gave way. The trapdoor flew open and Raven nearly plunged headlong down the well. Nodding her approval, she secured her weapons and headed down the ladder, prepared to have to fight her way out.

She motioned for Alexis to follow as soon as her feet touched the ground. Taking a deep breath, she opened the concealed door and stepped out into the sewers. The sudden silence took her by surprise. If this was an ambush, she couldn't spot it. She stepped onto the walkway and pressed her back against the wall. The darkness and quiet were nerve-racking, but there was no sudden thrust of a weapon, no sound of a crossbow's release, nothing, except for the faint light coming from the open door.

"Raven? Are you all right?"

She could hear the nervousness in her apprentice's voice. She decided to take a chance and drew out one of her enchanted gems. Summoning its full power, she flashed the light around the sewers as far as it would reach. There was no one waiting for them.

"Come on, it's safe. We want to get out of here before they decide to come back."

"Thank goodness, I was afraid that—" Alexis's reply was cut off in mid-sentence as a sudden roar filled the well. A shower of flaming debris poured down the shaft as the ceiling gave way, burying Alexis. Raven leapt back into the narrow chamber and pulled her companion's limp body from underneath the rubble.

She examined Alexis and noticed a nasty wound on the back of the young thief's head. She knew she shouldn't move her, but this was no place to treat her apprentice's injuries, either. Hoisting Alexis onto her shoulder, Raven hurried down the sewer. She turned every corner with trepidation, expecting at any second to run into a group of Black Leopards waiting to finish the job.

She reached the spot she'd been searching for and pushed hard on one of the tiles on the wall. It slid inward, releasing the catch on a hidden door. Catching it with her foot, she worked it open and carried Alexis inside. The corridor beyond sloped upward and led to a wooden door. Raven lifted the latch and walked into the house.

A quick glance revealed a rickety table, a rough bed, and an old dresser with a well-worn pitcher resting on it. She eased Alexis off her shoulders and laid her on the bed. Going over to the dresser, she brushed the dust off an old mirror. She tried to settle her thoughts and began chanting a spell. She hadn't attempted the spell in years so she stumbled through it twice before she recalled all the words. After a few moments, the image wavered and Bertok's face appeared.

"Bertok, I need you to come here. Now."

"Where are you?"

"Abandoned house. Silver Serpent Way between Copper Street and Red Stone Road. Be careful. Leopards prowl."

"Understood." The old man gave her a concerned look and then waved a hand in front of the mirror, breaking the spell. She stared at her soot-stained reflection for a moment and then set the mirror down. She poured some water into the bowl and pulled rags out of the dresser drawer before moving to the bed to deal with Alexis. Once she had finished cleaning and bandaging the wounds, she made the young thief as comfortable as possible. Satisfied she'd done all she could, she stepped into the back room and climbed up the stairs.

Thank Dashin I set this place up after Sean died. I was so afraid then someone might know where we used to hang out. She pulled the heavy curtains to one side in one of the upstairs rooms and peered through the broken glass. *And there it goes. I see the neighbors are busy trying to protect their homes and the Leopards are nowhere to be seen.*

She stood there staring at the smoldering remains as the flames died down. The longer she stood there, the hotter her need for revenge grew. Someone had violated her sanctuary … no, not someone, *Kazmer*. He was going to pay for this.

* * *

A soft knock on the door caught Raven's attention. She hurried downstairs and glanced out from behind the drawn curtains. Bertok's familiar shape was half-hidden in the shadows near the door. She opened it just enough for Bertok to squeeze through. As soon as he had cleared the mantle, she shut the door and slammed its locking bar back in place.

"I came as fast as I could, child. I hope I'm not too late."

"I'm just glad you're here. You're certain you weren't followed?"

"I'm as certain as I can be. However, even wary prey can fall to a skilled hunter." Bertok's gaze swept over the shack before he turned his attention to Alexis. "You know, considering the grief you give me about my home, I expected your sanctuary to be somewhat more … upscale than this."

"This is a hiding place, old man, not my sanctuary." She filled him in on recent events as Bertok began working on Alexis.

As Bertok continued his ministrations, all of Raven's frustrations came rushing out of her. She released her rage in one blazing torrent. As her rant wound down, she heard soft chanting coming from the hedge wizard and then he turned toward Raven. "I put her into a healing sleep. I'm glad you sent for me as soon as you did. Now, let me look you over."

"I'm fine, old man. I just need to get off my feet for a moment." She pulled one of the chairs out and lowered herself into it. Bertok paused for a second and then chose one of the others, eyeing the rickety chair with suspicion. He sat down, waiting for it to betray his girth, but they were quite sturdy.

"You let me be the judge of that, apprentice. I don't think you're in any position to tell me how you are. Now, stare straight ahead …"

After a short examination, he stood up and placed his hands on her head. As he muttered something, she felt warmth making its way through her body. She felt her muscles begin to relax and the bruises she'd received during the fight began to feel better. She caught herself trying to fall asleep under whatever Bertok was doing.

Shaking her head to try and focus herself, she pulled away and leaned back in her chair. "So, how's Alexis?"

Bertok frowned at Raven, as if to say he wasn't done healing her, but he turned and re-examined the young thief. "About as well as can be expected. I dealt with the worst of her injuries but she needs to rest. If she takes another blow to the head anytime soon, it'll undo everything I did this evening."

"That bad?"

"That bad. You're both lucky to be alive. I'm surprised, though. It's unlike the Leopards to leave an obvious escape route unguarded."

"They didn't leave it unguarded. They secured it."

"Yes, they did. However, they left enough slack for you to raise the trapdoor and reach the rope with a blade. That's an engraved invitation for a thief of your caliber."

Raven started to disagree, but stopped and pondered. "But why? Why attack my sanctuary only to let me escape?"

"Perhaps they were hoping you'd panic and lead them to something big and shiny? I'm certain you don't have the Dragonstone hidden at your lair."

"Of course not." She glanced out the window at the ruins of her former sanctuary and a bitter tone crept into her voice. "I did have most of my money hidden there, but not that. Old man, whatever the hell that stone is, it better be worth losing five years' work."

Bertok signed and leaned back in his chair. "Well, something or someone led them there, Raven."

Raven almost leapt from her chair and started pacing the floor. "How did they find me? I've been careful. Alexis has been careful. Hell, I've followed her a few times just to ensure she wasn't followed."

"If you weren't followed, then they tracked you another way. Besides me, did anyone else know of your interest in it? We know the king, his advisors, and Bishop Marius knew someone had stolen it, but they can be discounted for the moment."

"The only others who knew about the Dragonstone were Quentin, Galen, and Jerek." She paused for a second and then pushed on. "Quentin wouldn't betray me, considering he expects me to get revenge for the thieves' guild. Same with Galen. In fact, the only one would be Prince Geoffrey and I don't see him giving me up to the Leopards."

"Prince Geoffrey? How in Praxil's name did he find out?"

"I had a drink with him last night—right before he was taken to the dungeon." Raven paused and then slapped herself on the head. "Kazmer. I thought he was looking at the glasses on the table a little too close. If Galen deduced who stole the Dragonstone, Kazmer might have done the same. It appears he decided to keep me from aiding Prince Geoffrey."

Bertok frowned at that latest revelation. "You make the most interesting enemies, don't you?"

"It's a gift."

"I warned you about messing with Kazmer. If he suspects you were with the prince, you must have forced him to move his timetable up. If you can get him off-balance, you have a chance to defeat him."

"And why would a hedge wizard know so much about the head of the king's assassins?"

Bertok favored her with a smile. "In my business, it always pays to know who may hire you … and who may kill you."

"I'll keep that in mind."

"Did you bring anything with you other than your weapons? Is it possible you've picked up something that might have led them to you?"

"Just this." She tossed the velvet sack of gems and jewels to Bertok. "Not much left to start over again."

The old wizard spread everything out on the table. He picked up a couple of gems and held them up to the light. "These might have contained a spell once, but they're long since used up. I don't think you have to worry about these." He continued to examine the items until he came to a large diamond-and-amethyst necklace. Before his hand reached the item, the expression on his face changed. "There's strong magic on this one. Imperial College level, if I'm not mistaken. I'm not certain who cast the spell, but I'd hate to duel them. Where did you get this?"

Raven looked at the necklace lying on the table and her eyes grew cold. Only one word slipped out between her clenched teeth. "Ian."

"How did you acquire this?"

"He gave it to me a couple of nights ago, right after my run-in with Bloody Douglas. Said he'd been looking for me to apologize for being a jerk. That bastard! He took advantage of Jerek's death to foist that off on me."

She watched Bertok pull a few strange instruments out of the pouch on his hip. He assembled a small glass case and placed the jeweled necklace inside it. Raven noted the case was made of a thick leaded glass, like the stained glass in the cathedral. Once secured, Bertok arranged his instruments around the glass case and began to examine the necklace. His eyes grew narrower as he readjusted his instruments for another look.

"What's with the glass case, Bertok?"

"It should inhibit the spell on the necklace. I'm not certain it'll keep a determined seeker from tracing it, though. It'll take some of my supplies at home to neutralize it completely."

As he manipulated some of the instruments, Raven eyed

him with growing suspicion. "You know, for a hedge wizard you know a lot about the Imperial College."

"You know, for such an inquisitive apprentice you have a bad habit of doing insufficient research. Besides my shabby appearance and chronic lack of funds, why do you assume I'm a hedge wizard?"

Raven paused, taken back by the sudden turn in the conversation. "Most wizards trained by the Imperial College work at a court in one manner or another. They're not living in Lowtown."

"I noted you were wise enough to say 'most.' That's good. You're beginning to leave room for doubt. Now, ponder this, apprentice: What if a wizard, a former member of the Imperial Council, wanted to go into hiding? Perhaps he had powerful enemies who were seeking him? Where would someone like that hide?"

"If he or she was in danger, they would go somewhere wizards aren't expected to be." Raven's voice and eyebrows rose in unison as she continued. "You used to be on the Imperial Council?"

"I said, 'what if a wizard.' I didn't say *I* was that wizard."

"But you didn't say you weren't that wizard, either."

"Very good. There's hope for you yet. Now, I'd like to finish examining this necklace before daylight." He picked up a crystal wand from the table and held it, tip down, on top of the glass case. Raven noted it seemed to be filled with a clear liquid. Her eyes widened as the liquid began to change to a bright shade of blue. Bertok looked at the wand and nodded to himself.

"What the hell was all that?"

Bertok looked up at her, rubbing the bridge of his nose. "This is a very powerful tracking spell. Someone who knew what to look for could find you if you had this in your possession. Tell me, have you worn this at all?"

"No, it's a little too gaudy for my tastes. I was planning on fencing it."

"Well, that's a spot of good luck. Had you worn it enough,

the spell would have transferred to you from the necklace."

"Anyway, we don't have a lot of time. I was hoping to rescue Prince Geoffrey this evening. It'll have to wait until tomorrow night, but I can't wait any longer than that. Kazmer's made his move. If he suspects I saw him arrest Prince Geoffrey, he may eliminate the prince before I can do anything."

"I want you to stop by my place tomorrow night before you begin. I'll see if I can come up with something to even the odds a bit before you go back there."

"I'll do that. Besides I want to check on something before I go."

"Oh?"

"Where do you think I hid the Dragonstone? I wasn't going to bring it back to my place."

Bertok rose from his chair, hand pointed at Raven, but no sound came out of his mouth. Coming to a conclusion, he lowered himself back into his chair and favored her with a smile. "Levelheaded, planning ahead, and observant. All right, who are you and what have you done with Raven?"

"Very funny, old man."

Bertok shook his head. "Well, if it's good enough to hide something as valuable as the Dragonstone, it's probably a good place to hide something even more valuable. Can you give me a hand getting Alexis to my place? I've got a couple of spare bedrooms there. She can use one of them until she's recovered."

Raven looked out the window and saw the stars beginning to fade. It was only a couple of hours until sunrise at most. "Will you take the necklace to your place? Are your wards strong enough to protect you from that?"

"I don't know. I know if you want to keep *this* place hidden, we can't leave it here."

"Good point." She started toward the door and then paused. Spinning around, she headed to the upper floors. "Wait a moment and let me get changed. It would be safer if Perrin was accompanying you should we run into anyone out on the streets."

The old wizard's eyes widened in mock surprise. "That's a good idea. Are you sure you didn't get hit on the head as well? You're more sensible than normal."

That earned him a snarl from the dark-haired thief. "Keep it up, you old faker, and we'll see who gets hit in the head."

"Now, that's my Raven. Hurry up, child. I'll get Alexis ready to travel."

Chapter Twenty-Four

Raven paused as she reached the door leading out of the catacombs. She was still surprised she managed to stumble through the day without arousing her father's suspicions. She knew she looked like a mess by the time she reached Bertok's based on the wizard's reaction. He had taken one look at her and hustled her off for a quick nap. He also forced her to take one of his potions as soon as she awoke. She knew it was going to be a bad day tomorrow because the potion was drawing on her reserves. Still, it kept her head clear for now.

Just before she left Bertok's, she visited with Alexis while Bertok was off in another part of the house examining her rapier and katar for any damage. It took a load off her shoulders seeing her apprentice in good spirits. Alexis felt bad she wasn't going to be able to help, but Bertok insisted she remain in bed at least two more days. On her way out, she handed Bertok—over his vociferous protests—a note listing her remaining stores of gems and other items in case she didn't return. With everything taken care of, she'd left for the keep.

All right, Raven, you've procrastinated enough. You've got a prince to save. Time to play hero.

She eased the door open and examined the quiet hallway. According to Prince Geoffrey's directions, there was the side passage he said would take her to the armory. She knew the guards would be coming soon so there was no time to waste. She knew she needed to go halfway down this corridor and look for a bluish-green tapestry on her right. Using her gem, she sent a thin beam of light between her fingers illuminating a section of the floor ahead of her. After fifteen steps, she found a series of tapestries hanging on the left-hand wall. The third was a scene of a Sagran warship engaging a pirate ship, the bluish-green spray dominating the weaving. She pushed it aside and found a hidden door after a short search. She slipped a dagger tip into an indentation on the wall until she heard something click. The door swung open just enough for her to slip through.

She played her light around, examining the spiral staircase leading downward. She hurried down the stairs until she reached a small landing leading to a T intersection. She knew the left-hand passageway would lead to the dungeon while the right led toward the armory.

She paused in the gloom. There was a faint light coming from the direction of the dungeon. The light brightened her mood. She'd been afraid Kazmer might have made his move but if a guard was posted, it meant Prince Geoffrey was still alive. Steeling herself for what was to come, she drew her rapier and headed in that direction.

Reaching the end of the corridor, she found a narrow staircase descending into darkness. She knew there was a guard post halfway down but the absence of guards up to this point worried her. She leaned against the wall and glanced around with suspicion.

Something's not right. A prisoner as important as the Crown Prince should rate a number of guards. Unless Kazmer's trying not to draw attention to this place ...

Keeping her rapier at the ready, Raven crept down the stairs. She found the small room where the guards rested between shifts at the halfway point. There were no signs of recent occupation—the torches and the fireplace ashes were cold.

Strange. It looks like no one is manning this post. It still doesn't make sense, but I know the answers have to be at the bottom of this stairwell.

As she finished her inspection, a sudden flash of light startled her. Torchlight grew brighter in the doorway and footsteps could be heard coming down the stairs. She rushed next to the door and pressed her back against the wall. The light grew brighter as it reached the small landing outside. Her hand tightened on her rapier but the footsteps and the light continued down the stairs.

She kept her eyes on the doorway until she was certain no one waited outside. Scooting over to the doorway, she glanced toward the retreating light. Two people dressed in black stood before an iron door at a landing farther down the stairs. Their torch showed a small barred window in the door as they stood there.

Time to earn your keep, Raven. You may never get another chance like this.

She pulled out the small vial she's brought from Tybalt's from one of her pouches. She had to trust that the invisibility powder she'd made under Tybalt's supervision would work. She sheathed her rapier and dusted herself with the powder. She didn't have enough powder to practice beforehand so she hoped she'd covered herself well enough for it to work.

As the seconds ticked by, Raven became more and more frustrated. *Damn, I ought to feel something by now. I knew I should have tried it first.* She raised one hand to slam it against the wall when she realized she couldn't see her fist ... or her arm ... or anything else. The powder had worked.

Tybalt hadn't said how long the powder would last, so she had to go now. She stepped out onto the landing and tried to hurry down the stairs. It was then she realized how tricky it was walking down stairs without being able to see her feet. She almost stumbled a few times before she learned to ignore her body and concentrate on the two figures ahead of her.

Reaching the bottom, she heard the larger figure speaking to someone inside the room. After the challenge and proper response, the door's screeching hinges accompanied the heavy iron door's opening. She shadowed the smaller figure's entrance into the room. Stepping to the side, she just avoided being trampled by the two departing guards.

She let the new guards position themselves while she familiarized herself with the area. One guard stood next to the door, while the other went farther down the dimly lit hallway to stand in front of a solid-looking wooden door. This door had a similar barred window but a faint glow emanated from the room beyond.

I could use the rest of my sleeping powder, but if these aren't the only guards then any chance of reaching the prince is gone. They're not far enough apart to attack one without the other noticing, invisible or not. Besides, I can't see my hands or feet. I'm not certain I can sneak over there without tripping. I have no idea how long this invisibility powder is going to last, but I have to do something.

Placing a hand on the wall to guide her, she crept toward the guarded door. The farther she moved down the hall, the more overwhelming the stench became—a combination of rot and despair. She heard faint noises beyond the guards and said a quick prayer to the gods those were animals.

Easing past the guard at the door, she stood on tiptoe and peered through the window. A series of torches exposed a spiral staircase going down. The torches were too dim to show her how far down it went.

Great. Everything else has gone wrong tonight, why not this as well? At least these seem to be the only guards in the area.

Reaching for her belt, she took out several of the clay balls filled with sleeping powder. Holding her breath, she dropped one right at the guard's feet. As soon as she saw it hit the ground, she tossed the others in her hand at the guard by the door.

The guards jumped at the sound of the small clay balls breaking. Before they could react, the bluish powder enveloped them and they fell without a sound. She pulled them back from the main door and bound and gagged them for good measure.

Turning her attention to the interior door, she checked for any alarms but found nothing and began picking the lock. After a few seconds, she felt the tumblers give way to her attack. Being as careful as she could, she opened the door. For all its apparent age and decay, the door swung open without a sound, revealing the spiral staircase beyond.

Going to put her picks away, she noted she was becoming visible. She contemplated what might have happened if she hadn't attacked when she did. She ran a hand across her brow and took a deep breath to get her nerves under control. Once her hands stopped shaking, she drew her rapier and headed down the stairs.

She counted three complete circles in the staircase before spotting the landing ahead. She paused a few stairs above the landing. A series of torches flickered here, illuminating the landing and revealing five doors. Each was reinforced with heavy iron banding and secured with a large iron lock. A guard dozed in a chair propped up against the far wall, a ring of keys hanging on a hook above him. Listening to his snoring, she knew he'd never hear her approach.

Pulling a sap from one of her pouches, she crossed the landing in a few steps. The guard never paused in his snoring until she struck. He rolled off the chair and landed at her feet, a small trickle of blood leaking from the wound on the top of his head.

She grabbed the keys and a torch before she went to the nearest doorway. She had to try several keys before finding the one that opened it. She recoiled from the stench that rolled out of the room. Shining the light around revealed some half-rotted food and plenty of rat droppings, but nothing else. It took two more attempts before she found the door hiding Prince Geoffrey.

He looked up from the stone floor, a half-eaten bowl of ... *something* on the floor beside him. He tried to block the blinding light from his eyes, his hand shaking from exhaustion. "What? What do you want now? I've told you all I'm going to tell you."

"Prince Geoffrey? Your Highness? It's Raven. I've come to get you out of here."

A hysterical chuckle erupted, driving her back a few

paces. "Lies. More lies, Kazmer? I thought you were more subtle than this?"

"Your Highness, it is me. I've come for you."

The prince wiped a hand across his eyes and then stared up at Raven. "It *is* you. I never expected to see you again."

She rushed over and examined him. He'd been beaten, and by an expert. There was no permanent damage, nothing was broken, but he'd been pushed to the limits of his endurance. She started to assist him up before she noted the chain leading to the collar around his ankle.

Damn, they aren't taking any chances. She checked the ring of keys she had but none fit this lock. *Of course not. That would be too easy.*

Digging out her lock picks again, she went to work on the recalcitrant lock. After a few minutes of furious work, the lock sprang open and she eased the collar off his ankle. She was grateful to find his leggings had protected him up to a point. There was no sign of infection beneath the collar.

Slipping his arm over her shoulder, she helped him to his feet. She could feel him wince as he tried walking. Shifting her shoulder to steady him, she put more of his weight on her. With careful determination, she led him out of his cell and turned toward the stairs.

The sound of soft clapping stopped her in mid-step. As she watched, Kazmer stepped from the shadows of the stairwell and leaned against the stone wall. "Bravo, Raven. I've heard a lot about you. It's nice to see the stories didn't oversell you. You *are* quite the skilled thief."

Raven stared at the master of the Black Leopards, her eyes narrowing in anger. Memories of Jerek and his death came unbidden. She forced them away to concentrate on the current crisis. "So, how long were you waiting for me?"

"After realizing it must have been you with the prince that evening, I knew you would try to rescue him. After all, you're the best thief left in town not in hiding or dead. That's why we attacked your little hideaway. I knew you'd be forced to make this misguided attempt."

"You were taking a chance, then. After the attack on the Corconti, there's little love between the royal family and me. Your little band of assassins cost me a large number of friends."

"Yes, we found out much too late you had feelings for the Corconti chief's son. Not that his death bothers me, but it would have been a lot simpler to trap you if we'd had him as bait."

Raven eased the prince off her shoulder and helped him lean against a wall. Stepping away, she drew her rapier and began circling to the right. A feral grin spread across Kazmer's face as he drew his own weapon and took up a defensive position. "Oh dear, the little thief has drawn a weapon. It appears I've struck a nerve."

"You struck a nerve? I didn't think you had it in you. I thought you let others do all your dirty work."

Kazmer barked a humorless laugh. "You mean Ian? Pfah. He's a mere thief. I appreciate how hard he tries to make me happy. He's sort of like a small puppy. I'm going to hate to have to kill him once we recover the Dragonstone."

She continued to try and keep Kazmer's attention focused on her and not the prince. As the assassin stepped into the center of the room, she could see how he moved with care. *Not a single wasted movement. What is it with my opponents lately? I can't beat Kazmer. Hell, I knew I was in over my head against Raymond. I don't think Morgan in his prime could have beaten Kazmer. All I can do is try and make this a costly win for Kazmer. Maybe the prince can escape in the confusion.*

"You have the Dragonstone, don't you?" The assassin's voice broke through her thoughts. "If you hand it over, I might be persuaded to let you leave Sagras."

"So, you'd let me leave? Just like that."

A sly smile spread across his face as he moved toward her. "Well, almost 'just like that.' Of course, you'll have to leave the prince with me. After all, it'd be awkward to install Owen on the throne if Geoffrey is still alive." He extended his left hand toward Raven. "Now, prove you're as smart as

I think you are and give me the Dragonstone."

Raven had no intentions of handing over the enchanted stone. It was still back at Bertok's anyway but she shrugged her shoulders as if preparing to take off her backpack. At the last second, she saw Kazmer's smile change and she lifted her rapier almost by instinct. A sudden clang told her Kazmer had launched an attack and she'd somehow managed to parry it.

Raven almost didn't notice Kazmer's rush had taken him past her. She was still in shock over blocking the attack. Focusing her thoughts, she turned to find Kazmer looking at her with a mixture of amazement and enjoyment. He stared at his blade as if it had done something he hadn't expected and then looked back to her.

"You are a better swordswoman than I gave credit for. This night may turn out to be enjoyable after all." He brought his rapier up in a fancy salute and then took up a classic fighting stance. "En garde."

The next couple of minutes sped past in a blur for Raven. While there was no question that Kazmer was the aggressor, she found herself holding her own. It was almost if she knew what move he was preparing to use, even moves she'd never seen before. As she moved back from parrying his latest attack, she saw the assassin's face clearly. The look of frustration on his face told her he wasn't enjoying the fight anymore.

They squared off again. Raven noted the rapier she carried seemed almost weightless. *Must be the excitement of the fight.*

Kazmer's voice sounded raspy as his words came out around his gasps. "My compliments to your instructor. This has been a most informative fight. I shall have to hunt him down and kill him before he can teach anyone else."

Raven resisted the urge to be drawn into the conversation. She knew Kazmer was hoping to distract her again. Besides, she had her own problem keeping her breathing steady. Even with every trick Morgan had taught her, no training could have prepared her for a fight like this.

I've got to take the initiative. I've been lucky so far but sooner or later he's going to get through my defenses. Think, Raven! You're only going to get one chance at this.

Snapping her right wrist back, the wide triangular blade of her katar snapped into place, its familiar weight comforting her. Kazmer's smile grew wider as he recognized the punch dagger she'd brought into play and withdrew a main-gauche from his belt. She turned her body and held her right arm down her leg to hide the katar. Right now, she wanted Kazmer to wonder what she was going to do with it. Kazmer turned to put his left side forward, leading with the heavy dagger in a classic style.

She began circling Kazmer, varying her footwork and speed. She tried all the tricks she knew to get him off balance but every move was countered. She came to hate the smirk on his face. She started letting herself circle a little closer, trying to get into range. She had a slight advantage in being left-handed. Against a lesser opponent it would have been enough. Against a sword master like Kazmer, there was a tiny chance it might give her a momentary advantage when she started her attack. It all depended on if she could strike faster than he could counter.

She fought off the panicked impulse to attack before he could kill her. In the deadly game they played, whoever flinched first was going to die. She tightened and relaxed her fingers on the katar's cross handle to keep focused as she continued to move into range.

A movement behind Kazmer drew her attention for a split second, giving the assassin the opportunity he'd been looking for. He struck as her eyes wandered, driving the point of his rapier into her left shoulder. A short scream ripped its way out of her throat as the blade grated against bone. Pulling away, her shoulder felt like it was on fire and she felt the blood welling from the wound. Kazmer paused as if to admire his handiwork, giving her a moment to get herself together. It hurt like hell to hold her sword in position but there was no choice. She had to keep going.

Kazmer's voice broke through the fog in her mind. "You've been a good opponent, Raven, but this ends here."

She brought her sword into line with the assassin, still keeping the katar alongside her leg. With her wound, it was going to be a lot harder to initiate the attack, but she had no choice in the matter. Beginning to circle again, she kept trying to force Kazmer out of position.

As they circled, she noticed Prince Geoffrey had slid along the wall toward the stairwell and was holding on to a torch sconce. With a sick feeling in her stomach, she knew Kazmer could easily chase him down in his weakened condition before he reached the top of the stairs. Somehow, she had to keep Kazmer from following him.

She circled back to her left, trying to keep Kazmer from noticing the prince. She readied her attack when a sudden flash of light caught her attention again. Before Kazmer could take advantage of her distraction, the flaming torch struck the assassin square in the back of the head. The assassin flinched as a shower of sparks formed a halo about his head in the dim light and Raven seized her opportunity.

With a long lunge, she brought her rapier up, meeting his, and then rolled her arm up and inward, entangling both his rapier and main-gauche. Moving them to the side, she continued forward, twisting her hips and bringing her right hand up like she was throwing an uppercut. The foot-long blade of the katar found its mark, striking Kazmer just below his chin and driving it deep into his throat.

Raven saw the shocked look in his eyes just before the light fled from them. The assassin crumbled backward, landing in a heap on the floor. His collapse was so sudden, she almost followed him. Straightening up, she paused as her left shoulder let her know it was displeased with that amount of abuse. Catching her breath, she leaned forward and wiped the gore off her blade on Kazmer's clothing.

"Not bad for a mere thief," she muttered. Turning to the prince she started to say something … and then began to wonder why the torches were orbiting her head and the room was growing dim.

Raven realized she was falling just before she passed out.

Chapter Twenty-Five

Please tell me I'm still alive. If I hurt this bad and I'm dead, eternity is going to be a very miserable place.

Raven placed a hand on her throbbing forehead. She attempted to open her eyes but the bright light made her regret that decision. She tried to sit up, only to find hands restraining her.

"Take it easy there, lass. You've had a rough go of it."

"Who ... what ... the prince?"

A soft chuckle greeted her confusion and a cold compress was placed against her eyes. "Don't worry about Prince Geoffrey, lass. He's with friends—and so are you. You stirred up a beehive when you rescued the prince. Kazmer's death has the Leopards off balance for now. We're trying to take advantage of that."

"Then we should be moving." Her voice sounded as weak as she felt. She tried to get up again, only to be pushed back into place.

"No. You need to rest a bit longer. I don't think we can find a safer place given the commotion going on. I'm afraid your eyes will be sensitive to the light for a bit thanks to the potion we forced down you. That was a nasty wound you had. If his highness hadn't found us in time, the poison would have killed you."

"Poison?" Raven hated how weak her voice sounded. It made her feel even more vulnerable.

"Aye, poison. Kazmer wasn't taking any chances, it seems.

All of the blades we found on him were envenomed. It's a good thing we were able to sneak Tybalt into the keep without drawing too much attention. He identified the poison right off and fixed up a counter-brew."

Raven shot up in bed in spite of the pain in her head. "Tybalt?"

A familiar soft laugh sounded across the room. Raven could see the vague outline of the person sitting on the bed handing her the compress that had gone flying in her panic. She heard Tybalt's familiar footsteps approaching as she replaced the cold cloth. "I'm glad to see my patient doing so well. I predict a complete recovery if she can move like that. Hugh, if I could examine her in private ..."

Hugh? Raven stifled a gasp. The lord chamberlain himself was helping to care for her?!

"Of course, Tybalt. I'll be outside if you need anything." She felt Hugh get off the bed and heard footsteps leading off to the left before hearing the door shut. A chair scraping across the floor toward the bed told her where Tybalt was waiting.

"Apparently I owe you my life, Master Alchemist. You have my thanks."

"Nonsense. It's the least I could do for my apprentice."

Raven fought to keep her face expressionless. "Apprentice? I'm afraid you've confused me with someone else."

Tybalt's voice dropped into a conspiratorial whisper as he leaned forward. "Perrin, you can call yourself whatever you wish and wear whatever disguise you wish, but don't think you can fool me. I know Bertok's handiwork when I see it. Besides, I doubt you happened to find this vial filled with the same powder my apprentice worked so hard to create these past few weeks."

Raven fell back onto her pillow like a puppet with its strings cut. "I should have thrown that away when I was done with it."

"Perhaps. It seems you did a good job making this, though. You have the makings of a great alchemist, with a little more training."

Raven rolled over on her side. Easing one corner of the compress upward, she made out his vague shape sitting near her. She started to ask him something and then paused. "Wait a moment. You said you recognized Bertok's work? How do you know that old hedge wizard?"

Tybalt's laugh rang out in spite of his attempts to control himself. "First off, apprentice, I haven't always lived on the Hill. Second, Bertok may be many things but a hedge wizard is not one of them. Is that what he told you he was?"

Raven thought hard. "Come to think of it, we had a similar conversation just the other night. I accused him of being one when I saved his life in Lowtown several years ago. He never admitted to being anything, although he seems familiar enough with the workings of the Imperial College."

"Child, if he hasn't told you who he is, then I'll keep his secrets. But he's no hedge wizard. He's one of the most powerful wizards in the Empire. However, he also has powerful enemies, which explains why he's in Sagras. It's as far from the capital as he could get and still be within the Empire's boundaries. Believe me, not just anyone could create that medallion you're wearing or put that enchantment on your rapier. If I hadn't noted the glamour while I was treating you, I might not have realized who you were."

That brought Raven's thoughts back into focus. "Who have you told?"

"Told?" He chuckled again. "Why would I tell anyone? What you do on your own time is your business. If Bertok trusts you, who am I to disagree? You had plenty of opportunities to steal from me and never betrayed my trust."

A knock drew Tybalt's attention so he missed seeing Raven's flaming cheeks as she blushed at the compliment. While he went to open the door, a thousand thoughts competed for her attention. She didn't realize who'd entered the room until Prince Geoffrey spoke.

"How are you feeling?" She started to sit up, before he spoke again. "No, please, lay there and rest. You'll need your strength soon enough."

She noted his voice sounded stronger. "You seem much better, Your Highness."

"It's amazing what food and sleep will do for a person. Hugh is gathering our allies. My father and I are going to have that discussion we talked about a few nights ago. This time I'll make certain I have his attention."

Raven eased the compress off her eyes. Even though it was hard to focus, she could tell Geoffrey was more confident than the first time they'd met. He turned to the muscular man standing next to him. "Hugh, we need to relocate to another section of the keep. I'd rather avoid an incident until we're ready to meet my father."

"Agreed, Your Highness. Might I suggest the upper level of the northeast tower?"

"That's perfect. Have food and drink brought there. Not too many people, though. Let's not draw attention to ourselves."

"Understood, Your Highness. I know just the people to handle it."

Raven's eyes came more into focus and she noticed she was in a small room with stone walls. Everything in the room had a martial air about it. She guessed she was in one of the keep's barracks rooms.

"Do you feel well enough to travel, Raven?" She turned to see the prince still in the room, extending a hand to her. She reached out with some trepidation, letting him guide her to her feet. As she stood up, her knees wobbled and she was grateful for his assistance. The whole situation seemed surreal to her.

The prince looked at the remaining men. "Send two men ahead to ensure the way is clear. The rest of you take different routes, a few at a time, and we'll all meet at the top of the northeast tower. We know Owen won't go there."

"Why wouldn't your brother search there?" A puzzled expression ran across Raven's face as Geoffrey laughed aloud for the first time in days.

"Why, my little thief? That's the library. He wouldn't be caught dead in there."

* * *

The rest of the day was a blur to Raven. She remembered bits and pieces: being escorted by the prince, his arm securely wrapped around hers; climbing stairs and then eating something. The last thing she remembered was Tybalt giving her something that tasted horrible.

Opening her eyes, she discovered her headache was gone. She rolled over to her side and noticed the room was dark, except for a small lamp on a table with men sitting around it. She swung her feet off the bed and spotted Geoffrey and Hugh among them. A yawn escaped from her before she could stop it.

Prince Geoffrey turned his head and smiled at her. "I see our guest has woken up again."

She stretched and returned his smile. She took her time standing up, making sure she wasn't going to pitch over on her nose before joining them. "Sorry to have been such a bother, Your Highness."

"No bother at all. If Tybalt hadn't given you that potion, our planning session would have bored you to sleep long before now." His blue eyes twinkled as he spoke and she found herself smiling in spite of herself.

"At least that wouldn't have left this horrible taste in my mouth." Her features twisted as she ran her tongue over her teeth, trying to get rid of the last of it. "Now that I *am* awake, what's the plan?" She noted the others at the table viewed her with suspicion.

Hugh ignored the others and gave her a wide smile. "So, you're not quite done serving the prince?"

"Let's not go that far, my lord. I owe his highness a debt for saving my life. I like to pay my debts as soon as possible."

Prince Geoffrey turned to her, a look of admiration on his face. "No, Raven, I owe you for getting me out of that dungeon."

Before Raven could counter, Hugh's laugh brought them up short. "Well, now that everyone's done figuring out who owes whom, maybe we can concentrate on what's next?"Raven and Prince Geoffrey exchanged embarrassed glances and turned their attention to the group seated around the table. The prince picked up a dagger he'd been using as a pointer and twisted it in one hand. "I still say the best plan is the most straightforward. I take a selected group of men and confront my father in the throne room. You and the others seize the main corridor and ensure no one else interferes."

One of the men pointed at the rough map they'd drawn laying on the table. "But that leaves you vulnerable, Your Highness. What if he has assassins hidden in the room?"

"I don't believe my father would do that."

"Not your father ... your brother." Everyone at the table turned to stare at Raven. "Remember, he's the one who threw you into the dungeon. With Kazmer's death, the Black Leopards are relying on his patronage now. Your father isn't going to be happy when he finds they went against his wishes."

"How do you know that?" one of the other men at the table challenged her.

"I was in the keep for ... a different purpose when I overheard a meeting of the Privy Council. They're all in this up to their necks ... with one exception." She nodded pleasantly to Hugh. "They kept the lord chamberlain in the dark about the entire plan. Kazmer mentioned more than once the king hadn't approved of Prince Geoffrey's assassination. However, that's the only realistic way Owen could assume the throne. He has no chance at succession now with his plot exposed. His only option is to try and kill you, Your Highness, before you can confront your father."

Harsh muttering met Raven's words but Geoffrey silenced them with a sharp motion. "Let her speak. She hasn't led me astray yet."

"I've told you before how I feel about your brother. I

don't put anything past him."

A cloud crossed Geoffrey's face. Before he could speak, Hugh slapped him on the back and laughed as only he could. "By the gods, Geoffrey, you should keep this one close to you. She'd make a good conscience once you assume the throne. I won't be around forever. She's much more your age … and not hard on the eyes, either."

Geoffrey stood up and walked over to the water pitcher nearby, a red flush rising on his face. "Between Raven and you, I'm not certain I can survive all this honesty."

Raven looked at the rough map of the throne room. "My lord, besides the main doors, are there any other ways into the room?"

Hugh looked where she was pointing and scratched his chin for a moment. After a bit, he grabbed the quill out of the ink and made a few scratch marks on the parchment. "There's a door that leads to the king's chambers. There are rumors about hidden passages beyond the throne room but I've only been back there a few times. The king never took me into his confidence about them and I never asked." He made a few more marks on the map. "And, of course, there's the servants' entrance."

A plan began forming in Raven's head. "Your Highness, could your plan spare two men who are skilled with the crossbow?"

"I suppose so. For what purpose?"

"Hopefully for none, Your Highness. However, if we can take positions in the servants' area before you enter, we'll be in a good position to protect you from an ambush when you confront your father. Once all the attention is drawn to you, we can take up positions here, here, and here." She used the tip of the quill pen to point to a series of columns near the servant's entrance.

Hugh smiled at her again. "Are you certain you've never been in the military? I've been the chamberlain for years but I never considered that option. It's an obvious answer to the problem."

"That's because you think like a soldier, my lord. You're all about honorable battle. Me? I'm a thief. I prefer not to fight, but when I have to, I don't follow the rules and I play to win."

He gave her a quick wink. "Perhaps we should exchange trade secrets after this is over."

She felt her cheeks beginning to burn again so she changed the subject. "When do you intend to confront your father, Your Highness?"

"After his evening meal. His normal routine is to return to his chambers afterward. I think we can get him to meet us in the throne room. I know he'll listen to reason."

He had more confidence in his father's good nature that Raven did, but she kept her feelings to herself. She might hate him for causing Jerek's death but Kazmer's death had balanced the scales a bit. Ian would keep for later. Depriving King Marcus of not only the Dragonstone but also his right arm, Kazmer, would cripple the king's plans for Helion.

While the others continued their arguments, Hugh brought in two young guardsmen. The taller of the two introduced himself as Roland and the other as Thaddeus. Thaddeus merely grunted at her and leaned against the wall, arms crossed across his chest.

"Don't let their manners get to you, lass. They're probably the two best archers in the Royal Guard."

"If they'll follow instructions, their opinions of me don't bother me in the least."

Roland picked that moment to pipe up. "No problems there, miss. If the lord chamberlain says to follow you, then that's what Thad and I will do."

"Strip out of your armor. Put on some soft clothing and then report back to me."

The two young guardsmen exchanged surprised glances, then headed to another section of the library to change. Once they'd returned, Raven inspected them and their gear to ensure they weren't carrying anything that would make noise. She led them over to the table and explained her plan to them. Roland was enthusiastic, making a few suggestions of his own, while Thaddeus merely grunted and nodded.

Satisfied both crossbowmen understood the plan, she turned to Hugh. "When do we leave?"

"Now. You've got fifteen minutes to get into position before we leave to seize the entryway. All bets are off once that happens."

"We'll talk once this is over."

"If the gods favor our plan, we will indeed. Now, go!"

Raven motioned to her companions and they slipped out of the room. They found the stairwell leading down and headed toward the kitchens and the servants' passage. Hugh said it was all up to the gods, but she believed in evening up the odds whenever she could.

That is, provided the gods let her.

Chapter Twenty-Six

Raven scanned the throne room from the half-opened door to the kitchens. She didn't see anything suspicious but could not force herself to relax. She heard Roland's nervous breathing behind her and knew Thaddeus was farther down the corridor to ensure no one was following. She hated having to lock up the servants in the pantry, but it was for their own safety. Plus, it would discourage anyone from playing hero and spoiling things at the last minute.

A soft tap on her shoulder startled her. She spun around, dagger in hand, before she realized it was Roland. "Sorry. I was wondering how much longer?"

Raven let her breath out in a long, continuous exhalation. She hadn't realized how keyed up she was. After weighing the pros and cons about wringing his neck, she sheathed the dagger. "We wait until Prince Geoffrey's group enters the throne room. Let them draw everyone's attention before we go in. Just relax. It'll be soon enough."

As Roland withdrew, she let a wan smile reach her face. She remembered how antsy she had been the first time Sean had taken her on a thieving run. The fact he spoke to her by the end of the evening showed an unusual amount of patience. Training Alexis had been a stroll in the royal park compared to what she must have put Sean through.

A sudden commotion grabbed her attention. The royal chancellor retreated across the throne room, pleading with Prince Geoffrey. "Your Highness, you can't just barge in here like this with armed men. It just isn't done. I'm going to have to ask you all to leave."

"And, Andreas, once again I'm telling you to fetch my father so I may speak to him. Otherwise, I'm going to use you as a battering ram and break down the door to his personal chambers. The choice is up to you."

The chancellor blanched at Geoffrey's statement. He tried to muster up one last protest, but the look the prince gave him convinced him discretion was the better part of valor. He hurried toward the king's chambers and Geoffrey positioned his men around the room. Once he was satisfied, he took up a position at the foot of his father's throne to wait.

Roland started to push past Raven, but a viselike grip stopped him dead in his tracks. "Don't be in a hurry. Wait until the king arrives and see who enters with him. Someone might spot us if we move before then. Wait until he starts arguing with the prince."

Roland pulled back, rubbing his arm, while she returned her attention to the throne room. A few moments later, the chancellor rushed from the king's chambers and picked up his crosier. Rapping the butt of the staff on the polished marble floor, he waited for the echoes to quiet before announcing, "His August Majesty, King Marcus of Sagras." She watched as Prince Geoffrey and the others dropped to one knee, although to her delight they kept their heads unbowed, watching for any sign of treachery.

King Marcus slammed the door open as he strode into the room. He threw his cape over one shoulder with contempt as he sat down. "What is this, Geoffrey? Armed insurrection against the throne of Sagras?"

"That is not my intention, Father. But there are questions I must ask and I will have answers."

"You *must*? You *will*?" The king's voice rose in pitch as he looked at his son wide-eyed. "Do you dare give me commands? I am still the king and I am still your father. While I still breathe, you must do what *I* say, not the other way around."

"All right, Roland, you and Thaddeus take your positions," she whispered as she waved to the latter to join them. Then she opened the door for them to slip through and secured it behind her. She didn't pay much attention to the back-and-forth between father and son. Reaching her hiding place, she was pleased with what she observed. She had been afraid Geoffrey would let his father cow him but he was holding his own.

"Be that as it may, Father. I want to know by whose authority I was locked in the keep's dungeons for two days."

"Don't be ridiculous, Geoffrey. I think I would know if my son was a prisoner—although that assumes I notice you normally. Let's face facts. You'd have to get your nose out of those books long enough to pretend to be a threat. You're not important enough to be imprisoned."

"Kazmer thought I was enough of a threat to arrest me under the cover of darkness and spirit me off to the dungeons."

The king's face turned red as the seriousness of the accusation sunk in and he spun around, pinning Andreas with his glare. "Send someone to find Kazmer and have him report to me." Turning back to Geoffrey, he looked down his nose at his son. "You'd better be able to prove these charges. Kazmer is my most devoted servant. More loyal than some who claim to be in my service." Geoffrey's supporters looked around guiltily as King Marcus waved his hand, taking them all in.

After Andreas had left the room, Geoffrey turned back to his father. "I'm afraid Andreas may find it difficult to gain Kazmer's attention. Your pet assassin is dead."

Marcus looked at Geoffrey with genuine surprise. "So, you killed Kazmer? Then I expect Andreas will return with his next-in-command. Unless you managed to kill him also?"

"No, Father, nor did I kill Kazmer. The person who rescued me from the dungeons was forced to kill him."

"Oh, this person was *forced* to kill the leader of the Black Leopards?" The king's laughter rang out. "By the gods, Son, when you invent a story, you go all out. I should have had you appointed jester years ago. It seems those stories your mother read you as a child gave you a true sense of humor." The king dabbed at his eyes with the hem of his sleeve. "I must say, this is one of the few times I've enjoyed your company."

Raven found herself wincing at the king's words. She knew most of the Privy Council was unimpressed with Geoffrey, but to hear the same words coming from his father was painful. Not for the first time, she was grateful for her father's love and affection.

She could hear a commotion through the doors at the far end of the room over the bantering between father and son. Hugh and his men had engaged someone trying to reach the king. She knew Hugh only had a handful of men with him. They'd never withstand an all-out assault on their positions if these were the Royal Guards. Geoffrey needed to bring this to a head soon.

A sudden shout brought the fighting to a halt outside. The door at the far end of the room boomed open as Owen and one of the Black Leopards entered with the chancellor. Raven found her hands tightening and loosening on the hilt of her rapier as she watched Owen approach. He was too confident for someone about to be denounced in front of his own father.

Owen's smile became larger as he set eyes on Geoffrey before the throne. "Ah, Father, you've apprehended the traitor. I never should have doubted your skills."

"If there was a traitor to apprehend, I might have appreciated learning about it before he walked into my throne room and demanded an audience." King Marcus scowled at Owen, who paused for a second before continuing his advance.

"Father, we caught Geoffrey plotting against you with someone from the city's underworld. Kazmer presented me with evidence Geoffrey was plotting to use the stolen Dragonstone against you. Paid in full, no doubt, by one of our enemies."

Geoffrey fixed Owen with a cold stare. "Choose your words carefully, Brother. I hope you can produce this so-called evidence, because there will be a reckoning very soon.

I am still the Crown Prince, no matter how much you want to step in front of me."

"Be honest, Geoffrey. You're unfit to rule Sagras." Owen walked forward, dismissing Geoffrey's threatening look as he would a serf. His voice dropped into a conspiratorial tone as he approached. "You knew there was no way Father would leave you the throne. If you didn't seize this opportunity to gain it, you never would rule. Not that I blame you. It's the first regal thing you've ever done. Too bad it will be your last."

"Have you lost your mind, Owen? Or perhaps Kazmer has been poisoning you against the family. Did he promise to remove Father, too, to win your loyalty?"

"My good brother, Kazmer is a loyal servant of the throne of Sagras. He supports the throne with his every breath."

"He supported Father until he quit breathing, I'm certain of that."

Owen turned to face his father, a questioning look on his face. "Do I hear my brother's words right? The man who has a problem recognizing the proper end of a sword is claiming to have killed the head of the Black Leopards, the greatest swordsman in Sagras?"

King Marcus smiled a thin, cold smile. It seemed he was enjoying this too much for Raven's nerves. "He claims someone killed Kazmer. He has yet to name this elite warrior."

A look of panic crossed Owen's face before he composed himself. Turning back to Geoffrey, he resumed his mocking tone. "Well, since someone did free you from your cell, it's possible Kazmer could have been surprised and killed. That's not important now. What's important is what to do about your treachery?"

Geoffrey's calm voice cut through Owen's preening. "Even if you don't acknowledge my right of succession, Father is still king. He is the only one with the right to imprison me. By your own words, you knew I was imprisoned in the dungeon. Perhaps you want to explain to Father what gave you the right to assume his authority? And without

Kazmer, it's your word against mine, unless you can produce this evidence of yours."

Raven was watching Owen with care. She could see he was getting more agitated. He wasn't certain what to do without Kazmer whispering in his ear. She slid one of her daggers out of its sheath and held it at the ready, keeping a close eye on the prince and the Black Leopard standing off by himself.

Owen turned to his father, his face flushed. "Father, you have to believe me when I say there is evidence of Geoffrey's treachery. Ask him if he did not say he was going to stop your upcoming war by any means possible."

"Geoffrey, ... ?" King Marcus's words hung over the throne room like an executioner's axe.

"I did say I was willing to use any means possible to try and convince you against a fruitless war against nations that were not our enemies. Sagras is too small to stand against an alliance of the other city-states. It would cost us more in trade and money than we'd ever recoup, even if we forced the conquered lands to pay tribute."

"For someone who had nothing to do with the planning of this campaign, you seem very confident about your assertions." The king's voice dripped with sarcasm as he stared at Prince Geoffrey. He placed his fingers in front of his face for a moment, the fingertips coming together to form a steeple as he considered his next statement before continuing. "What if I told you our military was ready to move out in two days?"

"I'd say you're making a dreadful mistake."

Marcus stopped and stared at Geoffrey. "You get one chance. Why would that be a mistake?"

"You're woefully undersupplied. Wulfric's men are adequately trained but you're too dependent on foraging and booty. The fishing fleet cannot have supplied enough salted fish and I know from the daily reports there's insufficient salted pork and dried bread to sustain the army for any length of time. I don't doubt the fighting skill of the men in the barracks, but even they cannot fight on empty stomachs for too long."

"Spiridon has assured me that the Dragonstone would make us invincible. Besides, our military is still capable of seizing Helion before they can muster a defense. The other city-states will argue like jackals over a three-day-old corpse, giving us time to consolidate our gains. By the time they decide anything, it will be too late."

"That might be, Father. However, your reliance on the Dragonstone has locked you in to moving too soon. Before we can consolidate that much territory, the other states will have organized both their defenses and cut trade with us. We are unprepared to garrison that much territory, especially if Helion's army retreats rather than surrendering. The Ariatic Hills beyond Helion would give them a place to regroup and the cavern system there could hide them for years."

"Caverns. Hah. You've never been to Helion. How would you know about those caverns?" Owen tried to laugh Geoffrey down but his tone betrayed his nervousness. Owen was beginning to doubt his own vision of his brother.

"And what do you base these opinions on?" The king leaned forward, fixing his gaze on his son. If Raven hadn't known better, it appeared the king was impressed with Geoffrey.

"To answer Owen first, Father, I know of this because I have read about Helion and its surroundings in those books you disdain. I learned about those caverns when I was reading about the vineyards. If you truly want to seize Helion, you must seize the hill country first, otherwise you're sending a lot of our soldiers to die for nothing."

Geoffrey began pacing in front of the throne. "Father, I am against this campaign. I believe it will cause Sagras irreparable harm. However, if you insist on it, then I have no choice but to advise you how to do it right. It's true I don't spend all my time practicing with a sword, but that doesn't mean I have no interest in our military. After all, as your firstborn, I will be in charge of them someday and I don't want to lose a one needlessly."

Raven watched Owen throughout this entire exchange. He had come to denounce his brother and here "Geoffrey the bookworm" was showing a deeper understanding of warfare than he. She could see the panicked look growing on his face as Geoffrey matched his father argument for argument. It was only a matter of time before Geoffrey turned their father's attention back on Owen's crimes.

A sudden shout and a crashing door drew everyone's attention. Hugh and his remaining men were trying to barricade the entryway against the Royal Guardsmen coming to aid the king. Seizing the opportunity, Owen grabbed a dagger he had hidden in his flowing sleeve and leapt at his brother, a murderous rage etched on his face.

Raven didn't hesitate as Owen began his attack. Stepping around the pillar, her left arm flew forward and released the throwing dagger. A sudden *twang* sounded off to her right, telling her Roland had fired his crossbow.

Everything seemed to slow down as she watched the throwing dagger glistening in its flight across the room. The Black Leopard standing beside Owen crumpled backward as Roland's bolt took him square in the chest before he could finish drawing his sword. Her dagger struck Owen in the stomach just as he reached Geoffrey. Owen jerked when Raven's dagger hit and his own dagger struck Geoffrey on the shoulder.

Owen's scream ripped through the room as he fell to the floor, his hands clutching at the dagger's hilt protruding from his stomach. Geoffrey knelt next to him, holding a hand to his shoulder to staunch the blood from his wound. As Owen's cries turned into a ghastly gurgle, the sudden turn of events shocked the entire room into silence.

Raven rushed forward, flanked by Roland and Thaddeus. Raven noted Thaddeus's crossbow was still cocked and he was scanning the crowd just to be sure. While she began applying a compress to Geoffrey's shoulder, Thaddeus nudged Owen's body with a toe. "Yep, he's dead, all right."

A shriek rang out from the throne behind Raven. "What

have you done? Assassins! Murderers!" She almost didn't recognize King Marcus's voice but she heard his footsteps rushing up behind her. She threw herself forward, knocking Prince Geoffrey out of the way as the king's sword sliced through the air where she had just been.

"Oh, no, you demoness. You won't get away that easily. I'll pursue you to the ends of the earth to make you pay."

Raven drew her rapier and circled away from the wounded prince, trying to keep the king's attention on her. She heard movement and then Thaddeus's voice rang out. "Hold it right there. This is their affair. I'd recommend you all keep your hands where I can see them." The *twang* of a crossbow rang out, followed by a scream and the sound of a body thudding against the marble floor. Raven glanced to her left and saw Thaddeus cocking his crossbow with care as he kept his eyes upward. A figure dressed in black leather lay sprawled on the floor, a broken crossbow lying on the floor next to him. She looked up and noticed a series of nearly invisible balconies overlooking the throne room. Looking to her right, she saw Roland cranking away on his windlass to cock his crossbow with a sheepish look on his face.

After that momentary distraction, it took all her concentration to parry the king's furious attacks. Visions of Jerek and Alexis flashed in her mind, but this wasn't the time for personal vengeance. King Marcus's attacks were so undisciplined she could have killed him a dozen times over. She hoped to wear him down until his fury passed.

Circling the room one more time, Prince Geoffrey surprised her when he cut in front of her. Someone had tied a cloth bandage to hold the compress on his shoulder. He shook his head at her, then took up a defensive position. "Let me deal with him."

"Your Highness, he's not going to listen to anyone."

"I realize that. It's my responsibility, not yours, Raven. Withdraw."

The look he gave her bode no insubordination. She swallowed hard and backed up without another word. She'd seen several sides of Geoffrey, but never before would she have used the term "regal."

"Father, put down your weapon. She is not a murderer. She saved my life."

The king looked at Geoffrey, madness contorting his face. "Your life? *Your life?* What about Owen's life? Who is she to decide which of my children live or die? I know ... you put her up to it. You always were jealous of Owen." The king lifted his sword into position and stared down the blade at Geoffrey. "I am still the king and I hereby condemn you to death, Geoffrey. From this moment forward, you are no son of mine."

Geoffrey straightened as if a great weight had lifted off his shoulders. "You may not claim me as your son, Father, but claiming my life is not going to be that easy."

"Traitor! Rebel!" King Marcus rushed forward to strike Geoffrey, who barely got his sword up in time to deflect the blow. The king's madness seemed to give him superhuman strength as his attack drove Geoffrey backward. The prince weathered the initial onslaught and used the columns in the room to put some distance between his father and himself. Raven noted Geoffrey refused to get into a power versus power exchange. Instead he was relying on his training and stamina, forcing the king to chase him around the room.

Roland, Thaddeus, and she spent the next several minutes trying to ensure no one interfered with the two men. This had gone beyond the point of turning back. Either Geoffrey won on his own or Marcus would kill him or have him killed later. She turned back to watch the fight and saw the king and prince had come together. Their swords were interlocked and each tried to use their strength to force the other to retreat. Suddenly, Hugh cried out, "Watch out, Geoffrey, he's got a dagger!"

Geoffrey caught his father's hand only inches away from his stomach. The cold steel flashed in the torchlight illuminating the throne room. As they struggled, the king rammed his chin onto Geoffrey's shoulder. The prince cried out in pain, but refused to release his grip on the dagger. A cruel smile played on Marcus's face as he slammed his chin into Geoffrey's shoulder again and again.

Raven cringed at each blow and, against her better judgment, she started to move forward to help when the prince snaked a leg around his father's and the two went crashing to the ground. A scream of pain echoed through the room, but it was impossible to tell who it came from.

The king rose from the floor, staring at the unmoving body of his eldest son. Only when he turned to face the crowd in the throne room did he seem to notice the hilt of the dagger protruding from his chest. A look of surprise registered on his face, as if he wondered how it got there. His mouth opened and closed but no noise came out, then his eyes rolled up and he slowly fell to his knees before slumping over on his side.

Raven rushed over to Geoffrey to find he was hurt but alive. She felt some blood on her hand where he had struck his head on the cold marble in the fall. Hugh and the others roused themselves and came to assist her. Geoffrey put most of his weight on Hugh as they helped him to his feet. He motioned for them to take him to the throne. After he sat down, he motioned Hugh closer and the two conversed in voices too soft for Raven to hear. After they finished, Hugh stood next to the prince—no, the new king—and faced the people in the throne room.

"Those members of the Royal Guard here, if they will lay down their swords, his majesty is prepared to pardon you and return you to duty. Any who will not lay down their weapons will be declared in rebellion to the throne. Where do you stand?"

There was a moment of hesitation and then almost as one, they knelt on one knee facing the throne, their swords resting on the floor in front of them. Geoffrey looked at the guardsmen and warriors in the room and smiled. He motioned to Hugh again to continue.

"Now prove your loyalty. Find and seize the former members of the Privy Council. Let none escape the punishment they have brought upon themselves. Now, go!" Hugh's command had not ceased echoing before the room was empty, except for the chancellor, Roland, Thaddeus, and Raven.

Hugh turned to the chancellor. "Andreas, don't just stand there. Fetch the royal surgeon to deal with the king's wounds."

"Aye, Lord Chamberlain."

Raven had the unpleasant image of a long-legged spider rushing off as Andreas scuttled out of the room. Shuddering at that image, she turned back to the throne. King Geoffrey's breathing seemed to be settling down. He was beginning to unwind from his combat. She knew the magnitude of what had happened would hit him soon enough.

She moved to the foot of the throne and dropped to one knee. "Your Majesty, it's over."

In a weary voice, he spoke. "No, not quite. Hugh, place her under arrest."

Chapter Twenty-Seven

Raven sat in the dim room cursing herself for the thousandth time for ever trusting a noble from Sagras. Every one had proven untrustworthy and of questionable lineage. This latest betrayal was the hardest of all to accept, though.

Why are you surprised, Raven? Did you think he was going to offer you his hand?

Her sarcastic question stopped her in mid-pace. *That poison must have affected me worse than I thought to think something that ridiculous. No, what's surprising is the fact I'm surprised I'm here. I should have escaped while the prince … no, King Geoffrey … was fighting his father. I let my personal feelings get in the way and now I'm going to pay for it.*

She looked for any means of escape she might have missed the other ten times she'd examined the room. All they had taken were her weapons; she still had her pouches and backpack. *Either they're confident I can't escape or they're hoping I'll try. That would save everyone a lot of trouble, wouldn't it?*

Finishing her latest circuit, she heard footsteps approaching. She sat down and waited for the inevitable. *Hopefully, I can see Geoffrey one more time. I want to ask him why he waited so long to betray me.*

The footsteps stopped in front of her door and she heard a key turning in the lock. Two guards entered, followed by Hugh. He'd changed into his court finery and nodded to her in a curt manner. "His majesty would like to see you now."

"I have a choice?"

Hugh frowned at her. "You're not going to make this easy, are you?"

"I think I'm taking this very well all things considered. If I had known the reward for saving Geoffrey's life was arrest, I admit I might have thought twice about it. "

Hugh had the decency to blush. "Nevertheless, miss, I am here to escort you to the king."

Raven rose from the chair and curtsied to Hugh. "I'd be honored to accompany you, Lord Chamberlain." The pained look on Hugh's face brought her up short. Deep inside, she knew it wasn't Hugh's fault.

He motioned to the guards. "If the young lady will promise me she won't try anything stupid, I won't need your services anymore."

Raven found herself warming up to the older man. "I'll behave, Lord Chamberlain."

"That's Hugh, young lady!"

"Then, *Hugh*, I promise to behave."

"That's the Raven I remember. All right, you two, you may go. Let the king know we'll be there in a bit."

The guards exchanged confused glances, then hurried down the corridor. Hugh waited for them to disappear before turning to Raven. "If you'll be so kind to follow me?"

They moved through the quiet keep until they reached a short corridor. Raven was surprised when Hugh walked past all the doors and approached a large mosaic embedded in the far wall. He looked over his shoulder and then pushed a series of the tiles inward. With a soft grinding noise, a section of the mosaic slid to the left, revealing a dark stairwell leading downward.

Hugh lit a torch before motioning for Raven to follow him. He waited for her to enter and then moved a lever located on the wall. The hidden door slid back into place without a sound. *The keep protects its secrets. I was only a few feet away and couldn't spot anything until Hugh opened it. But where does this lead?*

She followed Hugh until they reached a landing at the

bottom. She looked around but only saw another hallway with a set of double-doors at the end. *We haven't gone far, so unless there's another stairwell, we're not near the dungeons. What's the point in bringing me here?* She started when she felt a soft tap on her shoulder.

"I believe we need to go that way. The door is not going to come to us."

She saw the twinkle in his eye and knew he was congratulating himself on being able to startle her. He noticed she was watching and fixed his stern expression back into place. Her amused expression let him know he wasn't fooling her.

They reached the doors and she leaned against the wall while Hugh knocked. A guard appeared and Hugh spoke to him in a low voice. After a short wait, the doors opened and she saw King Geoffrey and a large man in court garb across the room. They were pointing to a large map of Sagras and the surrounding countryside on the wall. She saw Geoffrey's left arm in a sling, but he didn't act as if he was in too much pain.

Geoffrey shook hands with his companion and as the man left, he noticed Hugh and Raven approaching. He motioned for them to sit at the table and told the servants to bring some wine. Once everyone was seated, he dismissed the servants and turned to the two of them. "Raven, so glad you could join me."

Raven was confused by his friendly tone. She fell back on her normal defense in a situation like this: sarcasm. "How could I turn down such a generous invitation? After all, it was delivered by such a gallant escort. My congratulations on your speedy recovery and, I must say, your new crown looks good on you."

Geoffrey seemed to ignore her tone. "The royal surgeon has horrible bedside manners but he knows his healing magic. I'll need to get the crown resized but there's plenty of time and I have you to thank for that."

"Yes. You do."

Geoffrey leaned forward over the table, facing her. "But, you see, we have a problem. What are we going to do with you?"

"Me? I'm just a common thief, Your Majesty. No one you need to concern yourself over."

Geoffrey's laugh boomed out in the quiet room. "Raven, you may be many things but common is *not* one of them. Let's see all the things a common thief has done." He began ticking off points on his fingers. "You stole an item bound for my father from the cathedral, robbed a number of loyal supporters to the throne, been a member of a criminal organization, broken into the royal keep numerous times, found your way unescorted into *my* personal chambers, penetrated the Royal Dungeon, killed the leader of the Black Leopards, assaulted members of the Royal Guard and the Black Leopards, and who knows what else you've done that I don't know about." Geoffrey took a deep breath after his recitation before continuing. "Now you've acquired a taste for regicide. If you're representative of the common thieves, Raven, I'm terrified of the experts."

Raven bowed her head as he named her offenses. After he wound down, she tipped her head upward and looked at him through her locks of black hair and tried to smile. "I guess I *have* been busy these past few months."

"Raven, if you had been any busier, I'd be wondering where my pants were. The problem is, my dear little thief, as much as I appreciate what you've done for me I have to decide your fate." Geoffrey rose from the chair and began pacing. "Well, Hugh, you're my lord chamberlain. Earn your pay and give me some advice."

The older man crossed his arms across his chest. "It's obvious we can't just let her go. I'll wager she knows more about the keep than anyone now that Kazmer is dead. We can't ensure she won't break in again. Hell, we still don't know how she's getting in. Therefore, there's only one logical solution, sire. You need to marry her."

Both Raven's and Geoffrey's heads snapped around to stare at Hugh, who was sitting there with a huge smile on his face. "After all, Sire, it would solve your problems."

Geoffrey and Raven exchanged embarrassed glances. After a few seconds, the king walked behind the chair he'd been sitting on and leaned against it, avoiding glancing Raven's way. "I admit, Hugh, that is *a* solution. She's certainly more attractive than the young princess from Bertyon Dad tried to marry me off to last year. But isn't that a bit drastic?"

"There is ample precedent, your majesty. At least unlike an arranged marriage, you know what she looks like. Some partners never meet before the wedding ceremony. Besides, it's obvious to my ancient eyes you two are attracted to each other."

Raven cleared her throat. "Hugh, maybe I'm old-fashioned but I always expected to marry because I was in love, not just to stay out of prison. Not that being married to his majesty would … well, what I mean …" She let her voice trail off as she realized she was only making herself blush worse.

"Oh well. That was the best solution. If you can't marry her perhaps you could elevate her, Your Majesty. A title and a position on your new privy council?"

"Hugh, I've only been king for about two hours and I'm already hearing from the nobles about who they think should be on the new council. I don't think I could appoint another non-noble … they're still pretty upset about your appointment. There could be an outright revolt if I ennoble Raven. She is a tad infamous right now."

The two men exchanged glances and Geoffrey lowered himself back into his chair. "So, that's not a good option, either. Lord Chamberlain, your suggestions have proven unsatisfactory so far. What other options await our lovely guest?"

"I'm afraid those were the only two I could think of that would benefit both of you. The rest only benefit Sagras. You're not going to like them."

Raven didn't like the sound of that. "And those would be … ?"

His voice dropped just above a whisper. "The dungeons, the galleys, exile … or death."

"You're right, Hugh, I don't like any of those."

The chamberlain turned to face the young man sitting near him. "Sire, we cannot allow her to remain in the city. Your brother had powerful allies and you have not had time to build your power base. You cannot give them something to rally around. If she remains, they'll swear you put her up to killing Owen. Without the noble's support, you couldn't control this city for long. You could be staring into the face of a civil war. Believe me, some will see the events of the night and think that removing a new king could be easier than an established one. "

"Am I not king, Hugh?"

"Aye, Sire, you are. But as much as the nobles owe you their loyalty, there are responsibilities you owe them—one of which is upholding the laws. If you do not render judgment on Raven, have no doubt they can afford the time and money it will take to hunt her down. Even if she avoided the nobles, there is still the underworld and Sagras' enemies to worry about. She knows these halls too well. If she is captured, there are ways to make her reveal the truth. She'll be a marked woman the second she steps out of the keep."

Raven turned to Geoffrey with a nervous smile on her face. "Somehow that whole marriage thing doesn't sound so bad compared to the alternatives."

Geoffrey favored her with a broad smile. "No, Raven, as enticing as the thought is, if I'm to woo you, I'd prefer to do it properly." He began pacing the room, hands clasped behind his back. Raven recognized the look on the king's face. Her father wore it often enough when he was working on a problem with solutions he didn't like.

After a bit, Geoffrey found himself back behind his chair, facing Raven. "I've no desire to imprison you or assign to the penal galleys and it would be rather churlish to condemn you for saving my life ... twice. Therefore, the only option is exile. I'm sorry, Raven, but it's as much for your own safety as the city's."

Raven found her voice after a few moments. "Of course,

Your Majesty. I appreciate your generosity. How long before I begin my exile?"

The king looked to Hugh and then back to Raven. "Can you avoid being spotted?"

Raven touched her silver medallion and smiled. "I can, Your Majesty."

"Very well. You have five days to get your affairs in order. I want to see you again privately before you leave, but it cannot be here. Where can I meet you?"

Raven paused for a moment and then grinned. "I have the perfect location. There's this bookseller in town …"

* * *

"That's so unfair, Raven. I can't believe he's exiling you after all you did for him."

Raven smiled as the young thief stomped around Bertok's sitting room. *A few weeks ago, I might have acted like that. Now, I'm just too tired to get worked up.*

As Alexis began another circuit, Bertok held up his hand. "Please, Alexis, this house is not that sturdy. I'd appreciate it lasting a little longer."

She stopped in mid-stride and whirled around, staring at the old wizard before shrugging and retreating to a nearby chair. "It's still not right."

The wizard held up a hand. "Considering the other options, it's the least onerous."

Before the young thief could continue, Raven jumped into the conversation. "Alexis, I always knew this could happen. When Geoffrey read off the charges against me, he had no options. Believe me, exile is not the worst that could have happened."

"But you saved his life!"

"Yes, and he's saving mine by letting me leave on my own terms. A couple of the nobles suggested dropping me over the wall stark naked and seeing how long I survived. King Geoffrey and Hugh may be on my side but, let's face it, the majority of the Hill wants me dead."

Bertok shifted in his chair to draw her attention. "So, what are you going to do?"

"There are a number of city-states in the empire I could visit. Then again, I've dreamed of seeing the Southern Isles. I can still sell the Dragonstone to raise some money."

"You're a little better off than you think, Raven."

She spun around to face her apprentice. "Oh?"

Alexis scuffed her feet before looking up at her mentor. "While you were gone, I went back to the lair. We didn't lose everything in the fire. There was a section that was almost untouched. I found where you had some gold and jewels hidden."

Raven whirled back to face Bertok. "I thought you were going to keep an eye on her. She wasn't supposed to be up wandering around."

"I'm as surprised as you are, Raven. She must have sneaked out."

"I thought you heard me, Bertok. I guess you snore too loudly."

Raven was about to fuss at her apprentice but the indignant look that spread across Bertok's face was priceless. Alexis went to one of Bertok's tables and removed a blanket from a chest hidden beneath it. Raven pawed through it with feigned casualness and found the chest filled with a number of sacks containing loose gems, jewelry, and gold coins. By her rough calculations, this would keep her comfortable for years.

"So, does this change your plans?" The old wizard leaned back in his chair, grabbing one of his pipes off a nearby table. As he began packing tobacco into it, he continued. "After all, you do have another option."

Alexis's eyes scanned back and forth between the pair. "I'd like to know what's going on. If I'm going into exile with Raven, it might help if we didn't have so many secrets."

"Excuse me? If *you're* going in to exile with *me*? I don't recall the king banishing you."

"Be reasonable, Raven. How can I be your apprentice if you're not here to teach me? Besides, you need me to keep you out of trouble."

It took a lot of effort but Raven convinced herself not to strangle Alexis. *Oh, if you thought your training's been tough, you've got another think coming.* She spotted the grin on Alexis's face and realized she'd fallen right into her young apprentice's trap.

"If the brat is coming along, what about you, Bertok? Your friend, Tybalt, thinks there's more to you than you like to admit."

"Tybalt always did have good taste and a loose tongue. I'm flattered, but no. I'm an old, fat man as you've so often noted. I'm comfortable here. I have a house, food, enough money to get by, and the occasional non-annoying visitor. With you leaving, I even might get some peace and quiet."

"But I thought you were going to finish training me?"

"I said I'd train you when you gave up being a thief and got serious about your studies. Tybalt offered to take you on as an apprentice also. Yes, we've been talking since he found out I'm here. Still, I think exile would be good for you. Get whatever this is out of your system and when you're ready, Tybalt and I will still be here."

Raven fell quiet as she considered life without Bertok around. *Other than Father, he's been the one constant in my life since Sean died. He's never been shy about giving me advice and he's right more often than I like to admit.* Looking up, she realized Bertok wasn't in the room. She glanced at Alexis, who pointed at the stairs. After a few moments, he returned carrying a leather jerkin, a tall pair of boots, and a silver dagger.

"I've been thinking. Given the circumstances, would you consider selling me the Dragonstone? You don't know how to use it and I'd rather it didn't fall into the wrong hands."

"And you think I should trade a one-of-a-kind mystical gem for some clothes?"

Bertok's face fell at her sarcastic reply. "Have you learned nothing the past few years? Do I have to retrain you to 'observe' or do you think you can remember your first lessons?"

Raven leaned back to escape the vehemence of his tirade. After he wound down, he laid the items out on a low table in front of her chair. She cleared her mind and stared at the items, noting the auras surrounding the clothing and a much stronger aura around the dagger. She took a deep breath to break her concentration, then turned to see the old wizard smiling at her.

"So you haven't forgotten everything I taught you."

"No, I pay attention when you're discussing something important."

Bertok turned to Alexis, a mock frown on his face. "You see? You see what I have to put up with? It's amazing I've known her this long without turning her into a newt."

"If you could turn anyone into a newt, you wouldn't be here in Lowtown, you old faker."

"Don't tempt me, apprentice. Besides, I think keeping the Dragonstone out of the royal family's hands is a good idea. Geoffrey may be more stable than his kin, but why take chances? The best way to resist temptation is to avoid being tempted."

"My goodness, you almost sounded poetic there."

"I'm old, but I'm not feebleminded yet. Now, do you want me to tell you about these items or would you rather figure them out by yourself?"

"By all means, please elucidate."

"Thank you." Pointing to the leather jerkin, he began. "This has been enchanted to the hardness of steel, yet it retains the suppleness of calfskin. It's not perfect protection, but considering the situations you find yourself in, it will help."

Raven stuck her tongue out at Bertok before picking up the jerkin, noting the workmanship. "You're certain this will hold up? It feels as light as dandelion fluff."

"You can put it on and test it, or you can take my word for it. Now, may I continue?"

Raven waved a hand at him. "Please go on with your tale."

"These boots belonged to a master thief in Wolf River. Not only do they provide magical protection for your legs, but they minimize sounds. They're no guarantee against a nightingale floor, but at least they won't hear you clomping down the hallway." Before Raven could point out she didn't *clomp*, he continued. "There is a bonus with these boots. If you use the command word, small claws extend from the toes to assist with climbing. Please note, I said 'assist' not 'do the climbing for you.'"

"A master thief? What if he wants them back?"

"Since he was knifed in bed by a jealous mistress, I think you're safe. As I said, the jerkin and boots provide protection ... if you're wearing them."

Alexis pointed at the dagger. "And I suppose this was owned by another thief who came to an untimely end?"

"That's a reasonable guess, but no. This is special. Not only is it enchanted to never lose its edge, it has an interesting property. Alexis, please pick up that piece of wood over there."

While the young thief was occupied, Bertok picked up a large candle. The red gem in the hilt began glowing when he lit the candle. As he brought the candle closer, a red beam of light shot from the gem. Speaking a command word, the beam intensified and began burning a small hole in the wood. Alexis held. Moving the dagger with care, he was able to cut a hole through the wood.

"Now, Alexis, if you'll flip the piece of wood around?"

She gave the wizard a puzzled look, but complied. He focused the beam and spoke a different word. A brighter beam of light shot out and ignited the wood in her hand.

Alexis tossed the wood down and stomped out the flames. "By all that's holy, Bertok, you could have warned me."

"Then the demonstration wouldn't have been as effective. Also, the brighter the source of light, the more intense the beam. Considering your choice of professions, I'm certain you can see its potential. Oh, and take these." He handed

Raven a bag with several large gems. "That should keep you off the streets for a while."

"If you ever get tired of being a hedge wizard, you'd have a great future as a fence."

"You flatter me, young lady. Now, take your apprentice and get out of here. I believe you have preparations to make before the king arrives."

Chapter Twenty-Eight

Perrin moved a stack of books off the shelf and began dusting. It was almost time to start dinner but she knew tonight was going to be different from the usual routine. Looking to her right, she watched Ronan carrying some extra books back to the storeroom.

This seemed so simple when I first proposed it to King Geoffrey. I was just going to walk up to Father and tell him the truth, but every time I've started to bring up the subject I've panicked. Why do I still feel like I'm five years old when I'm around him?

It's strange. I resented Fiana and Ronan when I first met them. Now, it's like they belong here. Father's moving on with his life, just like I'm trying to do with mine. Ronan is taking to the bookstore like a sailor to water.

Besides, I think I understand Father now. I know how much it hurt when Sean died. I can only imagine what he must have gone through when Mother died. I guess I never thought about how brave and strong he's been, taking care of the store and me all this time. I have to live a life Sean—and Jerek—would have been proud to share with me.

"Hurry up, Perrin, or I'll be done before you." Ronan gave her a shy grin before disappearing behind one of the display cases. They hadn't spent a lot of time together but he seemed like a good kid. She watched him taking some of the valuable books to the safe.

"Be careful, Ronan. Some of those books are brittle."

"I'll be careful." He reached the doorway and stopped.

"Have thieves ever broken in here? It seems they'd be more interested in gems and gold than old books."

"I don't think a thief has ever broken into the store. But you never know … someone might not want to pay. Hiring a thief might be less expensive than buying one of those."

"I was wondering because some guys said a thief was caught in the Royal Keep a week ago. Said it was a cute girl and she saved the prince's life. The nobles are trying to hush this up but Theo's dad heard about it from a scroll maker on the hill. Can you imagine? She must be the greatest thief in the world."

"Sounds like you've got a crush there, Ronan."

Ronan cheeks burned with embarrassment. "Why'd you have to say something like that? How would you break into some place with stone walls and guards and all that stuff? I can't imagine breaking into *this* place."

"That's because you're an honest kid. So, do you want some cute girl to rescue you if you get into trouble?"

"Perrin!"

She was trying to keep a straight face when a deep voice echoed out of the kitchen. "That's enough talk about thieves and princes. A little more work and a little less gossiping!"

They both turned at the same time. "Yes, Father."

Perrin turned toward Ronan with a surprised look on her face. "I'm sorry, Perrin. It's like they're already married the way Mom talks about him." He ducked his head and disappeared into the back with an armload of books.

Perrin stared at him as he disappeared. *I'm going to miss Ronan when I leave Sagras.*

"Perrin, are you done there? These potatoes aren't going to cook themselves."

"I was waiting for you to come here and finish up. I can't leave with the door open."

They exchanged smiles as they passed and she heard him telling Ronan good-bye. He had lit the fire in the stove for her and she began peeling the potatoes. After she had finished the bowl, she heard voices coming from the front of the shop. She crept closer to the stairs where she was able to see without fear of being exposed herself.

Two men stood just inside the doorway talking to her father. Plain clothes or not, there was no question they were Royal Guardsmen. The larger was speaking to her father while the other kept looking out the door. "You *are* Rory, the bookseller, correct?"

"I said so, yes. I also told you there is no dark-haired girl here. Now if you don't mind, we're getting ready to close."

"Is there anyone else here in the building with you?"

Rory let out an exasperated sigh. "My daughter is in the kitchen working on dinner, which I'm hoping to get to as soon as you leave. So, if you don't mind …?"

"I'm sorry. You'll have to see two more customers." The larger man nodded to the other, who motioned outside. A carriage with the curtains drawn pulled up and two men hurried inside, clutching their hooded cloaks tight. The two guardsmen exited the store and slipped inside the carriage to wait.

Perrin saw her father sigh deeply and face the two hooded figures. "Gentlemen, since you will not be denied, how may I help you?"

"Is there a more private room in which we can speak?"

"If you'll wait here, I'll lock the front door." Rory walked to the front and shut and locked the door without waiting for a reply. Returning to his unwanted guests, he led them toward the kitchen, where Perrin ducked back to set a pot on the stove.

"Gentlemen, this is the most private room I have besides my bedroom. What's so damn important it wouldn't wait until morning?"

The two hooded figures looked to each other and then pulled their hoods back, revealing the king of Sagras and his lord chamberlain. Rory paled as he realized who he'd been chastising. "Your Majesty, my lord, please forgive me, I had no idea."

Hugh motioned for him to sit down. "I was afraid the

313

arrangements had not been made ahead of time."

"Arrangements, Lord Chamberlain?"

"Please, call me Hugh. You were recommended as a very discrete person. We were supposed to meet someone here tonight. It appears they haven't arrived yet."

Rory gave the king a puzzled look. "Why meet here instead of your keep?"

"Let's just say the keep doesn't keep secrets very well, bookseller. This meeting must be handled with care. Some of my enemies would love to end my reign before it even begins."

Perrin poured hot water into the teapot and set the best porcelain cups on the table while the men sat in awkward silence. Once it had steeped, she poured the tea and then sat at the table.

"Your Majesty, may I present my daughter, Perrin."

Before the prince could respond, she came to a decision. "That's all right, Father, King Geoffrey and I have met."

"I must be going senile at an early age, my dear. I think I would remember meeting you."

Perrin's blue eyes twinkled in amusement. "You flatter me, Your Majesty. But we have met under different circumstances."

While the three men exchanged confused looks, she fished the silver medallion from beneath her blouse and spoke the command word. The whole room faded out of focus and when the room snapped back into clarity, she could see the effect on the three men. Her father sat there, his mouth hanging open. King Geoffrey had jumped backward, nearly knocking his chair over in his haste to retreat. Hugh sat there, a broad grin crossing his face as if he'd known all along.

"Gentlemen, I believe you came here to meet me?" Perrin was always surprised how much deeper her voice sounded as Raven.

"Perrin?"

"Raven?"

The king and her father exchanged glances as realization

set in. Rory wheeled around in his chair. *"Raven?* You're telling me *my* daughter is one of the most feared thieves in the city? Young lady, you've got a lot of explaining to do."

Perrin spoke the other command word, and her true features returned. "Yes, Father, I am Raven and have been for several years now. I don't have time to explain all my reasons, but believe me, hurting you was not one of them."

Hugh's voice cut through her father's angry stare. "That explains why no one ever found you. The transformation is remarkable, Raven. If you'll indulge an old man, this form flatters you more."

"The idea was to divert attention from myself. It appears I've done a poor job of that." Hugh chuckled as she leaned her head forward, letting her long red hair hide her face. "However, I don't regret exposing my secret if it helped save King Geoffrey's life."

"My daughter saved the king's life?" Perrin could hear how he was fighting a losing battle in trying to grasp everything transpiring this evening.

Hugh took a drink before responding. "Without your daughter's efforts, King Geoffrey would be dead right now. She's more hero than villain in this play. However, since you didn't expect us, this discussion is going to be awkward."

"I fail to understand how this could get any *more* awkward."

Geoffrey's cough drew everyone's attention. "Awkward or not, it doesn't change the fact I rendered a sentence against your daughter."

"Sentence? What is he talking about, Perrin?"

"I was arrested after the melee in the throne room. King Geoffrey is allowing me to go into exile for my punishment."

"Exile?"

"I'm afraid so, Rory." Hugh's sympathetic voice tried to calm Perrin's father. "His majesty has little choice in the matter. Your daughter has allies, but she also has some dangerous enemies. This is for her own protection. Although, with this new bit of information, it may not be necessary."

Perrin watched as Geoffrey's face went through a progression of emotions until it settled on hopeful anticipation. Slapping a hand on the table, he looked at Perrin and then back to Hugh. "You're right, Hugh. I knew there was a reason I kept you as my lord chamberlain." He turned to Rory, a broad smile fixed on his face. "If your daughter was willing to remain Perrin, there would be no reason to exile her. Her enemies would spend their lives looking for someone who doesn't exist."

She knew what her father wanted her to say from the expectant look on his face. She knew, deep in her heart, it was what King Geoffrey wanted, too. However, she had been debating this decision ever since her conversation with Bertok.

"No. It's time for me to quit hiding and begin living the life I've dreamed of living. A life beyond the walls of Sagras, a life seeing the world I've only read about while I've been here. You're getting remarried, Father, and Ronan is a great kid who *wants* to be a bookseller."

She turned to the king, a small frown on her face. "And, Your Majesty, if you do not exile me publicly, your enemies will use this as a wedge between you and the undecided nobles. There is already talk in the taverns you paid me to kill your brother, or that I used a spell to turn you against your father."

"You killed Prince Owen, Perrin?"

"Another time, Father." Perrin noted Rory had gone very pale with this latest revelation.

"You may have me under a spell, Raven … Perrin … whatever your name is, but it's not that kind of spell."

Hugh's raucous laughter drew attention from the king's flushed cheeks. "By the gods, Geoffrey, that's the first time you've admitted your feelings since I've met the young lady. If I were thirty years younger, I might have to challenge you for her hand." The old warrior gave Perrin a wink before turning serious again. "However, lass, think about what you're saying. If you are exiled, you'll never be allowed back into the city while Geoffrey rules, otherwise you face a death penalty."

"If Raven is exiled, I guarantee she'll never be seen in Sagras again. Then again, if Perrin returns to visit her family, I can't imagine the city guards blinking an eye." She tilted her head to the side and returned Hugh's wink.

"That doesn't answer the question. Why don't we exile Raven and let Perrin live in the city? It should be obvious no one wants to see you leave."

"But, you see, Hugh, that's why I have to leave. I am Raven because I like being Raven. I love the thrill of what I do, pitting my training and skills against the best the city had to offer. My goal has always been to acquire enough money to leave Sagras on my own terms. I wanted to travel and see some of these wonders of the world before I settle down. The funny thing is, I found myself giving more money to help people in the Commons and Lowtown than I kept. "

She turned to her father. "I want you to understand most of all. We've tiptoed around Mother's death for so long. We've been taking care of each other for too long. You'll have Fiana and Ronan with you. It's time maybe we both grew up a little."

The king's soft voice slipped into the conversation. "So you're saying I couldn't talk you into staying?" The intensity surprised Perrin. There was no questioning the sincerity on his face. He *was* a handsome man and she knew he had a strong sense of right and wrong. Still, the timing was wrong.

"Your Majesty, I would love the opportunity to get to know you better. But don't mistake what we've been through as a courtship. Time apart will help us determine our true feelings. Besides, as I said, there's nothing stopping me from visiting."

She picked up her cup of tea and held it to her face, letting her hair fall forward again. She watched the three men looking back and forth, afraid to be the first one to break the silence. After letting them suffer for a few minutes, she straightened her head and spoke. "I believe you wanted to see me about something this evening, Your Majesty?"

King Geoffrey looked at her with a confused look and then smacked himself in the forehead. "This sudden revelation made me forget why we came here. Hugh, do you have the letter?"

"Aye, Sire. You threatened me enough before we left the keep."

Geoffrey gave Hugh an annoyed look. "Perrin, or Raven, or whoever you are, this is for you." Hugh passed her a leather scroll case as the king continued. "You'll find a letter of credit in this, authorizing any bank in the Empire to provide you ten thousand Sagran crowns or their equivalent. It's not the reward I hoped to give you, but it's all I could access without going through the lord exchequer. He's still upset you broke into his house a few months ago."

Perrin laughed. "Yes, that would be a little awkward. Still, your generosity overwhelms me, Your Majesty."

"Nonsense. But, as Hugh and you have pointed out, this is neither the time nor the place to challenge the nobles. Oh, and please take this."

Geoffrey got up and walked over to Perrin. Before she could react, Geoffrey dropped to a knee in front of her, removed a ring from his right hand, and presented it to her. "Please accept this as a token of my appreciation. It's been in our family for generations. It designates you as my agent to anyone who sees it. Use it with care."

Perrin's fingers closed around the ring, her mind racing at its implication. She stared at the ring until she heard the sound of chairs moving. She looked up and saw Hugh and the king pulling their hoods up over their heads.

Hugh turned toward the flummoxed young woman. "Perrin, I believe Raven has an appointment at the keep in three hours. Please do be on time."

* * *

It was her first time back in the throne room since the night of the fight. She was surprised how crowded it was. The

318

room was filled with nobles and townspeople. Looking around, she saw not only the angry faces of the nobles, but also a number of people she knew from the Commons. The number of guardsmen surrounding her surprised her. Hugh had explained it was more for her safety than the king's. This would be the last opportunity for her enemies to reach her before she left the city.

Hugh walked to the front of the throne and turned to face the assembled crowd. "Bring the accused forward!"

The guards led Raven up to Hugh and then stepped away, forming a semicircle around her. She gazed at Hugh and King Geoffrey in their ceremonial robes. Hugh turned to where King Geoffrey was sitting. "The accused awaits your decision, Your Majesty."

"Thank you, Lord Chamberlain. The thief, Raven, stands here accused of numerous crimes against the throne and against the citizenry of Sagras. She deserves great punishment for any of them. But the worst of her crimes is the crime of regicide, for it was her hand that slew my brother."

Raven could feel the ripple running through the crowd behind her. Before the low muttering could grow though, King Geoffrey continued. "However, she is responsible for my life. She unraveled a plot against me and against Sagras. And while it was her hand that slew my brother, she prevented him from killing me. For that, she has earned my thanks."

The acoustics of the throne room carried Geoffrey's voice to the farthest corners. Looking at Raven, he spoke again. "Do you understand the crimes you've been accused of, thief?"

"Yes, Your Majesty."

"Do you have anything to say in your defense?"

Raven paused, as Hugh had instructed her, then lowered her head. "No, Your Majesty."

"Very well, is there anyone else who would speak either for or against the accused?" Some of the nobles opened their mouths as though to respond, but their resolve withered under the king's gaze. He turned back to Raven, still standing with her head bowed.

"Raven, since you admit your crimes and no one speaks in your defense, I hereby pronounce your sentence. You are banished from Sagras and all lands that fall under its jurisdiction for the rest of your life. If by noon tomorrow anyone finds you within the confines of Sagras, they are required by law to kill you or face forfeiture of their possessions and banishment of their family. This is my decision and my decision is final."

His words echoed through the room as the guards led the bowed thief out, escorted by the lord chamberlain. Once outside, Hugh dismissed the guards and led her toward the main entryway to the keep. As they walked down the deserted hallways, Raven raised her head, showing the big smile on her face.

As they reached the main gates, Hugh motioned for the guards to open them. "All right, Raven, you got your wish. I hope your exile is pleasurable."

He motioned for Raven to proceed on her way and turned to leave. Before he could take two steps, he was intercepted and found himself in a fierce hug that nearly knocked him off his feet. Looking down, he saw Raven's arms wrapped around him. "I'm going to miss you, Hugh." He reached down and patted her on the head. "I'm going to miss you, too. I think things are going to be too quiet here in Sagras without you." After a few moments, he dislodged her and held her at arm's length. "By the gods, your father is a damn lucky man. I'd have given most anything to have had a daughter like you. Now, go on. You've got a lot to do."

Raven smiled up at him. "Take good care of Geoffrey. He tends to get into trouble if you leave him alone too long." Before Hugh could answer, she disappeared into the gloom of the city.

* * *

Raven crossed the bridge over the Lentia River and headed into Hunter's Wood. Moving through the dense forest, she came upon a small clearing with a small campfire. A soft whinny greeted her as she entered and she could see four horses hobbled off to the side.

"Took you long enough to get here."

She spotted Alexis stepping out of the wood line, putting her sword away. She grinned at her apprentice. "At least you didn't disappear with all my money and leave me to walk."

"Don't think it didn't cross my mind."

"Believe me, it crossed my mind also."

The two spun around to see Quentin stepping out of the shadows. Raven noted his hands were empty. That told her there were snipers in the woods watching for any wrong move.

"What brings you out on a night like this, Quentin? Farming getting too boring?"

"You fulfilled our deal, Raven, but I believe you still owe Galen some information. Have you discovered who betrayed the thieves' guild?"

"Ian was working for Kazmer and had been before he joined the guild."

A look of amazement crossed Quentin's face at the revelation. "Ian? By the gods, I'm surprised he didn't pee all over himself every time Kazmer barked."

"I think there's a lot more to Ian than any of us gave him credit for. He had the smarts to get out of town before I could find him. I have a score to settle with that pile of horse droppings."

"Do you know where he has gone?"

"No. However, I do have some leads that I'm going to check on. That bastard set the Black Leopards on the Corconti because he was jealous of Jerek. He's got a lot to answer for."

"Indeed. Send me a message once in a while so I know how you're faring on your hunt."

"Quentin, have I ever held out on you before?"

"No. But, then again, they say travel changes a person."

"So they do. Perhaps you should try it sometime. They say the Southern Isles are a great spot to retire."

"Do they, now? Perhaps I shall look into it. When I retire, that is."

Raven walked over and extended a hand. "Good luck with your new career."

Quentin grabbed her hand and shook it. "Good luck with your hunting." He stepped back into the shadows and disappeared as if he'd never been there.

Alexis stepped forward, her face pale in the moonlight. "What the heck was that all about?"

"I'll tell you while we're riding." Raven walked over to one of the horses as Alexis doused the fire. Mounting the black horse, she grabbed the reins of one of the two pack-horses, while Alexis secured the other.

"Where are we heading, Raven?"

Raven stared up at the night sky as a shooting star made its way across the darkness. "I'm not sure, Alexis, but wherever we wind up I expect we'll get in trouble soon enough."

Alexis's laughter mixed with hers as they swung their horses to the north and set out through Hunter's Wood into the unknown.

ABOUT THE AUTHOR

RICHARD C. WHITE made his first professional sale in 1975 when he sold a sports article to the *Hallsville* [MO] *Top* while still in high school. He soon became the sports editor for the *Top*, writing articles and editorials for the paper. He was a sports reporter at the University of Central Missouri's radio station where he wrote/edited on-air copy and did interviews with local schools sports teams.

After college, Rich joined the United States Army. There he sold his first comic script to StarWarp Concepts, for *Troubleshooters, Incorporated*—and then went on to create his own small press company, NightWolf Graphics. Rich left the army in 1999 and joined a defense contractor, where he still works today.

Rich's first professional prose sales were in media tie-in works. His first story was "Assault on Avengers Mansion" for *The Ultimate Hulk* anthology in 1998, which he co-wrote with Steven A. Roman. He followed that with *Gauntlet: Dark Legacy: Paths of Evil*, an original novel based on the popular video game franchise. He has also written for anthologies based on the *Star Trek, Star Trek: The Next Generation*, and *Doctor Who* licenses.

Rich is a member of the Science Fiction and Fantasy Writers of America and the International Association of Media Tie-in Writers. He also serves on SFWA's "Writer Beware" committee.

When not writing, he shows an inordinate amount of interest in sharp pointy things. Rich picked up fencing with a foil at the University of Central Missouri along with being introduced to the Society for Creative Anachronism. Over the years he learned how to use a broadsword and shield, great sword, and pole arms. He also was an apprentice armorer and a herald for the Barony of the Darkwoods. Rich's current sword-related vice is Kendo, in which he has achieved the rank of *nidan* and is studying both *itto* (single-sword) and *nito* (two-sword) styles.

Rich's current work includes *Terra Incognito: A Guide to Building the Worlds of Your Imagination* (2015), a reference work for writers and gamers interested in world building; "No Rest for the Wicked" in *Battletech: Slack Tides* (2016); "Paladin" in *Robots* (2016) for the Origins Game Fair; *For a Few Gold Pieces More* (2017); and "War Stories" in *Liberty Girl: Fight for Freedom* (2017), featuring a WWII adventure of Heroic Publishing's Liberty Girl.